REVOLUTION

DIVIDED ELEMENTS - BOOK III

REVOLUTION

DIVIDED ELEMENTS - BOOK III

MIKHAEYLA KOPIEVSKY

13 5 7 9 10 8 6 4 2

KYRIJA
North Arm Cove, NSW, Australia
www.kyrija.com.au

A CIP catalogue record for this book is available from the National Library of Australia

ebook ISBN 978-0-9954218-0-6
paperback ISBN13 978-0-9954218-3-7
paperback ISBN10 0-9954218-3-7

Cover Illustration by Ethan Scott

For Elijah

ONE

In the darkness, hidden on the rooftops of Otpor, Anaiya is anonymous. Here, she is no-one—not the tainted protege of Kane 148, not the Heterodox co-conspirator of Otpor's rebellion, not Kaide's bright hope for a better future. Up here, there is no-one to demand something of her or be disappointed by her.

Perched on grimy tiles, five stories above the crumbling bitumen of the street, the night is broken by a single row of halogen lights. There are no prying eyes up here, no suspicious onlookers; nothing to regard her but the layers of residue she scrubs away with chemicals that sting her eyes and burn her nose. That and the Earth Elemental scrubbing at the same roofline just metres away.

It is possible that Sharna is a Cleaner—she has the scrappy build and sinewy arms for it. More likely, she's here for the same reason Anaiya is—to earn extra money off the ledger; hours of scraping away Otpor's pollution, all for the promise of ten glass rounds, tinted blue, not half a centimetre thick, and embossed with an intricate synthfly insignia.

Anaiya doesn't need the black-market money, not really: Kaide had promised to cover her expenses, bring her what she needs. But that has the feel of being indebted to him, being trapped. And she feels enough of that already.

Thoughts of the dark-eyed Air Elemental bring with them a kaleidoscope of mixed emotions. He has been her enemy, her reluctant partner-in-crime, and her lover. But, that had been before her execution, back when she was whole. Now, she is an Elemental without an Element, and Kaide is a knot of complications she hasn't figured out how to untangle.

The black-market cleaning jobs give her an excuse to escape the tension and confusion, give her a semblance of identity and purpose. More importantly, they offer her the night hours and hidden places she needs to survive in a city that doesn't know she is alive and would eliminate her if it did.

A series of beeps interrupts the silence. Ahead, Sharna disconnects the hose from her long-handled scourer and stows it using the straps on her backpack. Anaiya follows suit and together they make their way to the scaffolding and start the climb down. A small voice at the back of Anaiya's mind, in the part where her Peacekeeper memories lay shattered and dark, taunts her to perform a free-form lache and somersault down the rungs… But she pushes the thought away and lets her hands and feet plod the slower path.

It is brighter down at street level, and cleaner. The broken windows, random debris, and sand drifts of just a few months ago have been relegated to distant memory, and street lights shine with a renewed vigour in the absence of once-frequent blackouts. In this post-Resistance world, Otpor has returned to its utopia.

Anaiya grimaces. The city's false utopia is as thin as the polluted veneer on its rooftops.

"You coming back to the den?" Sharna asks. She stands in the middle of the street, the harsh white light of the streetlights picking up the grime on her coveralls and the deep lines of her ninth-lustrum face. It is only the second time she has spoken to Anaiya since their six-hour shift began; like all Earth Elementals, she has been conditioned to appreciate uncomplicated conversations, to display a lack of curiosity, to be satisfied with basic questions and easy answers. It suits both Anaiya's need for privacy and her crushing desire for simplicity.

"Maybe later."

Sharna shrugs and heads off along the brightly lit streets towards the boulevardes teeming with Elementals still revelling in a night-life no longer hamstrung by curfews.

If only everything else in my life was as uncomplicated. Anaiya readjusts her backpack and sets off in the opposite direction, sticking to the shadows and uninhabited side streets. At street level, the risk of being noticed makes her cautious. Even with her close-cropped purple hair, the eye lenses that turn her brown irises blue, and the bulky clothes that hide her athletic frame, she worries that a casual glance or unexpected encounter will bring her undone. She pulls her hood forward and ducks her head; she has no interest in testing whether a random Elemental will recognise the face of Otpor's second-most notorious Resistor.

Not that she worries an Earth Elemental will—they don't have the attention to detail and the imagination. Another reason she likes hanging around them.

As it always does, the path to Boileau Road and its strange Enclave tempts her feet towards the south-west. Some nights the urge is stronger to visit the exotic place of antiquities and organics, where wristplates sit detached from their lifelines, and books are things you can hold in your hand. And trees. Real, living trees. With thick, sturdy trunks, and slender arms that stretch laden with leaves and blossoms. Trees that survive hidden away behind tall walls, and thrive, even under Otpor's brown sun and in its recycled air.

But tonight is not that night. Her curiosity has been tempered by the long hours of hard work. And she doesn't have the imagination to pretend that the three-hundred-metre stretch of cobblestone street would not be cordoned off and guarded like it has been the last thirty-or-so times she's passed it.

She could return to Kaide's apartment, with its comfortable lounges and uncomfortable silences, but she doesn't have the energy for that, either—for the looks of concern, the feigned stability, the sexual tension full of promises and the past. Easier to take the meandering route through the shadows to Precinct 17, where the small intimate spaces and trendy izakaya give way to dimly lit drinking dens: large halls with basic bench-seats and long tables, cheap alcohol, low-key Unorthodoxy, and lots of laughter.

She waits in the doorway of an empty retail store, biding her time until someone approaches to enter the den, or someone from inside opens its doors. Whereas once her feet would have shifted with impatience, tonight she leans casually against the alcove's wall and lets the interplay of light and shadows create a familiar symphony in her mind.

Heavy beats and raucous carousing swell into focus as a heavyset Earth Elemental opens the door to exit the den. She could be a Labourer, or a Demolition grunt, or a Retail Worker—there is nothing in what she wears, or how she holds herself, or the drunken sway of her gait that gives away her competency. She has the kind of anonymity of all Earths, the kind of anonymity Anaiya craves.

Calling on her Peacekeeper muscle memory, Anaiya slinks in the shadows towards the den, avoiding the gaze of the Earth and reaching the door before it clicks shut. Squeezing in the small gap between it and the door frame, she pushes into the shadowy hall beyond, letting herself be swallowed by the noise and the casual abandon.

At the bar, she trades a clear blue round for three shot glasses brimming with tequila. The bartender, a fourth-lustrum boy with a round face and shock of auburn hair, winks at her as he slides them over, and even the blackness rotting away her core can't stop her from laughing in response.

She finds a spot at the end of a far table and settles down on the bench seat, nodding to the older Elementals who sit with their pints of amber and talk loudly of days gone by, when avatar sports had more grunt and nutrient boosters tasted like shit. She tunes out their inane gossiping and downs two of the tequilas in rapid succession, letting the alcohol and the cacophony of noise lull her into a deep, satisfying numbness.

Anaiya looks up as a familiar Earth takes a seat opposite her. Jiran has worked with her on a couple of cleaning jobs over the last month. He is three lustrums older than her, but the extra fifteen years have not dampened his physicality: his broad frame is as toned and intimidating as a fifth lustrum Border Watcher and his face is free of the pockmarks and inevitable corrosion that comes with the accumulation of synth toxin. Only his eyes and the weariness in his voice betray his age.

Words from Kane 148's journal float on the rush of tequila in her mind. *The Cooperative conditions the mind, even as its burden breaks the spirit.* After a while, even the ubiquitous alcohol, drugs, and entertainment lose their sheen.

"Just finished your shift?" he asks.

"Yeah, just finished a six-hour over near the promenade." Anaiya picks up the third glass of tequila and drains it. "You?"

"Nah," he says, looking around the den. "I'm looking for some extras. Lira's books are full for the next two weeks, and I need some extra cash to pay rent."

"Someone else is sub-contracting cleaning jobs in Precinct 17?"

It is how the black-market thrives: an older Elemental, usually in their eighth or ninth lustrum, with all the smarts but none of the physical prowess, maintains their employment and then secretly contracts out the work to desperate Elementals willing to share a fifty percent cut. It is a risky venture—a sniff of Unorthodoxy would see employment rights and profits reclaimed; but everyone seems to understand that their discretion and silence is lucrative for all involved—extra cash here, means more transactions there, and with everything off the books and the Cooperative's radar, there is more to keep and less to forfeit.

"No," Jiran says, turning back to Anaiya and taking a swig of his own drink. "But, I was hoping to convince a Demolitioner to give me their shift."

"Have you seen Lira tonight?" Anaiya asks, letting her own gaze drift across the crowded tables. "I wouldn't mind picking up my payment."

"Up for a big night?" Jiran grins.

Anaiya smiles, but she feels it fall short. It would be easy to stay at the den, drink until the inebriation leans her a temporary armour she can take back to Kaide's apartment, sneak in through the window of his spare bedroom, and sleep through the unasked questions the next morning. But she has been a coward for long enough.

"Not tonight, just don't want to have to wait two weeks again. Lira can be a slippery eel when it comes to releasing those glass beads."

Jiran laughs, the long, easy chuckle of someone who knows no greater frustration than the occasional cold shower and not enough money for the final round of drinks. "Yeah, she's a character, that one. How well do you know her?"

Anaiya pictures the diminutive Cleaner in her mind: close-cropped dark hair and piercing blue eyes; small mouth usually pursed in distrust or distaste; compact frame that still holds its tone; and sun-browned skin, except for the pale and wasted left arm. "Not well—I usually get my payments from other Earths. But I've heard that she's easy to find when you're looking for work, and hard to find when you're looking for payment."

"She's been at the game for a while. Most Earths would have taken a demotion after an injury like hers, but she made it work. Made it profitable."

"How long is *a while*?"

"About ten years ago, if you believe the stories."

It is the way he says *stories*—full of scandal and secrets—that catches Anaiya's curiosity. Like a thread just begging to be pulled. So she pulls it. "What stories?"

Jiran catches the elbow of a Server moving between the tables. "Six tequilas?" he asks, looking at Anaiya for confirmation. She nods and hands over another of her blue rounds to join Jiran's.

"So, Lira's bad arm?" he continues after the Server has moved away. "She got it after being detained for dex-possession—which she never had and they never found."

Once upon a time, the allegation would have caused Anaiya to scoff or would have goaded her into indignant outrage. "No story, there. We've all seen Peacekeeper…" *Brutality.* "Exuberance."

"Right?" Jiran leans forward. "Except the Peacekeeper who detained her was *the* Peacekeeper. The Original Resistor." Even now, especially now, Elementals are careful to not say Kane 148's name aloud. But Jiran doesn't have to say his name for Anaiya's heart to leap into her throat. There's a peace she still hasn't made with her former mentor—a confusion about who he had been and what he had expected her to be that seems to cloud everything.

"And," Jiran continues, oblivious to Anaiya's tension. "The best part is that Lira didn't get the injury when she was restrained. I mean, she was injured, obviously—two of them crash-tackled her in the Edges—but then they pushed her into a solo detention cell without medical attention. For four days."

Even under the growing warmth from the tequila, Anaiya shivers, unexpectedly caught in the memory of the fear and desperation she'd endured during her solo cell detention. She'd emerged desperate and crazed after just twenty-four hours. How had Lira survived four days?

"She would have been in there for longer, if it hadn't been for, you know, *him*."

Kane?

"Rumour is that he was the one who pulled the strings to release her. *And* that she was the reason he became an Earth Elemental."

Anaiya laughs, unable to hide her disbelief. Kane had changed a lot in the time between his Heterodoxy and Execution, but the thought of him turning Heterodox out of pity for an Earth Elemental was ridiculous. "There's no way…"

"Hey," Jiran replies, throwing his hands up in submission and leaning back. "I'm just telling you how the story goes. Wild, though, right? A Peacekeeper becoming Heterodox because he fell for a Cleaner?"

The Server returns, proffering the glasses of tequila. Anaiya takes her three and pulls them towards her, unconcerned as the clear liquid spills over the rim and pools on the laminate table. The standard narrative leaps to her mind, as it always does, delivered in the tight voice of the trainers during her conditioning: *Orthodoxy is right belief and right action. Unorthodoxy is wrong action. Heterodoxy is wrong belief. Unorthodoxy is negligence and recklessness. Heterodoxy is an illness, an unnatural mutation.* She downs the first shot of tequila quickly, but it doesn't flood her with the same promise of numbness.

"They were close after he went Heterodox?" she asks, the narrative still eating away at her thoughts. *Unorthodoxy can be rectified. Heterodoxy can only be terminated.*

Jiran knocks back his own tequila and smiles good-naturedly at the older Elemental who takes up a seat next to him. He reaches for his second glass and turns back to Anaiya. "No other reason for the rumour to start, hey?"

The noise of the drinking den swells around them. More

Earths have finished their shifts and flood the space with their too-loud voices and uninhibited laughter. Jiran turns back to the newcomer, engaging in easy conversation and leaving Anaiya to the dark thoughts that toss and pitch in her mind.

The idea of Kane turning Heterodox to woo an Earth Elemental is beyond belief, but it's harder to dismiss the possibility that he'd fallen for Lira after his Earth tendencies started showing. Anaiya knows how easy it is to fall down that tunnel with a realigned brain.

I wonder how true the story is... Because there is always a remnant of truth, even in the most outrageous rumour. It was how she and Eamon had ended up on the Execution Pillar less than three months ago: Star-crossed, Heterodox lovers plotting to bring down the Orthodoxy of Otpor. Not entirely true; not altogether untrue. It was hard to think of Eamon without shivering, without remembering how he had chained her inside an empty air recycler, led her bound through Otpor streets to his lynch-style justice, and pressed a knife to her throat while the erratic crowd cheered for her impending execution. Yes, they had both plotted for the Orthodoxy's downfall, but they had been far from star-crossed lovers.

She downs her second tequila and looks around the den for the elusive Lira. The once-empty tables are now full, and scores of Earth Elementals crowd around the long, plain bar. A few of the faces are familiar—Sharna with her messy, blonde hair pulled into a loose braid, flirting with a younger woman; one of the regular patrons, his features permanently clouded with a scowl, despite his loud and unabashed guffaws; and the Trainee Cleaner she worked with a couple of weeks ago and whose name she has already forgotten. But, no Lira.

No matter. Even if she were to find Lira, there is no subtle way to broach the subject with her. No easy way to say, *Hey Lira. I hear you used to hang out with Otpor's most hated Elemental.* At least, not without drawing her suspicion and risking her recognising the person asking as Otpor's second-most hated. *Still in Kane's shadow.* The thought is not as sharp as it used to be; the bitterness replaced with something softer but more persistent.

She stands up, leaving the last shotglass untouched. There are other ways to discover how many of the stories are true. *Or, at least, substantiated.*

She waves to Jiran, who flashes an easy smile and reaches for her abandoned tequila. Pushing through the throng, she ducks through the exit and back into the dark streets of the city. A warm buzz cloaks her body, born of the alcohol, the steady stretching of her legs, and the growing anticipation. She maintains a steady pace, keeping to the shadows, but takes the shortest route back to Kaide's apartment. Back to her hidden stash of rescued notes written at Kane 148's hand.

The darkness is fading, the sky a brown and purple bruise, when Anaiya begins the short climb to Kaide's second-floor apartment. Her unprotected elbows scrape against the rough bricks. She has lost so much of the finesse she possessed as a Fire Elemental. Once, that thought would have left her hurt, angry, and confused. But, perfect forms and pretty cat vaults don't hold the same value they used to.

Still, she worries that her clumsy efforts will wake Kaide. She holds her breath as she pushes her way through the window and drops to the floor. As soon as her feet make contact, she looks up, expecting to see Kaide in the doorway; disappointment and relief flaring in her core when he is not there.

It would be so much easier if he just didn't expect so much.

Sometimes, his belief in her is the only thing that adds meaning to her untethered life. Other times, the sheer weight of it threatens to drown her.

She pads on soft feet to the bureau and gently pulls it away from its place against the wall, grateful for the thick polyester carpet that silences her movements. The grate of the air vent comes away easily, and her hands pull free the hidden papers nestled inside. Her fingers no longer tremble at the touch of the Unorthodox paper or at the thought of the Heterodox writings they contain, but still her heart races.

Sitting on the floor with her back against the bureau, she unfolds the pages one by one and smooths out the creases. She has read them a hundred times before, looking for hidden meanings and obscure truths in the erratic thoughts and searching for answers to her own Heterodoxy. But all they had given her were more questions.

But, maybe Lira has the answers. *If the stories are true.* Anaiya can't remember seeing the Earth Elemental's name in Kane's writings, but she also knows the tunnelled focus that comes when looking at something with an agenda, and the things that can be missed…

Her eyes scan the words, no longer delving into their meaning, just looking for something that could be code for Lira, hoping that Kane's residual Fire tendencies had led him to choose a simple disguise.

When the pages yield no help, she pushes them away and reaches back into the vent for the glass screen tucked away in the darkness. It bears familiar scratches and takes a while to reboot, but it eventually stutters to life and the display fills with the digital files she had stolen from the archive. Remembering that moment still flushes her with adrenalin; that impulsive decision had set her on the path to her death, and to Kaide.

She glances to her right, to the wall that separates her room from his, and reaches out to touch it. Nothing but steel and plaster between them.

In the last few weeks there have been moments of intimacy, when the fire of connection between them felt as though it could obliterate the chasm that exists in the moments of quiet.

A chasm of my own designs.

And it is—carved with a cold heart that can't move past the betrayals and barrenness. She had thought that existing in between two Elements was a cruel punishment, but her Execution had stolen both Elements from her, and having no Element has torn her identity asunder. It is hard to give yourself to someone when you don't know what it is you are giving.

Sighing, she lowers her hand back to the glass screen and opens the same files she has pored over since her Execution. A rare few are digital documents that were no doubt confiscated from Kane 148's devices, but most are digital images of real pages; Kane's distinct handwriting is all over them, filling the margins and blank spaces, threatening to obscure the printed text that the volumes were intended for.

She has known forbidden books—strange volumes of fragile pages filled with their clunky, archaic-looking text and overly elaborate typeface. She has read salvaged pages torn from books left abandoned and forgotten in derelict warehouses, and seen volumes as thick as bricks hidden away in the Enclave on Boileau Road. All of them dangerous; Unorthodox in their structure, Heterodox in the words they held.

Just like me.

Most of the pages Kane had scrawled on were early manifestos of Otpor's Principals, the founding leaders of the Cooperative. And much of the scrawling had been emotive arguments and treatises on why the Orthodoxy was flawed and how the Fire Element was corrupted. These had been the focus of her fevered reading in the aftermath of her Execution, but now, in the early hours of morning, she skims past them, swiping at the screen until a more random collection of files appears.

Opening the first one brings up lines and lines of tiny text. The notes in the margins are sparse and Anaiya skims the print, swiping through the pages until she is confronted by something more beautiful and more shocking than Kane 148's words.

The dark lines of black ink are familiar, but instead of words of angst and frustration, they trace something more gentle, more striking across the page. The portrait is rendered in perfect detail, with a tenderness she would not have believed possible in her mentor. But, then again, she had known him when they were both Fire Elementals, when the softest emotion they knew was disappointment.

As beautiful as the ink outline is, it is the colours that arrest her. They remind her of the paint that dripped from concrete recyclers and pooled in the holes of their rotting surfaces during the Resistance. But, on the page, they are beautiful.

The face looks over a shoulder, half in shadow, half in light.

Eyes seem to peer from the paper, a shade of blue that would be pure fantasy if she hadn't already seen them in the flesh.

Lira. She is younger in the portrait. Her face bears no complacency or regret or resignation. Rather, it is set in a fierce determination and defiance.

So, the stories are true. Or hold some truth. She has learned that truth is not the immovable constant she once thought it to be, that it is instead a temperamental thing.

She stares at the picture, unable to swipe to the next page. This was a face Kane 148 had studied, had watched unobserved, had etched in his mind before etching it onto the paper. It would have been impossible to believe him capable of it—of the artistry, of the unlikely connection with another Element—if she were not capable of it herself.

She looks again to the wall that separates her from Kaide; it would be easy to go next door to him. She wants to. But she is too proud. Or too confused.

The dull thud of nearby footsteps pulls her gaze from the screen to the door. A bitter flash of guilt brings with it a silent recrimination that she should have sought him out first. But it is overwhelmed by relief. She puts aside the glass screen and stands up. The sound of footsteps quieten and the seconds stretch on in silence.

Has he changed his mind? Her gut twists at the thought of her coldness having pushed him too far away. She steps forward, then stops. Waiting for him to open the door. Wanting to open it herself.

She clenches her fists and forces her breath to come slower so that she can hear him through the brittle plastic of the door.

"What are you doing here?" Kaide asks, his voice a soft murmur through the door.

She opens her mouth to answer, her brain racing for the right words.

"I'm sorry."

And, despite the words being those on her tongue, it is not her voice that speaks them, but Seth's.

TWO

"I didn't know where else to go." Seth's voice comes muffled through the door. He sounds tired. He sounds *defeated*. It is a word Anaiya has never associated with the bright-eyed, passionate Elemental who introduced her to his Resistance.

Her chest tightens as she imagines him standing in the room on the other side of the door, with dull eyes and slumped shoulders. She had thought she'd loved him in the beginning, back when her realigned brain had flooded her with unfamiliar emotions and she'd fallen into stolen kisses and moments of vulnerability. Later, she'd hated him—not when she discovered he led the forbidden rebellion, not when he'd turned his back on her and declared her dead, but when he'd handed her over to his vengeance-crazed friend to publicly execute her in front of a rabid lynch mob.

But, she hadn't been executed then—her escape had come with a key secreted to her by Cress. She had thought Kaide was the orchestrator, hidden somewhere in the crowd and working to save her. But, he'd denied it. *"Cress and I are close,"* he'd said. *"But, she was always closer to Seth."*

"Where have you been?" Kaide says, his voice centring Anaiya's thoughts and grounding her emotions. She wonders whether he knows she is inside the apartment. Wonders how he feels about it. Seth has been an unspoken taboo topic between them, not exactly forbidden, but definitely uncomfortable. *How do you reasonably discuss your ex-lover, who tried to kill you and maybe tried to save you, with your current lover who actually did save you?*

"I couldn't stay here," Seth says, his voice softer and more muffled. Anaiya steps closer to the door and presses her ear to the surface. "It was too dangerous—too many Peacekeepers… Too many ghosts."

"So you just disappeared?"

"I didn't think you'd want me around."

The silence stretches after that. Anaiya holds her breath, desperate to hear what comes next.

"So, if here wasn't an option, where was?" Kaide asks. "I didn't think there were many places to avoid Fire Elementals or memories."

"Some places are easier than others. Set apart. Isolated. Where the drugs and alcohol make wish-star dreams seem like reality, and reality like a fading dream…"

The Enclave. He's been at the Enclave. Or, at least, one of the buildings attached to it.

For years, enclaves had been urban legends, and average ones at that. Secluded places where the rich and powerful could hide from the rabble. The whispered legends said they were gated communities with their own Peacekeepers to protect them, and Air artists to entertain them.

But, the Enclave was more than a myth, and the legends had it all wrong.

In the months since her Execution, she tried to sneak back into its world, but the tunnel access had been bricked up and Boileau Road closed, barricaded by bollards plastered with *Ongoing Repairs and Maintenance Work* signs and supervised by a rotating shift of Fire Elementals. Dressed in dark kevlar and as motionless as the concrete they guarded, they could pass for off-shift Border Protectors if the idea of them protecting such a tiny stretch of road wasn't so ridiculous.

"Then why come back?" Kaide asks, his voice calm and measured. Not that it fools Anaiya—she knows his emotions are a deep undercurrent. "It all sounds perfect."

"Can't hide forever. And sometimes dreams, no matter how

lifelike they seem, are just dreams. I'd forgotten what had started me on my path; I needed to remind myself why it was so important."

"I tried to remind you."

The voices are getting softer and less distinct. They've moved further into the apartment. Heart racing and fingers trembling, Anaiya reaches for the door handle and slowly presses it down, waiting for and dreading the click of the latch. It sounds too loud, even above her raging heart. She freezes, holding her breath and silently begging her heartbeat to slow. There are no sounds from beyond the door, nothing to indicate they have heard her, so she gently prises the unlatched door open.

"… liked the excitement more than the cause." Without the door as a barrier, Seth's voice sounds deeper and weighed down. "I should have realised it earlier. But it was nice to have someone who… didn't fight me. Lilith made me feel right, or righteous. And, after Rehhd, I was desperate for that."

The words hit like a sucker punch and she flinches. Memories of Rehhd always hit hard. She had been Anaiya's first Air contact after her original realignment, had introduced her into the world of Seth's resistance, and had quickly become suspicious of her. It was Rehhd and her vulnerable, authentic words on resistance that had eventually shifted Anaiya's perspective on the resistance and the Orthodoxy it was fighting. *Resistance leads to growth… Fighting the art strengthens the artist, and it is the artist, not the art, that needs to be strong.* She had been talking in code, so suspicious of Anaiya, yet so desperate to share her vision. She had been trying, in her way, to show Anaiya that Otpor's strength was in its citizens and not its ideology.

It had taken so long for Anaiya to grasp the true message of her words, and by the time she had, her mission had already Executed the speaker. The guilt from letting Rehhd go to the Execution Pillar, even in the aftermath of Seth being revealed as the resistance's true leader, had plagued her throughout her next realignment process and the months after. It still plagues her.

This is a bad idea. She doesn't want to hear what Seth has to say. Stepping back into that old world, that life, will only invite the same messy emotions and chaos she had barely escaped from.

And yet, she opens the door wider. The gap is smaller than half a hand's width, but enough to afford a limited view of the room beyond.

Seth has his back to her, hand raking through his short-cropped hair in a familiar gesture of unease. Kaide stands opposite, hands slung casually in his pockets, but reservation showing in the sharper angles of his jaw.

"So, she's still back there?" Kaide asks. "At Boileau Road?"

"As far as I know. With the Resistance dead, she'll get her excitement there, I suppose."

"Who would have guessed an Air could be so superficial?"

Seth barks a laugh, the noise sharp and joyless. It dies quickly and leaves a deeper silence behind.

"I'm sorry," he says after a while. "For all of it. For leaving, for not listening to you. For Eamon. And Anaiya."

Kaide glances over to the door of her room, his eyes widening at seeing her peering out behind it. The look of horror puts a chill to her heart. Her hand reaches for the door to shut it, but not before Seth turns.

In that moment, when Seth's gaze finds hers, time grinds down to its slowest speed. She slams the door shut with a crash that ratchets her heart rate higher. Stumbling back, eyes still glued to the door, she is only steps away when it opens again. She expects to see Kaide, his face darkened with the same fear and urgency she had seen just a minute ago. But it is her former lover, and not her current, that greets her.

Her hand flies up, unbidden, ready to reach forward and slam the door back into place. But, she stops at the last second, unsure whether it is the uselessness of the action or the hold of Seth's gaze that stays her hand.

His own pause, the frown that pulls at his tired features, suggests he hasn't recognised her yet or doesn't believe the impossibility standing before him. She could duck her head and push past him, leave him and his questions for Kaide to deal with. She glances back at the bureau, and to the glass screen and papers lying discarded on the floor next to it. Even if she were to leave now, what she would leave behind would reveal her as clearly as shedding her disguise.

She looks back at Seth, but his gaze has tracked with hers and fixes on the forbidden objects she has left exposed. And, when he looks to her, there is no more doubt or confusion clouding his eyes. He sees her.

She opens her mouth to intercept him, hand flying up to the voice modulator that may still conceal her true identity.

"Seth." Kaide's voice is low and dangerous. When Seth turns, she sees him standing just beyond the doorway, his body angled to her even though it is Seth he addresses. At the sound of his name, Seth makes to turn around, but pauses, never letting his gaze waver from Anaiya.

His face darkens. "An—" The syllable is strangled. Kaide pushes into the room and steps in between her and Seth.

"Seth," he says again, harder, more insistent; as if words are tangible things that can barricade or chain.

"I don't…" Seth's voice, by contrast, is hesitant, almost tremulous. He trails off into silence. Anaiya suffers in it, wanting to peer around Kaide's broad frame and see what emotions are clouding his face.

"Kaide." Seth says eventually; softly, deadly. "Is it really her?"

And Anaiya doesn't need to see his face to know his emotions, she feels them herself. The guilt and betrayal twist in her gut, swirling around tortured memories and banished thoughts. She takes a step back even as Kaide pushes Seth back through the door. "Not here," he says, and then throws a glance over his shoulder to Anaiya. There is an apology in that look, and something else—a sadness or resignation? She doesn't stick around to discern it. Turning her back on them both, she rushes to the window and, pausing only to confirm the alley is empty, leaps from it.

The den in Precinct 17 is noisier when Anaiya pushes through with a group of younger Elementals. The table she had occupied with Jiran a few hours earlier is full of new faces, and the broad-framed Earth is nowhere to be seen. *Probably trying to placate his missus after too many drinks and 'honest' observations.* The thought makes her smile and, with a little resistance, the sharp edges of her encounter with Seth start to file down.

Rather than find a seat pressed up against sweaty bodies of Elementals she doesn't know, Anaiya lingers at the end of the bar where the crowd is thinner and the air less cloying. The wait for drinks, however, is longer and so she spends her time casting her gaze over the den's patrons and imagining them as other Elemental competencies — A Cleaner as a Border Watcher, a Warehouse Manager as a Lab Technician, a Server as a Dancer — seeing if one identity fits better than the other, or whether both could be equally true. It has become her favourite distraction since losing her own identity. Both of her identities. *All of them.* Part distraction, part impossible wish-fulfilment.

She shakes her head free of the runaway thoughts; they are dangerous and painful threads to untangle.

The Server finally approaches and Anaiya hands over another glass round to purchase two steins of voybee's amber-coloured alcohol. It tastes as bad as she expects and it hits as hard as it should and, yet, her mind still tugs at the threads of her distraction.

What would I be? What could *I be?*

They are the easier questions. What Elemental hasn't imagined, if only in their Premie days, of what corps would be assigned to them, what competency they would be aligned to?

What am I now? What can *I be?*

They are the harder questions. Questions she had before her Execution. Questions that have only grown more insistent since.

She glances down at the metal cuff at her wrist, the skin still angry and swollen where Kaide had embedded it after her original one was torn from her skin and attached to a dead body in the city's morgue. Unlike the real wristplates on the arms of every Elemental in Otpor, hers is made of a lighter metal and, despite the very real pain she had felt when Kaide had sliced into her arm and slotted the cuff into place, there are no tiny wires that penetrate veins or wrap around nerve fibres. Just another way she is an Elemental in pretence only.

Everything on the outside — her fake wristplate, her fake

purple hair, her fake voice emanating from the sound modulator at her throat—it all works to present the picture of a normal, but forgettable, Elemental, and hide something altogether different.

"You shouldn't be here."

Anaiya looks up and is confronted by a sweating Server trying to squeeze through the narrow gap to the bar and struggling under a tray laden with empty glasses. Startling, from the gruff voice or the echo of her own thoughts, Anaiya grabs her drinks and moves out of the way, bumping into bodies and drawing looks of amusement and ire in turn.

This is a bad idea. She shouldn't be here. There are other places she can escape—abandoned apartments she's scouted on cleaning jobs, where she can plug in her fake lifeline and listen to the music Kaide had programmed on to a chip embedded in the wristplate. *"It's not that different, when you think about it," he'd said. "You just won't get real-time access to new stuff and you'll miss out on the direct chemical manipulation."*

It was like living a two-dimensional life in a three-dimensional world. But, there is nothing for it; it is who she is now.

"Do I know you?"

The words send ice through Anaiya's veins; they are the words she has dreaded since waking up from her Execution, the words she has hidden from in dark shadows and crowded Earth drinking dens where no-one should have the interest nor the eye for detail to see beyond her carefully curated disguise.

She turns slowly, hoping to find one of the Cleaners she has worked with, but instead finding someone just as familiar, but more problematic.

Lira.

Anaiya turns away, ready to push through the crowd, but the woman's hand reaches up and grabs her shoulder, peering closer at the dark eyes and purple hair.

"I do know you, don't I?" she says, but this time the words are barely a murmur above the noise of the crowd.

"I did a cleaning job for you earlier tonight," Anaiya says with affected nonchalance, taking a large swig of her drink and turning back to the bar. "You owe me ten blue rounds."

Lira snorts. "Everyone owes someone something."

"Heavy are the debts the entitled pass down," Anaiya murmurs into her glass. It is a throwaway line from one of Kane's notebooks, but seconds later, Lira pushes past the nearby Elementals to stand next to her. For a long time she just stands there, fingers tapping against her own tumbler, but not drinking.

"Who are you?"

"Just a Cleaner."

"No…" She leans close, keeping her gaze on Anaiya's profile. "Not just a Cleaner, Anaiyasha."

Anaiya whips her head towards the older woman and immediately regrets it as Lira's eyes widen slightly at the involuntary confirmation.

"I saw you die," Lira says, her words barely a whisper above the din.

"I'm not who you think I am," Anaiya says, too loudly. She steps away, leaving her drinks behind and pushing past Lira and away from the bar. Panic is tightening its grip around her chest, making it hard to think clearly, to do anything but scan the room for an exit. Finding Lira was supposed to give her answers, not lead her back to the Execution Pillar.

Lira's grip on her arm digs deep into the skin and causes her to pause.

"Well, in case you are," Lira says, low and harsh. "You should know that you were the only thing he talked about with hope and the last thing he thought of before he died."

Anaiya shakes out the older woman's clench once and for all, striding through the den without a thought for who might be watching her, and storming through the exit without a backward glance. The cool air hits like a brick and she stops in her tracks.

Stop running. It is one thing to have to remain hidden, it shouldn't mean she always has to run.

She had been fearless as a Fire Elemental. And impulsive as an Air Elemental. But, now, without an Element, she is neither.

Taking a deep breath and pushing down errant thoughts, she strides back into the den. Lira is still at the bar where she left her, standing alone and apart, despite the bodies that push and swell and cram into the space around her.

"I know you too," Anaiya says, her voice skimming above the din. "And I wasn't the only one he talked about."

Lira looks at her, her face free of the panic and fear that had flooded Anaiya when she'd heard Lira use the same words just minutes ago. The older woman frowns, squinting and leaning forward. "Shall we compare notes?" she murmurs.

It is a strange word to use, *notes*. Innocuous in its own way—Peacekeepers upload notes to citizen wristplates, sellers accept debt notes when funds are waiting to be cleared. But, each of these exist only in a digital format; a simple data array to convey static information. Not so the other kind of notes, the notes Kane 148 had written in the margins of books, the notes carefully and poetically crafted in Seth's journals, the love notes Kaide had scrawled for her on the back of the pages of ancient plays. Those hold more than just static data. The same words written in a different hand, in a darker tint where the stylus had pressed harder, on different paper with its different texture and scent—it all added something, gave meaning that existed beyond just words.

Had Lira receive these kind of notes from Kane? Does she still have some hidden away in places where their Unorthodoxy and Heterodoxy will not be easily found?

Lira's face softens in the silence of Anaiya's contemplation.

"Come," Lira murmurs again, the words not so much audible above the noise around them as they are clear by the movement of Lira's lips.

Anaiya, heart thrumming with the anticipation of finally getting answers, follows the older woman away from the crowd and into the street.

"How did you know him?" Anaiya asks.

She and Lira sit on uncomfortable, gaudy, plastic chairs in a room lit only by a small lamp perched on a table that seems to float above the floor. It is an anachronistic setting for an Earth Elemental, and yet Lira seems completely at ease in it. More than that, it seems to suit her.

"He restrained me," Lira says, looking down at her hands and smiling. "He thought I was holding dex."

"And?" Anaiya prompts when the other woman falls into silence.

"I wasn't. I was holding something far more dangerous. I tossed it before he and his partner reached me, but he went back to search for it. And when he found it, he came looking for me…It's funny," she says, looking back up at Anaiya, her smile faded, "in spite of all the lies the Cooperative feeds us, about Orthodoxy and Heterodoxy and everything in between, they are right when they say Heterodoxy is a virus. Revolutionary words are *infectious*. Or, at least, they can be—if your immunity is compromised."

Anaiya leans forward, resting her elbows on her knees. "I thought the original Heterodoxy was Kane's."

"The first Heterodox words were. But the first Revolutionary words came from a very Orthodox place."

Anaiya startles at somehow knowing the answer to this riddle. "The Cooperative." How many pages of early treatises and discourses penned by the Principals had she read in the days since discovering her mentor's notes?

"So, you're not as blind as the rest of them."

"What did you do? Steal a glass screen or data drive?" It is the only way Anaiya can think of an Earth getting their hands on Heterodoxy. Knowing what she now knows about Earths and their black-market trading, she imagines that high-quality tech would fetch more than a few measly blue rounds.

Lira smiles sadly. "That's the way it all started. Using fake cleaning contracts to get access to the right places and steal next-gen screens. Then I realised the content was more lucrative than the tech."

"How did you get your hands on it?" All the digitised versions of classified information were stored in secure lockers in the Evidence Hall buried three levels below the ground floor of Last Defence. And, Anaiya has experienced first-hand how difficult it is to gain access to those rooms, and to steal from them.

It is strange, *dangerous*, to be discussing these things out loud.

And, yet, the way Lira's words echo with her own experiences settles her nerves and her doubts.

Lira looks at her. Really looks. She leans forward and peers intently into Anaiya's eyes, never blinking, never looking away. Even in the soft light, the lines and marks of the synth toxin build-up are evident in Lira's face. Anaiya tries to pick her lustrum. As a Peacekeeper, the task was a simple exercise, but now her unaligned brain gets too distracted by the story of the face, unable to focus on just the facts. She could be in her seventh lustrum—Kane would have been in his eighth if he were still alive—but, something about Lira's energy makes her seem younger.

"There are places, you know," Lira says quietly, still leaning forward, but her stare now far-away. "Places you can't begin to imagine. Places that seem Heterodox just dreaming about. That seem like a dream, like you've stepped through to the other side of a mirror. Where things are like a reflection of this world, where they almost seem like they are part of this world, and yet they are so fundamentally different as to be a whole new reality."

Anaiya falls still. *I know places like that.* She wants to say it out loud, but holds her tongue. Her experience in the Enclave is a secret she holds even from Kaide.

"How different?" she whispers. It is impossible to think that Lira has seen that side of Otpor—an upmarket Air gallery would seem like a different world to an Earth Elemental. And, yet, Lira doesn't seem like just another Earth… not with her strange apartment, lyrical voice, poetic words, and shifting demeanour.

"Is that why we're here, Anaiya?" the older woman asks, blinking out of her reverie and leaning back in the moulded plastic chair. "To talk about places that shouldn't exist?" Anaiya shakes her head, feeling a twinge of disappointment. Some days she feels as though her time at the Enclave was a fever dream; something her corrupted brain had manufactured after her Execution. It would be easier to believe that it was nothing more than a fantasy, if it wasn't for the fragile leaf she kept hidden away at Kaide's apartment.

Even so, it would be nice to know she isn't alone in finding what was designed to stay hidden.

"He saw something in you," Lira says. "He used to talk

incessantly about how you were different. To an Orthodox mind, that would be an indictment. This world doesn't tolerate different. But, Kane—he saw it as a blessing."

The Air word sounds too comfortable on her tongue.

"He saw it as a lifeline. A way out of… of this." Lira throws her hands around, her eyes gazing out to the window and the skyline of Otpor beyond.

"Because I was different?"

Lira nods.

"But, you're different," Anaiya says. "And he was different. Why did he think I could do anything to change that?" She throws her own hand towards the city beyond.

"I don't know," Lira says, fixing Anaiya with her gaze. "But he was right, wasn't he? How else would you be sitting here, once a Peacekeeper, then a Heterodox betrayer, and now an Earth Elemental, resurrected from death?"

THREE

The floor of the abandoned apartment Anaiya is squatting in is cold and hard, its threadbare carpet no comfort to her sleepless body. With no furnishings and no air conditioning, even if she wanted to sleep, it would be near impossible. And, yet, it is not the discomfort that keeps her from sleep, but Lira's words. And the words of Kane that spill across the pages of the book Lira gifted her.

The older woman had smiled when she had handed over the slim notebook with its plain grey cover and faintly lined paper. It had been a sad smile, almost wistful; it played on Anaiya's mind as she fled to the fringes of Precinct 16, warning her of some hard truth or painful enlightenment Kane had recorded on his pages. And now, as she reads his words, she finds it, but it is not as she expected.

She had anticipated his words would be about her, about how she was supposed to change the world. Instead, the notebook is full of wild dreams and unimaginable futures. Of an Otpor without Elements.

My fire heart and my earth brain, like the sun-baked sands of the Wastelands. Beautiful and deadly in their uneasy alliance. Finding echoes in water ideas in air words, like forgotten rains, or air gracefulness and fire strength, like the firestorms that used to race across the crowded streets of Otpor. Before it was Otpor. Before it was crowded. Before identities were engineered to create an efficiency and compliance that takes away and subverts our true identity. And calls it Orthodoxy.

The words aren't a radical shift from what she has read in other remnants of Kane's writings—the themes of freedom and enlightenment abundant in each. But, in the other volumes she had read, his ideas had seemed to call for the eradication of the Fire Element, and later, for the return of Fire to the Orthodoxy. Both were equally shocking and impossible. And yet, she had believed in both of them—drawn to their truth by her newfound perspective on Peacekeeper violence and ruthlessness.

This new vision should be more shocking than the others.

Imagine a world where there are no Elements. Where not having an Element isn't defective, but normal.

The want of it hits like a lightning strike. She would do anything to feel normal again.

She stares at the pages for hours, mind ticking over Kane's words and their implications. He didn't want to remove the Fire Element, and he didn't want to restore the Orthodoxy. He wanted to dismantle it all, scratch away the conditioning until raw identities, bloody and vulnerable, were all that remained.

Finally, it is the hunger that drives her back to Kaide's apartment. Her body shakes with the lack of nutrients, but she knows that the real hunger is for someone to tell her they believe in her and that she doesn't need to be an Elemental to be worthy.

She waits in the darkened alley, peering up at the ajar window of the second bedroom, internally debating whether she is hungry enough to risk running into Seth again.

Seeing the light wink on in Kaide's room bolsters her courage. As always, she quickly scans the area to confirm no-one is watching, and then scales the wall. She pauses at the top and peers inside the room. Even with the dark shadows, she can see that it is empty.

Relief floods her body, turning tense limbs soft and pliable. With Kane 148's notebook tucked under her shirt, she glances to where her other Heterodox items are stashed, hidden in the vent behind the bureau that has been returned to its place. She doesn't stop, though; her feet practically skipping across the dense carpet to the door that is also slightly ajar.

Pushing it open, her eyes drink in the details afforded by the light still spilling from under Kaide's door—the faded carpet, the pin-striped wall skin, the comfortable lounges, and Seth.

He stands in the lounge room, holding a book like it is just another everyday object and not something that could see him interrogated by Truth Seekers for merely possessing it. He looks up as though sensing he is being watched—he always had an uncanny knack for that—and, this time, there is no surprise on his face.

"Hello, Anaiya."

The quiet words slam into her chest. It has been forever since they have spoken to each other; so long that the memory of it is a hazy collection of fragments—finding his hidden journals, scaling down the wall of his apartment building, being caught in the act and having to confront just how far their connection had been corrupted. The final threads of their relationship had been severed that night, leaving him with nothing to stop the execution order he had issued a few months later. Except maybe an echo that had seen him rescind it and give her a chance to escape.

"Back from the dead, hm?" Seth asks, not bothering to hide the hard edge to his words.

"You too, I see," she replies, stepping into the hallway. He smiles at that, but it is not the smile she remembers. She is not the only one who has changed since their original meeting in the weeks after her first realignment. *Death and betrayal will do that to you.* "Why *are* you here? Why leave your perfect paradise?"

Seth raises an eyebrow. "Never said it was perfect."

"You didn't need to; no Fire Elementals, no Peacekeepers—it's your dream-come-true."

He barks a short laugh and sinks to the lounge. "It was never supposed to be a permanent arrangement. Just a safehouse until the madness of your and Eamon's Executions had faded. They were still looking for 'accomplices' in those early weeks, and we didn't know whether we were on the Peacekeeper hunting list or not."

"So the paragons of high society and Otpor's elite just let you crash?" Anaiya blinks at the heavy sarcasm loaded in her voice. "They don't seem the type of Elementals to throw a pity party."

Seth shrugs non-comitally. "I'm sure they had their reasons. Just as they had their reasons for helping us with our plans to take down the Peacekeepers."

"And that turned out spectacularly well." The conversation is getting to her, bringing up past trauma and forcing it into high definition. She turns from him and starts towards Kaide's room.

"He's not there," Seth calls out.

"His light's on," she replies, not slowing. But, opening the door reveals an empty room. Reluctantly, she turns back to Seth. His head is bowed, his gaze on the book.

"He left it on, hoping you'd come back. He's out searching for you."

"Why would he be searching for me?"

"Because you could be lying in a gutter with a grade three laceration and no wristplate vitals to alert paramedics, no ability to attend the Infirmary even if you needed to. Or because you could be locked away in a solo detention cell, being tortured by Niamh who would have no qualms breaking an Elemental he had already Executed. Or because—"

"Alright, Seth, I get it," she snaps.

He lifts his head lazily, as though the conversation is of no more interest than the pages he toys with.

"I'm sure you do, Anaiya."

As a Peacekeeper, she would have smacked the insolent look off his face, wrapped him in a headlock, and given him a bloodied nose for the hell of it. Even in the absence of alignment to an Element, part of her still thrums with a vague desire to do something similar. To rip the book out of his hand and turn it into a weapon of sorts.

Tch, tch, Anaiya. Control the Fire.

She smiles at the irony of her old mantra and it deepens when she sees Seth's look of surprise in response. He still sees her as a Peacekeeper, still expects her to act like one. Be one. He doesn't know she is cast adrift. That she is no-one.

What would he think of her if he knew? What would he think of Kane 148's vision for a brave new world of Air Peacekeepers and Fire Dancers?

"What are you reading?" she asks.

The look of surprise remains, but he holds up the thick fabric-bound book, its title emblazoned in gold on the cover. *War and Peace.*

"A titan of the ages," he says, his voice taking on a quality as though he's reciting it. "Less a chronicle of history than portent of the future, I suppose." He drops the book to his side, fingers tapping against its corner. "Why? Were you expecting another piece of Kane's legacy?"

When she had first met Seth, he had spoken of Kane's words with a reverence and fervour. Now, his voice is as muted as the light in his eyes. *Because he fears he has let down Kane in bringing about his vision, or because he has been betrayed by it?*

A loud click interrupts and saves her from having to answer Seth's question and her own. They both turn as Kaide slides the door open and steps into the apartment. He looks tired and dejected, and then his gaze falls on her. The relief that sweeps across his face and softens his features quickly transitions to annoyance, or maybe thinly veiled anger. Seth was right, he was out looking for her, was worried about her. And is now pissed at her.

She steps forward to… Explain? Placate? Apologise? None of them are options she wants to take in front of Seth. He stands with his arms crossed against his chest, regarding Kaide with sympathy and what looks like the smug satisfaction of *I told you so.*

"Not now, Seth," Kaide warns, his voice low and tainted with exhaustion. The door slides back into place and he turns back to Anaiya. "Nice to see you again, Anaiya. Is this a social call or are you here for research purposes?"

She notes the low-key sarcasm, knows it's his way of hiding his hurt. She opens her mouth to say something. Then closes it. Opens it again, and stops, exhaling softly. He doesn't move, just waits patiently for her answer.

Sighing again, she walks up to him, never looking away. She reaches for his hand and tugs at it. He raises an eyebrow and pulls his hand back, but doesn't disengage. She smiles, and pulls again, feeling the tension stretch along her arm and through her shoulder.

And this time he gives, lets her pull him towards her. She turns and leads him towards his bedroom. In her peripheral vision, Seth stands with his head bowed and fingers tapping again at the cover of his forbidden book. But, she ignores him, not slowing and not looking back.

"What's going on inside there?" Kaide taps a single finger gently against her forehead. They lie tangled in the sheets of his bed and each other's limbs. "You've been ignoring me for weeks, all secretive and silent." It's not an accusation, just a softly spoken account of the truth. "What brought you back, Anaiya?"

Her fingers, which had been drawing invisible lines across his naked skin, fall still at his words. *He thinks I came back for Seth.*

She pulls back. "It's not what you think."

"And what am I thinking?"

"Trust me. It's not that."

"Then what is it, Anaiya?" His voice holds the illusion of a tease, but she's not relying on his voice to tell her the truth, but his eyes. And in his eyes, just centimetres from hers, she sees the vulnerability.

"What drew you to the Resistance?" she asks.

His eyes widen a little at that.

"I mean," she continues, ignoring his surprise. "What was the real motivation? What was your end goal?"

He falls silent, and the surprise in his eyes turns to quiet contemplation. "I wanted the violence to end," he says simply.

"Really?" she whispers, genuinely surprised.

He tilts his head towards the bedroom door. "Seth was the visionary. The Kane devotee." He looks back to her, a strange kind of apology in his eyes. "I just wanted the oppression and retribution to stop. To end the senseless, useless, *endless* violence."

She bites down on her lip, trying to hold back the questions that burn in her mind. "Why was it so important to you?"

He pauses, pulls her hand into his and intertwines them. "Was Rehhd, and Eamon, and Seth in his own way, not enough?"

The names from their shared past bring with them difficult memories of betrayals, executions, and exile. Their stories should have been enough. For most Elementals, they would have been more than enough. But Kaide is not most Elementals.

"Was there anything else, beyond the personal impact? Anything else that made it important to you?"

They have their secrets between them, but their deepest moments of vulnerability always come back to the fact that they are both damaged goods. Both with corrupted brains and Unorthodox minds.

He sighs, an exorcising of old demons. "I wanted there to be more than this." He nods towards the window. "To Earth versus Water and Fire versus Air. To narrow boundaries, and ever narrower mindsets. Our alignments are more subtle and more complex than the simple dichotomies we live by. The Elements were designed to co-exist in harmony, but that vision has been corrupted."

She leans her head against his chest so that he can't see her disappointment. He still believes in the sanctity of the Elements. It is not the Orthodoxy he rails against, but the artificial conflicts it has created.

"You think an Air could connect with a Fire?" she murmurs into the silence.

"I think the lines are blurrier between us than what most think. That it's not all straight edges, but rough surfaces; bumps and grooves and burrs that allow for friction *and* connection."

She closes her eyes and listens to the steady thrum vibrating in his chest. He is not ready to hear Kane's vision of an Otpor without Elements.

Doubt creeps into her thoughts. What if she has misunderstood? What if she has let her own desperate, fractured mind conjure an interpretation that is less Kane's vision and more her own in an attempt to make sense of her unalignment?

Kaide's arms tighten around her and she lets herself be drawn into his embrace. It is easier to hide from hard truths and unsteady footings than dwell in the murky, mind-bending visions of her former mentor.

And, yet, even as Kaide erases her anxieties with his gentle touch and firm kisses, her mind still whispers to her its uncertainty.

"You know this, Anaiyasha." They are the words from her dreams. Half-remembered conversations with Otpor's first betrayer

and original Resistor. *"Your identity is not something that is dictated by others. Your identity is something you find yourself."*

The sun casts a dull, brown light across the sheets when Anaiya awakes. Kaide is long gone, the spot next to her cold with his absence.

She squints against the light, the temptation to drift back to sleep insistent. All night she'd slept in fits of bad dreams; visions of Kane's Execution morphing with her own and leaving her tired and edgy.

Kaide had tried to comfort her, tried to quell the tremors of her body with the sheer force of his connection with her. But she had pushed him away. Not because she didn't crave his touch or his comfort, but because she was too cold and distant inside for it to thaw her.

It is why she seeks him and runs from him in the same breath.

Sounds of movement beyond the bedroom door push energy to her limbs and pull her out of bed. She can still catch him, still make amends, or at least dull the razors that litter the emotional space between them.

She opens the bedroom door and strides into the lounge room. "Kaide, I'm—" The words die on her tongue.

"We have to stop this routine," Seth says dryly. "It's getting tired."

Shit. In between the reconnection and the nightmares, she had forgotten he was here. She bites down a retort and pulls down the hem of her pyjama shorts. "Good morning, Seth."

"He left hours ago," he says. "I'm surprised you didn't hear him, stomping around the place like a Border Watcher on patrol. But, maybe loud is your thing. Muse knows, it was last night."

Remnants of her Fire Element prevent her from blushing, but she still bristles at the attempt to unnerve her.

"Not the sex," he says, deadpan. *He's funnier than I remember.* "That was pretty quiet. But the after-talk—all that talk of Orthodoxy and alignment. Not what I'd be thinking about afterwards, but each to their own, I guess."

The urge to storm past him and out of the apartment is so strong it puts pins and needles to her feet. But the daylight hours are not hers anymore, and what pretence of freedom she had is gone, so she turns on her heel to seek the shelter of Kaide's room.

Her hand is on the door handle, ready to close it, when Seth speaks again. "He was wrong, you know; the Orthodoxy doesn't need reinforcing or saving. It needs dismantling."

FOUR

Anaiya stands very still. It is surreal to hear Seth echo her own desires so clearly.

"I don't know if you've noticed," she murmurs, keeping her voice low and soft to hide the tremors, "but the Cooperative doesn't take well to efforts that seek to bring it and its ideology down."

"I had," he replies, meeting her gaze evenly. "I've also noticed how some of their retaliations aren't as successful as they would like."

She knows he is referring to her, but she can't help but think of Kane 148. Executing him was supposed to have wiped out Heterodoxy, to have eradicated what was supposed to be an anomaly from the public consciousness. And yet, just a decade later, three others had been Executed for the same crime, and more who were guiltier still roamed Otpor's streets. Or hid in its apartments.

"What drew you to Kane?" It is a corollary to the question she asked Kaide just hours ago. Maybe the more important question.

And, just as it had with Kaide, her question takes Seth by surprise. His face drops the infuriating smirk and his eyes shift from cold to guarded. For a long while, he just stands there regarding her. And then he seems to let go of the fight and, for a moment, he's the same Seth she kissed in the shadows of Otpor's cemetery.

"He was in this world, but not of it. He lived it and understood it and was regulated by it, but he didn't conform to it. It didn't *define* him. Which is ironic—"

"Since the entire purpose of this world is to define people."

He stares at her, his expression again transformed; less guarded now, more thoughtful. "Yes."

They are caught in a moment—taken back in time to when they first connected. When they were both someone who saw the world a little differently and had the inner inferno, that cataclysmic combination of Fire and Air, to bend it to their will.

"I always knew you were different, Anaiya," he murmurs.

She'd heard it before. From him. Back in the day before all the betrayal and death. There was no going back to that time, and she had no desire to relive it.

"What would you do to change it?" she asks instead.

"No point trying to change you, Anaiya—you're as intransigent and persistent as the sand drifts."

"Not me. The Orthodoxy."

"Why?" His voice is flat and bitter. "Looking to start a revolution?"

"Yes." She is surprised when she hears the words aloud.

He doesn't flinch. "Me too."

It feels… uncomfortable, to be sharing this with Seth instead of Kaide. But Kaide is not here and is too pragmatic for radical notions of revolution.

And, it's not like she is actually planning a revolution with Seth. Just testing how crazy she is to be falling back under Kane 148's influence.

"Did you ever meet him?"

They sit on opposite sides of the room, forsaking the comfortable lounges for the less comfortable threads of the carpet.

"No. All I know of Kane is what the Cooperative force-feed me with their docutainments and what I've read in his journals. They don't exactly align, but I know which truth rings true."

Does it, though? And, this is where her uncertainty lies. It's easy to say something rings true when it mirrors your own truth;

harder to know when it is genuine enlightenment or when it is self-fulfilling prophecy and delusion.

"Why did it resonate with you?"

He isn't compromised like she and Kaide are. No hypoxia, no realignment. No reason, beyond the usual, to be anti-establishment. Most of Otpor's rebels had been in it for the thrill, some for the drama. But that isn't Seth. He is too invested. Too *connected*.

"He spoke my language."

She smiles, grudgingly, at that. It is true; there is the same fervour in their words, in the way they looked at and interpreted the world. She had fallen for Seth's words before she had fallen for him.

"It's strange, no?" she murmurs. "That a Fire Elemental, who became an Earth Elemental, writes like a Literacy competent with the soul of a Composer."

He barks a short laugh and looks down at his hands. They fidget at the shredded hems of his jeans, where the rough surfaces of Otpor streets have torn them up from too much friction. "No stranger than a Fire Elemental who became an Air Elemental and then an Earth, who speaks of revolution like a Water."

She can't tell whether he's being genuine or sarcastic.

"Why are you talking about revolution, Anaiya? Hasn't your rebellion cost you enough? Why rail so hard against our resistance only to resurrect it? Why now?"

She pauses and drops her own gaze. "I found more of his writing."

"How?"

Seth has every right to be incredulous. Kane had been Heterodox for only a year or two before his Execution, and his writings are rare. No doubt Seth thought he held all of them, all that hadn't been confiscated and held by the Cooperative in hidden archives. He wouldn't expect there to be more, wouldn't conceive of Anaiya finding any on her own; she wouldn't know where to look or what to look for.

"What do you think his vision was?" she asks instead.

"Why are you asking me, Anaiya?"

She hears the real question beneath it. *Why aren't you talking about this with Kaide?* "Because you've read his notes—"

"Not all of them, apparently," he says dryly.

"You know his words. You've pored over them. You've dissected them and reassembled them, turned them inside out and then turned them into your own. You *know* him. Not like I know him. You know *Kane the Resistor*; you know that microcosm of his life, probably better than anyone. I can't get any clarity on his vision—all the extra stuff, the history, gets in the way. But you don't have that distraction."

The look of what she has assumed was contempt, or frustration, has faded from Seth's face. He leans back against the wall, quietly contemplative.

"What are you really asking, Anaiya?"

They are circling each other, unable to get to the heart of the matter with all the distrust between them. She can't speak plainly, and he won't either. *There has to be another way.*

"Did you ever read *Romeo and Juliet*?" she asks, ignoring the way his gaze narrows, waiting for his nod of confirmation. "Kaide gave me some pages he'd salvaged."

"And?"

"And, he thinks it's a story of how some things are worth fighting for and dying for. But, I think it's about the stupidity of naming things and expecting them to only ever conform to that name." *What's in a name? That which we call a rose by any other name would smell as sweet.* "It's the same with Kane's vision—with every reading, the words seem to flip on their axis. I thought I knew what he was fighting for the first time I read his words. And then, I thought I'd figured out his *real* motivations. But, now I'm not so sure."

"Because of the new stuff you found."

"Yes."

"Are you sure it's his?"

"Yes."

"What did it say?"

She shakes her head. Seth sighs. The silence engulfs them again. They stay that way until Kaide returns to the apartment twenty minutes later.

"Am I interrupting something? Again?"

Seth stands up and shoves his hands into his jeans pockets. "Just comparing notes on literary classics."

"Oh yeah?" Kaide says, shrugging out of his jacket and throwing it over the arm of the nearest chair. He strolls over to Anaiya, winks at her as he offers her his hand and hauls her up.

"I found more of Kane's note," she says.

There are a hundred questions he could ask, questions that Seth has already asked, some she has already answered. But his first question is a much simpler one. "Are you OK?"

She nods and he squeezes her hand gently before letting go.

"So, what words of wisdom did our inspirational leader leave us this time?" With Kaide standing at the apex of their impromptu triangle, the room feels smaller and Seth closer.

"Not sure," Seth says, arms folded across his chest. "Anaiya's not divulging any of the details."

Kaide frowns at her and she shakes her head. "I was asking Seth for his take on Kane's vision."

His frown deepens at the echo of the same question she had asked him the night before, but he shrugs it off and turns his attention to Seth. "And what about you? Are you divulging any details?"

In a normal world and a normal situation, the rejoinder would have produced smiles all around. But, here, in this small room with the three of them damaged, betrayed, and corrupted, there is nothing but sombre silence and the very tangible feeling of things balancing on a precipice.

It is a silent reminder of times past, when the three of them would sit in izakaya on the Ravignan Strip, drinking tequila, and comparing battle scars. Nights with experimental music, and pool games, and three-metre-high murals of forbidden words and decaying walls.

The last memory makes her grimace. That was the problem—their shared desire for revolution coexisted with a shared history of…

Her thoughts trail off, unable to find the right words to describe the weight that hangs between them. *Weight.* It is a Peacekeeper word, something to describe the heaviness of tension and feeling of impending violence. *No, not violence. That* is a Peacekeeper thing. Weight isn't always about violence. *But, it is always about unbalance. Tipping points. Shifts from what is stable and predictable to… what is not.*

The hesitant conversation is an uneasy but familiar detente of wanting to share their secrets, but not trusting each other. *At least, I don't.* She stops herself from looking towards the bedroom where the desiccated leaf from the Enclave lays pressed between the sheets of her own journal. She should have told Kaide when she first found it…

"I'll divulge my details," Seth says, "if Anaiya divulges hers."

Kaide looks to her, his brow furrowed, but in that way of his when he's grappling with a tricky concept or question. There is no demand in his stance or pleading in his features. He looks to her, not pushing for the answer he wants, just waiting for the answer she's willing to give.

Just tell them. It's what she wants. Why she started the conversation in the first place.

"Sure," she says. "You answer my question, and I'll answer yours."

"What was the question again?" Seth asks.

He's being facetious. Anaiya bites down a juvenile retort and fixes him with a glare. "What do you think Kane's vision for resistance was? His real vision—the future he imagined, that he wanted to force into existence?"

"He didn't want to force anything into existence," Seth says. "But, sometimes the truth takes on its own energy and forces its own path."

"Truth. What is the truth?"

Seth opens his mouth to answer, but she cuts him off. "No. What was *his* truth?"

"He saw the world differently. He saw beyond the pretence and the superficiality."

"And what did he want to do about it?"

"I don't know, Anaiya—you tell me, you've got his notes."

Kaide clears his throat. Until now, he's been a silent observer, an independent umpire watching her and Seth fight it out. She expects him to intervene, but he merely shakes his head. Seth rolls his eyes and folds his arms across his chest.

"Why ask me? What makes you think I have answers that you don't?"

"Because, you took his words and turned them into a rebellion. You saw something in them, you found your own truth in them."

Even Kaide startles at that. She has been too candid. Too raw. But the time for politeness is over. "You don't have to be a Water Elemental to figure it out—you're a Literary competency, you've read what? Hundreds of manuscripts? And yet, you've only started one rebellion. On the back of what? A few notebooks?" She shakes her head. "So, what did you *see*?"

"The Orthodoxy wasn't working," Seth spits.

"The Fire Element had overreached," Kaide adds, his tone calmer. There is an apology in it; he worries that her old alignment will see his truth as an insult.

"No," Seth says quietly, not looking at either of them.

Kaide frowns and turns to him, but Anaiya remains still.

"No?" Kaide asks, confusion twisting his tone.

"No," Anaiya whispers.

Kaide looks to her, but it is Seth's gaze she holds. He knows what she knows. He knows the truth of Kane 148's resistance.

"He didn't want to bring the Fire Element back into Orthodoxy, or to destroy it," she murmurs.

Seth drops his arms to his sides and sighs. "He wanted to destroy it all."

FIVE

The revelation pushes them into a tense silence. Of all the Heterodox ideas they have dreamt up and shared over their conflicted history, this is the most dangerous. The quiet stretches between the three of them, filling the space with sounds from beyond the apartment, sounds that had been drowned out by their earlier argument and that now rush into focus: noises in the hallway, heavy boots rushing up stairs.

Anaiya's muscle memory kicks in before she can fully rationalise what is happening. In one fluid movement, she pivots on her right foot, dives forward, and somersaults to the open doorway of Kaide's bedroom. She has just enough time to pull herself in behind the door when she hears the loud beep of the apartment's access panel being jacked by Peacekeepers.

"Get on the floor!" The rough voice explodes into the apartment and Anaiya's heart feels a beat away from shattering her chest. With a trembling hand, she slides open the wardrobe door at her back and crawls inside. Closing the door plunges her into near-darkness, save the sliver of light that comes from leaving the door open the tiniest of cracks through which to hear more clearly what is happening out in the lounge room.

In the early weeks after her resurrection, she and Kaide had prepared for moments just like this—had found the perfect hiding spots and practiced drills until it became second nature. But, when no Peacekeepers had arrived to take her away and things settled into a new kind of normalcy, complacency had crept in. They had thought the threat was over.

Had they been too loud? Too careless with their talk of Kane 148 and revolution? Had someone heard them?

"Where's the female?" The harsh male voice barks again. "Where is she?"

"There is no female." Anaiya hears the effort in Kaide's voice—his tone forceful enough to be convincing, but not so strong as to warrant a Peacekeeper reprisal.

"Where is she?" a second voice roars.

"It's just us." Kaide's voice has changed. He sounds desperate, his voice strangled and strained. Have they got him a restraint hold? Are they stepping on the small of his back with their heavy black boots, and applying just enough pressure to immobilise his diaphragm and expel the air from his lungs?

"We won't ask again. What have you done with the female?"

"There is no female." Seth is shouting, his voice full of panic and rage. "It's just us." He is too loud, too confrontational.

What have they done to Kaide? Why is he quiet? Why does Seth sound so desperate?

Anaiya's muscles scream with the effort of staying still. There is no saving them from the tight confines of the wardrobe, but stepping from its protection would only cement the certainty of their deaths. Staying hidden is the only chance of survival she can give them.

How did they find us? How did they find us?

They had been so careful for so long. What had she unleashed by sharing Kane 148's vision aloud? What retribution had she brought down on all of them?

It is hard to breath. The tiny space presses in tighter and empties of oxygen. Her chest is so tight it feels as if her ribcage is made of iron. And every cell in her body feels afire.

She will never survive losing him. She will never survive knowing it has been her recklessness that has stolen him from her, has led him to the Execution Pillar he saved her from only months ago.

"It's the wrong apartment." The second voice barely penetrates into the room. "Next floor up."

Anaiya's blood thrums so loudly, she can't make out the rest of the exchange. She presses her ear closer to the crack, staring at the numbers that flash on her fake wristplate—one minute passes...two...five...ten...twenty... Its constant rhythm is the only thing that keeps her sane.

Twenty-seven minutes later, she hears the door to Kaide's bedroom close. Her heart stutters again and her muscles tense with a readiness she hasn't felt in a lifetime.

Footsteps thud closer. She pulls herself quietly into a crouch, ready to spring forward and launch across the room and out of the window at any hint of an escape opportunity.

"It's okay, Anaiya." Kaide's voice murmurs into the darkness, and everything inside her liquefies. He slides open the door, and she has no energy to spring forward into his arms. Instead, she falls backwards against the wall of the wardrobe and covers her face, a torrent of silent tears streaming down her cheeks.

Seth pours the last of the tequila into the small jar sitting on the lounge room table and sinks back into the armchair. Holding the jar up tothe naked lightbulb makes the warped glass shimmer and the imperfections shine like rivers of gold.

Anaiya sits on the lounge next to him, cradling her own tumbler of tequila and running her finger around its lip. The two of them have sat in silence since Kaide left them to buy more tequila. They are intoxicated enough to be sharing the same space and not sniping at each other, but still too sober to deal with the Peacekeeper scare.

Both he and Kaide had been injected with restraint serum before the Peacekeepers had realised they were in the wrong apartment. Scrolling through Kaide's incident file on his wristplate had confirmed the error: a charge of domestic battery recorded at 2243 and rescinded at 2245.

An hour later, and even with the alcohol warming her blood,

Anaiya still shivers at the alternative scenarios her brain tortures her with.

"It will always be like this unless someone strips it away," Seth says softly, bitterly.

Anaiya lifts her glass and lets a rivulet of tequila scorch away her tremors. Talking about revolution seems more reckless, now.

Still, it strikes her as strange that she and Seth are on the same page about Kane's vision. That they have seen what he had seen—a vision of Otpor without Elements.

She sneaks a sideways glance at him. When she had first crossed the threshold from Fire to Air, it had thrown her into chaos. Her connection, her absolute loyalty and commitment to her former Element had made her chafe and then rail against her realignment.

Everything in Otpor has always been about identity, and having your identity erased is like being a synthfly with your wings ripped off. Still alive, but useless. Still a synthfly, without really *being* a synthfly.

Seth is as attached to his Air identity as she had been to her Fire. It would be worse for him. Harder. Where her revelation had been triggered and aided by the physical and psycho-social realignment process, Seth doesn't have that. All he has are Kane's words.

And, yet, here they are. Former lovers, once enemies, eternal resistors; sharing the same impossible, Heterodox dream, given to them by a dead revolutionary who has created proteges out of them both.

"When did you know?" she asks.

He looks up and then back to his drink.

Was it before he agreed with Eamon to Execute her? Before he handed Cress the keys to free her? Before... "It's why you came back, isn't it?" *Why you left the Enclave, and Lilith, behind. Why you sought out Kaide.* "What did you find there?"

"Find where, Anaiya?" he murmurs, not looking up.

"At—" She almost says, *the Enclave,* but catches herself. There is no way the Enclave's strange and superior residents would allow low-level Elementals into the Enclave. "At the Danish Prince. What did you find at the Danish Prince?"

"You know about it, don't you?"

"The izakaya? You know I do. You saw me there."

But, the wry look on his face tells her that he knows what she is hiding. And, again, they are at a stalemate. Each protecting a secret and waiting for the other to share first.

"Not the izakaya," Seth says, his voice a whisper. "The Enclave."

She stays quiet.

"Danai mentioned you saw the inner sanctum," Seth says, and then barks a laugh. "It pissed Lilith off no end. She begged to see it, but 'rules were rules'. *Exclusive is not exclusive if everyone gets to see it.*"

"Then…" Confusion addles her mind and her voice trails off. "Then how did you find the truth? Where did you find it?"

"In the echo."

The Echo. It was a beautiful and strange way to describe it. It is the perfect way to describe it.

Hours later, with dusk approaching, her mind still returns to it. It swims in the silences, when the whispered conversation between her, Seth, and Kaide falters under the weight of what they are contemplating; when the tequila feels less like a kite on a wind and more like a sodden blanket.

Kaide struggles with it. She can see it in his rigid posture and the way his hands clench and unclench, the way his fingers worry at loose threads of the lounge cushions, the frowns and sighs and questioning looks thrown her way. He had felt the same terror, imagined the same nightmare that she had when the Peacekeepers had stormed into the apartment. And, unlike Seth and Anaiya, he couldn't see what they saw in Kane's notes. Couldn't hear the echo.

The truth of Kane's vision was not obvious, but Seth was right—it had ripples. If you knew where to look, you could find them—in the way an Earth Elemental would pause at a Samedi Market stall to appreciate a piece of abstract art, or the way an Air Designer would apply Water-like precision to the final touches of their commission. The anomalies—not common enough to be obvious, not rare enough to be invisible—hinted at the defectiveness of the Orthodoxy and its strict division between Elements.

These were the ripples of Kane 148's vision. Ripples that would create crevasses, if they could just find a crack.

"We need to resurrect it," Seth says.

Kaide shakes his head. "How many more have to die for this doomed rebellion? This battle is over. We don't fight, we adapt. Adapt or die."

The fatalism sits uneasily with Anaiya, but maybe he is right. Maybe all roads from Kane 148's lead only to Execution.

"No," Seth whispers harshly. "Adaptation is surrender. This is not the future we fought for. This is not a future we should *settle* for." The alcohol has made him more emotional. Not aggressive, but more earnest. He's desperate for Kaide to see through the same lens.

"There is no way for it to succeed." Kaide, in contrast, sounds tired and reluctant. Pragmatic. *The Water in him.* "Any move we make will be swiftly dealt with. They know our moves, our 'red flags'. Know how to shut us down and disable us. What happened tonight would be a synthfly sting compared to what they would do to us. Our resistance has failed. Twice."

She expects Seth to argue, but he smiles sadly. "Third time lucky?"

It is a magnanimous gesture, a surrender of sorts. She wonders whether he hears in Kaide's words an accusation. Wonders how deep the guilt travels; for Rehhd's death, and Eamon's. And hers.

"It doesn't have to be the same rebellion," she murmurs. "It never could be." The words come unbidden, flowing under the influence of the tequila and caught up in the current of their conversation. "We're not trying to erase the Fire Element anymore. It's not the same fight. It's not the same end-game.

"Niamh, if he's expecting anything at all, which is unlikely given the current state of affairs and the size of his ego, will be expecting what he's seen before—a passive resistance, localised to the Air Element in the Northern Area, targeting the Fire Element. He'll be expecting something known. And predictable. But we don't have to rebuild this revolution in the image of the ones that have failed."

Kaide and Seth regard her silently, their frowns replaced by their own unique expressions of thoughtful consideration—Kaide chewing his lip, Seth raking hands through his hair.

"And," she continues, swirling the last of the tequila in her jar, "maybe they failed because *they* were the wrong rebellions. Maybe we don't need another rebellion. A rebellion only changes who's in charge. Maybe what we need, what *Otpor* needs, is a revolution."

They sleep, in fits, in the lulls between passion and frustration. The next morning comes too quickly, bringing with it a fierce brown light that sneaks in under the faded curtains and pounds against Anaiya's eyelids, forcing them to open despite the hammering of her head and roiling of her stomach.

Squinting against the glare, she pushes herself up. She doesn't remember migrating to the lounge from the armchair, but the woven blanket across her legs suggests that Kaide has moved her.

She looks around for him. But the room is empty and the open doors to the bedrooms offer no sight of either him or Seth. She is alone.

Memories of their discussion come back to her in fragments.

"Who will lead this revolution? We are too recognisable, it's too dangerous."

"We don't need a leader, we're not creating a new world order; we're just dismantling the current one."

"We can't leave behind a vacuum. Nothing survives in a vacuum."

The last one was Kaide's.

"Not a vacuum," she had countered. *"Just a factory reset. Everything has come from a starting point. Everyone can return to it."*

Because, that's what had happened to her. What she is living; what she has lived *twice.*

Just a return to the original state.

But, returning to the original state is not without its complications. *Or chaos.*

Seth craves the chaos. He needs it—to sate the guilt and anger and frustration. He has wanted to rain down chaos ever since Rehhd was Executed.

From the ashes, the phoenix emerges. He had murmured it constantly the night before. It had been his mantra with the first resistance, when Otpor's true golden age was supposed to have emerged from the ashes of a defeated Fire Element. Now, he wants to burn everything down.

"Yes, yes," Kaide had placated. *"But, let's not confuse the phoenix with Icarus."*

The words had meant nothing to Anaiya, but they had tempered Seth's emotions and drawn the three of them back into silence. Each pondering the impossible question on their own terms. *How to start a leaderless revolution without tipping Otpor into fatal chaos?*

No less impossible was her own, more personal, version of that question. *How do I survive in this world without an Element and not descend into insanity?*

She presses her hands to her temples and ignored the protests of her tired and hungover body. With a groan, she stands and drags her feet to the second bedroom and to the bureau that hides Kane 148's notes.

Hours dissolve in the pages at her hands, with only the soft rustling of paper to mark their passing. It is easy to lose herself in his words—to get caught up in the beautiful turns of phrase; fall into an easy fiction of the mentor she never really, *truly*, knew; get swept away by ideologies that make her new state of uncertainty seem like a strange ideal.

"Find the answers you're looking for?" Kaide leans against the doorframe, arms loosely folded across his chest, eyes soft but red from no sleep.

Anaiya looks up, a sea of random pages scattered on the floor around her. "No." She sighs. "Did you?"

Kaide shakes his head. He steps towards her then stops, exhales slowly. "Truthfully, Anaiya, I'm not even sure of the questions we're asking. Or why we're asking them."

"Because this life is a lie. And worse, it's a lie designed only to benefit a small elite who seduce us into compliance and apathy with alcohol, drugs, entertainment, and false security. They feed us this easy lie and coat it with so much glucose that we've become addicted to it."

"No one is disputing this world is not fair or that the Cooperative, and its ideology, are not flawed. But, what is that we are seeking? A new Cooperative? A new ideology?"

She stays silent.

"No," he continues. "Because this is not about creating an alternative to what we have, but about tearing what we have down."

"Is that so bad?"

"No… But I need to know what we achieve by doing it. *Why* we are doing it."

"Because it's the truth. The Elements are not right." She remembers Kane 148's words: *The inherent defects of the Element will not remain hidden forever. A new world order will be established.* "They are not natural."

It's nothing that Kaide does not already know, has not already read himself. After all, he was the one who had slipped her the note written on those same pages. And yet he shakes his head.

"Soylent is not natural. Nutriboosters are not natural. Lys is not natural. Wallscreens are not natural. Lifelines are not natural. Would you tear these down too? Is being unnatural all that condemns them? Condemns the Orthodoxy?"

She stands up, too agitated to remain seated. His calm demeanour and challenging words are throwing her off-balance, wrapping her up in confusion, and ratcheting higher her frustrations. *Why can't you get it? Why are you being so argumentative? So* resistant?

He raises his hands in surrender. She closes her eyes and takes a deep breath.

"No," she says, her jaw tight. "The oppression and injustice and violence are what condemns it. The Peacekeepers barging into apartments and sticking you with restraint syringes and trampling over your body, and brutalising you with no conscience, no regret for their error, no reprimands, no shame or guilt or *pause*.."

"Anaiya," he says softly. "Six months ago, I would have agreed with you. I would have been the one telling *you* that same thing. But the Peacekeeper reprisals are over and the violence is no more than over-enthusiastic restraints. The Elements are playing by the rules now."

"So, what?" she demands, unable to reign in the anger bubbling up from her core. "You're *happy* with this? You think this is the golden age we were promised? You think this is the way we were supposed to live?"

He holds her gaze, his stance still relaxed, his expression still calm, until she feels some of the anger leach from her own body. Slowly her shoulders relax and Kaide responds by stepping forward. She expects him to wrap her up in his fierce embrace, but he walks past her and towards the bureau. He doesn't push it open, just reaches down and pulls at the bottom drawer. Moving aside the multi-coloured blankets and old t-shirts, he retrieves a small plaque.

She steps closer. The plaque is two hand-spans tall, three hand-spans wide. Thicker than a piece of paper, but only just. Almost impossible dimensions to fit the masterpiece that has been painted on it. Two groups of people stand facing each other across an invisible divide; the first group with their bellies swollen and Premies grabbing at their hands look away, while the second group press forward, pointing strange, slender implements at them. The backdrop is painted in vivid colours and thick, bold strokes, while the figures themselves are flat and two-dimensional, painted in white and greys and black.

"It's beautiful," she says simply.

Kaide smiles but keeps his gaze down on the plaque. "It's just a copy. One of a handful floating around, hidden in strange places. The original itself was painted long ago, at least a century before the Singularity. Even it was a copy, a re-interpretation of another painting completed one hundred and fifty years previous."

"Who did it?"

"The first original, the true original, was painted by someone called Goya. The next original, by someone called Picasso. And this, painted after gazing on a photograph of that original printed in a book and hidden in a warehouse, was painted by me."

She stares at him, but he keeps his head down. "I wanted to

know what it was to paint. To create using a physical medium. Like Sound Creation. Except, here I was directly manipulating the physical, not just recording it and distorting it." He sighs softly. "It took me months. I must have gone through fifty or more versions— each one a disaster in its own way, each one better by shades than the one before. I didn't sleep for two days when I painted this one. Sat in a small room off Rue Dethorini, no wallscreen, no distractions. Just the book, this canvas, and some paint."

"It's incredible. It really—"

Kaide shifts his hands, bringing them both to the top of the plaque and bringing them down hard. The painting tears apart, flakes of paint and material falling away where the rend is most violent. She reaches out to grab at him, at his hands. But he brushes her aside and tears the painting again. And again. Until it is a jumbled mess of grey and coloured pieces floating to the floor.

"Kai—"

Finally, he looks at her. Sad, but not angry. "It's easy to destroy something, Anaiya. Harder to create something worthy."

He lets the last of the remnants fall, pulls her into a tight embrace, and leaves silently.

SIX

The den in Precinct 17 is as raucous as always. Lira is nowhere to be seen, but again, that is not unusual. Impatient, but determined, Anaiya pushes down her frustration and attempts to stroll casually to the bar. It has been weeks since her last shift and her collection of blue rounds is diminished, but she hands over two of them in exchange for a pitcher of Vieu Corbowe and pushes her way through the crowd to the nearest empty seat.

The rush of noise and onslaught of sensations is a strange comfort. For so long she has hidden away in Kaide's apartment, poring over Kane 148's words and the pages he had written them on—the ancient texts, the early constitutions, the treatises and philosophical ramblings. Searching for the answer to Kaide's question, which has suddenly become her question—what happens after the revolution?

Her hoard of Kane's notes revealed a thousand different facets of his angst and disillusionment and rebellion, but yielded no answers. It would be easy to conclude that he struggled with the same uncertainty that she did, that he had all the questions but none of the answers.

But that was not Kane, not at the end. He was calm and centred: a man with a mission, not just a target.

"Nanshe?"

The name rolls over the noise of the den, tickling at her

hearing, but not really registering.

"Nanshe?" Louder, now. She looks over, seeing Sharna approaching, a smile on her face.

Damn it, Anaiya. Focus. She had taken the name Nanshe as her cover when creating her Earth persona—close enough to her *Nisha* diminutive to capture her attention, distant enough from her real name to avoid unnecessary attention.

"Hey, Sharna." The woman still wears faded jeans and a blue t-shirt—her unofficial Cleaning uniform. "You just back from a shift?"

"Yeah," she replies, sitting down next to Anaiya. "Could have used an extra pair of hands—they've got us doing the Daniel Towers on Rue Lagache, which are a real bitch."

"Rue Lagache?" The name is familiar. *Why is it familiar? Lagache, Lagache, Lagache.* The intersection with Rue Jouvenay. Boileau Road. *The Enclave.* With all the recent distractions—Seth's return, finding Lira, Peacekeeper encounters, talk of revolution—she had forgotten about the Enclave. Remembering it now reignites her curiosity. The hidden sanctuary was full of forbidden artefacts that would stay inaccessible unless she could find a way inside.

"You still need help?"

"Looking for some extra rounds?"

Anaiya spins her last two rounds across her knuckles and through her fingers. "Current stash is running low."

"I'm supposed to be back on in six hours," Sharna says. "I know you don't like working daylight hours, but you can have it if you want it. Eighty percent cut—I don't need the full commission."

Anaiya doesn't need the sweetener—the Boileau Road connection is more than enough. Still, the extra rounds won't hurt, and settling for anything else would make her look too eager. She nods. "Count me in."

"Then, it's all yours," Sharna says and slides over ten blue glass rounds.

Anaiya frowns, unsure of whether to take them. Sharna laughs. "It's okay, Nanshe. I trust you."

I trust you. She says it so casually. Like it's the most normal thing in the world to trust someone.

Sharna stands up. "The meeting point is on the corner of

Jouvenay. Tell Jiran I sent you."

"Jiran?"

Sharna laughs again. "Just don't get too distracted by all that eye candy while you're ten storeys up. Things can go bad quick when you're that high."

Eye candy? Sharna thinks Jiran is attractive?

Anaiya laughs. "No distractions. I promise." *At least, not the kind you're thinking of.*

Sharna winks and disappears through the crowd. For a long time, Anaiya just sits there flipping and stacking the rounds in quick staccato bursts of movement, finding a meditative rhythm in the clicks and clacks, and letting her mind pick through this unexpected opportunity.

It will still be dark enough in the pre-dawn hours to move through the streets unnoticed, but she will lack the extra cover from the throngs of Elemental who moved in the night. Jiran is a known quantity, so sharing the roof with him in daylight is not as daunting as it could be. But, she will finish the shift well after sunrise, and the site is blocks from her nearest safehouse and even further from Kaide's apartment.

Still, it is a chance to get closer to the Enclave; her first real chance, now that the tunnels are bricked up and the road sealed and guarded.

Kane's notes aren't the only places to find answers. And if something inside the Enclave can help her figure out what kind of revolution Otpor needs and what kind of new world order needs to be established in the aftermath, then it is worth the risk.

Watching the sky over Otpor shift from an inky black to russet brown serves as a warning and a reprieve. It has been months since she has felt the kind of freedom that comes from sitting above the city with the sunlight bearing down and a nor-westerly brushing against her skin and pushing against the persistent haze of pollution.

Jiran seems oblivious to the change in setting, to the way the early sunlight casts a softer and longer shadow. Maybe it is a quirk of being an Earth Elemental, or maybe just a quirk of Jiran's.

He is easy company. Not as quiet as Sharna, but not annoying either—offering only an occasional observation, always about the job at hand, or good-natured ribbing at Anaiya's steady pace: *"They pay us per hour, not per tile. Try and leave a little bit of work for the next crew."* She likes the familiarity of it, the lack of urgency and tension. It is an entirely comfortable and benign kind of enjoyment: simple, easy, safe. Everything her life is not.

As the hours drag on and the heat bears down, Jiran's energy seems to falter. The conversation becomes more sparse and the acrid stench of the chemicals more potent. The weight of her cleaning rig (which was barely a nuisance at the start of the shift) has turned to lead in her cramped hands and her legs ache with the effort of maintaining balance on the slick tiles. She should feel as tired as Jiran looks, but the adrenalin still buzzes along her veins. Not as strong as it had been when she first started the shift, but still enough to keep her steps light.

It spikes again when the alarm on Jiran's wristplate beeps to signal end of shift. She turns away from the morning sun, to where the rooftops seem to converge and Jouvenay intersects Boileau.

"Thank fuck that's over," Jiran mutters. He looks exhausted, but he wears his wry smile like a badge. He would have made good patrol partner; the best Peacekeepers were always able to move past the events of a shift the minute it was over.

"Not for me," Anaiya replies, introducing her cover story and shrugging when Jiran looks wide-eyed to her. "I picked up another shift a few blocks west."

"You're going to back-up after a shift like that?"

"If I knew how bad it was going to be, I would have said no."

"Sharna didn't tell you?"

"No, but she offered me an eighty percent cut." It is her turn to smile wryly when Jiran laughs. "I should have known, huh?"

"Well," he says, packing away his gear and grinning wider, "I'm off to spend at least three of these blue rounds on cheap voybee, and then to sleep for fifteen hours if I can swing it."

Anaiya laughs and packs up her own gear. "See you on the flip side, J."

He throws her a wave and heads towards the scaffolding fifty metres away. She doesn't wait til he reaches it before she sets off on her own path.

The tiles are more sticky, less slick, as she angles towards Jouveneay. She stays low and moves slowly, keeping below the roofline and hidden from the street. At this late-morning hour, with the heat well-established and the nor-easterly long deceased, the small windows that look out over her are dark and shuttered; no doubt sealing away all the cold, conditioned air blasting through small vents inside.

Steadily, she makes her way closer to her target. The endless swathe of grimy tiles finally opens up to reveal Jouvenay Street fifteen-or-so metres ahead. Her gaze tracks to where she imagines the trees growing just beyond, hidden away in the Enclave, their limbs desperately reaching up to catch the weak rays of light.

And then her gaze picks out the Border Watchers; this close, she can't pretend they are anything else. Rigid and alert, they stand spaced out along the roofs of Boileau Road buildings like sentinels.

Once, she had wanted to be one of them, had searched for them atop the ramparts of the Border Wall and imagined being up there with them. Now, they trigger a fear that sends her stumbling back and crashing to the tiles. Ignoring the pain flaring in her side, she scrambles to a more stable position and slowly lifts her head until the Watchers come back into view.

There is no reason for them to be there. No reason except for the Enclave beyond.

What are they protecting against? Who called in the favour? And why did Niamh agree?

Her former patrol partner obviously has a hand in this. Niamh, now Deputy Fire Commissioner, has been overstepping and extending the reach of his power for months; his rise to the position and orchestration of her Execution had been the pinnacle, but he's always had a way of bending the rules to suit his ambition.

It is easy to remember him as the precocious Premie in the Nursery, trying (and failing) to beat her at simple games of skill and speed. Easier still to remember him as the Niamh who overcame what little weakness he had to become a fearless and ruthless Peacekeeper. *Fearless. Ruthless.* Once, they were words of respect and reverence. Now, indictments of subjugation and sadism.

But, it is this Niamh—the Fire Elemental at the height of his power and still hungry for more—that flashes in her mind. The Niamh who led a black-ops mission that created her Heterodoxy; the Niamh who killed a Water Commissioner with his own hands; who killed her, less directly and more publicly, if only for a few brief minutes before she was secretly resurrected.

That he is involved in the over-saturated protection detail is obvious. But who approached who? *How much does he know?*

Niamh with a little knowledge would be dangerous; with too much knowledge, unstoppable. It is a terrifying scenario, but one she doesn't have time to contemplate here, in broad daylight, on top of a roof, within sight distance of Border Watchers.

She crawls on her belly back along the roofline. The grime that had gripped the soles of her shoes now clings to the cottonex of her t-shirt. She should have kept her Cleaner's apron on. *Ah, regrets.* Her grin borders on a grimace as she mentally beats down memories of her true regrets.

When she is far enough away, she scrambles to her feet. Even though Jiran should be well-gone by now, she can't risk him seeing her, so she takes a longer path back, scanning the streetscape below. She searches for markers that will guide her to a quiet alley— somewhere safe where she can descend without notice, somewhere close to one of her empty apartment hideaways. Scaling an adjacent roof line gets her nearer to the river, the warehouses she had scouted in the weeks before her Execution looming into view.

The sight tugs at hidden threads in her mind. She had discovered the warehouses after figuring out how Seth's rebels were moving and stockpiling the pituarmagn for their attack. Enough mood-altering chemical to dose the entire city and turn them into a weapon aimed at Peacekeepers.

Except, it didn't. Yes, there was the attack, and the intoxicated frenzy had been bad enough—*bad enough to land me on the Execution Pillar*—but, it had only involved a few hundred Elementals. Significant, but not three-warehouses-worth-of-pituarmagn significant. *What had happened to the rest of it?* She stares at the concrete silos and their pockmarked facades. *Are they still full?*

The thought makes her pause. If they *are* still full, there can only be two reasons why—either they still plan to use it, or they can't use it because it doesn't work.

Both options twist in her gut. The first presents an opportunity and a challenge—a way to manipulate Elementals into bringing down the Orthodoxy if they can just steal it from the Enclave's reach. The second—a dead end before she's barely had a chance to pull together a workable plan.

Forestalling the pessimism of the latter, she focuses on the first possibility—enough pituarmagn to start a revolution *and* replace it with a new collective mentality. A new world order.

The first thrill of hope quickens in her belly. She pushes aside the Air emotion and draws on the remnants of her Fire pragmatism. She needs more information. And there is someone who can give it to her.

Anaiya returns to Kaide's apartment in the last hour before the changeover in Peacekeeper shifts. She knows they will be less alert, if only by degrees, and the darkness is deep enough to hide her from wandering eyes.

She arrives to find the lights from his bedroom casting a glow into the alley, and the uncertainty that had caused her feet to drag moments before dissipates. Even at a hidden distance, Kaide has a calming effect on her; he is the reason tempering her impulse, the calm to her storm.

Her hands grasp clumsily at the brickwork in her haste to scale the wall. She finds Kaide sitting in the armchair by the lounge room window, his head bent down over a book and his hair falling dangerously close to his eyes.

How strange this life is; how strange that, in a way, she finds it normal.

He looks up at her. "Hey, Anaiya."

Her feet tingle with the urge to run to him, but she holds back.

Control the Fire... Except, these days, it seems that she is not so much controlling it as she has extinguished it.

And yet, the fire in her belly tells her otherwise. She hasn't extinguished it, she's just concentrated it all towards one, and only one, target: Retribution.

Kaide frowns at her. Not frustrated; concerned. And that is him—so self-assured and centred; comfortable in his own skin and his footprint in the world. Like she used to be.

"You okay?" he asks, setting the book down and holding her gaze in that way of his that brooks no lies.

She breaks the connection and scans the apartment. "Is Seth around?"

Kaide sighs. "Is this going to be a regular thing? Because I'm starting to feel incidental to this new relationship of yours."

He keeps his voice light, but she hears the smallest hint of tension in it, sees it in the crinkles at the corners of his eyes, and the slight slump of his shoulders. It is the first indication he's given—or that she's paid attention to—that suggests he doesn't have it all under control, that he's also finding his feet in this strange new world.

Pushing down her own insecurities, she walks over to him and perches on the chair's arm, letting her legs dangle and resting her head on his shoulder. It is the closest thing to intimacy and vulnerability she will risk.

"I'm sorry," she mumbles, the words catching in her throat. Words that are still so unnatural, even though the regret they articulate is all too familiar.

He stiffens against her, just briefly, and then rests his own head on hers.

"Why are you looking for Seth?" he asks, his voice clear of the jealousy that had tinted it earlier.

"I think he knows the way we can tear down the Orthodoxy and build something up in its place."

SEVEN

"You told her about the pituarmagn?" Seth's voice is urgent, but he keeps it low. The three of them sit on the rooftop of Kaide's apartment building. It was Anaiya's idea—no chance of any planted surveillance (she knew the risks of hidden Soundmatchers) or other Elementals hearing forbidden things through thin walls.

"He didn't tell me," she says, closing her eyes and letting the night-time breeze wick away the sweat beading on her skin. "You did. Remember? At the open-mic night at Soylent?"

She waits for his response and, when it doesn't come, she opens her eyes. Kaide frowns at Seth, but Seth stares at Anaiya.

"Before we met Kaide and Cress," he murmurs, his face unreadable. "Before we showed you the mural."

The memories of that night are sharp and clear. She hadn't known it at the time, but, as she and Seth had walked down that darkened street, she had been walking the edge of a precipice.

More than her deployment, more than even her realignment, that moment had defined the end of her old life and beginning of her new life. In that moment, no-one had forced her to take the next step, no-one had made the decision for her. It was the first time she had taken control of the chaos spinning around her, had finally chosen to stay loyal to her original Element and its promise to erase the legacy of her Heterodox mentor. In that moment she had chosen her doomed mission over the charismatic Air who had tapped into her new identity and forged an impossible connection.

And suddenly Seth's face isn't so unreadable. She sees him remembering the same details and reliving that same moment where everything changed.

"I remember," he murmurs and looks away, breaking his gaze with her.

"Okay," Kaide says, drawing out the word and looking from Seth to Anaiya and back again. "So, now that we're on the same page about the pituarmagn history, why don't you tell us what happened to the stockpile."

"Nothing, as far as I know," Seth replies. "We never got a chance to distribute it. Eamon went rogue and we had to quickly adapt to the new plan." His eyes flick to Anaiya and, again, for a brief moment, they are caught in each other's gaze and the shared memory of their past transgressions. Some memories bite harder than others.

It is difficult not to feel the echo of their last encounter, when she'd tried to escape a makeshift prison in an abandoned recycler; her foot connecting with his ribcage, his fist connecting with her jaw. The physical scars always heal quicker.

"We couldn't move that much product on twelve hours' notice without suspicion," he continued, "so we used the successful test batches that we'd stored in the Edges. Not that they were really successful; only ten to fifteen percent of the crowd were affected — most were just angry Earth Elementals jacked up on dex or jaydeedioxy."

"The batch didn't work?" Kaide asks. "But we tested it. It passed the trials."

"Sure," Seth says, shrugging. "It worked on a small sample under controlled conditions. But, out there on the streets, with Eamon and Lilith whipping the crowd into a frenzy, and a… a…" He looks to Anaiya and hangs his head, falling silent.

A bound and beaten Peacekeeper being dragged through them?

Anaiya closes her eyes again, grateful for the breeze that distracts her mind and stops it from falling into a fatal spiral.

"So, what failed?" she asks, her voice sounding distant and fuzzy. "The pituarmagn or the stimulus?"

Once again, an uncomfortable silence answers her question, but this time she keeps her eyes shut.

"It could have been either," Seth says eventually. "Or both."

"So, you have no plans to use it again?" Kaide asks.

"No." Seth doesn't hesitate before answering, his voice betraying no deception.

"Does the Enclave?" Anaiya asks, her eyes still closed.

Seth is slower to answer this time. "No…" The word is drawn out and she can hear his own confusion settle in. "Why would they? It didn't work. Plus, they don't need it; the Resistance is over."

Anaiya opens her eyes. "But, it did work—once. It did work when you tested it."

"Yes," Seth says.

"Sort of," Kaide says at the same time.

"It wasn't one hundred percent, but it worked well enough," Seth counters.

"Maybe," Kaide replies, still hesitant to agree. He turns to Anaiya and shrugs; a silent apology. This is something he hasn't shared with her before. "We got it to a point where we were seeing some effect—"

"Like at Soylent?" Anaiya interrupts, remembering the way the music and pituarmagn had manipulated her emotions.

"More," Seth says.

"And," Kaide continues, "We thought we could make up the balance with the music."

"But then we lost our Sound Developer to an… *unexpected* distraction."

Kaide shoots Seth a dark look, but Anaiya shakes her head at him. It's not the fight they need to have, and no good will come of it.

"It wouldn't have mattered," Kaide says, turning to Anaiya. "The pituarmagn was flawed, and we needed a Symbiotic, not a damaged Sound Developer."

"Do you think we could figure out what was wrong with the pituarmagn?" she asked him.

"Maybe. There's no time pressure, now. And Peacekeeper scrutiny isn't as aggressive."

"Will it be enough?" Seth murmurs, the fight in his voice gone.

"Could we really get the mix to a point where we don't need a Symbiotic?"

Kaide chews his lip and taps his fingers against his thigh. Anaiya reaches out and squeezes it. He smiles at her and squeezes her hand back.

"We have a Symbiotic," she murmurs.

Kaide shakes his head. "I'm not that good, Anaiya. Not even before my hypoxia—"

It is her turn to shake her head. "No, not you. Me. I'm a Symbiotic. I have complete affinity with Sound Creation."

Seth laughs, but Kaide regards her thoughtfully. Unlike Seth, he's heard enough of her music to know her Sound Creator title wasn't all a Peacekeeper facade.

"You were assessed?" he asks.

"By a Trainer, not a Neural Technician," she confirms. "The Observer thought the chance of a hypoxic having that level of affinity with a new competency was *negligible.*"

"Because it is," Seth says.

Anaiya ignores the barb and fixes him with a stare. "Good thing I wasn't hypoxic, then. Do you still have any of your test pituarmagn available?"

"Some. Why?"

"So I can prove it to you."

The familiar space inside Veritas heaves with bodies in motion. The izakaya on the Ravignan Strip is just how Anaiya remembers it: a large, dimly lit space—almost cavernous—full of eclectic furniture to accommodate large groups or the occasional Air loner indulging in their thoughts and feelings. Fourth- and fifth-lustrum Elementals mix easily with sixth- and seventh-lustrum Elementals, their faces animated, the bright and gaudy colours of their clothes dull in the dim, yellow light of the bar. The room pulses with activity; she can almost feel the currents of energy and taste the abandon.

Seth leans against the bar, hands in his pocket, and an easy smile on his face. Every now and then, he throws a casual remark to

Yve as she organises the Servers or mixes new and exotic concoctions, but his gaze never strays too long from sweeping across the crowd.

If it were anyone else, Anaiya knows that he would ignore them altogether, but he allows Yve to distract him. And she knows as well as he that it is a futile effort to sate the guilt that will always be hungry. Guilt for Rehhd, for not stopping her Execution, for inviting Anaiya into the Resistance and triggering this whole, bloody mess.

"You ready?" Kaide's voice pulls her attention away from the wallscreen of his apartment and back to the glass screen on the table before them.

The two of them sit side by side on the lounge, not touching, but close enough for her to draw comfort from him.

"No," she says wryly.

"It was your idea to prove your *unparalleled* music ability."

"I never said *unparalleled*. I said *Symbiotic.*"

"Same, same. Have you been practicing?"

It was all she had been doing. Ever since the three of them had hatched their crazy plan to test the idea in public.

"There's no point in having her test it on us," Seth had said, leaning back and appraising her with something softer than his usual animosity and distrust. *"We both want her to succeed, we both want her to fail. It will colour our conclusions."*

"He's right," Kaide had said after a while. *"The test needs to be blind."*

The plan itself had taken less than an hour to flesh out. Kaide had set out the parameters to ensure the credibility of the experiment—a large enough sample size, a neutral location, an established baseline, and independent indicators. Seth had provided the challenge—to manipulate a room full of Air Elementals, primed for a good time and inebriated with synthetic alcohol designed to induce euphoria, into a state of melancholy.

For weeks, she had locked herself away in Kaide's apartment, head bent over the glass screen, fingers scrambling over its scratched surface to build and refine and tear down and build again new symphonies. Every day, she asked Kaide to go out into the city and find her new sounds, darker sounds, that she could weave into the melody—a solitary Elemental crying; the death throes of a synthfly; the slow, deep rumbling of the last subworm on an empty track.

She had used everything she knew about the pituarmagn—the way it could tap into the primal, pre-conditioning part of the brain, could bring it to the fore and make pliable the more structured neural pathways. It was something she had seen at work in an izakaya not so different to the one she now watches on the wallscreen, but over the weeks she realised that she'd been exposed to a variant of it on a much more targeted and persistent scale. Her own realignment.

"You'll be fine, Anaiya."

She smiles at Kaide. He thinks her silence is a product of anxiety, nerves over the performance.

"You will," he says. "The piece is phenomenal. You are a much better Sound Creator than I ever was."

She remembers the way his body reacted when she'd first played it to him. They had sat facing each other on the rooftop of his apartment building, knees touching and analogue ear phones connecting them to the screen that rested between them. He had smiled and remarked at how it reminded him of their time pretending to be lovers. And then she had played her symphony. His eyes had widened, the pupils expanding like a flower in bloom. His shoulders dropped and his hands fell still in his lap.

He had looked at her differently after that.

"Kaide—"

"You'll be amazing."

She could reach out, lay a hand on his; give him some shadow of the affection he continues to show her. It would be so easy.

Instead, she smiles at him, a false act of bravado. "Let's find out, shall we?"

Kaide nods and looks away, the moment over. Guilt and melancholy flash bright in her chest. She lets them burrow their way to her core and fester as Kaide taps out a message to Seth.

It had been Kaide's idea to play the symphony in real-time rather than a recording. *"You're an adaptive creator—it's like you're not so much creating sounds as you are turning the outside world into music. If you play live, the symphony will evolve. You'll be able to refine it as you go."*

On the wallscreen, Seth glances down at his wristplate and nods. He had used his connection with Yve to gain after-hours access to the izakaya and lace the synth alcohol with the test-batch pituarmagn. Tasteless, odourless, and colourless, the chemical will remain completely benign unless the right emotional trigger is applied. Unless she can manipulate specific neural pathways with music only a Symbiotic can create.

Beside Anaiya, Kaide lifts the glass screen, plugs his lifeline into it and places it in her hands. The sound creation icon pulses, waiting to be activated.

Her hands tremble over the screen. She closes her eyes, drawing deeper on the darkness and hopelessness swirling in her core. Feeling them burn up through her body and coat her mind. Her hand presses down on the screen before she opens her eyes.

And then she plays.

The music swells through the earpiece; growing, softening, sharpening, fading with every swipe and tap and flourish. At first she is hesitant, too distracted by the scenes playing out on the wallscreen, but slowly she is drawn into the world of her glass screen—the icons and keys, the flashes of light and colour as the symphony is translated into an intricate visualisation.

She feels herself being pulled into the wake of the music, feels her body respond to its seduction, drawing her mind deeper and deeper into its darkness. The deeper she goes, the sharper the memories become.

…Kane on the Execution Pillar, eyes rolling back and head slumping forward…

…Losing to Niamh that first time trial afterwards, and knowing with a harsh certainty that she would never beat him again…

…Seth silhouetted in an unfamiliar alley, their tenuous connection still unbroken, still full of possibility, before the lockdown party…

…Lying in Kaide's arms, unable to bridge the final chasm that will allow her to connect with him…

It is the silence that brings her back to the present. The glass screen sits cold and transparent in her lap and Kaide is rigid beside her.

She startles, worried that she has ruined the experiment, or worse, that she has brought them into danger.

Her eyes flick up to the wall screen, searching for the signs of the mess she has inadvertently created. *You were supposed to be watching. You were supposed to be adapting the music to their response.*

She finds Seth. No longer leaning casually against the bar, he stands behind it, cradling Yve who slumps against him and weeps openly.

Around them, it is as if the rest of the izakaya is trapped in amber. Groups have fractured into isolated Elementals, the dancing and flirting and carousing halted, the energy and activity traded for something more subdued and sombre.

Melancholy.

EIGHT

"It's not enough." Kaide doesn't look at Anaiya when he speaks. He and Seth sit cross-legged on the threadbare carpet of the apartment, whispering harshly at each other, desperate to avoid being overheard by sleepless neighbours.

"Not enough? She turned an entire izakaya of synthed-up Air Elementals into silent, miserable—"

"It's not enough, Seth. Manipulating Airs and Earths is easy. We respond with the slightest provocation. We can't be sure it will work when we need it to."

Both of them ignore her, as though she is incidental to their conversation.

"Why are you so against this?" Seth demands. "The original Resistance was your idea. You were the one who saw the need for revolution, and now you have it at your fingertips. Why won't you grab it?"

"We grab it now and it will be like grabbing sand. We'll hold it for the briefest of moments, and then it will run through our fingers and back to the ground."

"You can't—"

"Kaide's right," Anaiya says, finally drawing their attention. "We'll only get one chance at this. We can't risk it all on Airs being Airs."

Kaide smiles at the obvious dig, but Seth just sits there, raking his hands through his hair in a poor attempt to control his frustration.

"We need a plan," Kaide says. "A real plan. Not some desperate, roll of the dice, *we just need this to work, please Creator let this work*, brain spasm. But a real plan. What needs to happen, what we need to do, when we should deploy. There are still too many questions without answers: What do we need them to do? What do we need them to *feel*?"

"But, you believe she can make them feel it?" Seth looks over to her. Like them, she sits on the carpet, forgoing the comfort of the lounges for the solidity of the floor. She remembers a time when she awoke to see him sitting on the floor of his own apartment. When he had told her that there was still beauty to be found in this world and then taken her to the Edges. She had connected with him that night.

"Yes," Kaide says, turning from Seth to look at Anaiya. "She's clearly Symbiotic, as impossible as that is. And she may well be the missing link. But, unless we know where to point this weapon, we will all end up on the Execution Pillar. Again."

"So, what do you suggest we do?" Seth asks, the acid gone from his voice.

"The first pituarmagn attack worked, even though it was flawed, because there was a real emotion to tap into: Elementals were *angry* at Peacekeepers. The pituarmagn was just a nudge to push them to act on the emotion and direct it towards it natural target."

"How do we manipulate an emotion when one doesn't already exist?" Seth murmurs.

"And how do we direct it towards a target that has no physical manifestation—when it is an amorphous concept that is complex and subtle and that changes shape depending on the Elemental complying with it?" Kaide finishes.

Anaiya presses her fingers to her temples, trying to order her thoughts against the weight of frustration. If a new pituarmagn attack is to work, they will need to manipulate a specific emotion in Otpor's Elementals and target that emotion towards a specific enemy. But, Orthodoxy isn't so much a target as a state of being— deeply ingrained in every Elemental and personalised. There could be no single emotion attached to it—it ran the gamut of all emotions. There could be no single target—

"We can't turn Elementals against themselves," Seth murmurs, coming to the same natural conclusion she had. It is why the original resistance to remove the Fire Element was misguided and doomed from the beginning—Peacekeepers and other Fire corps enforce the Orthodoxy, but don't maintain it. Orthodoxy persists not because Elementals feared the Fire, but because the Orthodoxy has become indivisible with their own identity.

"No," she concedes. "But we have to turn them against that part of themselves that believes the lie. The same way we've turned against it. We have to show them that the Orthodoxy is a metal burr that needs to be pulled from the skin."

"How do we do that?" Kaide asks softly. "How do we undo lustrums of conditioning? The pituarmagn will heighten an emotion, but the emotion needs to be present in some form for it to work. How do we make them reject the Orthodoxy?"

"We need them to see the lie," Seth says. "We need them to see the corruption and subjugation the lie makes possible."

It is early morning when Seth leaves. As the door clicks into place, Anaiya looks over to Kaide. He looks tired, which is not unexpected—the three of them have spent the last six hours thrashing out the first stages of their nascent plan. But it is not his tiredness that gives her pause, but the overwhelming sense that Kaide is a man who is stepping in one direction while a magnet pulls him back in the opposite direction.

She knows that sensation. She felt it in the early days of her realignment—hesitation and fear battling loyalty and determination. He's not sure of the path he's on, the path they've decided is theirs to carve out. And, yet, he's still treading it with them. It was Kaide who kept the conversation going when she and Seth had run out of ideas, who forced them to challenge their assumptions, and found ways to plug the holes in their theories.

"Why are you doing this?" she asks, pushing herself up to

stand on tired legs.

He shrugs and falls back into the lounge, closing his eyes and cradling his head in his hands.

Anaiya steps towards him, her shadow casting a long, dark shadow across his forearms. She sinks down beside him, the movement or proximity tempting him to drop his hands and open his eyes.

"Seth misspoke when he said I wanted a revolution," he murmurs, not looking at her but down at his hands now resting in his lap. "The resistance was never about an uprising. It was supposed to be a circuit breaker. Something to stop the Peacekeepers from their escalating violence, something to force the Orthodoxy to be reinstated.

"I dreamt up the Resistance when I thought Peacekeepers were the enemy, when I thought the violence would get worse and that making a stand—even if that stand was just some paint on a wall—was important. I just wanted a better life."

"And now?"

He is so still it seems that he will never answer. And then he turns to her and fixes her with that gaze of his—the vulnerability and earnestness and uncomplicated honesty a sharper spike to her guilt.

"Now, I know that Peacekeepers are as complicated as the rest of us; or, at least, have the capacity to be. I know that making a stand is a romanticised notion with real consequences; consequences that can exact a heftier price than the thing you're making a stand against.

"I thought your Execution had ended it. Things were getting better; no more reprisals, no more curfews, no ongoing escalation of Peacekeeper brutality. The Resistance had done its job, served as a catalyst to shake things up. Your death was the reset, it pushed everything back to the original status quo." He smiles bitterly and shakes his head. "I never liked the original status quo. And Kane's words made me hate it. I saw in his words the vision for that 'better life'."

"But?" Anaiya says hesitantly, voicing the qualification heard but not spoken.

"But, now I'm wondering whether chasing this platonic ideal of a better life will destroy the chance of my own, personal 'better life'." He looks over at her. "You asked me why I am doing this? I'm doing this because I'm invested in this vision of yours—I can see how it is the culmination of Kane's vision and a re-framing of what it is to be a citizen of Otpor, beyond what it is to be an Elemental. But mostly I'm doing this because I'm invested in *you*. I know what this means to you, Anaiya. And I *know* what you mean to me."

She breaks eye contact and stares down at her lap.

"But," Kaide continues, "I also know I can't really tell you that. Because every time I inch closer to you, you pull further away. Because you see intimacy as entrapment and connection as constraint."

The truth of his assessment hits hard and her stomach clenches with the guilt of it.

"Lucky for you," he says, standing up and walking to his bedroom. "I'm prepared to stay silent and wait for you to re-establish the connection."

NINE

"You've been… *absent*." Lira slides a shotglass brimming with tequila across the laminate to Anaiya. The older woman's anachronistic apartment is dimly lit; the alcohol shimmers while a playlist of Air tracks hums along softly in the background. "I was worried."

That I'd turn you in or that I'd been discovered? The older woman had been surprised when Anaiya turned up unannounced, but she'd asked no questions and let her inside.

"I need more information. From him, about his vision."

For days, her mind had been stuck in the same loop. *We show them the target. We show them what they are and what they've done.* But who is the target? If the Orthodoxy itself is to be undone, who is the enemy that holds it together? Who is the head that needs to be severed? And would severing it only make way for a new head, or many, to take its place?

The older woman clicks her tongue, as if dispelling a bad taste, and shakes her head. "You have all that is available, there is no more to give."

"But there are no real answers. No plan to implement. I need the full picture."

Lira downs the rest of her tequila and fixes her gaze on Anaiya's. Sighing, she sets the glass back onto the table and taps her fingers against its rim. "Eventually, the trainee must let go of her mentor's hand and make the climb alone. He trusted you to create a plan. *You* were his answer."

"But, I have no answers. I'm more confused now than I've ever been." She lowers her voice to a harsh whisper, "I don't even know who I'm supposed to be fighting against."

"You're not fighting against a someone, you're fighting against a something. Something you can't hold, can't steal."

"But someone's feeding it."

"We're all feeding it. Every compliance, every quiet obedience to our conditioned nature, every eye turned blind to the inaccuracies and inconsistencies—it strengthens the Orthodoxy and weakens our resistance."

"But if it is so broken, why doesn't it fail?"

"Because it's not broken for everyone."

Lira is right—there are those who benefit from the Orthodoxy, from keeping Elements in their pre-ordained boxes. Like Commissioners, who depended on it to reach the upper echelons of power. And like Niamh, who murdered a Water Commissioner with no fear of retribution. And even they seem like expendable pawns to the likes of Farasei and Danai and the Elementals in the Enclave.

"Have you heard the stories of the Enclaves?" she asks Lira.

The older woman pauses as she refills her shotglass. Slowly, she returns the bottle to the table. "Some stories are more than legend."

"And some legends underestimate reality."

They stare at each other, each trying to gauge the depth of the secrets they hint at.

"Who told you about it?" Anaiya asks.

Lira toys with her drink, swirling the amber liquid around, but never spilling it. "Not told," she whispers, her voice raspy with the liquor. "Seen."

It is a bold claim. Maybe she is trying to mess with Anaiya's head, maybe she has her own hidden agenda. But, it doesn't fit with what Anaiya knows of her. And there are ways to verify if her words are hubris or truth.

"What exactly did you see?"

"Things that once existed but have long been extinct. Things that were written at the beginning of time as we know it, and before." Lira's voice takes on a dreamy quality, from the tequila or the memory. "Words from pages I'd never seen and wouldn't see again until Kane came along. Stories of star-crossed lovers..."

The turn of phrase sparks a rush of adrenalin in Anaiya. "Where civil blood makes civil hands unclean."

She knows these words; knows this story. It is the story that brought her closer to Kaide, the story that had saved her on the Execution Pillar, and resurrected her after her death.

Lira leans back in her chair and appraises her. And Anaiya can imagine what she is thinking—it is one thing to have seen a Heterodox text, another to have seen inside a secret Enclave.

Anaiya pushes aside the final shred of secrecy and self-preservation that has stayed her tongue until now. "Did you see the tree?"

Lira lurches forward as if Anaiya has tugged her closer by an invisible thread. "You've been inside?"

Anaiya nods, remembering the narrow cobblestone streets, the decorative building facades, the trees. Remembering the way its inhabitants spoke of the Elementals on the outside—"*they are what they are conditioned to be... everything in its place, everything in balance*". The memories come as fragments, disjointed and rough around the edges. While her Execution hadn't terminated her life, it had damaged her—messed with her identity and her mind. She remembered most of what had happened before her resurrection, but other memories required specific triggers to resurface. Like memories of the Enclave.

"The apartments—paintings on the wall, implements on wooden tables, *real* wooden tables. And shelves of books." The memories are rushing at her. "Something on the table, like a soylent brick, but denser, and softer. Sweeter. And a wristplate. Unconnected. Just sitting there, transmitting without a body to receive it." She sounds hypoxic. She has said too much.

Fighting against the flood of memories and the rush of adrenalin that comes with recalling them, Anaiya forces her lips closed and her tongue still. It makes no difference; still the memories assault her. *"You forget your place,* Elemental". Danai had spat the word, as if an Elemental was something beneath him, separate to him.

"Boileau Road?" Lira asks.

"Is there another?" Anaiya murmurs.

"When I was a Premie, I heard rumours there were three. Boileau Road was my first, and then, a year after Kane's Execution, I stumbled across the one in Southern Area. I've never found the third, not that I've looked for it. Perhaps it is genuinely a rumour."

Anaiya pushes aside her own memories, her mind focusing on what Lira has revealed. "The Enclave in the Southern Area. Do you have any contracts nearby?"

"There is nothing for you there. Nothing you have not already seen, nothing you don't already know."

"Maybe," Anaiya murmurs. But the conversation and the memories have unlocked more than a shrouded part of her mind. She sees Farasei and Danai on the balcony as Eamon dragged her through the streets. Remembers their privileged boredom, their arrogance and apathy.

And she knows she has found her target.

It feels like an age since Anaiya has travelled out of the Northern Area. She had waited until pre-dawn, when the subworm was free to ride and she didn't need a wristplate or lifeline to gain access.

The Earth carriage is full when she boards at Brochant, not far from Lira's apartment. Servers, Cleaners, Warehouse Managers—they all press up against each other and jostle in the too-small space.

Anaiya stands near the door, crowded in by a portly man in his seventh lustrum. His tattered polyester suit and stained kydex satchel brushes against her as he slumps with his head down and shoulders forward, struggling to stay standing as the subworm rattles along its tracks. Around them, laughter and loud chatter fill the space to suffocation. She shuffles, turning her body and pressing closer to the door, letting the noise wash over her, letting the river of lights on the subworm tunnel wall create its own, alternative melody in her mind.

It is only when the worm arrives at Duroc does she realise that the man is no longer next to her and the carriage has largely emptied. The doors open with a hiss, the air-conditioned chill traded for the muggy, stale air of the station. She exits with a handful of Earths and together they make their way up the stairs.

She has chosen a subworm station a few blocks from where Lira's Second Enclave is located. At this hour, Peacekeeper patrols will be light, but with few other Elementals on the streets, she will be easily spotted by any who take the time to look. She pauses on the stairs, suddenly undecided about her next move.

She pulls at her purple fringe, tugs her hoodie forward, and hunches over like the rest of the bone-wearied Earth Elementals making their way to their homes or second shifts. And with her blood running hot in her veins, she steps out into the street.

Her eyes appraise the streetscape, searching for a place to wait, to hide, until the dawn hours arrive and her detection is less likely. She follows the meagre stream of Elementals down the main street, ducking into the nearest alley and scanning for an easy ascent.

There are few windows recessed into the walls, and even those are dark. The building on the left is only four storeys high—an easy challenge for a Peacekeeper, but Anaiya's muscles are not as conditioned as they used to be, and her coordination is less precise than she would like. Scaling Kaide's apartment wall isn't the kind of practice she's needed.

Sighing, she flexes her fingers and rolls her wrists, bending and stretching on her knees in quick succession, before leaping for the nearest ledge and cat vaulting to the one opposite. Awkwardly, she finds her own kind of rhythm, leaping from wall to wall, ledge to ledge, like a low-level Premie, until she reaches the roof.

Up here, she can breathe easier; untethered, unseen. This is her new comfort zone.

She creeps along the tiles, her frayed nerves soothed by the steady rhythm and deep shadows. Eventually, she finds what she is looking for—a mostly empty apartment building three blocks from the Enclave. The smell of stale water, mould, and backed-up septic hits her as she climbs through the bathroom window. There is no residual electricity in the apartment, so she makes her way into the lounge room by feel.

The adrenalin coursing through her body makes it impossible to sleep and so she lies on the threadbare carpet and watches the glow of the streetlights flicker on the walls and ceiling. Only when the dawn light appears does she pick herself up from the floor, stretch out aching muscles, and clamber back down to the street.

Even in the early morning, the precinct is busier with Elementals on their way to work—cleaning the streets, setting up stalls, hustling toward subworm stations. It is easier to blend in.

She heads towards Rue Delariv, working from her imprecise memory of Lira's instructions and desperately wishing she had her real wristplate with its coordinates function. The nearby streets open up into a courtyard. Here, all the Elementals look the same—thick-set, broad shoulders, slow gait, easy smiles. Except for one. He stands out in all the ways she has learnt to avoid.

He sees her, blinking in disbelief before frowning and folding his arms over his chest. She slows her own approach, looking around for patrolling Peacekeepers and finding only Earth Elementals, the occasional low-level Water Elemental, and Seth.

There is no reason for him to be here. She sees him thinking the same of her with his scowl. He glances over his shoulder, towards where Lira's Enclave is supposed to be situated. Turning back, he catches her looking in the same direction and his scowl softens to a frown of puzzlement.

She walks slowly towards him. It is absurd to think they have stumbled on the same rumour at the same time. Absurd to think that Seth, with all his history with the other Enclave, could just come across this place by accident, by pure chance. That his furtive glance to its location was the normal furtive glance of someone in danger, undirected and unconscious.

He knows this place. Has known about it for a long time.

What exactly do you know?

She is twenty steps from him when his eyes widen. Drawing on her old Peacekeeper discipline, she resists the urge to turn around and see what has caused his reaction. Angling slightly away, she strides past him and across the courtyard. The northern edge of the courtyard is busier; she waits until she has weaved amongst the small crowd before turning back.

Seth is still where she passed him, standing in the middle of the courtyard, but he is no longer alone. Seeing Lilith standing next to him causes her chest to tighten—with fear that she has let down her guard, been too trusting. That she has let Seth lead her back to the Execution Pillar.

And yet, even as tight as her chest clenches at seeing Lilith, it is seeing Danai with them that steals the oxygen from her lungs. Danai who had been at the first Enclave, who had sponsored Seth's rebellion, and had watched impassioned as Eamon had led her bruised and bloodied through the streets of the Northern Area to her lynch-mob justice.

It is seeing Danai that reveals the depth of Seth's deception. On shaky legs, she pushes through the small crowd and away from Seth and his co-conspirators. How much has he told them? And what will they do with it?

Her thoughts fracture, her mind unable to pull together coherent conclusions through the rising panic. With no answers and no plan, only one thought cycles loud and clear—*Get word to Kaide. Then disappear.*

TEN

It is dangerous moving about the streets during daylight hours. But danger is a relative concept, and Anaiya can't imagine feeling more exposed than she already does.

She avoids going back to Kaide's apartment—he won't be there and Seth will be expecting her to return. Instead, she pulls up the hood of her jacket, fans her fringe lower across her forehead, and shuffles along the street towards Kaide's sound studio.

The city is busier now; it is easier to stay hidden in the crowds of Elementals. Still, she glances furtively from under her hood, her chest tightening at every glimpse of a Fire Elemental. Around her, the weight is light: the crowd moves without tension and the hum of conversation flows easily. Most of it washes over her, drowned out by hectic thoughts, second-guesses, and imagined scenarios of how it's all going to end in disaster. But some snatches of conversation puncture through like flashes of lightning.

"I want to get to the markets early to catch the Trinkateur near the river."

"The demolition job won't be finished until next week at the earliest."

"What I want to know, is when are those Water technicians going to come up with something to hide these awful toxin scars?"

The weight is light, because their lives are *normal*. Normal lives she had been willing to turn upside down to give them an unfamiliar and uncomfortable truth. She was stupid for ever considering it; why throw away what her resurrection had gifted her? Why reject her second chance? The chance to escape the Orthodoxy; to live in a peaceful Otpor with a man who wanted her in his life…

To live in a cage. To always be hiding. To condemn the rest of the world to live a lie.

The fire in her belly urges her to walk faster, but she pushes it down and maintains the slow, meandering pace of the Elementals around her.

Fuck Seth. And Fuck his Enclave. I am going to take down this Orthodoxy.

By the time she reaches the building that houses Kaide's studio, her head is swimming with an untethered, almost manic rage. The crowd is thinner here and blessedly free from Fire Elementals. Pulling a small blue stone from her pocket, she launches it at the studio's window in one quick, fluid motion, and continues walking. She hears the sharp crash as it breaks through the glass pane and the tinkling of glass shards falling to the street, but she doesn't look around. Lengthening her stride, she pushes on towards the Edges.

The temperature drop that always accompanies the entry to the Edges provides a much-needed salve to Anaiya's raw emotion. She trails her hand along the rough, concrete shells of the air recyclers, just like she had an age ago, when she had been working to take down a resistance, not looking to start one.

She finds the recycler that has become her and Kaide's emergency meeting point—the same one where he had found her after Rehhd's Execution. Back then she had been just a Sound Creator in a Peacekeeper's uniform—neither identity fitting her properly, and both chafing against each other. The Edges had been the only place where both of them could co-exist a little easier, the place where all of her Unorthodoxy and Heterodoxy came alive—in her music, in Kane 148's notes stashed in the crevasses, and in the pup that licked at her hand and snuggled up inside her hoodie.

Delacroix. He had saved her from spiralling into a mess of anxiety and despair. Kaide had looked for him after her resurrection, but the pup had disappeared once and for all. Maybe back to the Wasteland, where other packs roamed more freely.

She pauses briefly, scanning the surrounds and whistling softly. In all her previous visits, she has never seen him; never heard the same plaintive mewling of a hungry pup that had first led her to discover him, or seen any half-chewed rat carcasses to suggest a pup was nearby. Nothing that was born naturally and created to forge their own future lasted long in Otpor.

Sighing, she turns back to the recycler and uses the pock marks to climb to its zenith. With her jangled thoughts finally slowing and the adrenalin leaching from her body, she settles down on the hard surface and waits. Time passes in a fallible way without a wristplate to force it into the precise passage of seconds and minutes; eventually, the heat of the late-morning sun wears down her patience, and she vaults down to the collar where the rush of wind from the turbines below obliterates the sweat on her skin and causes her to shiver.

The noise echoing against the concrete around her makes it impossible to think; she hunkers down against the nearest wall and closes her eyes, focusing on the only thing she can control: her breath.

Inhale, exhale. Inhale, exhale.

A touch at her wrist startles her. Reflexively, she pulls her arm away and smashes it back into her assailant. Too late, she realises that it is Kaide. He falls back against the concrete floor, his hand cradling his cheek, his eyes wide in surprise.

She scrambles towards him, her frantic apologies lost underneath the noise of the turbine. With gentle hands, she prises away his own and looks at the cheek, fingers pressing with the lightest touch to test for fractures. Sighing with relief, she falls back on her heels. It will bruise and swell, but there are no breaks.

Kaide reaches up and covers her hand with his, wincing, but not dropping his hand. Slowly, he circles it around hers and pulls it down to rest on his knee.

"What's going on?" he mouths.

Taking a deep breath, she stands up, pulling him up with her. Together they climb to the top of the recycler where the noise is not as overwhelming.

"I'm sorry," she says as they stand facing each other.

He smiles and then winces. "It's not the first time you've hit me, Anaiya."

She smiles back. "It is the first time I didn't mean to."

He sits down and waits for her to join him.

"What's going on, Anaiya? Why the blue stone? Why not just wait for me at the apartment?"

She had known when she threw the stone that he would come with questions. Had known that she would need to finally share the secrets she has guarded so closely. Still, in the harsh light of midday, in the expanse of the Edges, where there is nowhere to hide and nothing to shield her from Kaide's reaction or judgement, she baulks.

He was right; she is always pulling away from him, the threat of real connection like the tip of a needle against her jugular.

She shakes away the last of her reservations. He is worthy of her secrets: she can trust him with them, can trust that he will not betray her to Seth. And yet, her words come stilted and hesitant. Starting at the beginning, she tells him of the nights she infiltrated the Enclave at Boileau Road — of the books she found inside, and the trees that grow like fabled giants in its courtyard. She tells him of Lira and the Second Enclave. And then she tells of him of finding Seth and Lilith and Danai in the square outside its walls.

For a long time he is silent. And then, as if what she has told him weighs too heavy, he slumps forward and cradles his head in his hands.

"I don't understand," he says. "He came back voluntarily, seeking forgiveness. He found you by accident."

"Maybe it was not his plan when he came back," she murmurs. "Maybe he just found what he needed to resurrect his rebellion. What better way to bring down the Fire Element than to show them to be completely incompetent. Unable to succeed in their most basic role of Executing the Heterodox?"

Kaide looks up at her, uncertainty in his eyes. "But, he found a better revolution with us. Right? We offered him the chance not to just take down the Fire Element, but the entire Orthodoxy. And he *wanted* it. He convinced *me* to want it. Why would he give that up?"

She expects to feel the familiar claws of betrayal—she had overcome her deepest fears to tell him her secrets, had finally reached out to make the connection, and he sat there building up his own resistance to the truth. But, she doesn't feel betrayed. Just tired. And confused.

"I don't know," she concedes. "But why else would he meet with Lilith and Danai? The two people that helped him stage his last rebellion? And why would he do it without telling us?"

Kaide sighs and looks down in his lap. "Why don't we ask him?"

"Because he might use the opportunity to finish what he started last time?"

"What if we didn't do it at my apartment? Do you have one of your apartments that we could use? One you could ditch if things don't go as planned?"

She thinks of the handful of empty apartments she has used over the past few months, mentally recalling the catalogue of their unique characteristics and ranking them based on their isolation, proximity, ease of access to a get-away location, distance to either of the enclaves, and likelihood of Seth being familiar with the area.

"Yes," she says, picturing a studio apartment on the top floor of a condemned apartment building in Precinct 20 near Dumas Station and the old necropolis.

"You could last there for a week-or-so?"

She nods, the thought of confronting Seth settling comfortably in her mind.

"I'll leave nutrient boosters here for you and—"

"I can take care of the rest," she says. "Just try and bring him between mid-afternoon and midnight."

"And if he has a good reason for it all?"

"That's the easy question, Kaide. What do we do if he doesn't?"

The question hangs in the air, unanswered. Not because there isn't an answer, but because there is only one. The same answer she has been grappling with and hiding from and suffocating under since seeing Seth with his friends in the courtyard.

If she has unwittingly walked into his trap, her life is forfeit—either condemned to a life of hiding in the shadows away from everything she knows and craves, or ended in a public execution at the hands of her enemies.

ELEVEN

The sound of footfalls on the landing outside the Precinct 20 apartment arrive just after sunset, not two hours since she had left Kaide behind in the Edges. It is too soon to be him and no-one else knows she is here, yet she moves silently towards the window, ready to make her escape. It would not be unusual for dex addicts to use empty apartments for their sessions: the descent into violence is easier to contain in an empty room where no-one will notice the broken windows or pay attention to the holes in the walls or blood stains on the carpet.

Fleeing, if only for a few hours, is not ideal, and yet it is her only good option. Fighting two or more dex junkies would only draw attention or get her injured—distractions she doesn't have time for.

Perhaps they will pass. There are many empty rooms in the building, the chances of them choosing the apartment she occupies is—

"Anaiya?" Kaide's voice calls softly as the door creaks open.

Her heart falls. Something is wrong. He shouldn't be here, not so soon, not without—

Seth. He follows Kaide into the apartment with his hands up in defence. "I didn't betray you, Anaiya. What you saw, it wasn't what you think."

She looks over to Kaide who shrugs. "Just hear him out," he

says. "He came to find me straight away, to explain."

Her ears strain for the sound of other footsteps on the stairwell; she tears her gaze away from the men in front of her and searches for others in the street below. Her future-searching skills have dulled; it has been so long since she has used them, since her perfect conditioning ensured accuracy. She pushes her mind to see what will come next, where the hidden assailants will emerge from, but all she sees are Kaide and Seth, eyes shining with an emotion she can't quite place. Even with her realignment to the Air Element, she has never truly mastered the subtler emotions.

"I went to see if we could get the pituarmagn," Seth says. "We'll need all of it if we are to succeed."

"Why didn't you tell us?"

"Probably for the same reasons you didn't tell us you were heading to the Second Enclave."

She has no reply for that. Theirs is a trust that has been broken too many times to be fully repaired.

"We don't have to like each other," Kaide says softly. "We don't even have to trust each other implicitly. We just need to work together."

Neither she nor Seth respond.

"It was your plan," Kaide continues, his voice stronger. "You both came up with it. It doesn't happen unless you are both on board—so, figure it out."

And with that, he steps out of the apartment and shuts the door.

"I'm sorry, Anaiya. I should have told you."

She shakes her head and rests against the windowsill. "I know you're not the only one with secrets. Or trust issues." The words are spoken to Seth, but they could just as easily be shared with Kaide. *So many secrets…* "But that's the problem, isn't it? Maybe there's just too much… *stuff* between us." He looks away, staring past her and out the window. "No room left for trust," she continues softly. "Not the real kind of trust you need to work with someone. Not when lives are on the line."

"There have always been lives on the line," Seth says—not a rebuke or an accusation.

"We were never good at protecting them," she murmurs, feeling the familiar drop in her gut that always comes with remembering the people left dead or damaged in the wake of the Resistance or her realignment.

"Or each other." He finally looks up at her and her gut drops further.

"Maybe. But, I think we protected each other—in our own messed up way—when it counted." *Like in the izakaya basement, before Peacekeepers stormed in, or in the streets before the Northern Edges, before Eamon slit my throat.*

He frowns a little, but stays silent, the uneasy detente returned.

"It's not enough, is it?" he says after a while.

She shakes her head. *Not enough to mend the betrayals.*

The room has turned cold; the clouds have arrived to block the sun and usher in the nor-westerly. Long shadows shrink and disappear in the faded light.

"I hope Kaide has some good reading material to keep himself occupied," Seth says too loudly into the silence.

Anaiya laughs. "I don't think this is what he would call 'figuring it out'."

"He has more faith in us than he should."

The mood in the room falls sombre again. They may not trust each other, but their connection hadn't been built on nothing; they see the world in the same way, or almost the same way, like looking at it from opposite sides of the mirror. The same shapes and colours and dimensions, just in reverse.

"You're good for him," Seth says.

"Ha!"

He smiles wryly. "Not in the keeping-him-up-all-night-worrying sense. But he's different around you, he's… I don't know, more present. Like you're tethering him in the real world, getting him out of his head."

"What do you mean? He's always been in this world. Look at

his music. The role he played in the Resistance."

"They're all concepts. Kaide's always found it easy to connect with concepts—they're complex but not complicated; easy to define, easy to walk away from. I've never seen him connect to another Elemental the way he connects with you. Once upon a time, I was the messiest distraction he had, but I'm nothing compared to you."

She raises an eyebrow at him and he smiles.

It is nice to feel comfortable around him again, to enjoy these brief moments of levity and banter. But she still can't shake the cold feeling she had first felt when seeing him in the square with Lilith, and that had spiked when he'd walked into the apartment with Kaide. Enjoying Seth's company again and being able to smile around him isn't the same as being ready to trust him. She hasn't trusted anyone since her mentor was Executed. She still doesn't trust anyone.

Except for Kaide.

The thought sneaks up on her. In spite of the secrets and tensions between them, she trusts him. Trusts him enough to still be here, in this room with Seth, regardless of the trepidation still lingering.

"Maybe we don't need to trust each other," she says, staring at the door to the apartment and imagining Kaide standing patiently behind it. "Maybe it's enough to trust him."

"I'd trust him with my life," Seth says quietly. "I did, even when everyone around me said not to."

"He doesn't deserve either of us," she says, turning back to Seth.

"No, but he's relying on both of us to come up with a plan."

"Maybe two isn't enough to bring down the Orthodoxy." The words taste bitter and the sense of defeat settles uncomfortably around her shoulders.

"It doesn't have to be just the two of us."

"One more isn't going to make a whole lot of difference."

"I wasn't talking about Kaide. I was talking about the Enclave."

"You can't be serious." Anaiya stares at him, waiting for him to crack a smile at his poor attempt at a joke or, at the very least, a hint that he is being sarcastic. "You do remember what happened last time you worked with the Enclave?"

"I don't mean we should *work with* the Enclave—they clearly have no moral compass and there's no longer an incentive for them to work with us. But we can *use* them. Think about it—they have the resources, the anonymity, and they're immune from Peacekeeper scrutiny and enforcement."

"But, how do we access that? They're not going to offer it to us, and there's no way we can ask without giving away our plans and risking them passing that on to Niamh and his Peacekeepers."

"We need to access their pituarmagn stores; if they haven't moved them, or have plans of their own to use them."

Anaiya shakes his head. "Unlikely. They'll want it there as a back-up, but they won't use it now."

"Because they're keen to keep the Fire Element onside?"

"I doubt the Fire Element are leading that relationship. No, they won't use it because they don't need to. They got what they wanted." She shivers and shuts the window against the cooling air, slinking down from the sill to the floor.

"But why stop with your Execution? That was their chance to trigger their own revolution, to ride out their social-disruption experiment."

Anaiya snaps her head up. "Their what?"

"You know, their 'manifestation of anarchy', their watch-from-afar entertainment, match to a fire."

"They said that?"

"Not as poetically as I just did."

She would be tempted to roll her eyes if everything didn't seem suddenly sharper and urgent. "What, exactly, did they say?"

Seth frowns, his earlier levity tempered. "*They* didn't really say anything, I mostly heard it from Lilith—about Danai being bored and looking to pull down arrogant Peacekeepers."

In his words, she can hear the echoes of the overheard conversations that had drifted down the avenue of the Boileau Road Enclave during her first visit. *"Peacekeepers! What are they, but overzealous bullies?" "Danai sees it all as entertainment, he is reckless..."*

Seth shrugs. "Every time I saw him, he seemed entertained by the notion of Air Elementals going up against the Peacekeepers; the possibility of a shift in power. I knew he didn't hold the same convictions as us, but I didn't care. He held the keys. If he was happy to open the door, I was happy to enter."

"They didn't want the chaos," Anaiya says quietly. "Danai maybe was entertained by it, but the others only let him dabble because it served their end. It was their pathway to re-establishing the status quo."

"Not possible; they were helping us bring down that status quo."

Anaiya shakes her head. "That's what you wanted to believe, but think about it—were you really fighting the status quo, or rebelling against a movement away from it?"

Seth frowns and settles down on the floor opposite her. "The Peacekeeper violence?"

"It was never the status quo, not really. It was an anomaly—it was as Unorthodox as the crimes Peacekeepers were chasing. It broke from the norm, but it was never the norm."

She sees his face change and knows that he is getting it. "Your resistance was never about dismantling the Orthodoxy; it was about returning it. Putting Peacekeepers back in their place."

"And now they are."

"No more violence, no more curfews."

"But that was never the real problem."

"It was for the Enclave."

He looks up at her, understanding dawning on his face. "They wanted the Orthodoxy returned. Not because it is right, but because it suits them."

She nods. "Because it is an *anaesthetic*. With everyone compliant, with everyone blissfully unaware and *satisfied* with their indulgent lifestyles, the Enclave remains anonymous. No one listens to the urban legend, and even if they do, no-one bothers to really check them out."

"They keep their machine well-oiled," Seth murmurs, closing his eyes and resting his head back on the wall, "and sit back, unobserved and unknown, to feast on the spoils."

It is the perfect quote, full of a poetry and emotion that fits the moment. "Who wrote that?" she asks, expecting him to rattle off the name of a long-dead Literacy. She has come to know so many of them over the past few months—Shakespeare, Dostoyevsky, Rimbaud, Morrison. Each with their own voice, their unique take on the worlds they inhabited and imagined, their particular shades of colour and beauty.

Seth opens his eyes and looks at her sadly. "Kane 148."

"The Enclaves are our target, aren't they? The target we need to direct outrage towards. The thing that will get Elementals to see the lie as a swindle—a poor joke played on them to keep the Enclave elite."

It is the conclusion she had come to at Lira's, but hearing him share the same revelation is the validation she has so desperately craved.

"We need to get more information on them, more evidence," he says, the passion building in his voice.

"You need to go back to the Second Enclave."

TWELVE

"Have you heard from him, yet?" Anaiya asks as Kaide walks into his apartment. He shakes his head, shrugs out of his jacket, and tosses a small backpack on the lounge next to her.

"It's only been a week," Kaide says, sitting down next to her. "He'll make contact when he can."

He's worried that she's still nervous about trusting Seth. She's not, just impatient for things to move to the next stage.

He peers over at the glass screen in her lap. "Any progress?"

She looks down at the jumble of lines, symbols, and colours on the screen. After agreeing that the Enclave should be the target, the three of them had tried to nail down what emotion Anaiya should try to manipulate. *Fear. Outrage. Disobedience.* All were considered and debated heatedly, before they were all eventually rejected. They needed something like Heterodoxy itself, something that would replicate and sustain itself without further manipulation. They only had one shot at the pituarmagn distribution; if the manipulation didn't trigger something deeper, more primal, more powerful, then it would end in failure, just like its predecessor.

For days they had tossed around ideas, arguing why they would or wouldn't work.

"We need something like this," Seth had said, pulling up a picture of a fractal on his glass screen. The colours were luminous, but it was the pattern that had arrested her: an entire universe growing more detailed and intricate with each replication, the same emotion copied over and over and over, finding new pathways, new manifestations, at every point.

She knew that emotion. *Betrayal.*

But knowing it and translating it into a singular piece of music were two entirely different things.

"It feels impossible," she says to Kaide. "It's not simple like anger or even like melancholy. It's multi-dimensional: to feel betrayal you have to feel both a depth of connection *and* the pain that comes from the unexpected severing of that connection. A pain so intense, that it destroys the connection and its echo—the trust, the loyalty… your convictions and self-esteem." She falls silent, the air suddenly thick with the betrayal they've both experienced; at the hands of others, at the hands of each other.

"Maybe it *is* impossible," she says with frustration, pushing the glass screen away from her.

"Not impossible," Kaide replies. "Difficult, but not impossible. When Seth and I first came up with the idea for a Resistance, it was easy—the idea is *always* the easy part. Same with Sound Development: knowing what you want the final outcome to be, knowing what you want to create or change or generate is easy. Because it all lives up here." He taps gently just above her temple. "Up here, there is nothing to stop your ideas. Nothing but your own fear or disillusionment. The hard part comes when you try to push the idea from here," he taps again, then runs his hand down her cheek, her neck, along her shoulder, and down her arm, "to here."

She shivers, her skin flushing and tingling with the echo of his touch. He turns her hand over to face palm up and traces languid circles on her skin. "Here is where it all becomes real. When it's not an untethered idea but something *you* need to bring about, that you have to give structure and form and texture to.

"Easy things are like cheap things—disposable. You need to fight for the things of value."

He lets go of her hand and shakes his head. He smiles, but she can see it is forced. Something he does to shake off his own dark emotions or to make her feel better.

She smiles back, but hers is also a lie. She can feel the sadness around its edges.

"What have you got there?" she asks, nodding towards the backpack.

He follows her gaze. "I was feeling kind of useless—Seth infiltrating the Enclave, you working on your masterpiece. I'm not used to sitting back and doing nothing.

"So…" He pulls the backpack onto his lap and unzips it. "I did my own digging. I didn't find anything new in my stash, or Seth's, but then I figured Eamon and Rehhd probably had their own." He reaches into the bag and produces a handful of books and papers. "Turns out I was right."

"What's in them?"

"Not sure. I'm hoping something about the Enclaves."

"Really? You think it's possible?"

"Maybe." He flicks through a thin, soft-bound book. "A lot of these are personal journals—random writings, observations, ideas in various stages of development. If the Enclaves have been around for a while, there will be some mention of them somewhere."

Anaiya reaches over and picks up a heavier looking volume. It reminds her of the ones she had spied at Lira's apartment.

"How long do you think the Enclave has been around?" Kaide muses.

"I don't know," she replies, caught up in thoughts of Lira and their last conversation.

"How big were the trees?"

"Big."

"Big, as in they looked like they had always been there?"

She remembers the way the pavement stones had buckled around their trunks, like they and not the trees were the things out of place.

"Yes."

"Maybe the Enclaves have been around for more than a while; maybe since the Emancipation. At least, it's possible the Boileau Road Enclave has been."

He rummages around in the bag again and produces another handful of thicker volumes. "A lot of the books we found, besides Kane 148's notes and some texts salvaged from pre-Singularity times, were early writings of the Cooperative—initial drafts of the constitution, philosophical debates about conditioning, plans for the new Otpor."

"And?"

He hands her a rusty-coloured volume. "These writings were all about making sense in a strange new world. About planning for something better and figuring out how all the pieces would come together. If the Enclave was part of that plan, then it would be written down somewhere—maybe here." He taps the book in her hands. "Maybe there."

"And if it wasn't part of the plan?"

He shrugs. "Look at Kane's notes. And Seth's journals. Sometimes not having a plan is a bigger motivation to write than having one. Sometimes it's the writing that gives voice to hidden strategies and unspoken ideas."

She stares at him, watching as he chews on his lip, imagining him turning over ideas and questions and memories in his mind.

"But what if the Enclave of old is nothing like the Enclaves today?" she asks, riffling the pages. "How will the musings of long-dead Elementals help us?"

He clicks his tongue and smiles sadly at her. "You, of all Elementals, should know, Anaiya. If you're going to take down your enemy, you have to know them first. And the best way to know who they are now is to understand where they have come from."

Weeks pass, ricocheting Anaiya between hope and self-loathing. The books Kaide brings home yield no help and word from Seth is scarce. What little he communicates back, during quick visits or messages to Kaide, is not enough to get them closer to the pituarmagn supply or to 'knowing their enemy'.

With every day that passes, she finds it harder to pick up the glass screen. Hours spent deep-diving into her personal and imagined experiences of betrayal has… *emptied* her. Seeing Kaide recoil from her when her music builds and bounces off the plaster walls brings bittersweet relief—validating her efforts, but strangling their fragile connection.

Only when the brown sky turns dark, and the hint of an evening northerly presses against her sweat-stained skin, can she shake off the feeling that she's drowning inside the four walls and escape into the city's skyline.

It is easy to slink along the rooftops of Precinct 16 undetected: with the lights all trained on the street-level izakaya and galleries, Peacekeeper patrols are focused on the movement of Elementals on the ground.

The anonymity emboldens her and she tracks towards Boileau Road. Her feet skip along the tiles, maintaining her easy pace despite the adrenalin building in her core and the guilt tingling in her chest; this is a risk she doesn't need to take. And yet, days spent thinking only about the Enclave has made her desperate to see it again.

She approaches from the west. It is a more difficult route—the gaps are wider spaced, the roof pitches steeper, the shadows deeper. Worst still, it is a dangerous route. The buildings that surround the Enclave are tall—rising like sentinels that jealously guard the secrets beyond their walls. A fall from one would be fatal, even if the drop didn't kill her.

Her steps falter and she pushes the uneasy thoughts away, working her mind to dredge up her Peacekeeper memories and revel in the thrill of the chase.

The gap between the roof of the building she is on and that of the building in the Enclave's block is impossible. The intervening street is ten metres wide, maybe more. Challenging enough for an active Peacekeeper, one who hadn't let the hard angles of their body go soft. But, as much as the horizontal jump is a weight at her stomach, the real challenge is vertical. The building opposite is ten storeys higher, easily dwarfing the six-storey admin building she stands on.

She hums to herself, softly, the low notes barely audible above her breathing and heartbeat. The words of the nursery rhyme circle in her mind. *Can't go over it, can't go over it. Can't go around it, can't go around it. Have to go through it. Guess I'll go through it.*

There are only two floors with balconies on the building

opposite, two garlands that slink around the tenth and fifth floors. She can make the jump to one of the balconies, the distance reduced to a more reasonable seven metres, but she'll need to choose the right one. Dark windows are a good sign, but there's no certainty the rooms beyond are uninhabited.

She waits. And waits. The itch to move—to fidget or pace or just leap—isn't as sharp as it used to be. She can still feel it—a small, hard pea buried under a hundred mattresses—and it tugs at her thoughts, but only softly. A vague call to rub it, not the urgent insistence to scratch, scratch, scratch.

Lights occasionally flicker on and off, some brighter than others, but two windows stay dark. She hums again, a different tune. *Stripey one, spotty two; I choose her, I choose you. Slinky one, sturdy two; she's a liar, he is true.*

With each word, she had tracked her gaze between the two windows, the last word falling on the one closer to the middle. Her decision made, Anaiya pulls herself to her feet and stretches out sleepy limbs. Inhaling deeply, she paces back along the roof. The pitch will make the run up difficult; if she overestimates, her footfalls will sound the alarm to anyone inside. In a predominantly Air precinct, she can only hope they will assume Peacekeepers or a bad drug trip.

She closes her eyes and visualises the flame at her core. It's not there anymore, it died when they first realigned her, but imagining it there gives her the confidence she needs and wakes up her muscle memory.

Shaking off the last of her nerves and uncertainty, she pushes off and runs towards the edge of the roof. Her feet are light and they navigate the slope easily. Her eyes fixate on the horizon, where the roof disappears and becomes the building ahead.

Her heart is thundering. *Not panic, just anticipation. Readiness.* The edge is closer. Three metres. Two metres. One.

Her mind goes blank at the last step. There is nothing but the fire in her muscles, the breeze against her skin, the balcony ahead, and the drop below. And then she is flying, her arms and legs circling in the air, desperate to propel her closer to the balcony.

Ice fills her veins almost immediately. The balcony is too far away, her trajectory failing too soon. She is not going to make it.

She flails wildly, limbs clawing at the air. Panic suffocates her, her vision narrowing until all she can see is the dull metal of the balcony's railing.

It all happens in the space of a few seconds, but the fear stretches time to its limits.

Save me, she begs silently. To the Ultimate Muse, to herself, to whatever will hear and heed her.

She is closer, hope exploding in her chest. If she can just… stretch a little further… reach… reach. *Reach.*

Her hands smack painfully against the railing. The impact threatens to release her tenuous grasp, but she fights her body's instincts and curls her fingers tighter, swinging her legs up to the lip of the balcony and scrambling up and over the railing.

She slumps down on the tiles, breathing heavily and cradling her battered body. Memories of seeking refuge on another balcony flood her mind, taking her back to the moment she had escaped Eamon's lynch-mob justice and watched the chaos of the first pituarmagn attack unfold.

Slowly, she shakes off the grip of the past and stands on shaky legs. Tonight is different from that night. Tonight, there is no Trainee Peacekeeper with a restraint syringe ready to pull her away. Tonight she is not running from Execution. And this is just her first step.

THIRTEEN

The door to the balcony slides easily and noiselessly along its track. The fluttering in Anaiya's belly settles as the darkness and silence stretch beyond into the empty apartment. There is no furniture, no movement, no inhabitants.

Empty apartments aren't unusual in Otpor, but here, in the richer part of an upmarket precinct, it feels stranger. Especially an apartment with a balcony. *Balcony, yes, but the view isn't great.* Maybe that's it: maybe the lower floors are empty, just scaffolding to support the apartments above with their expansive views and lofty isolation.

It is a problem she hadn't anticipated. The plan to make her way up to the roof was built on the assumption that the unoccupancy rate would be spread fairly evenly throughout the building, allowing her to sneak her way up the floors. But, if all the occupancy was concentrated in the upper floors, the roof was effectively sealed off.

She presses her eye to the apartment door's peep-hole. The darkness fills the hallway—no overhead lights or wall sconces, no light escaping under other doorways. Turning on the battery-powered diode of her fake wristplate gives her some relief from the darkness. It is not as bright as the genuine article, and it will eventually falter without her biorhythms to sustain it, but it is enough to guide her to the stairwell.

As the door to the stairwell clicks shut behind her, she pauses. The chances of running into someone in the stairwell are slim. She could chance it, climbing the fifteen levels between her and the roof. But, if someone was to intercept her, her only escape would be into a well-lit, highly populated floor.

She hums again, peering down the stairwell to the depths below. *Can't go over it, can't go through it, guess I'll go under it.*

Slinking down the stairs, her footfalls are soft thuds against the concrete. She should be more alert, but her mind is distracted—internally debating whether she has made the right decision, knowing that time wasted on the wrong option leaves her open to being discovered. Maybe she should have tried to access the roof. Maybe there is no way under.

And yet, it is not an impossible proposition: she had first accessed the Enclave by stumbling upon an avenue of interconnecting basements. It is conceivable there is another subterranean access point; plus, with only six floors to descend, it is less likely she will run into any interference.

So, she keeps angling down until her feet hit the basement. Like most basements, it is fairly nondescript—plumbing, electricity, heating, storage. She shines her wristplate light around the space, finding nothing to suggest a doorway to the Enclave.

She pulls the boxes aside and empties the storage cabinets of spare parts and chemicals. Leaning her shoulder in, she pushes against the nearest one, cringing at the sound of metal gouging lines into the floor tiles. Behind it, there is nothing but a blank brick wall, so she steps back and moves to the next one.

Biting down against the ache in her shoulder, she pushes them aside, one after the other, discovering nothing but dusty bricks, rusted screws, and cracked tiles. Groaning softly, she sinks to her knees and rests back on her haunches.

She shouldn't be here. It had been a stupid idea—triggered more by her frustration than any real strategy. She needs to be smarter; there's too much at stake, too much she can lose.

And, yet, the words don't ring true. Yes, if she is found, her pretence will be unravelled, and she will be Executed. *But, there are worse fates than dying.*

Execution is a terrible fate; but living a dead life, a life locked away and anonymous and inhibited, always hiding, *always afraid of discovery*—that is worse. Her finger picks at the edge of a broken floor tile, revelling in its sharp and uneven edges. *Dying would be… a release*; a way out, a reprieve from all the messy emotions and feelings of impotence and inadequacy. There is nothing in this world for her—no corps, no identity, no purpose. Kane 148 had left her. Delacroix was dead. She had betrayed everyone she has ever had any kind of relationship with—Niamh, Rehhd, Seth, Kaide.

Her mind trips up on the last name. Picturing a life without Kaide… is to imagine a life cut short, a thread knotted before its end, a story interrupted before its natural conclusion.

In a world with nothing left for her, there is still Kaide.

She pushes herself up to her feet, brushing the dirt from her jeans. It is time to go. Glancing down at her hands, she startles at the blood at her fingertips. The tile near her feet is tainted crimson at the edges, the jagged line of the cracked tile like a knife's blade. She has dislodged the corner, pulling the small piece out of alignment and revealing the substrata. Not the concrete she had expected, but something more exotic and yet familiar.

Bending down, she pushes her finger into the small space, skin grazing along the slightly textured surface of the timber.

Timber. It is a word as exotic as the object it refers to.

She taps against it, pushing her ear closer to hear the long, hollow echo.

Slowly she stands up and looks around the room, searching for something to punch through the wood. Fixing her gaze on the empty shelves, she rips off her wristplate and jams the metal edge into the screws of the nearest stack. Twisting furiously, she loosens the first and then the second, not stopping until the metal shelf falls heavy into her waiting arms.

Bracing against the noise and the attention it will draw, she slams the shelf down on to the cracked tile and the timber flooring below. The tile shatters and the wood splinters, but still it takes her five attempts before the ground gives way and she falls to the real basement below.

She walks fast. Never quite running, but pushing herself faster in case an unknown someone has heard her and is now following. It isn't long before the tunnel comes to an end, the brick walls narrowing to a fine taper. But, unlike her entry to the tunnel, her exit requires no brute force.

The simple, metal grate moves aside easily, large enough to push through once she wriggles and contorts her body. The streets are quieter than the last time she was here, not that they were particularly busy then. But, tonight, there is no-one wandering the cobblestone lanes, no murmured conversations, no clandestine meetings. The doors to the apartment buildings are closed, the windows dark. This is not the Enclave she knows.

Ahead, soft light spills onto an intersection. She pads towards it, gaze sweeping for any movement, but finding none. Reaching the intersection, she pushes herself up against the brickwork of the nearest building and peers around the corner.

It takes her a moment to orient herself, the view looking familiar but off-centre. Her eyes drink in the light at the very end of the street, taking in the details of the illuminated buildings. The ornate building on the left, with its large double doors and strands of small twinkling lights, is the back entrance to the Danish Prince izakaya… which makes the six-storey building on the block diagonally opposite the same one she had broken into all those months ago; its black angles are occasionally lit up by light escaping from an unshuttered window, but mostly it is a dark shell.

What is going on?

Turning away from the light, Anaiya walks back down the cobblestone road towards the grate. Stopping a metre-or-so away, she stares up at the darkened apartment building that sits on the corner of the block, drawn to its facade of uneven brickwork. To her Air eyes, it is an arresting pattern, a wall embossed in geometric shadows. To her Fire eyes, it is a staircase.

REVOLUTION

She climbs the wall easily, her hands and feet finding purchase with every reach. Breaking into the first floor is a simple task, the window sash opening with the gentlest of pushes. She eases into the room, listening for any indication of presence. It is hard to hear beyond the insistent beating of her heart.

She moves further into the room, her finger hovering over her wristplate, tempted to turn on the diode. She holds off, waiting until her eyes grow accustomed to the darkness. The room is empty. There is nothing, no remnants of the past, no evidence of the Enclave. Nothing. And, yet, the space feels lived in. She can sense it. She can *smell* it—it lacks the dank, musty scent of the long-abandoned apartments she has squatted in over the last few months; there is still the hint of life, and activity, and *home*.

Slowly, she makes her way through the rest of the building. Checking lifeless apartments for anything that will help her understand the anomaly that is this silent Enclave. But all she finds are hollowed-out apartments, devoid of any furniture, ornaments, or knick-knacks. And yet, unlike the empty apartments she has squatted in during her avoidance stints over the past few months, there are no layers of dust, no signs of neglect. These apartments may be empty now, but they haven't been empty long.

It rattles her. Heart beating a little faster, she strolls out of the apartment's front door and back towards the light. If she is to find some answers, she'll need to forsake the empty apartments for ones that are still lived in.

The next wall Anaiya scales is a more difficult challenge than the last, but not impossible. She swings herself into the darkened apartment two floors below one of the illuminated windows. This close to the izakaya, she needs to move with more stealth.

Crouching down on the plush carpet, she crawls towards the far wall where she hopes to find a door, her fingers burying into deep, soft fibres as they sweep to navigate the space in the darkness.

Her eyes begin to differentiate between the shadows, just as her hand connects with something solid. It is not the door she is looking for, nor the wall it is set in, but a four-poster bed. She looks around wildly, shadows materialising into objects—the bed, a dressing bureau, a large chest with heavy blankets thrown haphazardly on top.

She falls still, straining to hear anything over her heartbeat. The doorway is visible now, just a metre-or-so away. She looks from it to the window and back again. Her heart still thundering in her chest, she crawls closer to the door. Hand reaching up for the handle, she pauses, pressing her ear to the door to hear for what could be beyond. If only her heart would stop beating so damned loud.

And then she hears it, a clattering of sorts; metal on metal, metal on plastic, plastic on something dense. And then murmured conversations, two distinct voices. Now three.

She scrambles away from the door, desperate to reach the window, when she hears the creak of the door opening. With ice in her veins, she launches herself forward and rolls under the bed, shielding her eyes from the light that fills the room.

"It doesn't matter what you tell him," a male voice says, the sound too loud in contrast to the muffled murmurs of just seconds ago. "Farasei will never leave this place. It is his *Le Hameau.*"

"He is a fool," a softer voice murmurs.

"Perhaps." The timber of the bed creaks as someone sits down on it.

"Perhaps?"

"He makes some good points. What damage has been done, is done. There is no-one left to discover us."

"You don't worry that our forgotten urban legend is gaining more prominence with the Elementals than it should?"

"Urban legends never gain any traction—they are forgotten almost as soon as they emerge. And what legends exist only scratch at the surface—there's not enough substance in them to suggest the real truth. And it is only the real truth that can undo us."

There is a long sigh, the bed creaks again. "In any case, our place isn't here anymore. Almost all of the hamlet have relocated to the Second Enclave.

"And we will leave." The light in the room flicks off. "Farasei can have his hameau. We'll join the others next week."

There had been moments during the night when Anaiya thought seriously about moving out from her hiding place and attempting to reach the window. But every creak of the bed and soft murmur held her in place.

In the confined, dark space, she recalls the overheard conversation and tries to make sense of it. The Enclave was emptying out, because of her, because of what she saw and what she could have said. But even what she saw wasn't the real issue. There was a deeper secret here, more dangerous than trees and books and paintings.

What could be more damning than living an isolated, privileged life full of Heterodox artefacts?

It had unnerved her to hear Farasei's name mentioned. She wonders whether his was the third voice. She can picture his easy smile and sharp eyes, the silent scrutiny he had worn while Eamon prepared to slice her jugular open. What had he said to her all those months ago at the Danish Prince? *I am an interested spectator, but violence and destruction aren't my thing.* To think he had been in the same apartment makes her nauseous.

It was uncanny that he also used to say 'Elemental' with that distinct inflection. She replays the conversation between the two Elementals again. *"You don't worry that our forgotten urban legend is gaining more prominence with the Elementals than it should?"*

The Elementals. Not 'the other Elementals', or even 'the lesser Elementals'. *The Elementals.* It was a strange distinction…

She shifts onto her side, moving slowly and silently. It is hard to stay awake. In the dark stillness and endless quiet broken only by soft, sleep-drenched murmurs, she feels her eyes grow heavy and her body lose its tension. She struggles to remain alert, to push her mind to find the answers at the centre of the knot she is desperate to untangle.

If only she wasn't so tired. If only the floor wasn't so soft and warm.

Her body startles, eyes blinking against the warm light that illuminates everything around her. Sleep tears away from her like a bandage ripped before the scab has healed, and her heart explodes in a chest that feels too small and fragile to contain it. She glances around wildly, finding a small vantage point through the space between the floor and the linen that drapes from the bed. The door from the bedroom is ajar. She holds her breath, forcing her heart to beat slower, and listens.

She stays there, watching the minutes pass by on her wristplate, wondering whether the battery is dying or whether time really is moving that slowly. After fifteen minutes of hearing nothing but her shallow breath and distant voices, Anaiya lifts up the linen and looks around, pushing her tired brain to future-search. All her instincts assure her that the threat is removed, that whoever occupies the apartment is in another room and distracted by a wallscreen. And yet, her body remains stuck in place.

You can't stay here, Anaiya. You have to move.

Taking a deep breath, she rolls along the plush carpet and springs up to a crouch, moving quickly to hide behind the door. With trembling fingers, she pushes it shut, stopping just before the mechanism can click into place.

She glances over her shoulder to the window. The muted brown light of mid-morning glints off the brass handles of the window sash and the silver coils of the lifeline tangled around the wristplate on the bedside table.

The voices in the room beyond grow louder. There is no more time left. Before she can think strategically, Anaiya sprints across the room, snatches up the untethered wristplate, securing it in her hoodie, and climbs out the open window. Her feet scrabble awkwardly to find a foothold in the brickwork, her hands grasping the window ledge, fingers cramping with the effort of holding on.

Three storeys up is not an impossible height, but an awkward fall will be disabling—maybe for ten minutes, maybe for weeks. Fingers screaming with pain, she grips the ledge tighter and pulls her knees up, bracing her feet against the wall. In her mind, she can see the perfect form of the quadrupedal landing, the way she would have performed it as a Peacekeeper.

She inhales deeply—*Doesn't have to be flawless, just has to be landed*—and pushes off from the wall. The twist is too loose and the crouch seconds too late, but she lands it. Her feet thud into the stones, her ankle rolling underneath her. There is a hiss as she breathes in quickly, heat burning through her foot and up her calf.

With her injury hobbling her, she won't make it back to the grate on the other side of the Enclave without being seen, and limping into the Danish Prince, even with its deep shadows and soft lighting, is a death wish. There is nowhere for her to go, no dark corners to hide in, no abandoned apartments to squat in. This will all end the same way it had last time, with her dead.

Her gaze tracks to the part of the street where the original tunnel entrance had been. The hatch is still there. It shouldn't surprise her—there was no need to barricade it when the tunnel below was bricked off. Limping as fast as she can, she makes haste towards it, reefing up the hatch and sagging with relief when she sees the tight space that still exists below. With no time to second guess her decision, she lowers herself down and closes the hatch above her. She will escape from the Enclave when her foot feels better and the night arrives to hide her, but for now, she waits.

The hours are easier to pass in the cramped space underneath the road than underneath the bed in the apartment she has just escaped from. From here, she can see glimpses of life in the Enclave, hear snatches of uninhibited conversations. Occasionally it captures her attention—a particularly bright swathe of fabric fluttering in the breeze, an unlikely, shrill voice piercing the quieter hum of the hamlet—but mostly she fixates on the stolen wristplate.

It is almost identical to the one she wears—the same dull metal and reflective glass plate—a perfect replica, right down to the bevelled edges that hide the lack of subdermal wires.

Like her fake, it has some genuine functionality—a working time and date stamp (although the stolen wristplate presents its date in duplicate—the Fifth Day, 3 Piscia 205AE paired with Vendredi 5 Fevrier 2305AD), sound modulation, brightness modulation. She taps and swipes at the glass screen, her attempts to access secondary functions frustrated by an authentication protocol she doesn't understand.

She turns it over, and then back again. Wraps the lifeline around her wrist and uncoils it, appreciating the heavier weight to it, running her finger along the links that shine brighter and less tarnished than hers.

The screen flashes bright, the date and time disappearing to make way for a word—Sidirus. *A name? A function? A place?*

A melody starts to swell from the wristplate, high-pitched and overly simple. She smothers it with her hand, frantically looking for the sound modulator function that is now suddenly absent. The volume grows. Cursing, she shrugs out of her hoodie and wraps the dense material around the wrist cuff, the lifeline left dangling. The music stops abruptly, but distantly Anaiya can hear a muffled voice. She presses her ear to the bundled hoodie and belatedly realises that the sound is coming from the lifeline.

With trembling fingers, she brings the lifeline closer to her ear.

"Chara? Chara, can you hear me? Where are you? Chara?"

Long after the voice fades, Anaiya still stands rigid, staring down at the wristplate she is too scared to unbundle from her hoodie. Whatever it looks like, it is not identical to her fake piece of metal.

So many questions crash into her thoughts—*Why would elite Elementals need fake wristplates? Why would fake wristplates have full functionality like comms? How can it even work without biorhythms to sustain it?* She can't answer any of them, she doesn't have the right knowledge, the right skill set.

She needs Kaide. But he's separated from her by three cobblestoned streets, three precincts, and the final arc of the sun to the horizon.

The hours between dusk and nightfall drag nails along her nerves.

So many hours of being still and silent, entombed in a cramped space below the surface—it leaves her gasping for space. Real, *open*, space. For movement. For the chance to do something, get somewhere, find the answers she needs, pursue the next puzzle piece. She wants it so bad, she could claw away the walls with the desire of it.

And, yet, she waits. Waits until the shadows that had dripped down between the grate are obliterated by a deeper black. Until it is a faint light that interrupts the darkness, and not the other way around.

She should wait until the night has given way to the early hours, when the Enclave is less busy, when there is less chance someone will see her. But, the throbbing in her ankle has long since disappeared and she has waited long enough.

Her hoodie is still heavy with the stolen wristplate. She has spent the last hour-or-so debating whether she should take it with her. If it sounds again while she is moving through the Enclave, the cover that the night provides will mean nothing; but leaving it behind means leaving behind the chance of discovering what secrets the Enclave's elite are hiding.

Shrugging out of her t-shirt, she wraps the wristplate as tightly as she can and stuffs it back into the pocket of her hoodie.

The grate moves aside easily and she slips up into the street, forcing herself to resist the rising adrenalin to push it back into place. Her legs tremble with the effort of moving slowly. It is the simplest of movements and yet, tonight, it becomes an impossible collection of micro-decisions that are too easily over-thought and second-guessed: she is walking too slow; she needs to shorten her stride; she needs to keep her head down, no, not that much; she should walk away from the main streets; she should keep away from the shadows of the side streets; everything is too obvious, everything is too risky.

She can see the abandoned street ahead, the one with rows of abandoned apartment buildings, the one that leads to her tunnel. In a few more steps, she can disappear into the deeper shadows and slink along the dark walls with no fear of discovery.

Reaching the intersection, she fights the urge to look behind her and slips quietly into the darkness. The shadows wrap around her like an embrace and her body relaxes into it. All the tension and torment of sneaking through enemy territory—the second-guesses, the physical and mental strain of just walking and never looking behind—it all just sloughs away from her, like an old skin she has outgrown and has no more use for.

With each step towards the tunnel, she forgets where she has come from and starts planning her next step. She'll go to Kaide's; it's dark enough and she can make her way without incident. He'll know what to do with the wristplate, maybe hack it like Niamh once hacked hers to get some covert surveillance…

"You don't belong here." The voice cuts through everything. She knows it can only be addressing her, and yet she keeps walking. Hoping. She is so close.

"I said," the voice calls louder, something about it familiar, "you don't belong here."

Dread washes like an oil slick from her head to the pit of her belly, her body unable to move. She could run, make it back to the vent, make it out of range before they could catch her and identify her. She should run. She needs to run.

"Wabi-sabi? Is that you?"

The words—a familiar diminutive Farasei had gifted her before her Execution—are a trigger, releasing her body from its immobilisation. She runs, her feet pounding furiously on the cobblestones, her eyes trained only on the spot where she knows the drain will be. She pulls her hoodie up, hoping it camouflages her in the dark, and races along the street until the hole appears.

She throws herself at it, the small dimensions and rough stones tearing along her skin and beating muscles already tired and cramped. Wriggling and pushing desperately, she crashes through and falls heavily to the ground below. An echo of her earlier injury twinges brightly, but is quickly overcome by the adrenalin that picks her up and pushes her onward.

The walls of the tunnel close in on her and her reality is reduced to the endless darkness: the thudding of her feet against the tunnel's floor; her rapid, shallow breathing; and her incessant, galloping heartbeat.

She doesn't know how long it takes her to get back to the basement. Forgetting her original caution, she tears up the stairs and through the ground-floor lobby. Bursting through the front door, she gulps in the cool, dry air, her lungs burning with every breath.

Too late, she remembers the Peacekeeper sentries. They react immediately—two females, full Peacekeepers, not a Trainee in sight. They are in better shape than her, more in tune with their bodies, more practiced. But what Anaiya lacks in conditioning, she makes up with pure adrenalin.

Her limbs ache to be let loose in the free-run, but she holds on to the hope that they won't recognise her, won't know who she really is, so she sticks to sprinting.

They are getting closer. So close, they destroy any option of going back to Kaide's. She needs to lose them and she needs to be smart about it.

She changes trajectory, turning west. Turning towards the Edges.

FOURTEEN

The Peacekeepers drop back after a few minutes of pursuit, no doubt to return to their post, but it is not long before she hears the shouts of the backup Peacekeepers that have been called in to continue the chase.

Still, it gives her a head start and puts some good distance between her and them. Enough distance for her to make it to the first row of recyclers in the Edges without eyes on her. Gravel crunches underfoot, but she doesn't worry about the noise—the walls of concrete around her bounce the sounds in all directions, sending them crashing and merging and refracting until it is an indistinguishable mess that could originate from anywhere. She just has to keep out of sight.

She turns a tight corner, feet sliding, stones skittering. Hands grabbing at the recycler, she pulls herself up roughly; the jagged edges of the concrete gouge lines into her skin. She ignores it all— the pain, the exhaustion, the panic—and forces her body to keep climbing until her hands hit the smooth, uncorrupted edge of the platform and the rush of recycled air pummels her sweat-drenched temples.

She rolls into the indented collar, pulling up short just before the ventilation wall. She could sit up, but doesn't; just pulls her knees into her chest and curls around them, bracing against the rush of air and shivering at its cold touch. The noise of it is so dense, it obliterates all other senses.

There is no way to know whether her pursuers have found her, whether they know who she is, whether they are coming for her now. She clamps her eyes shut, bites down on her hoodie, letting the material stuff her mouth. It tastes of sweat and dirt and the bitter flash of concrete dust. She bites down further and lets it muffle the scream that tears along her throat.

It dredges up from the centre of her core, releasing all the emotions she has pushed down and drowned over the years. She could scream forever, scream until her voice gave out and then some.

No.

She bites down harder on the hoodie, clenching her teeth against the material and killing the scream. She can't stay here. Not if she wants to live.

The Peacekeepers would have checked the building, would have discovered the broken basement floor and the tunnel leading to the Enclave. They would have called it in. Would have made contact with the Peacekeepers who were pursuing her.

If she doesn't move now, she'll have a contingent of Peacekeepers making their way to the Edges and scouring every recycler until she is found.

Climbing to the top of the recycler drains the last reserve of energy from her body already wracked by fear and exhaustion. Slowly, she comes to a crouch and looks around. The city lies thirty-or-so metres away to the east, its lights a bright halo catching in the residual pollution. In the opposite direction lie a few scattered water sub-stations, sitting like metal cubicles along the Syn River; large enough to be easily spotted, but not enough to hide her. And in between, dominating the landscape, are the air recyclers. Spaced five to ten metres apart, some jumps she could make if she wasn't so tired, others are impossible regardless.

She glances down to the ground, relieved and terrified that she can't see her pursuers. She'll need to scale back down the recycler and make her way along the ground to safety. Except, safety is back in the city, and the only way to get there is past the line of Peacekeepers that will be making their way into the Edges.

Half scrambling, half falling, she hits the ground hard. Her knees shake with the jolt of the impact and she stumbles forward.

Easy. Easy. She needs to move fast, but she also needs to move with stealth. She heads away from the city, pacing towards the Border Wall and looking for an alternative path that will circumnavigate the Edges and lead her back to the city.

Ten minutes into her escape, she hears them: soft, rhythmic footfalls on the gravel. She pauses, hoping the silence of her own journey will halt theirs, but still they come.

She runs faster, getting closer to the Border Wall even as she angles south-west, trying to find a back route to the city. Her chest aches, her heart close to bursting—with the exertion, with the tiredness, with the realisation that she can't outrun them. She can hear their advance, and even with the refracting sound, she knows they are sliding south-west to match her trajectory and cut her off.

She pushes deeper into the Edges, the Border Wall growing more immense with every metre gained. As it grows, her opportunities for evasion shrink; the closer she gets to the Wall, the greater her chances of being cornered.

Fighting against every instinct to put more space between her and her pursuers, she stretches her angle, turning west. And then her feet falter, her chest aching with the sudden realisation that she has traded one immovable obstacle for another. While she may have avoided being cornered against the Border Wall, there is nothing to stop her from now being cornered by the Syn River.

Even as she pushes herself to run, she can picture it— Peacekeepers emerging from the dark avenues between the air recyclers, rushing her as she scrambles backwards, the loose stones of the river rampart skittering to the ground, to the water below…

With all her escape options evaporating, her heart flutters with the unexpected emergence of another. It is desperate, but so is she.

With everything she has, she races for the river. Her feet pound on the loose-packed gravel, followed in quick succession by the sound of her pursuit; the thudding footfalls interspersed with shouted orders and constant communications.

The lines of the rampart appear beyond the final cluster of air recyclers. There is no time to assess the terrain, and there is no point in future-searching. Half a metre away, she launches herself at the low-lying wall, feels the stones skittle under her feet as they touch down on the narrow girth and then push her upwards again. She pivots her body mid-air and lets it drop, throwing her hands out at the last moment and falling into a hanging ledge grip.

The inner wall is smoother, its surface worn down by the constant flow of water, and it takes her precious minutes to find imperfections she can use as footholds.

The voices of her pursuers are louder now, breaking around the final row of air recyclers and erupting in the open space above the river. "We've lost the soundprint. Start checking the recyclers in sectors A5 and B1."

Anaiya's feet touch the surface of the river and plunge below, icy water invading her clothes and whipping across her skin. She slowly moves her feet underwater, seeking another foothold and finding none.

Ignoring the protests in her aching arms and fighting against the shivers that have started to ripple along her upper torso and shoulders, she takes the full weight of her body with her arms and slowly manoeuvres downward until her waist is covered by the watermark.

There are more Peacekeepers, now. Their voices loud and insistent, calling out directions and confirming checks of the nearby recyclers.

Closing her eyes, she draws a deep breath and slips silently under the cold, dark water.

The current below the surface pulls aggressively at her—trying to tear away her tenuous grip as she struggles to find gaps in the rampart stones to guide her way underwater.

Her chest, already tight with adrenalin, presses close to bursting as the air in her lungs begs to escape. Slowly, she lifts her head above water to take a breath; lights from the Peacekeepers' wristplates bounce around the river, and the sounds of coordinated sweeps echo off the nearby recyclers.

Plunging below the water, despite its angry current and icy grip, is a blessing.

She tries to move faster, to cover more distance with the limited air that burns in her lungs. Her limbs are turning numb, her fingers scrabbling more clumsily for purchase. She opens her eyes in an attempt to look at them, but finds only darkness.

Her mind is sluggish—unable to pull her thoughts into order, unable to find clarity with the pins and needles of pain drilling into her temples.

She pulls a hand from the rampart and brings it closer to her face, desperate to see it, to reassure herself that her fingers are still attached.

It happens quickly: one second, she is a loose piece of scaffolding attached to the river wall; the next, she has succumbed to the river's insistent current and is set adrift in its icy depths. In her panic, she opens her mouth, drawing in a deep gulp of dirty cold water. She is spinning, tumbling, careening wildly, trying to find up in a world that is dark and silent and airless.

Her foot strikes out, hitting something hard and jettisoning her in a different direction. Breaking the surface of the water, she coughs and splutters, and with barely a breath in between, she is plunged underwater again.

The nightmare continues in this vicious cycle—the river holding her underwater in its cold and dark watery grave until it smashes her body against the heavy stones of the wall and spits her to the surface in a spluttering, desperate mess, before its current grabs her again and pulls her under.

Her underwater thrashing starts to slow; her body is too exhausted, too numb to continue in this losing fight. Stretches pass in a mix of unconsciousness and blinding light.

And then the river relaxes its fight; its desperate race to leave the city slows and its current becomes less streamlined. Anaiya's body cashes more frequently into the ramparts, shocking her into temporary moments of lucidity.

The river is narrower here. Her legs smash against the wall and, for a moment, she is snagged. Something in the deepest, most primal part of her brain latches on to the change and she rolls her body towards the underwater obstacle.

The lights are blinding here; while she can't feel her limbs, she can see them flailing in the dark water and flashing white, stares at them as if she were a distant and independent observer. She clambers up the ancient stone steps of the rampart, disjointed and disoriented. There is no relief at escaping the river—just a vague observation that it no longer holds her.

She blinks against the lights; the realisation that she is in the city comes slow and dull. Stumbling forward, her mind is a mess of fractured sensations. She is so cold…so cold…so cold… And there is a new darkness waiting for her—warmer than the icy clutches of the river, so warm, so inviting. She could curl up in a warmth like that, snuggle up beside that darkness. If only for a little while. Just a little while…Just a little…

"Easy, easy." The voice is low and distant. She's drowning and this voice is the only thing reaching for her. She swims through the darkness of her fever dream, pushing against the current that wants to drag her under.

"Anaiya, easy. You're okay. You'll be okay." The voice is clearer, the darkness not as deep.

Her eyes flutter open, blinking in the soft, yellow glow of the nearby lamp. Slowly, details filter into consciousness—the teal walls and rows of shelves. She knows this room.

Sharp, stabbing pain erupts in her skull. She groans and closes her eyes.

"Hey." It's Kaide's voice, soft and reassuring. "I'm here. I've got you." He squeezes her hand. She focuses on the gentle pressure, letting it file down the harshest edges of the pain.

"What happened?" She rasps, her throat aching with the effort of speaking.

"We were hoping you could tell us."

She waits until the pain in her head subsides and opens her eyes again. Kaide sits beside the bed on a chair dragged in from the spare room. Even in the muted light, she can see the strain and sleeplessness etched into his features. His eyes flit to the doorway. Seth is there, leaning against the frame, looking as tired as Kaide.

"I found you lying drenched and unconscious in the service alley," Seth says. "I thought you were dead."

"What happened, Anaiya?"

She tries to dredge the memories from beneath the fuzz in her mind. *Drenched. Unconscious.* Her brain trips over the words, pushing uselessly against the barriers to her thoughts. There is something there… something just beyond her reach… a flash of a fragment of a memory. Water, dark and cold. Rising up her skin like cold hands grabbing, clutching at her flesh to drag her to her death. Drag her to the bottom of the river. She had clung to something hard and slippery, trying to crawl from the water's grasp, but it had pulled her back in.

The river.

The image flashes bright and clear—scrabbling at the rampart stones slick with water and slime, sinking under the water and desperately trying to break its surface again without thrashing about, and drifting, half-drowning, as it snaked out of the Edges, until she could finally crawl from its hold. Other memories rush at her like a torrent—the pursuit, the Enclave, the wristplate, the overheard conversations, Farasei.

Every memory plunges her in icy waters all over again. She clenches her eyes shut, the pain in her skull growing sharper as the pressure in her chest grows tighter.

And then there is nothing to hold back the sobs that torture her body all over again; not her shattered resolve or broken bravado, not Kaide's strong arms as he wraps her up in a fierce embrace and tries to silence the tremors. She buries her face into his shoulder. "I've ruined everything." The words tear up her throat and flash bitter on her tongue.

She mumbles them again, her lips trembling and slurring the words. Over and over she repeats it, louder and louder, until Kaide pulls away and stares at her with a soft concern that cuts her wound open again.

"What have you done, Anaiya? What have you ruined?"

FIFTEEN

"So, Farasei and some Peacekeepers may or may not know that you're still alive."

"Seth." Kaide shoots a warning glance at him.

The three of them sit in Anaiya's room, its walls and ceiling padded with wads of polysilk and cottonex to provide extra levels of soundproofing. Seth's face had clouded as she recounted the story of the Enclave and her escape, but now it practically thunders.

"What? That's basically the gist, right?" Seth turns to Anaiya. "You risked everything, you risked *us*, for what? For a chance to stretch your legs? Satisfy your curiosity?"

"Seth!"

Anaiya puts a hand on Kaide's leg; Seth has every right to be angry and intervening will only exacerbate the tensions already simmering between them. "What about the wristplate? Did it survive the river?"

"Maybe," Kaide replies. "Hard to tell. I thought it was just another fake like yours, which raised its own questions. But, if it has the kind of functionality you've just described, then I'll have to do some tests, see how it's powered and whether its power core can be fixed or recharged."

"Why would we waste time on this?" Seth's agitation bubbles over again. "This won't help us. We need to focus on getting access to the pituarmagn, and figuring out the distribution lines, without raising suspicion—which was difficult enough before Anaiya's moment of insanity-slash-clusterfuck. We need to figure out the sound manipulation, we need to figure out the distribution lines, and perfecting the sound manipulation. We *need* to develop our visual catalyst, the all-encapsulating image of the enemy; *them*, not their technology."

"I thought we could hack it," Anaiya says softly. Her skull is throbbing again; everything seems too complicated, too impossible.

"What do you mean, *hack it?*" Kaide leans forward, blocking her view to Seth.

"Like what Niamh did to my wristplate, after I found Kane's notes in the Evidence Hall." She pauses, uncertain about whether to continue. "Like what I did with the Soundmatcher—using it as a covert listening device."

Seth groans. "How will that help us?"

"There is a bigger secret to the Enclave, beyond the fact that it exists and is full of Heterodox elitism. They were worried about a bigger secret being uncovered."

Kaide frowns. "What secret?"

"I don't know. That's why I thought we could hack the wristplate."

"What's the point of hacking the wristplate," Seth interrupts, "if we can't get back inside to return it, or collect it? They know you broke into the Enclave. They know the Enclave has been breached twice, now. There is no way you, or anyone, is getting back into that Enclave."

Kaide sighs and leans back into the lounge, and Anaiya is faced again with Seth.

"Good thing there is more than one Enclave," she says.

"So, that's the plan, yeah?" Kaide looks to both Anaiya and Seth to get their assent. "Seth, you'll do some reconnaissance in the second Enclave, figure out the security detail on the pituarmagn supply, and get an indication of what distribution lines are available and feasible. Anaiya, you'll keep working on your sound manipulation—we need to test for Earth receptivity and see whether we need to tweak it for Fire and Water. And I'll get to work on the wristplate and secure the apartment in the Southern Area."

Of all the decisions they had made that night, the last one is the most disconcerting. There is no certainty that either Farasei or the Peacekeepers had positively identified her, but even the small likelihood poses risks they can't take. Seth had kept his resurrected relationship with Kaide secret; if anyone suspects something, Lilith or Danai will come asking questions. Until then, his position is still safe.

But, Farasei knows Anaiya's connection to Kaide; he had seen them together that night at the Danish Prince. And Kaide has long been a person of interest in Peacekeeper investigations into Heterodoxy. All that is needed is for the two parties to talk— something more likely than it should be, given the Border Watchers on the rooftops and Peacekeepers at the entrances.

Kaide is compromised and so is their apartment.

That they need to make difficult decisions is without question. But the pace at which everything is changing unsettles her. And she can tell by their furrowed brows, clenched fists, and bouncing knees that Kaide and Seth share her reservations.

"Are we moving too fast?" she asks hesitantly.

Kaide sighs and leans back against the wall, his shoulder brushing hers, the touch reassuring. Even Seth's posture seems to collapse in on itself, the rigid and righteous frustration of an hour ago now completely absent.

"We could always lie low for a while," Seth says reluctantly.

"It wouldn't hurt," Kaide murmurs. "We don't have the time pressure we had last time; there are no Peacekeeper reprisals, no imploding resistance…"

The three of them lapse into an uncomfortable silence, each dealing with the implications of acting versus waiting. Anaiya tries to picture what kind of shift will indicate that it is okay to come out of hibernation and kick start their revolution.

"There will never be a good time to do this. Revolution will never be safe."

Kaide smiles sadly and intertwines his hand in hers. He looks to Seth, who nods and sets his face into a mask of determination.

"So, we stick with the plan. And we meet again at the Southern Area apartment in two weeks' time."

SIXTEEN

Anaiya's shadow stretches over the pavement, uninterrupted for a brief few seconds, before the fat warehouses cast their own shadows to obliterate it. The street is quiet, the early morning hour enticing only a handful of Earth Elementals towards the subworm station. She knows that as they draw closer to the station the crowd will increase, but for now she is happy to enjoy the first flush of heat from the sun and pretend she is just another Earth Elemental minding her own business and trudging her way to work.

She glances to her right. A few paces over and just a few steps behind shuffles Kaide. Like her, he is dressed in the fashion of Earth Elementals—simple denim jeans, loose and long-sleeved cottonex shirt, sturdy boots. It strikes her how easy it is to be treated as an Element when adopting the same clothing and same movement.

Is that all that separates us? Our threads and our gait?

A kilometre later, the simple brickwork of the Port Vinchen station appears between the warehouses. As expected, a small but steady stream of Earth Elementals make their way down the stairs, disappearing into the subterranean tunnel below. She pauses, letting the flow of Elementals diverge and then converge around her, and seeks out the recessed doorway Kaide had scouted the night before. Taking up position in its shadows, she watches as Kaide is swept along in the current of Elementals to the station's entrance.

She looks down at her wristplate, noting the time, knowing

Kaide is probably doing the same. There aren't many subworm stations that remain fire-risks, but some—the small ones in unimportant precincts at the outer reaches of the city—still have enough celluloid to warrant rudimentary fire detection and suppression systems. Like this one.

While Kaide had spent the previous night scouting the street for the right audio-projection spot, she had been crawling through supply vents to drop the last of the pituarmagn from his old testing stash into the main line of the water sprinklers.

Reaching into her pockets, she retrieves two palm-sized speakers and connects them together with the cord Kaide had given to her. There is a slight tremor in her fingers as she links them into her lifeline. Their cheap, plastic shells clatter against the concrete as she sets them down on each side of the recess. With less than one minute to go, she taps open the music file on her wristplate and keeps her finger poised above the broadcast button.

Thirty seconds. Twenty seconds. *Please let this work. Please let this work.* Ten seconds.

The low-pitched, frequent beeping is the first indicator that Kaide's part of the plan to set off the fire response system has worked. And then comes the retreating tide of Elementals; they exit the station en masse and, unbeknownst to them, sprayed with the pituarmagn ejected from the station's sprinklers.

Taking a deep breath, Anaiya presses firmly on the button flashing on her wristplate screen. The speakers at her feet emit a sharp crackling sound and, seconds later, the station's alarm is drowned out by her Melancholy piece.

She had argued that they should test the Betrayal piece—she is still so unsure of its potency, never knowing whether her own reaction or even Kaide's is because of the music or the residual emotion stored deep within them. But, Kaide had argued against the idea—*"We're not testing whether the Betrayal piece will work—it's too soon and too dangerous. We just need to see whether one piece of music can have an equivalent effect on different Elements. We need to know whether this plan will only ever work on Air Elementals or whether we actually have a chance of deploying it more widely."*

He was right, of course. And now, with her music swelling in the natural acoustics of the streetscape and only five minutes to test the impact, she is grateful. The weight of expectation is heavier than she expected, she can't imagine how much heavier it would weigh with an untested piece.

The Elementals that stream out of the station appear no different to when they walked in, but she is not a trustworthy observer—*"too much bias"*, Kaide had said. So, she switches her wristplate to the recording function and captures the first few minutes, stopping only when she sees Kaide emerge.

He approaches with his shoulders hunched and his eyes downcast. Her gut twists. It has failed. And if the weight of expectation had been heavy, the weight of responsibility falls heavier still.

She shuts down the broadcast, bending quickly to disconnect the speakers and secret them away in her hoodie. Without glancing again at Kaide, she steps out into the street and lets herself get lost in the crowd.

How had she got it so wrong? The Air test had been such a resounding success. *Are the Elements so different that they need different sound triggers for the pituarmagn manipulation to work?* Developing one successful piece had been hard enough—but four? And if the Elements are so different, perhaps their revolution never really had a chance…

A touch at her hand brings her out of her thoughts. The crowd is gone—it is just her and Kaide walking along one of the quieter boulevardes back towards their apartment. The breeze has picked up, making the warmth of Kaide's hand more noticeable as he interlinks it with hers. She braces herself and looks over at him.

Gone is the defeated posture. He is smiling.

"And that, my dear Anaiya," he says, his voice low and jubilant, "is why you don't need a Neural Interpreter to tell you that you are a Symbiotic."

An hour later, Kaide is still smiling. With Anaiya's wristplate hooked up to the wall screen at their new apartment, it is easy to confirm that the test has worked. Earth Elementals, who had entered the subworm station burdened with nothing but resignation and listlessness, emerge hunched over and defeated. The fire and the siren should have woken them up and shattered their apathy; they should have emerged excited and energised. Even from beyond the cold glass of the wall screen, their melancholy is suffocating.

"The pituarmagn was definitely an enhancer," Kaide says, sitting on the edge of the lounge and bouncing his knee. "I mean, the piece affected me when you played it back in my apartment. But, with the chemicals in my system, it hit me harder than a Peacekeeper ever has."

Anaiya smiles, it is hard to stay ambivalent when Kaide is grinning at her. But, she is not as excited or as confident; they are still so far from where they need to be. Creating a chemically induced reaction to music isn't enough—they still need a way to target it.

She looks back down to the pages spread in front of her on the floor. Everything that even mildly hinted at an Enclave, or elite group, or separatist minority, appears excised from the collection of volumes and diaries and notebooks.

And, yet, she can't stop going back to look, to search again for something she has missed. There is a secret at the heart of the Enclave, something that could tear it down if it became known, maybe destroy the Orthodoxy if that knowledge came with a pituarmagn attack. If there is something in the pages that will guide her in how to uncover it, she'll suffer the frustration of reading and re-reading the same lines over and over.

"What do you know about parents?" she asks, glancing up at Kaide.

"What?"

"So much of the early Orthodoxy talks about them. Even Kane's notes rail against 'the heavy handedness of an authoritarian parent'. But, all I know of parents is what I see out in the Edges, with rats abandoning their progeny to avoid being eaten by them. I don't get it."

Kaide looks down at her collection of papers, tilting his head and frowning. "Are they all Orthodoxy notes?"

She shrugs and looks down, shuffling the papers and re-ordering them. "Mostly. Some of Kane's notes are in there, where they reference the same things."

"Maybe check out some of the old stories."

"Hmm?"

"The literary narratives, like the *Romeo and Juliet* pages, or the *King Lear* pages. They're pre-Emancipation and they both have parent characters. Maybe you'll get your insight there?"

"Maybe," she offers half-heartedly, returning to the notes.

"Seth might have a few more—he'll definitely know of more. You can ask him about it later tonight, he's coming over."

That snaps her focus back to him. "He is?"

"He's got some news, and he wanted to see the vision from this morning's test."

"What news?"

"He didn't provide details. Just something about the lines and a due date."

"Do you think it's good news?"

Kaide chews his lip. He's not telling her, but she can tell he has doubts. "We'll soon find out."

"Well, it's a step up from the apartment you dragged me to a few weeks ago," Seth says, stepping into the lounge room and looking around. He pauses when he sees Anaiya sitting cross-legged on the floor, the papers still strewn around her, the recovered pages of *Romeo and Juliet* in her lap. Walking over he crouches down and rifles through a few of the pages lying randomly at the edges.

She smiles despite herself. As a Literacy competent, Seth was always going to be drawn to the written word no matter his mood or baggage.

"I'm reading up on parents," she says.

His mouth quirks and he sits down on the carpet across from her. "Interesting choice."

She lays down *Romeo and Juliet* and sighs. "Probably just chasing a shadow." She is tempted to leave it at that, but her frustrated efforts are difficult to silence. "It's just that you see it everywhere—sometimes explicitly, like here." She reaches over and picks up the pages of the early Cooperative manifesto. "And here." She taps at a page from an early Otpor ordinance. "Sometimes not so explicit—just a vague kind of reference to an entity that knows better, that has the right answers."

"The Principals," Kaide says, stepping into the room.

Anaiya and Seth look up at him.

"The Principals," she murmurs, something clicking into place. Everything she knows of them, that anyone knows of them, is captured in the childhood rhyme drilled into impressionable minds incubating in the Nursery. *Otpor, great and fearless, home to good and strong. Saved from the Singularity to know what's right from wrong. Guided by our Principals, who led us to the truth. Nurtured by the Orthodoxy in our old age and our youth.*

Her heart is racing, grasping a truth that her mind is still trying to make sense of. Haltingly, she puts voice to the pieces as they come together. "Everything in the official documents talks about the Principals being the guiding lights—the ones who navigated Otpor to prosperity after the Singularity. They're the 'parent who knows better', the benevolent authority that protects."

She pauses, trying to collect her maddening thoughts, waiting for Seth or Kaide to interrupt her, or correct her, or somehow make sense of her incoherent thoughts. But they don't and so she continues.

"But, in the pre-Emancipation narratives, parents are not these benevolent protectors. They're selfish, and crazed, and manipulative, and short-sighted. Like the Capulets, or even Lear himself."

"Miss Havisham was the great manipulator," Seth muses. "The Lisbons were suffocating, and distant; and Charlotte Haze—"

"I told you he'd know more," Kaide says, settling down into the lounge.

"I have no idea who these people are," Anaiya says, "but it's all the same, right? The parents of the Orthodoxy, the *Principals*, have always been portrayed as righteous, unimpeachable superiors who knew the right path and led us to a better future, always protecting us. But, these other parents, they're more complex—they're selfish, suffocating, cruel. Their paths are not always righteous, they don't always lead to better futures—even though they sell them as better. And their reasons are never about protecting their children, but advancing their own interests."

Seth stares at her. She can see his mind working over her words, rearranging them and restructuring them into a frame he can make sense of.

"How does that help us, Anaiya?" Kaide asks from the lounge.

"So, in the narratives, parents are always telling their progeny to do one thing, but do something else entirely, themselves."

"And?" he prompts.

"What do we know about what happened to the Principals?"

"Not much," he admits. "But why does it matter?"

Seth tilts his head and frowns. "The Enclave follow their own rules."

She nods.

"They set themselves above, and apart," he continues.

"What if they've been setting themselves apart for generations?" she asks. "The *children* needed to be aligned and conditioned, *they* needed a set of rules to obey. But parents don't follow the rules.

"What if the Principals were never aligned? What if, since Emancipation, they've produced their own progeny? Their own generation of unaligned…" She falters. *Their own generation of unaligned Elementals. Except that Elementals can't be unaligned.* The very definition of Elemental implies alignment.

She snaps her focus to Seth. "Have you ever heard someone from the Enclave say Elementals with a weird emphasis? Like '*those Elementals*'?"

"*'Elementals are unpredictable'*?"

She nods. "Like we are something else, something other."

Seth's eyes are shining. "And they are above us, and apart."

"You've both lost me," Kaide calls from the lounge.

"It's the Enclave secret," Anaiya says, looking to Seth for support, and continuing when he nods. "They're not Elementals. They're like the Principals—setting themselves apart, setting rules for others that they never intend on following themselves."

"It's why they have fake wristplates," Kaide says softly.

Anaiya meets his gaze and smiles. "And trees," Anaiya adds.

"They have trees?" Seth asks, visibly surprised.

Kaide laughs and leans back into the lounge. Anaiya smiles. "And books, and paintings—real paintings, and something I'm pretty sure is what all these stories call 'bread'."

"The Enclave are our Principals," says Seth.

Anaiya nods. "They're our target."

"This changes everything," Kaide murmurs.

Seth nods, and then his face falls. "It does. It changes everything."

"What is it?" Kaide asks, frowning at Seth and his sudden change of mood.

"I couldn't figure it out." Seth paces across the small space between the walls of the apartment.

"Figure what out?" Kaide asks.

Seth sighs and rakes his hands through his hair. "There was a party at the Aery—the penthouse—a few nights ago. Danai was there and for a while it was just him, Lilith and me. He said something about failed plans and new beginnings, lamenting the loss of the Danish Prince.

"I saw that as my opportunity to get some information, so I made an offhand comment about how some parts of the plan must still linger—the pituarmagn, the distribution lines. Danai just laughed, said that if they could dump something as perfect as *Le Hameau* they could dump the pituarmagn."

"What did he mean *dump it*?" Anaiya asks. Nothing he has said explains his twitchiness.

"That's the problem—I don't know, now. I thought he meant they were going to just leave it sitting there wasting away like Boileau Road, or maybe distribute it as per the original plan if they were getting nervous—get it into the izakayas and drinking dens by altering the distribution manifestos."

Anaiya is impressed—using the pituarmagn as a precursor ingredient for synthetic alcohol is perfect. The degrees of separation between the source and the final product would be enough to keep the rebellion agitators and the Enclave hidden from scrutiny. And no-one will question emotional responses from Elementals, particularly Earth and Air, under the influence of what can only be assumed to be alcohol.

"Dumping it the original way has zero impact without the music manipulation," Seth continues. "It's an easy way to get rid of the product and still make some money from it. It's the smart play by Elementals who have the means to work around the law but still fear its reach. But, if the law doesn't apply to them—I mean, if we're right, and they're above the highest law, beyond even the Orthodoxy—then *dumping the pituarmagn* could mean anything."

"They may not fear the law," Anaiya says, "but they definitely fear attention. They hide away for a reason, wear their fake wristplates and barricade themselves away in the Enclaves—they don't want to be known."

"So, they don't care about losing money on the pituarmagn and they don't fear the repercussions of trying to move it," Kaide says, tapping his fingers against his thigh. "If they're worried about discovery, or tying up loose ends, they'll just want to get rid of it the quickest and easiest way they can, the simplest way that avoids any scrutiny by ordinary Elementals."

Anaiya thinks of the silo where the pituarmagn is stored, the crumbling stone walls and the smelly back streets, the rows of service alleys and the ever-present gurgling of the Syn River flowing just a few metres away.

"They're going to dump it in the river."

SEVENTEEN

Anaiya sighs and puts the glass screen down. Leaning back, she closes her eyes and allows herself to enjoy the late-afternoon sun take away the hint of an oncoming chill. The warmth is a small comfort. It has been a week since Seth revealed the Enclave's plan to dump the pituarmagn. The revelation had spawned a number of theories about what 'dumping' it actually meant and what it would look like, but in the end the three of them had decided two scenarios were most likely—the original plan, where an undetectable pituarmagn would be mixed in the synthetic alcohols sold in izakayas and drinking dens; and Anaiya's, where the Enclave would run a simple line through an under-utilised service street and spill the chemical into the Syn River.

"*We plan for both*," Kaide had said.

"*And push for the original*," Anaiya had added. Dumping the pituarmagn in izakayas and dens as synthetic alcohol worked in their favour—they didn't have to worry about distribution lines, the risk was all on the Enclave who seemed invulnerable, and the end result was what they wanted: pituarmagn in the nervous system of most of Otpor's Elementals.

But even that, their ideal outcome, needed a working music manipulation.

She stares out westward over the cityscape. Somewhere close to Boulevarde Exelmans, Kaide and Seth are scouting opportunities to siphon the pituarmagn from the silo.

Focus. A successful pituarmagn rescue needed a successful piece of music.

Readjusting her earphones, she braces herself before she replays her creation. It's a hard piece to listen to—even harder because she doesn't know whether her aversion to it is because it isn't working or because it is. She needs an outside opinion; from someone who isn't Kaide or Seth. Someone she hasn't betrayed, but who she can trust.

Easier to stop the Syn River from flowing.

Still, there is another option, albeit a risky one. She glances up again, her gaze tracking north this time. It is a reckless move, and she knows that if Kaide was here, his silent eyes would accuse her of as much. But, she needs the reassurance, the validation that she won't be the weak link to let down their only chance at revolution.

It takes her all of ten minutes to eject the portable drive, stash the glass screen back in the apartment, change into one of Kaide's hoodies, and head out into the street. It's too early to take the subworm and too light to free-run along the rooftops, so she pulls the hood forward, ducks her head, and moves through the city at the easy pace of every other Earth Elemental.

The sky has taken on the dark umber that comes before dusk and the air is cool against her cheeks. There is life out on the streets—Earth Elementals closing up their stalls, a few Water Elementals in the precincts closer to the central river area, the ever-present Peacekeepers and Infrastructure Protectors with their Fire postures and open disdain, and the occasional group of Air Elementals clustering around galleries and izakaya.

She watches them, taking in their idiosyncrasies; the things that mark them as individuals, the things that mark them as a particular Element. She wonders what will be left behind after their pituarmagn manipulation, what will survive when the betrayal piece strips away the lies and engineered identities.

The sky is a deep, rich brown, almost black, by the time she reaches the drinking den of Precinct 17. It is the hour of shift change and there are enough Earth Elementals around for her to sneak in unnoticed and without a working wristplate. She scans the hall, finding a handful of familiar faces, but no-one who knows her well enough to approach her, and no-one she wants to see.

This could work.

She saunters up to the bar, switching her gait to an amble when she catches herself, paranoid the quintessential Air movement will draw attention to her.

The Earth drinking dens aren't like Air izakaya—there's no freaky visual art rotating on wall screen tiles, no download/upload docks implanted in the bar top, no blissed-out Elementals absorbed by their own space. But, there is the end part of the bar where a lone music terminal throws out typical Earth music. The heavy bass beats and simple rhythm are overwhelmed by the usual hum of chatter, but not completely. Beneath the dominant sounds, the music lingers, finding hidden passages into the deeper parts of the mind. As a subconscious manipulation, it is perfect.

She weaves easily through the crowd and leans casually against the bar. The music terminal is a basic set-up; embedded in the wall, it presents a scratched glass screen and a line of docking ports to accept lifelines, back-up speakers, and data drives.

"What are you looking for?"

Anaiya startles and looks up. An Earth Server wearing a red bandanna and tight scowl taps her palm on the bar top. "Well? What do you want?"

"Uh, um…" Anaiya stammers, unprepared for being caught out.

"It doesn't take a Water Elemental to figure it out. You only have three choices: voybee, tequila, or genievre."

"Oh. Tequila."

The Server's scowl deepens and she taps the bar top again, more pointedly. Anaiya hastily rummages around her pocket, desperately hoping that a few glass rounds languish there forgotten. She checks the other pocket, fingers desperately scrabbling, relief blooming when they find two smooth, cool rounds. She places them on the counter and the Server snatches them up and turns away to pour the drink.

Adrenalin still thick and her heart rate still rapid, Anaiya doesn't wait any longer. She sticks her hand back into her pocket, pulls out the small data drive, and jams it into one of the ports. If the terminal is like any of the Air and Fire tech she's used, the system should download any files with the right signature and put them in a processing queue.

She glances over at the Server; the drink is almost poured and the woman is distracted in chatter with another Server. Anaiya turns her back to the terminal and rests her arm on the bar top, her arm extending behind her back and fingers grasping the end of the drive.

The Server finishes pouring the drink and turns back around. *Please let that be long enough.* Anaiya pinches the drive between her fingers and pulls it from the port.

"Your tequila." The liquid sloshes over the rim of the glass as the Server slides it across the bar to Anaiya.

Anaiya nods and picks it up with her left hand, plunging her right hand into her pocket and releasing the drive. She steps away from the bar and finds a seat at a table near the exit. After months of visiting the den, she knows that the music is on a loop—the same song coming back around every few hours. Depending on how far into the playlist the current song is, she will have to wait either five minutes or three hours to see whether her ill-devised plan has worked.

"You're looking a little empty."

Anaiya smiles as Jiran sits down across from her and slides over another glass of tequila. It has been over an hour since she ejected the drive from the terminal and still her piece hasn't played, but the playlist hasn't looped back around either, so there is still hope.

"Was feeling a little empty," she replies, picking up the glass. "Thanks."

Jiran shrugs and looks around. "Haven't seen you around in ages. You waiting for Lira?"

She takes a sip of her drink, giving herself time to think. It is a good cover story—she can explain her absence away with not needing black-market money, and her reappearance with needing it now.

She nods, putting the glass down. "You seen her?"

"Not lately."

Anaiya notices the way his mouth pulls a little tight. "How's that working out for you?"

He shrugs and laughs casually. "Money on the side is always good money, but I'm doing alright."

"You still trying to impress your woman with that upgraded apartment?"

Jiran laughs again, but the sound is forced and his eyes are guarded. "Nah. That ended a couple of weeks ago." He takes a long swig of his own drink. "Turns out she found someone who could afford her expensive tastes." Another long swig and the glass is empty. "I spent all my money, everything, on her. Her Air-designed clothes, her ugly beads."

His voice grows louder, his face flashing briefly with ugly emotions. It takes Anaiya by surprise. The Jiran she knows is easygoing and self-deprecating, occasionally open about his personal life but only ever to get a laugh.

And then she hears it—her music, barely audible over the rising chatter of Earth Elementals. Around the den, little pockets of laughter and easy conversation have shifted and the space is dotted with angry faces and aggressive postures. A burly man at the next table leans in menacingly; at the bar, a young woman throws her hands around, sending a drink smashing to the floor. And Lira.

The older woman stands near the exit, her eyes locked on Anaiya, her betrayal less angry and more sad.

And then the music changes and a typical Earth song starts to play. The volume level in the den drops a little and the tension keeping the affected Elementals rigid is dissipating, but the guarded eyes remain and the conversations stay less jovial.

"It's no big deal," Jiran says, snapping Anaiya's attention back. "Her loss, right?" He barks a laugh and stares down at his hands.

"Yeah," Anaiya replies unsteadily. "Sometimes you don't know what you're throwing away. Or what you're trading it for."

"Yeah." Jiran stares down at his empty glass. "We all learn eventually, though, don't we?" He stands up and heads back to the bar. Anaiya watches him retreat and then looks over to the exit.

Lira still stands there, staring at her. She carries her sadness lighter now, but it is still there. Anaiya stands up and walks over to her.

"This was you?" Lira asks softly.

Anaiya nods.

"You've been busy."

Anaiya nods again.

A silence stretches between the two of them. As the seconds pass, Lira draws herself up and her face settles into its usual mask of nonchalant indifference. But, like the others, her eyes stay guarded.

"You felt it?" Anaiya asks, her voice still unsteady.

"I did."

"We should talk."

"We should."

Lira's hands are steady as she pours Anaiya a drink. The smell of genievre wafts in the air of Lira's apartment, pulling at Anaiya's thoughts. She had gone to the drinking den to test her music, to see a hint of it reflected in the Earth Elementals there. Without the pituarmagn, the effect should have been mild. And yet...

"That was quite the stunt, Anaiya." Lira pours herself a glass and sits down. "What exactly were you doing?"

Anaiya swirls the glass, watching the lights overhead reflect and refract in the clear liquid. There are so many ways to answer Lira's question, so many versions of the truth, or lies, she could spin. How much can she reveal, how much does she need to keep hidden?

"Just testing what music I can get Earth Elementals to listen to."

"That was some powerful music."

"I'm not sure everyone felt the same."

"Enough of us did."

She knows Lira wants answers. But she has questions of her own.

"What did you feel?"

Lira sighs and sets down her glass. She opens her mouth, and then sighs again. "In that moment, when I saw you, I saw Kane." Her shoulders slump forward. "And all I could remember was him leaving me. Throwing himself to the rats for his precious ideology. Handing himself over to the Execution Pillar. Letting them take him from me. I hated him for that. For leaving me. For betraying me."

They both fall silent; thoughts of Kane 148 fill the space between them and lull them into a sombre, reflective mood. His legacy looms so large, it is hard for Anaiya to disentangle it from her real memories of him.

"Who were you before you met him?"

Lira laughs. The residual distrust is gone and her eyes shine bright with the genievre. "I was what I've always been, a Cleaner."

"So what changed?"

"Besides finding a whole world of Unorthodoxy, or finding Kane, the Original Resistor?"

"We both have that in common."

Lira smiles sadly. "And more."

She is right—neither of them have stayed true to their original alignments. Lira is no more an Earth than Anaiya is a Fire. She would pass it off as Kane's influence, but Lira is not the only Elemental she knows that doesn't act like she should, and she hadn't been the only one affected by the music at the den.

"I used to joke he made me who I became," Lira says softly, a smile playing on her lips. "That he knocked the Orthodoxy out of me when he tackled me in the Edges. But, I think that maybe my alignment never really stuck. And maybe that tackle just knocked free the last thread tying me to it."

It could be Anaiya's story; a feeling that something was never right, a situation—not of her doing—that messed with her mind, and an easy reliance on blaming her connection with Kane for all of it. But maybe her connection to the Orthodoxy was only tenuous, despite all her loyalty and dedicated efforts to protect it. Maybe her Heterodoxy wasn't the radical shift she believed it to be, but just the severing of the last thread that connected her to the Orthodoxy.

"Do you think the alignment process is flawed?" she muses

aloud.

"No more than the Orthodoxy is." It is a flippant comment, a product more of the alcohol than anything else, but it circles in her thoughts as the night wears on. And, as she makes her way back to the Southern Area, it buries in her mind and refuses to budge.

EIGHTEEN

"Anaiya was right. They're going to dump it in the river, and soon. We have to siphon it now." The words rush from Seth as soon as the door to the apartment closes behind him. He has spent the last two weeks trying to glean hints of the Enclave's plans without drawing suspicion, each attempt less successful than the previous. Until now.

Anaiya looks up from the pages of *The Virgin Suicides* that Seth had brought her on his last visit — *"Some more messed-up parents for your reading pleasure"* — her mind already racing with questions.

"We're not ready," Kaide says, walking into the room from the balcony and sitting down next to Anaiya. "We have a half-formed plan on how to tap the silo and nowhere to store the chemical we manage to steal."

"Siphoning makes for a guaranteed outcome," Seth says. "What other option do we have?"

"There's no way to get access, Seth. You saw the site as well as I did, it's on lock-down."

Anaiya puts the book down and closes her eyes, turning the problem over in her mind. Dumping the pituarmagn in the river is a dead end — the chemical would become too diluted to have any effect, And even if *some* effect were possible, it would only reach a quarter of the population via the limited water substations along the downriver stretch before it flowed out beyond the Border Wall and into the Wasteland.

They could potentially siphon it to an empty air recycler, not unlike the one Eamon had imprisoned her in before her Execution, but they would need to run their own lines, and figure out a way to actually store it so it remained viable, and then a way to transport it when they were ready to launch their attack...

"It's impossible," she says aloud. "There is no way to take advantage if they dump it in the river. There's nothing we can do, nothing that makes sense. And even the options that don't make sense would take months to organise and a team of ten people to implement."

Kaide sighs and leans back into the lounge while Seth paces the small room. Finally, he stops and leans against the wall.

"Airs were never built to lead revolutions," Seth says, his voice a mix of sarcasm and defeat. "Start them, yes. Be their figureheads, yes. But, leading them requires a more methodical mind. It's a shame you're not a Fire Elemental anymore, Anaiya; we could really use your incisive pragmatism right now."

She smiles at the good-natured barb. "Airs. Good at planning parties; bringing down the Orthodoxy, not so much." The thought gives her pause, the words sparking a tiny seed of possibility.

"What if we could make them change their mind?"

"About dumping it?" Kaide asks.

"About dumping it in the river," Anaiya clarifies. "What if we could convince them to go back to their original plan?"

"I can't show any more interest in the stash without tipping them off," Seth says. "Lilith is already asking questions."

Anaiya shakes her head. "We don't need to directly convince them. The reason why they're dumping it in the river is to avoid visibility, right? Because they think it's more covert than the original plan to distribute it to izakayas and drinking dens. What if we change that? Make dumping it in the river the riskier move?"

"What are you proposing?" Kaide asks.

She looks to Seth and shrugs. "Let's throw a party."

The lights strung across the river shine like stars. From the fourth floor of the apartment building Kaide has secured as temporary accommodation, they cast a soft glow that plays on the angles of his face. He is smiling. It is not a smile she has seen him wear before. In all the time she has known him, his smiles have been sad, or knowing, or resigned, or fleeting. Always fragile or ironic. Never this, never joyous or free.

He looks over to her and his smile widens. "You checking me out, Anaiya?"

She grins. "Maybe. What's got you so happy, anyway? You know this might not work."

"I like this," he says, looking down at the revelry below. Music swells in the air and the buzz of Air Elementals completes the carnival atmosphere. "It reminds me of what Otpor used to be like. And I like experiencing it with you, because I can imagine this is what Otpor will be like after all this is over."

After it is over. It's hard to think ahead that far, to imagine the possibility of what life will be like, what it *could* be like if they succeed… or if they fail.

"How many more days do you think it will take for them to fall back to their original plan?" she asks.

It has been three days and nights since the first lights were strung and the party commenced. In the beginning, only a handful of Elementals had turned up, drawn by the novelty and cheap drinks. As word spread, the crowd grew, and despite the occasional Peacekeeper intervention to break up fights or impose noise restrictions, it continued to grow.

"Another couple of days, maybe four at most." Kaide shifts his gaze from the party below to the silo behind it. "Seth says they're getting pretty twitchy. The Boileau Road Enclave is all but empty, they want to cut away the rest of their loose and fraying threads."

"And the broadcast hack is ready to go?" Getting the pituarmagn distributed around Otpor would achieve nothing if they couldn't broadcast her music manipulation and target the resulting sense of betrayal towards the Enclave and the Orthodoxy.

"It was never really disabled; if you had been Executed on Eamon's makeshift stage instead of the Pillar, the recordings would have been shown on every Elemental wallscreen channel for twenty-four hours."

She nods. They have been over this before, but it's not only the Enclave residents who are getting twitchy.

"And the code wouldn't have changed?" she asks.

By Kaide's account, Eamon had used his connections to get the emergency broadcast code the Cooperative had used during the initial resistance. It was the code that had forced Kane 148 docutainments and narrative features to play endlessly on every wallscreen across the city when the Resistance had first emerged. As an emergency broadcast, there was a twenty-four-hour failsafe—a guarantee there would be no interruption, no opportunity for dissidents to shut down the propaganda.

Kaide shrugs. "They could have changed it. But there's been no reason for them to."

"And the visuals?"

Kaide reaches over and puts a hand on her shoulder. "We're ready, Anaiya. If we can fix the pituarmagn distribution, Otpor will learn of their betrayal."

He thinks she is nervous, that she is overthinking things or dwelling on the negatives. But she has run high-stakes missions before, has been on the cusp of success where everything looked positive and her focus has shifeds from what was in front of her to what lay beyond.

And she has been burned.

NINETEEN

"They're moving it," Seth shouts, barging in to the apartment.

Anaiya looks over her shoulder from her position on the balcony. "Out here," she calls to him. She shakes out her legs and shifts to a different position. Hours of sitting on the cool tiles have lulled her body into a deep numbness. She should have moved inside earlier, but the street party—even three days later—is still intoxicating and she struggles to take her eyes from it.

"Wait, where's Kaide?" Seth steps out and settles down across from her. It is a small balcony, and even though they sit at opposite ends, if they were to stretch out their legs, their feet would touch. She tilts her head and looks at him. Their relationship is one that has spanned a wide spectrum; she has loved him and she has hated him, sought him out and avoided him. But, this strange detente of theirs—the distrust and honesty—it is the one she is most comfortable with.

"Kaide's on silo watch," she says, nodding towards the storage facility's silhouette. "He'll be back in a couple of hours. Are they really moving it?"

"Farasei turned up at the Enclave last night. The party is making all of them nervous. There are no celebrations, no revelry. Lilith is pissed." He laughs. "They want to move on—and they can't do it until Boileau Road and everything linked to it is buried."

"You're sure?"

"As sure as I can be. Lilith's the one with the connections, so I can only go off what she says."

"And what is she saying?"

"That they can't wait any longer. That they're pissed at Air Elementals and desperate for her to do something. She asked me if I knew who was behind the party." He smiles.

"What did you say?"

"Something about Air parties taking on a life of their own. That even if we knew who started it, we wouldn't know who is keeping it alive."

"That would have gone down well."

Seth grins. "Yeah, there are a few things that Lilith doesn't like, and telling her she can't do something, and jeopardising her leverage with the Enclave are probably top two."

"What else did she say?"

"She didn't need to say anything else. If they're impatient to move it and they're not risking the plan to dump it in the river, they're not going to waste time coming up with another plan, when they already have one waiting."

Anaiya frowns and looks down at the party. Everything he says makes sense. If they are as impatient as Lilith says, they wouldn't waste time on another plan; if moving the pituarmagn to the izakaya and drinking dens was good enough the first time, their arrogance wouldn't see them reconsider it as a viable option this time.

"We did it?" she whispers.

Seth shrugs. "So far, so good."

"We should tell Kaide."

"Now?"

Anaiya stands up. "There's no point in him staying out in the cold watching a silo that's not going to be tapped."

It was late on the Second Day when the trucks came rumbling down Boulevarde Exelmans. From her vantage point on the balcony, Anaiya caught glimpses of them as their big metallic bodies glinted in the dying sunlight. Three days later, the party on the riverside service street breathed its last; with no more cheap alcohol, an expired novelty factor, and a slew of new events popping up in the izakayas to the north, there was nothing to keep the crowd interested.

The silence is almost eerie as she and Kaide make their way to the nearby Javel subworm station. Anaiya presses close against his back as he swipes his wristplate against the terminal to open the barrier gate.

They walk to the platform without speaking, holding hands like every other Air couple, but keeping alert to any suggestion of scrutiny or Peacekeeping presence. It is late, but not late enough that the platform is empty. Most of the Elementals are Earths: Cleaners, Demolitioners, and Production Liners heading to their next shift with their high-vis vests reflecting the fluorescent lights of the subworm line. A few Airs gather at the far end of the platform where their designated carriages will align, their mood more upbeat, their chatter louder than the Earth Elementals that outnumber them. Unlike their Earth counterparts, they are no doubt heading to the more vibrant izakayas of the Northern precincts. It makes her and Kaide's journey an easier one to hide.

The subworm rattles into the station a few minutes later and she and Kaide follow the other Airs into the carriage. It is strange that she can't identify their competencies—once, she would have been able to tell a Dancer or a Graphics or a Sound Development competency just by observing their stance, their word choices, their clothes. Now, she either can't differentiate their characteristics as easily, or her mind doesn't devote as much energy to it.

She leans into Kaide, feeling a comfortable weight as he rests his chin on the top of her head and wraps his arms around her. She presses her face against his chest and closes her eyes. To everyone else in the carriage, it is nothing out of the ordinary—just another pair of Air lovers on their way to some party or other distraction in the north. But the subterfuge allows Anaiya to remain undetected from those who might recognise her. It also allows her to hide the small rivers of anxiety that tumble in her core, and gives her time to collect her racing thoughts.

Last night, Seth had tested the pituarmagn distribution at a Northern Area izakaya, Kaide in a Southern. Both ordered their drink of choice and plugged in their earphones to listen to the betrayal piece. "I couldn't look at anyone," Seth had said later that night in the riverside apartment. "Everything about the izakaya—the Elementals around me, the movement, the mood—it was too much. I got caught up in my own head and everything just reminded me of that time." He didn't need to elaborate. He had flinched when Kaide first opened the door to let him in and hadn't been able to look at Anaiya in the eye until at least an hour later.

Kaide had reported the same: "It was like the betrayal was in my bloodstream." Even Anaiya, having worked on the symphony for weeks and knowing it so well she would dream about it nightly, had been physically affected when testing it for distribution in a Precinct 12 drinking den.

The journey to Alesia station passes in a blur of anxiety and anticipation. Light flashes in sharp staccato as the worm pushes through the tunnels before emerging into the dark night of the northern precincts. When it finally groans into the quiet terminal, there are only a few Elementals left in its carriages. They all disembark without fuss and go in their separate directions once they escape the shadows of the station.

Anaiya and Kaide keep silent as they walk hand-in-hand towards the Edges. Somewhere out here is a decommissioned air recycler that houses an array of Water-tech data servers.

After five minutes of walking in the darkness, Kaide drops Anaiya's hand and reaches into his pocket. A faint buzzing tickles at her ears, like a synthfly flying too close or a fluorescent globe taking too long to flicker on. The small device pulses with light, the frequency of flashes synchronised with the peaks and troughs of the buzzing. Like most of Kaide's tech innovations, it was designed with music in mind, but had quickly found a more interesting application.

The scanner had been created to detect and record the barely audible sounds—the whisper of sand across the broken ground, the creaking of the corroded concrete as it shifted to rubble, the distant gurgle of the river. Now, they use it to detect hidden treasure.

The buzzing erupts into a frenzied static, the pulsing light hitting and reflecting off the nearby recyclers with such rapid frequency it almost bathes them in steady light.

Kaide moves closer to one of the recyclers, his steps growing bolder as the noise and light reach their crescendo, and then he switches off the device, plunging them both back into darkness and silence.

"This is the one," he finally says.

Anaiya steps forward, following his voice until her eyes adjust to the more subtle light from their wristplates. She puts her hand on the recycler's exterior and leans closer. Beyond the thick concrete shell lies the switch that will send her music to every Elemental in Otpor and trigger their revolution.

"You've got the code?" Kaide asks.

She taps on her wristplate to bring up the complex string of characters.

"And you remember how to key it in and download the package?"

They've been over the details so many times that, if not for the adrenalin jacking up her nervous system, she would roll her eyes. As it is, the monotonous repetition of Kaide's instructions help her to tamp down the jittering and gain some focus.

"Look for a server that has a serial number starting with 1611-512," she recites. "Find a port that can receive my lifeline extension, wait for the menu screen to load the transmission log and then key in the code directly."

Kaide smiles grimly. "Remember, because this is the server and not an admin terminal, you'll only have one minute to key it in. If you make any mistakes, the system will shut down and an alarm will go off."

She nods; they had been over this as well. Since finishing her betrayal piece, she has used her music-creation time to train her fingers in how to glide over a screen and input seventy-four characters in less than sixty seconds. She glances down at the code again. The string is there just to centre her, to remind her of her starting point. Once the transmission log screen loads, there will be no time to refer back to her wristplate; she will be relying on the muscle memory of the pattern she will recreate on the screen.

Just like music.

"You ready?" Kaide is trying to appear calm for her sake, but even in the dim light she can see the way his nervousness pulls his shoulders forward and makes him light on his feet.

Not trusting her voice, she nods.

"I'll see you in a couple of minutes, then."

On impulse, she reaches forward and grabs Kaide's hand, squeezing it briefly, then quickly drops it and turns away before he can pull her closer.

The touch of the recycler, in contrast, is cold and unforgiving. She grabs at the pitted surface, pulling herself up to the collar. It seems an age to reach the indentation, and she is not sure whether it is the vagaries of time or her failing Peacekeeper skills.

As she climbs onto the lip, she turns her face away to shield it from the buffeting winds and pauses. The building hum she hears is not the rumbling of turbines or the rush of wind, but the reverberating echo of the data centre inside.

The descent to the recycler's floor goes much quicker, Anaiya's eyes drawn to the constellation of lights that flash and shimmer below. Rows and rows of data cabinets are stacked three and four units high, pillar fans whir at high speeds to keep the data towers cool, and thick plaits of cable run along the floor like the ancient serpents in Kaide's novels.

She half falls, half scrambles the final few metres, hitting the floor too hard, her feet tangling in the thick cords of cable. Only when she looks up does she realise the enormity of her task.

Look for a server that has a serial number starting with 1611-512. Easier to find a grain of soylent in a sand drift.

The process of scanning for numbers quickly becomes meditative, allowing her mind to wander. She imagines seeing Kaide's face when she emerges from the recycler, the smile that will shift the lines of worry into something more joyous. She would like that.

The sleek plastic is cool under her touch as she wipes away the fine layers of dust to reveal the serial number of each server. Numbers run and merge together, some close to the fabled 1611, but never close enough to pull her from her thoughts.

He has been dreaming of the days beyond. Not that he speaks of it often, and always catching himself mid-sentence when he does, but often enough for it to give him that far-away stare when he looks out the window at sunset.

And damn him if it isn't contagious. As her fingers trail over the numbers, her mind conjures imagined futures: her and Kaide wandering the streets just to enjoy the evening breeze; music flowing from izakaya unburdened from their locks; nights spent sitting on river ramparts, watching the inky water rush past as the lights of the city bounce off the rippling current.

There is a seduction in the way the images whisper to her, in their all-too-easy-to-believe simplicity. Her post-Orthodoxy world is not a world of revolution, just simple pleasures and the absence of a fear that has become as habitual as breathing.

Her fingers are thick with dust and she wipes them on her jeans, casting her eyes over the numbers revealed on the nearest stack. *1592,1704, 1307, 1611.* She checks the last number, reading out the full string of digits. *1611-512.*

The flashing lights and pale green glow of the display panel burst into focus, every detail of the data box erupting into sharp definition. The sound of her thrumming pulse fills her ears and her stomach flutters with adrenalin. With trembling fingers, she unwraps her lifeline and secures the end attachment firmly into place. Tapping on the wristplate, she brings up the access key one last time. She stares at it until it shifts from a complex string of characters to a melody. And then she injects her lifeline into the port.

The display screen flashes bright, the loading screen appearing briefly before the transmission log starts to run. Her eyes scan frantically for the data entry field, the place to code in the access key. Lines of data scroll up the screen, precious seconds ticking past. And then, in the bottom corner, a tiny window opens. The keyboard is smaller than she has prepared for and she hesitates, even though time is already against her. The keys are a quarter the size, barely large enough for her fingers to hit each cleanly. She will need to not only be faster than she had anticipated. She will have to be deadly accurate.

Her body tenses as the ring finger on her right hand hits the first key. *I'm going to mess this up. It's not going to work. It's too small. There's not enough time.*

But even as the thoughts tumble through her panicked mind, her fingers continue with the rhythm she has started, tapping out the code's string without hesitation, even as her heart seizes with every connection she worries is an error.

No alarm sounds and there is no change in the screen, so she continues until the last character is keyed. She drops her hands and lets them hang limp at her side, shivering as they tremble with the adrenalin she has held at bay.

The screen flashes three times in quick succession and then goes blank. She tries to remember what Kaide had said would happen after the code had been entered. She knows the screen should have changed, but she hadn't really paid attention to the details. The alarm was the key indicator; not hearing it was supposed to be her confirmation of success.

She should be buzzing with elation. Despite the false start, the delayed entry, and the impossibly small keys, she has hacked into Otpor's communication servers and uploaded her music. And yet, she finds herself rooted to the spot, staring at the blank screen, her mind returning to all the moments she had tapped off-centre, so certain that she had mashed two keys together or fallen too heavy on an adjacent key.

But she can only stare at an empty screen for so long. The chill of the recycler and the whirr of the data stacks pull her from her disbelief and force her to move.

The climb to the recycler's lip goes by in a blur, her mind occupied with what she will tell Kaide. She had imagined his joy at seeing her return, the relief at hearing the confirmation of her success. Now, her doubts fill her mind, and she fears he will see the defeat in her eyes and that it will rob him of what little hope he has left.

It is the fear of seeing the joy evaporate from him that keeps her eyes averted as she descends the exterior of the recycler. Her hands and feet beat a steady rhythm, finding the grooves and pits in the concrete as she takes her time to return to the ground.

She waits for him to call to her, expects him to congratulate her or ask her how it all went. But the night is silent and so is Kaide.

At the last minute, five metres from the gravel floor, she looks down. Kaide's figure stands shadowy over by a nearby recycler. In the darkness, he seems to dominate the space rather than meld into it, his stature casual confidence and languid alertness.

The image sits uneasily with her as she jumps to the ground. It reminds her less of Kaide and more of...

"Hello Ani, long time no see."

Niamh.

TWENTY

Seeing her former patrol partner slings Anaiya back to the last time they had locked eyes. She had been shackled to the Execution Pillar—not the makeshift imitation that Eamon and Lilith had rigged up in backwater streets, but the real one of cold stone that still juts from the city centre under the lights of the Trocadero—and Niamh had stood unmoved behind her, adorned in the uniform of his new promotion. Deputy Commissioner suited him, suited his ambition.

"Death becomes you, An—"

She doesn't wait for him to finish. He still thinks she is a Peacekeeper, that her ego will push her to engage. But she knows her only chance is in running. A Peacekeeper would find it shameful to run from conflict; Niamh would never consider it. And that is why it is her best option.

Her calves sting with the sudden burst of urgency, her feet pounding heavy on the gravel-packed ground. She knows the pathways of the Edges well; she has spent most of her post-Peacekeeper life wandering and finding solace in them, and now they hide her from her pursuer. There is little advantage she holds over Niamh—he is faster, more singular in his desire, quicker to manipulate his environment. But he still thinks like a Peacekeeper—rigid in his assessment and depending too much on future-searching and its rational conclusions based on a thousand similar scenarios.

Still, he is quick to react. Even with her meagre lead, she can hear the heavy footfalls as he races after her, gaining with every second that passes.

The lights of the city twinkle ahead, promising sanctuary if she can just get to them. She starts to falter, knows that Niamh is gaining. Her lungs burn with the effort of sprinting. She runs the twisting lines between recyclers and casts her gaze around frantically—looking for a place to hide or a weapon to wield. The Edges doesn't offer an abundance of either; nothing but concrete behemoths, humming sub-stations, and sand and gravel underfoot. Spaces for rats to scurry or pups to scamper.

The wild, feral growl of a dog erupts in the night, echoing and bouncing against the recyclers. The sound trips up her heart and pulls her out of rhythm. *Delacroix?* And then Niamh's scream pierces the night. The primal urgency in that sound triggers a final flood of adrenalin through her veins, gifting her the energy and urgency to sprint the last hundred metres to the city's edge. Only when she reaches the crowded streets of Precinct 14 does she look over her shoulder, her body sagging with relief at seeing the Edges empty of Niamh's advance.

The fear of Niamh discovering her again stops her from fleeing back to the riverside apartment. Instead, she slinks into the nearest drinking den tucked away in a cross street—close enough to the main street to provide a crowd big enough to hide amongst, but not so close as to be a natural route for Peacekeeper reinforcements.

Inside, the den is like every other she has been in—long tables lined in wonky, but generally straight lines, a large bar that runs along the back wall, music barely audible over the raucous Elementals, and a single wallscreen close to the small hallway leading to the bathrooms.

She finds a seat at an emptier table over near the wallscreen and grabs at one of the empty glasses littering its top, using it as a basic alibi to prevent wayward glances or difficult questions.

Gripping the glass in both hands, she lets the cold surface soothe her trembling hands as she focuses on controlling her breathing.

As the shock and tension slowly leach from her body, dangerous questions come into sharper focus. *Where is Kaide? How did Niamh know how to find us? Where to find us? Why was he there alone?*

Her fingers start to tremble again and she grips the glass tighter. It has all been a monumental mess, right from the beginning: leaving Kaide alone and unprotected, the stupid data server and its tiny keyboard, the errors she is certain she made in entering the code…

She glances up at the wallscreen, almost as a delayed reaction, wanting desperately to see the space dominated by the visuals she, Kaide, and Seth had put together on the Enclave, to hear her music peeking out from under all the other noise. The hope of it makes her sit up straighter, makes her chest tighter.

The screen flickers with the usual Earth Elemental fare—brutal avatar sports with wild colours and excessive violence. She stares at it, waiting for it to change, begging for it to change.

When the broadcast eventually fades, it seems as if the screen will shift to the normal sequence of commercials. The screen flashes with an image of the quintessential Earth Elemental—all brawny and laconic—grinning as she sets up her street stall. And then the music swells. Image after image shows Earth Elementals, all from different competencies, all of them exhibiting the stereotypical characteristics she had once associated with the 'baser' Element—the bluster, the 'putting on a brave face' when faced with adversity, the simple living, the simple pleasures.

Maybe it's because she was expecting to see the betrayal package, with its revelations about the Enclave and the lies the Cooperative have told Otpor citizens for generations, or maybe it's because of the adrenalin that has been coursing through her body for close to twenty minutes, but a cold dread washes over her. This is not her package that is playing, but it is *a* package.

The screen fills with a sweeping panorama over Otpor, taking in the jagged edges of Stricken Core, the sleek lines of Last Defence, the imposing Border Wall, and the rows of bridges over the Syn

River. Opaque lettering fills the screen, spelling out the nation's core tenets: Liberty, Egality, Fraternity, or Death. And then a voice, barely audible over the noise of the den and the package soundtrack: "The Cooperative maintains the Orthodoxy that provides these fundamental privileges." The screen divides into quadrants, faces appearing in each.

Anaiya's blood runs cold. These are not the faces of the Earth Elementals from the earlier vision, but of Otpor's most hated. The Resistors: Kane, Rehhd, Eamon, and herself. The images are all in greyscale—tightly cropped profile pictures manipulated to accentuate angles and shadows and create a feeling of menace. Rehhd and Eamon look away from the camera, caught in covert surveillance. But Anaiya and Kane seem to stare straight through the screen, their Peacekeeping uniforms obscured from their official photographs. In each of their faces is a look of defiance and arrogance.

The music is louder now, and she belatedly realises the noise of the den has grown quieter. Around her, Earth Elementals crowd the space. Some continue as they were, but others stare fixed at the screen, their drinks and conversations forgotten. It flickers again, the greyscale of the quadrants bursting to colour as the profile pictures of the Resistors change to footage of their Executions.

Cheers break out in the den and a chant of "bring them down" starts to build. But not before Anaiya hears the final words of the package. "And the Cooperative will always bring down its Resistors."

TWENTY-ONE

Twenty minutes later, the den is back to its usual hive of chatter and drinking. But the mood has shifted—conversation drifts from avatar sports and after-hours parties to talk of protection, commitment, and standing up for 'what's right'; the casual vibe has been replaced by an edgy alertness.

Anaiya sits rigid at the table, gripping the same empty glass and staring down at the table, avoiding eye contact with everyone and desperately trying to be inconspicuous. Earth Elementals aren't typically astute; uninterested in forensically analysing the details, too distractible to focus for the time needed to make sense of complexity. But they aren't stupid. While Anaiya's look and demeanour has changed since her Peacekeeping days, and there is no reason for any of the den's patrons to think the Peacekeeper Resistor is anything other than dead, her heart still races and a cold sweat breaks at the thought of being caught out in her deception. Caught out by pituarmagn-charged Elementals who have just overdosed on a dense package of anti-resistance propaganda.

On shaking legs, she stands slowly up from the bench and steps into the crowd behind her. Her shoulder knocks into an older Earth who mutters something laced with obscenities. It sets heavier the stone in her gut. And suddenly she realises why.

There is a weight.

Peacekeepers are conditioned and trained to recognise weight—the subtle shift in a crowd's energy, the way an angry crowd about to riot weighed heavy, while a death vigil weighed light.

She had thought it a lost skill of hers—so many of them had been corrupted or faded after her Execution. But, she knows this feeling, and grasps the weight.

Her mind shutters against all superfluous thoughts, her gaze tunnelling in on the lowest risk pathway between her and the den's exit, a singular mantra screaming silently in her brain. *Get out. Get out. Get out.*

"She was always gonna follow in his footsteps." The brash and insolent voice sounds close; it takes a discipline she thought long gone to not turn towards it. "I mean, she was always gonna be messed up—they gave her a front-row seat to his Execution for fuck's sake. He'd probably already infected her with his Heterodoxy by then."

She picks up her pace, risking some attention if it will just get her out of the den more quickly.

"Peacekeepers who can't protect the Orthodoxy are better dead," another voice declares. "We need them to protect us from Resistors, not join them."

She is close now, almost at the door.

"The Cooperative provides and protects as always." "We will never surrender our way of life." "Death to all Resistors."

She barges her way through the final strides to the exit, pushing through into the night without a second thought for the dangers that may lurk out in the open. She exhales deeply, her lungs expelling the tension she has held for almost an hour now.

Her head swivels south, tempted to find Kaide and let him brush away her fears and console her in the wake of their crushing defeat. But, she doesn't know if he will be there. Like her, he would have avoided the apartment to ensure it remained off Peacekeeper radars in case he was followed. *Let that be the worst of it.*

There is something perverse in hoping that Kaide was only followed by Peacekeepers, but the thought of him captured and detained is like a punch to the gut, stealing all her oxygen and making her nauseous. She knows what will happen to him in detention; she's seen his scars and has her own to match. She pushes the image away before it can derail her.

If Kaide got away, he would be like her—lying low until the heat died down. She can rendezvous with him in a few days. Until then, she needs a haven. There are a dozen empty apartments she can bunker down in, but the prospect of being alone adds an extra layer of weight she doesn't want to bear. Being alone with nothing to distract her from thoughts of Niamh, and Enclave propaganda, and resistance Executions... it's all a deep, black hole she doesn't want to fall down.

Besides her empty safehouses, there is only one other place she can go where she will be safe. With thoughts of Kane 148 hanging like a dense cloud, she picks her way through the quiet back streets to Lira's apartment.

"I'd ask if you want a drink," Lira says after she opens her apartment door and ushers her inside, "but I think we both know that's a bad idea."

Anaiya is so tired. It weighs down her limbs and turns her bones cold. It also strips away the last of her caution. She sinks down into the most comfortable looking chair in the apartment, flinching as the hard plastic pushes against weary muscles. "You know about the chemical distribution?"

"I know what I saw a few weeks ago at the den, and I know what I felt twenty minutes ago after seeing Kane's face flash up on my wallscreen. And it wasn't the flush of lost love or regret or melancholy I usually feel when I see his face or hear his story."

"It wasn't me," Anaiya sighs, leaning back in the chair and closing her eyes.

"I would hope not." Lira's sarcasm, while only subtle, is like nails on soft flesh. Anaiya flinches, but keeps her eyes shut. *Maybe this was a bad idea.* "I'd hope that if you were trying to manipulate an emotion, it wouldn't be slavish obedience to the Cooperative and its Orthodoxy."

She doesn't feel the trembling start; one minute she is sitting numb in Lira's ridiculous plastic chair, the next her body is shaking, pitching back and forth in violent convulsions, her body too overwhelmed with exhaustion to function. Random details flash into focus—the retro lamp in the corner, the red-bound book half hidden on a shelf of soylent bricks, a water-stain on the wall just above the window. Details that burn bright, flickering as the convulsions escalate. Details that burn into her retinas, before everything turns to black.

"Easy, child." Lira's voice drifts on the edge of the darkness. "No harm is here."

Slowly, Anaiya opens her eyes and orients herself. The unforgiving plastic chair is gone, the anachronistic ornaments absent. The light in here is softer. Everything is softer.

"Where am I?"

"You turned up here last night—"

"This is your apartment?"

Lira chuckles. "It's not to your liking?"

Anaiya sits up in the large, plush bed, fingers trailing across the fine-woven blanket draped across her legs. A textured, patterned wall skin trails across the room in one large swathe, coloured a rich dark blue that shimmers with gold flecks in the lamplight.

"It's just not what I was expecting."

"Oh, Anaiya. You, more than most, should know that an Elemental doesn't have to fit neatly into just one box."

It's true. Elementals like Lira, and Kaide, and herself don't fit the conditioning they were given. "But, most do."

Like Seth, who even with his dreams of revolution is still a quintessential Air. And Niamh, who even with his designs and ambition is still a quintessential Fire.

Lira smiles and shrugs. "I'll get you some water."

Anaiya leans back against the headboard and stares at the ceiling. *Why do some Elementals stick to their conditioning and others resist?*

"What did you feel when you saw the propaganda package?"

she calls out.

Lira comes back, holding out the glass of water. "I felt like someone plugged a new reality into my brain."

"And you felt the same at the izakaya the other day?"

"No."

"No? But I thought you said—"

"No. The other day, I felt like someone plugged a new emotion into my brain. A new reality is something else entirely. And I didn't like either sensation."

Anaiya presses her palms to her eyes and groans. "It's all a big mess."

"What is? What's going on, Anaiya?"

She could stay quiet; it would be better to stay quiet. But everything feels like it is crashing down on her. Her secret is out, their revolution plan is over, and she is cut off from everyone. And she just wants Kane back, wants her mentor to tell her what to do, to tell her how to make it better. But all she has is Lira, and while it is the most fragile of threads that connects her to Kane, it is still a thread. And it pulls the words from her lips in a rush.

She tells Lira everything—the Enclave, the plans for revolution, Niamh discovering her, the failed manipulation. It comes out in one, long, uninterrupted stream of consciousness, pitching with emotion and tightening her throat until the words come out strained and raspy. Retelling it has made her realise the extent of her failure and it leaves her exhausted and defeated.

Lira stays silent, staring at Anaiya with a look she can't decipher, and then she sighs. "Maybe we need that drink after all." She steps out of the room and returns with two glasses of genievre. The bittersweet, heady scent reaches Anaiya before Lira can offer her the glass. She downs the contents, grunting as its liquid fire races down her throat.

The older woman smiles and hands over her own untouched glass. "Here. You need it more than I do."

Anaiya takes it gratefully and cradles it in her hands before taking a sip. "I messed up, Lira. It's all messed up. It's worse than messed up; it's over."

Lira sighs again, the lines on her face deepening. "It's

definitely not good. But it's only over if you want it to be."

"Lira—"

"I know. I know it's a shitshow. I also know that you've always known this path was never going to be easy. In this world, things aren't over until you're dead. And even when you're dead, it's not over. Unless you want it to be."

The silence washes over them. Anaiya stares down at her drink.

"There's no shame in it," Lira continues, "if you want it to be over. You've suffered what no-one else alive has suffered for this resistance. There's no shame in not wanting to pull that thread any longer. Or in thinking that there's nothing good that will come from getting to its end."

Anaiya puts the glass on the bedside table and throws off the blanket. "The end of Orthodoxy would have been glorious. It's all a lie anyway, isn't it? Just a tool for the rich and powerful to stay rich and powerful."

She stands up, desperate to do something with the frustration that makes her limbs itch for action. "But it's a dead end. I tried to pull it down—it was the perfect plan; it was the only plan that would work. And they hijacked it and turned it against us. There's no more pituarmagn access, and even if we had some, we'd be fighting against the reinforced conditioning they just broadcast to every wallscreen in Otpor."

"So, you need a new plan."

"There is no new plan. I told you, it was the best plan, the *only* plan."

Lira grunts and stands up. She is old and small, but still formidable. Anaiya sighs and follows her into the lounge room, not making it far before Lira slams something small and hard into her chest.

"You weren't the only one who stole from the Enclave, remember?"

Anaiya glances down and takes the book from Lira's grip. "You have a real thing for red books, don't you?"

"They seem to have the best stories."

The book is just larger than her palm, its binding thin and

creased, the bright red of the cover interrupted only by the stylised image of a man's face in yellow and black. *Guerrilla Warfare.*

Lira reaches over and flicks to one of the earlier pages, tapping at the text. "*Popular forces can win a war against the army. It is not necessary to wait until all conditions for making revolution exist; the insurrection can create them. Abandon the defeatist attitude of revolutionaries who remain inactive and take refuge in the pretext that against a professional army nothing can be done, who sit down to wait until all necessary conditions are given without working to accelerate them.*" She reaches under Anaiya's chin and lifts her face so that they stand eye to eye. "You picked a fight with the Cooperative on the kind of scale and with the kind of weapons they would use. If you want to beat them, stop giving them the advantage. Stop thinking about the one big strike, and start planning for smaller, more targeted strikes. A bridge is made up of bricks, after all. You don't need to annihilate the structure to send it tumbling; you just need to remove the cornerstones."

Two weeks later, Anaiya leaves Lira's apartment, her hair dyed black and her jeans and hoodie replaced with a worn pair of grey corduroy pants and a black knitted jumper with a frayed hem and flecks of white on the sleeves where harsh chemicals have bleached the colour. There is an uncomfortable vulnerability in not being able to shrug into the loose folds of her old jacket and pull down its hood to shroud her eyes. She struggles to not hunch over, to pull at her fringe, to stick to the dark shadows and empty streets.

Niamh will be looking for her, will be expecting her to rely on her Peacekeeper skills and tactics. Her best chance of evading him is being nondescript in the open, not stealth in the shadows.

Still, she picks at the frayed threads at her wrist as she walks through the Precincts towards the riverside apartment. For the briefest of moments she had considered the subworm, but Niamh knew she'd used it during her realignment mission and the thought of being trapped in the small confines of a worm segment terrifies her.

She could walk the distance in just under ninety minutes, but being exposed for that long is too risky. Especially with the number of Peacekeeper patrols out on the streets. In a crowd of lumbering Earths and vibrant Airs, their dark kevlar uniforms and alert stance make them easy to spot; their presence is like the shadow cast by the Border Wall when morning light bathes everywhere else with tepid warmth.

It is hard to know whether their edginess comes from a directive from their Deputy Commissioner to find a dead-resistor-walking, or whether it's just the natural biorhythm of Elementals designed to always be alert.

Her awareness of them is always in peripheral vision; she doesn't let her gaze linger long enough to see if she recognises any of them, to see if they are looking for any resemblance in her to the Anaiya that perished on the Execution Pillar all those months ago.

After three impromptu detours into drinking dens in the seventh and eighth precincts and a hasty retreat down a side street in the riverside market district of Precinct 15 (a brief burst of paranoia that still lingers in her accelerated heart rate), she arrives at the riverside apartment she shares with Kaide. Her mind whispers *home*, but she silences it. All of her homes have been taken from her and she's come to realise that it only hurts if you care about what has been taken.

She waits on the corner opposite, staring into the window of a low-end fashion store; to all appearances, she is debating whether or not to purchase the orange polyester dress with its magenta trim and sleek profile, but her focus is not on the dress, but the reflection of the building in the glass. For a few minutes, she watches and waits, looking for any hint of Peacekeeper surveillance, of anything amiss, off.

Each minute she lingers is another chance to be discovered; she feels the anticipation and fear of it like synthfly larvae crawling on her skin. She has waited too long. Dropping her gaze, she walks away from the shop front and crosses the street. The apartment lift is working, but some Peacekeeper habits are difficult to shake and she takes the stairs. Four flights up, the nondescript polywood door rushes into focus. She pauses, straining to hear anything that would suggest a disturbance, straining to hear Kaide's voice. But everything is silent.

She fumbles in her pockets for the analogue key Kaide had given her. The lock is hidden behind the proxy panel that comes away with a gentle click when she applies a double tap of pressure to its centre. The key slots into its entry, bolts sliding up and down into place along the haphazard ridges of metal. A quarter turn to the right and the door clicks open.

Pushing through into the lounge room, she casts her gaze around, expecting to find the room trashed, or at least disturbed. But everything is as she remembers. Nothing out of place. But, also, no sign of Kaide.

He's out looking for me. He's at his old studio. He's meeting with Seth to formulate the new plan.

Every option is feasible, but there is a desperate edge to each of them. She clings to them, not because they could be true, but because she fears the alternative.

In the shadows of her mind, the image of seeing Niamh at the base of the recycler plays over and over. She sees him standing casually against the corroded concrete, the Edges silent, no sign of Kaide. Kaide…He wouldn't have left her alone… Not when so much was at stake, not if Peacekeepers were in the vicinity, not if Niamh had arrived.

"They've got Kaide."

TWENTY-TWO

They've got Kaide.

It isn't Anaiya who utters the words, but Seth. He emerges from the bedroom, face lined with sleeplessness and worry. "Peacekeepers took him."

"How do you know?"

"Because they tried to take me," Seth says, his tone, his stance dejected as he pads across the room and sinks into the lounge.

"How did you escape?"

She sinks down on the lounge next to him, her unsteady legs no longer able to support her.

"Farasei. He smuggled me out via the inner sanctum. Said something about *this narrative being too simple and redundant*." He turns weary eyes to her. "He sends his regards, by the way."

She sits forward, closing her eyes and rubbing her temples. "He's playing with us."

"Yeah. But keeping a rat alive, if only to toy with it, gives the rat a chance to bite back."

"Niamh was at the recycler."

Seth's head snaps up. "He saw you?"

"He called me by name. Chased me through the Edges."

Flashes of memory spring up from her subconscious—the way the deep shadows of the Edges gave way to the city light, the tightness in her chest as Niamh pursued her through the maze of recyclers, the primal growl of a dog piercing the night.

"He let you get away?"

She shakes her head, feeling the energy drain from her body as a dense numbness takes hold. She recounts the story again, in less detail than she had to Lira and with a lot less emotion. This is just a factual retelling, focusing on the details that will matter to Seth, avoiding anything that will disturb the rock that sits heavy in the pit of her stomach and smothers the emotions building under the pressure.

When she finishes, Seth looks more dejected than when he stepped into the lounge room. "If Niamh has Kaide, and knows you're alive, and knows you were at the recycler with him to sabotage the emergency broadcast…"

"Don't say it," she murmurs, closing her eyes and biting down the rush of emotion that is sticking in her throat.

"He's dead, Anaiya. If Niamh has him, he's killed him."

Because that's what Niamh does—eliminates loose ends that can come back to strangle him:the Water Commissioner who led the unauthorised realignment of Anaiya; Jenna, the Peacekeeper who knew his dirty secrets; even Anaiya herself, not that he'd known that particular Execution had been unsuccessful.

Until now.

The apartment walls close in on her, stealing the air and overwhelming her with the very real, very visceral feeling of being trapped. She wants to scream until her lungs explode, wants to run through the streets to let the energy burn away her despair, wants to let the wail escape her constricted throat; but she can't risk drawing unwanted attention, or being seen by a Peacekeeper, or letting Seth see her true emotions. All her desires squashed and suffocated under all the things she can't do, can't risk, can't shake.

She walks up to the wall and punches it, relishing the sudden pain, the searing heat, and then the onslaught of micro-aggressions as the individual bones and tendons do their own screaming. Seth stands up without looking at her and comes back with a bottle of tequila.

"Let's get fucked up."

The first shot of tequila is a fire in her throat, forcing its way past all the messy emotions still gripping it tight. It helps to push her emotions most of the way back into their box, but the pain in her hand quickly swells to fill the void.

"Is it broken?" Seth asks, reaching over to fill her empty glass and then his own.

She tries to flex it, winces, and then picks up the glass in her other hand. "Maybe. Probably." The next shot is less a firestorm and more a river of molten steel.

Seth downs his glass and taps it back against the table. He stands up abruptly and heads to the bedroom. Anaiya downs her glass and pours another, the pungent alcohol sloshing onto the table as her left hand shakes with the effort of trying to maintain a steady grip and a coordinated pour. She wipes the mess with her sleeve. It is reckless to drink so much with a possible fracture, but the pain in her hand is less problematic than the demons in her head, so she picks up the glass and downs it.

When Seth returns to the lounge room, he is holding a plastic bracket and one of Kaide's old t-shirts. "It's not as good as the medical supplies Cress steals from the Infirmary, but it will do."

He sits next to her on the lounge and reaches for her hand. She flinches as he slides the double-angled bracket over the metacarpals and first row of knuckles on her right hand. Tearing the t-shirt into long strips, he folds one strip into a thicker wad and wedges it in the gap between the bracket and the underside of her hand. She groans as the pain flares at the sudden increase in pressure, but doesn't pull away.

"It will feel better soon." Seth's fingers move from her hand to her lower forearm. He holds the end of one strip against the skin and stretches it as he wraps it around her arm, moving in tight circles down to her wrist.

"How do you know how to do this?"

"Sometimes going to the Infirmary is not an option when you've been running from Peacekeepers. You learn pretty quickly to improvise." He picks up the next strip and wraps it tightly around the end of the last strip before moving down to her hand. "I haven't needed to do it in a while…"

"Where did you find the bracket?" The words come strangled through gritted teeth as Seth wraps the strips around the makeshift splint.

"It was holding up one of the small shelves in the bedroom."

"The one with his books?"

Seth nods, keeping his focus on the bandaging. And her stomach plummets as if the ground has fallen away from her. In the first few weeks of moving into the apartment, Kaide had encouraged her to find something that would make the small apartment feel like her home. In time, the trio of shelves that had housed Kaide's books had become a haven for her eclectic collection of market knick-knacks. They had lain in bed and laughed at the ugly plastic sculpture of Stricken Core and admired the sleek lines of the metal wind chimes.

Please don't be dead.

"What did Farasei say?"

Seth finishes bandaging her hand, tying it off near her thumb, and gently returns it to her lap. He squeezes his eyes shut, to shut out the conversation or to ward off his own emotions. The knot in Anaiya's gut tightens again, and even with the tequila turning everything else warm and fuzzy, her throat aches. Without Kaide, they are both adrift in a river.

"I told you," Seth mumbles. "He said that I wasn't the only one that Peacekeepers are looking for. That they had Kaide. That this ending wasn't as entertaining as the one he preferred. And to send his regards to his favourite Peacekeeper-turned-Resistor."

He opens his eyes only to stare down at his hands. Shaking his head, he fills their empty glasses, but Anaiya doesn't drink, just stares down at the shimmering liquid.

"How did they know your connection to Kaide?"

Seth shrugs. "Wristplate proximity, I guess."

"No, they tried that when I was on the realignment mission. It didn't work—your connection was third degree, at best. And you've had even less recorded proximity since Rehhd's Execution." The tequila is exerting its influence, her words slurring on the hard consonants. "There's no way they would know you were connected to him. I mean, Jenna had her suspicions, but Niamh killed her." She squeezes her eyes shut, trying to push away the intoxication she had been chasing only minutes ago. "And Jenna was only suspicious of your connection to Rehhd. Kaide was too openly connected to others for any one connection to be notable.

"Only the other Resistance members knew the connection. And they loved you. They chose you over Kaide. They'd never betray you. Not to Peacekeepers. And they wouldn't even *know* of the Enclave, except…"

Her inebriated mind finally catches up to the rush of words spilling from her tongue. She stares at Seth, who looks stricken. "Except for Lilith."

"Would she…?"

"What? Betray me?" He picks up his glass and downs it, then picks up Anaiya's untouched glass and downs that. "I don't know, you tell me—seems as if you two have more in common than I realised."

The barb stings, but her inebriation quickly dulls it. "But why would she? Why would she incite a public lynching of a Peacekeeper, rally a crowd to focus their rage on all Fire Elementals, only to turn you over to them?"

"Maybe she is one of them?" The bitterness in his voice washes harmlessly over her. She shakes her head, the movement too vehement, too wobbly, with all the alcohol in her system.

"No, not even I went that far; I pretended to be one of you, but never to the point where I actively put Peacekeepers or Fire Elementals in danger."

"So, if Lilith didn't rat me out to Peacekeepers, who did?"

Anaiya's brain hurts with the effort of untangling all the loose threads. It could have only been Lilith—she had been the only one who knew about the Enclave and the rebellion. But it can't be Lilith—there is no way she is a Peacekeeper operative, no way that Niamh would repeat the failed realignment procedure, not with a broken Peacekeeper and dead Water Commissioner on his hands. And if she isn't a realigned Peacekeeper, then her enmity towards the Fire Element is genuine, and there could be no reason for her to cooperate with them. Like all resistance members, she would rather die.

Or at least hide. Not all resistance members faced the Execution Pillar. Not when they had the Enclave to shelter them.

"How did Lilith get involved with the Enclave, anyway? How did she even *find* them?" It had taken power cuts and transmission strikes to give Anaiya her slim window of opportunity the first time she had accessed Boileau Road, and the discovery of the subterranean tunnels after that. Lira had literally fallen into one after slipping from a roof. And both of them had been unwanted intruders, tolerated with a kind of curiosity at best, openly reviled at worst. Never welcomed as a guest or treated with the kind of familiarity Lilith was gifted.

"She didn't hand you over to the Peacekeepers," she says suddenly, ignoring Seth as he starts to answer her question. "She told the Enclave. And they handed you over to the Peacekeepers."

Seth scoffs. "That doesn't make sense, either. Why would the Enclave take us in and protect us after the rebellion, only to hand us over to the same Element whose downfall they were sponsoring less than a year ago? Why would they stir up more trouble between the Elements when they have finally achieved their status quo of blissful ignorance and compliance?"

The two of them stare at each other, the same revelation dawning on them.

"Because," Anaiya murmurs, voicing what she knows Seth is also thinking, "we were just about to upset the balance."

TWENTY-THREE

"They knew about the pituarmagn attack." Seth stands up and sways on unsteady legs before grabbing at the wall to steady himself.

"You told Lilith," Anaiya accuses.

"No! No." He sits back down. "I told her nothing. You know the cover story I told her—she thought Kaide had rejected my attempts at reconciliation. And she knew nothing about your reappearance."

Anaiya groans, her mind still too fuzzy to get to the answers lying just outside her grasp. "I need to sober up."

"I'll get it," Seth mumbles, looking pointedly at her compromised hand. He strides awkwardly out of the room and returns a minute later with a small atomiser. Anaiya reaches for it with her left hand and pumps two short bursts under her tongue.

"Better than a cold shower," she says, shaking her head clear as the chemicals wick away the residual intoxication. The onslaught of pain from her hand comes throbbing back into focus, generating a ball of nausea in the pit of her stomach. Clenching her teeth, she pushes the atomiser across the table to Seth.

He shakes his head. "I'm happy to remain numb, thank you very much."

She can't blame him; partly because the whole situation is so fucked up—any sane person would avoid it at all costs—and partly because he is a quintessential Air Elemental who can't offer her the kind of incisive analysis she needs right now.

She needs Kaide.

Her stomach tightens again, not with nausea, but fear and longing. He would be able to cut through all the maddening thoughts and strip away the static, get to the heart of the problem and find a practical solution.

"How did the Enclave know about the attack?" she wonders aloud. "We only ever discussed it here. They would have to hack your wristplates to get streaming audio, and there's been no opportunity for them to have installed the hack since your interviews after Rehhd's detention, yeah?"

Seth nods, leaning back into the lounge and closing his eyes. The alcohol will lull him to sleep soon. She reaches over and slaps his thigh with her good hand.

"Fuck! What was that for?"

"Stay awake. Were you ever restrained after those interviews?"

"No," he mumbles and closes his eyes again.

Even if he had been, Peacekeepers would have swooped on him much earlier, with all the plotting he had done around the rebellion.

"So, no wristplate hack…" Something scratches at the back of her mind, her brain still catching up after the fog of intoxication has lifted. *Wristplate, wristplate, wristplate.*

She startles and sits rigid. Very slowly, she moves closer to Seth, picks up the atomiser from the table, and flicks him on the ear.

"Fuck, Anaiya. Can you stop—"

She shoots two sharp bursts of the adrenalin into his mouth and shoves her hand over it to stop the coughing and spluttering. Urgently she shakes her head and, satisfied the chemical has worked and he will keep silent, she takes away her hand and puts a finger to her lips. Leaning close to his ear, she whispers, "What did Kaide do with the wristplate I stole from the Enclave?"

Seth pulls back from her. "It's not here," he says. "He was working on it at his studio." His face drops. "Where we discussed the pituarmagn attack."

It all hits like a sucker punch. "That's how they got him," she murmurs. "Niamh didn't get him at the recycler; if he had, he wouldn't have been there at the base waiting for me. He didn't know I was there. He was just waiting for whoever it was—you or Kaide—they thought was tampering with the broadcast feed.

"Kaide would have returned to his studio, knowing, like I did, not to return to the apartment in case he was followed. They would have soundmatched your voices." She stops. "No. That's not it; if they had soundmatched, they would have picked you up sooner somewhere else, from your wristplate location pings. They must be triangulating the location of the stolen wristplate. Which explains why it took some time in finding Kaide—he hadn't been to the studio in weeks."

"Why do you care, Anaiya? Why does it matter?" This time he stands up without swaying, his agitation leeching into his voice and stance. "It means *nothing*. It helps *nothing*. It won't bring Kaide back. It won't bring the Orthodoxy down. This revelation is all for *nothing*."

"No," she replies, her own anger lacing her voice. "It isn't for nothing. Nothing changes—we bring the Orthodoxy *and* the Enclave down. And, if bringing them down gives us justice and retribution for Kaide, all the better for it."

It is dawn when she leaves Seth asleep on the lounge and heads towards the bedroom on weary legs. Curling up in the sheets and blankets that still smell like Kaide layers on fresh torment, but she only curls in tighter, burying her head into the pillows and letting out the sobs she has held back for hours.

She dozes in fits, dreamwalking in the space between waking and sleeping. Vivid images weave amongst each other and overlap—soundmatchers and wristplates, Enclaves and Execution Pillars, enemies and lovers—her tired mind playing out the scenarios of the plan she and Seth had hatched and confusing them with old memories.

The midday sun forces its way into the room, sharpening the edge of her discontent and leaving her no option but to finally open her eyes and face the day she has tried to avoid. The bed remains empty beside her, and the reminder of Kaide's absence seems to grab her in a tight fist and crumple her. She draws a shaky breath, fighting the tiredness and the slippery slope of emotion it presents, and clambers out of the bed.

Silence follows her as she steps into the lounge room. A half-empty bottle of tequila and mismatched glasses are the only evidence of Seth ever being there. She is grateful he is not here now to witness her suffering.

She pulls at the bandages and splint that bind her hand, relief and pain competing with each tug against bruised ligaments. The skin below is mottled and swollen, singing with fresh pain as she gingerly stretches out her fingers.

Leaving behind the tequila bottle and the glasses, she makes her way to the kitchenette. Finding a fresh glass, she fills it with water from the tap and leans against the counter, drinking like she hasn't seen water in years and savouring its cool relief against her parched throat. She pours another, letting the water overflow the rim of the glass and run over her hands. She stares at it, at the way it cascades in thick ribbons, the way it plays with the light and blurs the lines of cuts and bruises.

Only when the cold sets an uncomfortable tingling to her hands does she shut the water off and drink from the too-full glass. Slowly, she drains it dry. And then she throws the empty glass to the floor and watches it shatter into pieces like so many grains of sand it came from.

Turning her back on it all, she walks back to the bedroom. With the little strength she has in her left hand, she tugs at the blankets and sheets and pillows until the mattress is bare. Taking the heaviest blanket, she awkwardly drapes it over the curtain rod of the small window above the bed, pushing and pulling it into place until most of the sunlight is barred from the room.

The bed is cold and hard when she lies back down on it. But it is as it should be. Closing her eyes, she lets the throbbing of her hand, with its steady rhythm, rob her of her thoughts and lead her back to sleep.

"You took the bandage off," Seth says when he arrives back at the apartment.

Anaiya looks up from her book and then back down to her bruised hand. "Not broken. I think it's just ligament damage."

She sits cross-legged on the lounge, Kaide's collection of salvaged Heterodox stories propped open in her lap.

"How did you go with the wristplate?"

Seth shakes his head and sinks into the armchair. "My guess is they picked it up when they nabbed Kaide."

The pang of disappointment flares in her core, but she is not truly surprised. She should have realised earlier—if the wristplate was how they discovered the pituarmagn attack, and how they found Kaide, they wouldn't have left it behind. Something about the conclusion pricks at her thoughts. "*Who* would have picked it up?"

"Hm?" Seth isn't listening, peering down at the book in her lap, no doubt trying to read the text upside down, trying to figure out what it is and where it came from. But Anaiya's brain is tripping over something else, something unexpected.

"Who would have picked it up? Because whoever picked it up would have known what it is, and where it came from."

"So?"

"So, whoever picked it up would know about the Enclave."

"And?"

"And there's no way your average Peacekeeper knows about the Enclave."

Seth finally looks up at her. "What makes you say that?"

"Because I was a Peacekeeper for more than a generation, and I only ever heard random whispers and rumours, never considered it anything more than an urban legend. And the Enclave are working pretty hard to keep it that way—their biggest priority, beyond maintaining a status quo that sustains their privilege, is to remain hidden."

"So who picked up the wristplate?"

"There's no way an Enclave member would deign to do their own dirty work." She thinks of Farasei and Danai and their entourage of disinterested onlookers during the execution Eamon and Lilith had planned for her. "So, we'd have to assume it's a very elite cadre of Peacekeepers who are in concert with, or at least beholden, to the Enclave."

"What does that mean for us?"

"It means they're operating off the official grid, that they can act outside the rules." An unauthorised op, just like the one Niamh had recruited her to when she had first been realigned.

"Act outside the rules. Like killing Kaide without a trial or witnesses."

Anaiya's chest twinges as the thought of Kaide rushes to the front of her mind and temporarily obliterates everything else.

"Yes," she says, swallowing against the small, hard lump that swells in her throat. "And us, if they were to find us."

Seth sinks down to floor and leans back against the wall, closing his eyes and pressing his palms to his temples. "It's never going to work, is it? They'll always be more resourced than us, always have the advantage of the system against us."

His despair infects her own thoughts, shutting down the last threads of hope she had still been clinging to. It *is* impossible. Just two abandoned and adrift fugitives against the two most powerful forces in Otpor—the blanket authority of the Peacekeepers and the hidden strings of the Enclave.

She glances around the room and reaches for Lira's strange book with the yellow face on the cover. The page that Lira had read aloud to her is still folded into a small triangle at its corner.

Abandon the defeatist attitude of revolutionaries who remain inactive and take refuge in the pretext that against a professional army nothing can be done, who sit down to wait until all necessary conditions are given without working to accelerate them.

She runs her finger over the text, skimming the words, looking for answers. Drawing the book up to her chest, she reads aloud.

"The fundamental characteristic of a guerrilla band is mobility. This permits it in a few minutes to move far from a specific theatre and in a few

hours far even from the region, if that becomes necessary; permits it constantly to change front and avoid any type of encirclement. As the circumstances of the war require, the guerrilla band can dedicate itself exclusively to fleeing from an encirclement, which is the enemy's only way of forcing the band into a decisive fight that could be unfavourable; it can also change the battle into a counter-encirclement (small bands of men are presumably surrounded by the enemy when suddenly the enemy is surrounded by stronger contingents; or men located in a safe place serve as a lure, leading to the encirclement and annihilation of the entire troops and supply of an attacking force). Characteristic of this war of mobility is the so-called minuet, named from the analogy with the dance."

"What is that?"

"A book—" She stops short, not yet ready to divulge her relationship with Lira. "I found at the Enclave," she finishes lamely. But Seth doesn't seem to notice her hesitation or her weak explanation; he reaches for the book and she lets him take it.

"This was at the Enclave?" he murmurs, thumbing through the pages. Anaiya stays silent, watching his face change as his gaze flits over the text. "This has to be the most Heterodox thing in existence. It's more than just a treatise… it's a manual on how to defeat the Cooperative." He pauses and looks up at her. "Do you think it could work?"

"We don't engage in their fight. No more big, epic plans on a national stage. Rapid, strategic strikes on specific targets."

"Smash and grab tactics."

She nods.

"It's high risk…"

"Yes and no. They're already after us, so hiding isn't that much safer. Targeting the Enclave will generate more heat on us, but they won't be able to use the general Peacekeeping corps, so we'll only ever be up against a black-ops Task Force."

"Who have extra-judicial killing authority."

"Yeah, but who will be no more than five bodies on the ground. Niamh won't risk being compromised by more than that. If we stay smart, and stay hidden, we can take down the Enclave one piece at a time. Or, worst case, push them off-balance; get them to a point where they're so annoyed and frustrated, they slip up. And reveal themselves."

TWENTY-FOUR

Walking in to Veritas is like walking into a memory. The izakaya is silent in the pre-dawn hour, empty of the patrons that would have crammed the place just a few hours ago. But full of ghosts.

Seth feels it too. She sees it in the way he stiffens when entering the basement level, the way his head swivels to the spot where the Trainee Peacekeeper had sat blindfolded and shackled against the wall, and then to where all the dark secrets had spilled. Rehhd and Eamon's idiocy, Seth's true position of power, Anaiya's betrayal, Kaide's complicity.

A cold panic grips her heart. Memories of Peacekeeper backup arriving, of the sharp sting of the needle at her neck, the rush of warmth and darkness—it is all too vivid. She starts to tremble, remembering the solo detention cell she had woken in, a metal coffin that had pressed in from all sides.

The air is too thin in the basement; her lungs pitch with desperation, trying to suck in more oxygen, but it is like trying to grasp water in an open fist.

A touch at her wrist short circuits the rising panic. Seth tentatively wraps his hand around hers and squeezes. She looks over to him, his face shadowed in the unlit basement.

"I'm supposed to be the one who's nervous, remember?"

She flashes a weak smile, squeezes his hand, and lets go. He is being kind when he doesn't need to be, when his own memories would be raging at him to be anything but. He is not the Seth she saved that night, but he is not the Seth that let Eamon lead her to his makeshift Execution Pillar either.

"Where's your Surgeon?"

He barks his own nervous laugh and looks around. "Cress said the Technician had the time and the address. But black-market Waters are notoriously late. Part of their Unorthodoxy, I guess."

He is trying to be funny, but she can hear the anxiety in his voice.

"Does it hurt afterwards?" he asks.

They had discussed all the ways removing a wristplate would change the way Seth could operate; the adjustments he would need to make, the way his life would change, the opportunities and constraints. But, this was the first time he had asked about pain.

"Nothing that some Nurozav or a bottle of tequila won't fix. It will feel like the wires are still plugged in through the flesh. For me, it felt like they were burrowing at times, burning hot or like ice. But not all the time, and it eventually faded."

Seth nods and takes a seat on the bottom step of the staircase leading up to the bar. They had agreed that removing his wristplate was their best option. The risk of a black-ops Task Force using the standard Peacekeeping scanner app to find them was too high. It was how she had found Lilith after her stint at the Evidence Hall listening to old Truth Seeker interviews.

"So, what's our first strike?"

They have debated and interrogated their next-step options a hundred times over in the past forty-eight hours, but she humours him, if only to help turn his mind from the procedure he's about to go through.

"Best option is hitting the old Boileau Road Enclave. It's practically empty, so it's a soft target. But it still holds enough to be a point of intrigue and frustration."

"It will be—"

The sounds of metal screeching along concrete cuts him short as the basement door opens.

Anaiya slinks back into the shadows as two Technicians enter the basement. One is altogether too familiar—Vincent, who had confirmed her wristplate hack after Niamh had got to her, who had passed on her desperate message to Kaide before her Execution, and who had resurrected her with a dead woman's wristplate. His presence makes sense—there couldn't be too many Unorthodox Technicians with wristplate hacking ability that the Resistance would trust. But, the presence of the second technician, a tall wiry female with short-cropped platinum hair, does not.

"Who is she?" Seth asks, standing up and walking over to them.

"She's here to administer the anaesthetic and to restart your heart if anything goes wrong." Vincent looks over to Anaiya. "Who's she?"

Anaiya fights the urge to step further back into the shadows and pull up her hood.

"Insurance," Seth says, pulling Vincent's attention back to him. "In case you get any ideas while I'm 'dead'".

"I don't know why I keep getting involved with you lot. I was supposed to be done after the last clusterfuck of Kaide's." He peers over to the shadows again, no doubt searching to confirm what he probably already suspects.

"You've received your payment. Double the last, I've been assured. So, let's put an end to the mindless chatter and get on with this, shall we?"

Vincent nods to the other Technician, who drops her satchel to the floor and busies herself with moving crates into the centre of the space.

"How long will it take?" Seth asks as he steps towards the makeshift gurney, stepping over cords and around the bright lamps the Technician has propped up nearby.

"The removal is practically instantaneous. Once your wristplate records the full loss of vitality, I'll disengage it. The actual procedure will only take twenty minutes. But you'll be unconscious for an hour or two." He squeezes a large dollop of sanitiser on his hands and rubs them together vigorously. "We'll stick around for ten minutes-or-so after we've removed the wristplate, just in case you start haemorrhaging or go into cardiac arrest. But after that, you're on your own."

Seth lies down on the crates and looks over to Anaiya. "If I don't make it back, *avenge us both*."

She would roll her eyes at the melodrama if it wasn't such a real possibility. "I'll see you in a couple of hours."

He barely flinches as the Technician injects the needle into his neck and seconds later his eyes close, his face relaxes, and his whole body goes limp. Vincent picks up his hand to read the vitals flashing on the wristplate, the bright red statistics flashing more and more urgently.

The convulsions explode without warning, pitching Seth's body into violent spasms that tip him from the crates and onto the floor. His head smashes into the hard floor, opening up a gash on the left side of his skull. The Technicians pounce on him, bearing their weight down to stop his thrashing from doing more damage. Anaiya rips off her hoodie and races from her shadows, bundling the material up and placing it under his head.

"Keep him still," Vincent grunts. "We're going to have to start the procedure now, or his heart won't make it."

While Anaiya and the other Technician hold down Seth's raging body, Vincent races to unpack his kit. Scalpels and endoscopes shimmer in the flashing red light, nestled beside a portable defibrillator, rolls of gauze and bandages, and an assortment of vials.

Her own arm tingles as she watches him slice into the skin around Seth's wristplate. Rivulets of blood snake down to the floor and Seth's body gives up its trembling. His wristplate light is dull now, blinking slowly, the stats fuzzy and vague. And then it turns black.

Even though she had been prepared for it, Anaiya's heart still stutters at the sight.

"What's going on?"

"He had a reaction to the anaesthetic," Vincent says, still moving his scalpel around the edge of the wristplate. "Instead of slowing down his biorhythms, it's spiked them first. Without the wristplate functionality, there's no way of knowing whether the loss of vitality is the fiction we've manipulated or a real mortality event."

The wristplate comes away in his hands, leaving behind a mess of bloody skin and tissue. Long, fine filaments glimmer in the bright light of the lamps, stretched taut and wavering with the pressure as Vincent pulls at them with long, tapered forceps. The sight of it all makes it difficult for Anaiya to process what the Technician is saying.

"You don't know if he's dying?"

"I don't know if he's dead."

She is reaching past him and for the defibrillator before her brain has formed a fully coherent plan.

"Escher."

The other Technician reacts immediately to the sound of her name, rushing Anaiya and tackling her to the ground. The pain in her shoulder is lessened only by the surprise at the strength of a Water Elemental and the panic that still rages at the sight of Seth's limp body.

"We can't bring him back online," Escher whispers harshly. "It will register the compromised wristplate, and it will either set off an alarm or communicate the nearest coordinates. Either way, his wristplate gets flagged, and so does he."

Anaiya stops pushing against the Technician, the logic of the reprimand killing her rage and leaving behind a flat, dull-edged panic in its place. Seth's wristplate lies discarded on the floor, the lifeline curled up like a bloodied snake on the concrete, and still Vincent pulls at the thin wires burrowing in his arm, swearing when they don't come away cleanly. The globules of flesh that cling to the red-stained silver stands speak of an internal damage she can't comprehend.

"Should it take this long?" Her voice is high and reedy. "Why is it so messy?"

"The anaesthetic was supposed to dilate his bioframe, but the seizure has left a residual tension." Water Elementals are renowned for being unflappable, and while Vincent's voice is still evenly pitched, the clipped syllables are the equivalent of an Air Elemental having a meltdown. All the dull edges of her panic file blade sharp.

"And?"

"And retrieving the wristplate connections has collateral damage."

"Is it fatal?"

"We'll find out soon enough. Escher, prep the defib—we can't rely on the biorhythms to reset once the anaesthetic wears off."

The Technician scrambles over to the defibrillator, her fingers setting off a series of beeps as she punches at tiny buttons. "Ready," she says as the machine's display flashes brightly.

"Get me the endoscope, I think we've got a tear in the heart." He pulls a wire free and moves his scalpel to Seth's chest, pulling up his shirt and pressing the blade into the flesh. Escher passes him a long thin tube, plugging one end into a glass screen as Vincent inserts the other into the incision.

Anaiya shuffles closer, peering at the glass screen as the scope transmits the vision of Seth's internals; the bright red tubes of his arteries, the heart that sits silent, and the bent piece of wire that has become dislocated from one of the strands Vincent has pulled free.

"What do we do?" He asks, turning to Escher.

"Is everything else free?"

"Yes."

"Defibrillating will depolarise the muscle, but it could also tear free that filament and have it slice through the aorta or pulmonary artery on its way."

"How did the lifeline connectors even get to his heart?" Anaiya asks.

Vincent throws her a look of exasperation. "Do they teach you nothing in the Fire corps?"

Escher frowns at her, but moves into the space opposite Vincent. "We need to resuscitate manually."

"The connectors aren't entirely inorganic," Vincent says, removing the endoscope and quickly stitching the entry incision. "The metal is interwoven with a bioplasm. After installation in the first lustrum, the connectors not only grow with the body, they grow towards the heart, programmed to seek out the highest concentration of iron."

"I'll manage oxygen supply," Escher says urgently, drawing Vincent's attention away from Anaiya. "You need to start chest compressions now."

It happens quickly: Vincent bearing down on Seth's chest in short, sharp bursts of strength, Escher pumping air into his lungs with two breaths to every compression.

Anaiya waits for his eyes to open, for him to lurch up coughing and spluttering like they always did in the movies playing on wallscreens throughout Otpor.

"The anaesthetic is interfering, it's still too strong." Escher says it with the same level of emotion and urgency that Anaiya would observe the colour of the walls.

"Or he is already dead." Vincent says it in the same tone, but continues to apply bursts of pressure.

"We can't wait until it wears off."

"You can't leave," Anaiya yells.

"We *are* going to leave," Vincent says.

"You will kill him!"

"He may already be dead."

"But what if he's not?"

Escher looks up at her. "Thirty compressions to the chest, followed by two bursts of air. You will tire after twenty minutes; after an hour, the chances of him waking up is less than ten per cent; and after two hours you will likely die yourself." She rocks back on her heels and stands up. Vincent sighs and follows.

"Vincent—"

"Save your breath, Anaiya. You'll need it."

TWENTY-FIVE

The pain in Anaiya's arms is unlike anything she'd thought possible. She can feel the muscles tearing even as she continues to push down on Seth's chest. The exhaustion is compromising her ability to revive him—her compressions shallower, her breaths weaker. She isn't ready to relinquish her last hope, to face the possibility that the enemy has taken both Kaide and Seth from her, that their good fight is over. But she is so bone-weary, so utterly exhausted.

One more round of compressions. It has become a mantra. Repeated in the seconds just before she pinches his nose shut and closes her mouth over his.

She needs a back-up plan. Even if her fatigue doesn't undo her, time will. The izakaya will open in less than two hours. She needs to be long gone before then, and she won't be able to leave behind a dead body.

She finishes the second breath and fights the resistance of her shaking arms to return to his chest. *One more round.* Seth's body jerks, a stream of vomit coursing from his lips. Anaiya jerks back, looking down at the wet patch on her hoodie and then to Seth.

His body is convulsing again, the vomit gurgling in his throat. And she realises that saving him from cardiac arrest will mean nothing if he chokes to death on his own vomit.

Rolling him on his side, she thrusts her hand into his mouth, fingers desperately scooping to clear his airway. She pulls her hand free and bends as close as she dares to listen for breathing. His body has fallen still, but the faint, warm breath is unmistakable in the cold basement.

Her body collapses backwards, relief a small twinge against the crushing tiredness and building despair at how she is going to move his unconscious body when she can't lift her own arm.

"Where are we?"

Anaiya clamps a hand over Seth's mouth. It is an over-reaction given the volume of music that pushes through the walls and fills the room. After an hour of monitoring Seth's breathing and heartbeat, she had recovered enough to move him upstairs and into Yve's office.

She had needed to kick the door in, the heavy polymaterial needing multiple strikes before it yielded. The pain had since softened into a dull throb and she worries the strain will cause problems, but for now she focuses on Seth.

"Still in Veritas."

He struggles to sit up. "Yve's office?"

Anaiya nods and gently pushes him back to lounge. "You're not in great shape; you need to lie down."

"What happened?"

"You had a reaction to the anaesthetic. Vincent got your wristplate off, but your heart failed. They tried to resuscitate you, but it was taking too long, so they took off."

He groans as he pulls his shirt up. The skin is stained with the dried blood of the procedure, but the wound looks clean.

"How am I alive?"

"I finished the resuscitation. Your heart started beating again. But you still don't have an all-clear; the resusc took too long, your brain was without oxygen for at least fifteen minutes. And you probably have a few bruised ribs thrown in for free. You're going to be laid low for days, maybe weeks."

"No… No, Anaiya. I need—"

"You need to stay here. For a little while. And I have to go.

Yve will be here in a few hours; she can't find me here. I wrapped your arm as best I could and found you some nutrient shots." She taps the syringes she found when rummaging through Yve's desk. "Meet me at Lei Zhardan at midnight on the Third Day when you've recovered. You'll need Yve to source you more nutrients, fresh bandages, and synth alcohol to clean the wound. Infection is probably as big a risk as your heart giving out, so you'll need to keep an eye on it. And—"

"What am I going to tell her?"

"Yve?"

"She doesn't know about all of this. I don't want to involve her in it again, not after Rehhd. She's been compromised enough…"

Anaiya nods slowly. Everyone connected to them is a potential Peacekeeper target, and a weapon that can be manipulated against them. "Maybe it's for the best. But, she knows you're being targeted by Peacekeepers, right?"

"Yes."

"And that you were here?"

He shakes his head.

"Well, that complicates things." They need a back story for him, something believable that will make it easy for Yve to help him without putting her in more danger and without putting Seth on the official radar. "Do you trust me?"

Seth closes his eyes. "You saved my life."

"Give me your other arm."

He groans again as he pulls his right arm across his chest. Anaiya reaches for one of the glasses on Yve's desk and slams it against the hard angles to shatter it. It comes away in three clean pieces.

"What are you doing, Anaiya?"

"You need to be injured, enough to need all the things you need now to keep you alive. If she knows you're in hiding, and that you're injured, she'll protect you. She doesn't need to know about the wristplate. Or anything else."

He closes his eyes and nods. Anaiya presses the tip of the largest shard against his skin and slices, watching as the blood blooms and runs a red river down his arm. She quickly wraps the wound with the remaining gauze and bandages.

"I'll smash the basement window on my way out. It will set off the alarm and call Yve and maybe an Infrastructure Protector. If there's nothing stolen and no other damage, the Infrastructure Protector won't be a problem." She ties off the bandage and secures it under one of the folds. "When Yve finds you, tell her you were running from Peacekeepers, broke into the basement, and cut your arm in the process."

"What if she doesn't believe me?"

Anaiya stands up and looks around. She is running out of time. "I've given you your backstory; it's up to you to make it believable."

Seth closes his eyes. She can see the toll it is taking on him, worries that their last-minute intervention won't be enough. "Seth?"

"Mm?" he mumbles.

"Can you make it believable?"

He doesn't respond. She bends close to check he is still breathing, that his heart is still beating. Even with her ear against his chest, it is hard to hear anything above the rush of blood in her own ears. Hard to tell in the warm office whether she can feel a faint breath against her cheek. She holds her breath, begging her heart to slow, and listens again.

It is so faint; she is still not certain that it's reality and not false hope she can hear. But she can't wait any longer. There is nothing more she can do for him and every minute she stays puts them both in the path of a greater danger.

And, so, she leaves.

TWENTY-SIX

Descending the steps to Lei Zhardan de Ruiso, Anaiya maintains the silence and stealth she has kept the last four weeks, and while her footsteps are still light, her heart is heavy. She had known it was next to impossible that Seth would show up in the first week; his wounds and recovery would have kept him at Veritas. The next week, she had been optimistic—he had been alert after waking up from the procedure, and she was sure he had just been sleeping when she had left him.

But since then, she had become less sure. Perhaps the internal injuries were worse than she had assumed, or perhaps infection had taken hold.

And now, almost a month later, she can't help but let her mind entertain more fatal reasons as to why he has not yet met her. He is dead. He was discovered and handed over to Peacekeepers. *And is dead*. Every bad option she can think of, all of them ending in Seth dead, all of them pushing themselves to the forefront of her mind.

As dominant as they are, she still clings to the hope that it is just his recovery that has been delayed. It is why she still comes to the concrete garden. Although, she doesn't stay as long as she used to, and she wonders how long she will continue to risk detection by coming back.

The shadows are deeper in the courtyard, hiding her from errant gazes and lending her anonymity in case someone does glance down. She moves to the ablutions basin and sits on its wide rim, trailing her hand in the inky water, grimacing at its cold bite, but keeping her hand submerged.

If only sins were so easily erased. The same thought had come to her when she had come to the gardens more than a year ago, after she had first encountered Kaide in the Edges in the weeks following Rehhd's Execution. She had returned to it again, when she had first agreed to work with him and Seth. An unlikely partnership, a reluctant detente. It was why she had chosen this place to meet Seth. It felt… *fitting.*

Also fitting that she should fail at this last hurdle, without vengeance and redemption.

The cold of the concrete and the water have lulled her into a bitter melancholy. Once, she had not known the word nor its meaning, now it plagues her with impunity. She resists its drag and stands up. The midnight hour is well past and, like all the Third Days in the weeks before, Seth has not arrived.

Next week. He'll show up next week. The words are hollow, adding weight to her feet and making the ascent to street level laborious. No longer protected by the shadows, she pulls her hood up again and makes for the darker and quieter lanes to the south.

She takes a different route than the one she has tracked previously. Since leaving Seth at the izakaya, she hasn't stayed in the same apartment for more than four days at a stretch. Each one scouted on the way to and from the garden, each with its unique advantage—distance from the garden, lack of frequent and nearby Peacekeeper patrols, easy access via low and wide balconies.

Tonight's apartment is more derelict than the others she has used, but its largely crumbling facade will gift her unobtrusive entry, the heavy wall warping the front door and stopping it from closing properly.

It is the only bright spot in a long, disappointing week. She no longer has the energy to free-run.

She slows two blocks away from the apartment. While the late hour makes it less likely she'll be seen, it also makes it more likely to be noticed if she is seen. And something tickling between her shoulder blades warns her that she *has* been seen.

It is easier to be jumpy at night, to hear something else in the sounds that carry and echo along empty streets. And yet…

She turns too quickly, stumbling on tired legs, her deteriorating Peacekeeper finesse failing her again. The sight of her assailant, camouflaged in black to seem more shadow than substance, drills spikes of fear into her chest. Something clatters loud and sharp behind her, but she can't take her gaze from the advancing attacker.

Distantly, she feels the scrape of the concrete as she scrambles back. But she is too slow, as if time is working against her. And, not just her. Even her assailant is caught up in its current; their arm comes up as their elbow bends, dark folds of material rippling and metal glinting in the muted light.

She brings her own arm up to shield herself, knowing the futility of it but unable to stop herself. The blade sails closer and slices across her forearm, pain singing in bright clarity and freeing them both from time's warped grasp.

The assailant advances faster now, another blade in their hand, which is already pulled back for the throw. So close, they will not miss the more vital organs left unprotected.

Anaiya scrabbles for the fallen blade beside her, crying with relief as her hand clasps the rough-textured handle.

She doesn't get a chance to use it. The assailant crumples to the ground with a sickening thud. Blood pools from a hidden head wound, and a large chunk of concrete lays stained nearby. A lone figure stands in the space behind.

"I'd say we're even, butterfly," Seth says. "Again."

TWENTY-SEVEN

The trip through the western precincts is tense, fraught with unspoken fears and hidden dangers. Anaiya leads the way, searching the streets that back on to the Edges for an apartment block, far enough away from the fallen assassin and capable of providing quick and simple access for both of them. In a narrow lane nestled behind rows of warehouses, she presses him into a small alcove and waits. The unexpected change in pace and forced proximity releases a rush of emotions Anaiya hadn't realised she had been holding back.

She closes her eyes and breathes slowly, waiting for the wave of emotion to subside, waiting for her muscles to relax and the tension to leach from her body. Opening her eyes, she glances at Seth. He seems oblivious to her torment, eyes scanning the streetscape for hidden dangers. He looks tired and rough around the edges, his face a little drawn, his chin scruffy with stubble. She hadn't realised how much she'd missed him.

The pre-dawn hour eventually calls the Earth Elementals from the apartment buildings to start their shifts. Just as Anaiya has done so many times before, she waits until there is enough Elementals to create a sense of crowd and limit the level of familiarity.

"Keep your head down," she whispers to Seth and pulls him to the crowd, becoming part of the lumbering journey towards nearby warehouses. They follow along quietly, matching the casual gait of those around them while Anaiya scans for a suitable safehouse. She finds one a few blocks down, dragging Seth out of the crowd and into one of the apartment buildings before its entry door can fully close behind the Demolition Grunt who is exiting.

They clamber up the entire ten flights of stairs before searching for an empty apartment. The top floor offers no prestige, with nothing but warehouses and uglier, taller apartment building to fill the view. Here, it is the lower floors that are in demand, offering Earths expediency to get to their shifts and a way to avoid more exertion when they return.

Her instincts reward them with an empty apartment far from the stairwell, the door ajar and the interior bereft of any comforts.

Anaiya slumps to the thin carpet while Seth moves the door, with some effort, into its locking position.

"I thought you were dead," Anaiya says, wrapping her slashed arm with the bandages Seth tosses over, her voice husky with the residual emotion still lingering after the alcove.

He slumps down beside her. "I thought the same of you."

They are close enough that their shoulders are touching. She leans in a little, settling against the solidness or him, reassuring herself that he is really there and that she is not alone. She pulls the blade from the inside of her boot and hands it across to him. "Have you seen anything like it before?"

He turns it over in his hands and shakes his head, handing it back to her.

It is heavier than she would have expected, but its clean lines and shiny appearance are familiar. "I saw something like it, once. In the Boileu Road Enclave. It makes sense that Niamh's special cadre would use them. Can do damage from a distance, easy to retrieve, leaving wounds that could come from striking any sharp material, and nothing to link it to whoever wields it."

She throws it across the room, watching it thunk into the stained plaster wall, wobble for a bit, and then fall to floor.

"We can protect ourselves against them," she murmurs, thinking of her old kevlar Peacekeeper uniform, the way it protected against the shards of brick and cleaved pieces of metal during complicated free-runs. "And darker clothes will be better."

"What's your plan, Anaiya?"

"They took what was important to us. We take what's important to them—control for Niamh; anonymity for the Enclave."

"And how do you propose we do that?"

She frowns, chewing on her lip. "Not sure yet. But we need to be properly prepared."

Moving through the streets of Precinct 4 is a strange kind of homecoming. Anaiya and Seth keep their heads down, sticking to the streets shared by different corps and Elements, rather than the Peacekeeper dominated streets she had lived in after her graduation.

The western part of the Precinct hasn't changed in the time since her realignment and deployment—the same shopfronts and izakaya dotted along the wider streets—and yet it seems an entirely different place. Not because it has changed, but because she has.

Her eyes drift to the west, and beyond to where her old apartment block is situated. For more than a generation, she had lived her empty life, moving from its sparse confines, to patrols, to izakaya, and then back again. She looks away. Once, it had been enough. She hadn't realised how empty it was until now.

"Are we close?" Seth whispers. His nerves are starting to get the better of him, his eyes darting constantly, his shoulders becoming more and more hunched.

"A few more streets. Stop slouching."

They move between the small crowds, weaving around Elementals who are making their way to evening shifts, drinking dens, and subworm stations. The sunset hour is the busiest, and while the light risks them being seen, the crowds will provide enough distraction for Peacekeeper eyes.

Neon signs blink on around them and the murmur of music that has been drifting in the air for the last twenty minutes begins to swell. They need to hurry; the Earth-run shopfronts will be closing soon.

Anaiya looks around; the washroom is only a few blocks away and no Peacekeepers are visible. She picks up her pace, pulling Seth with her. His hand is too small in hers. She pushes away the usual pang that comes with thinking of Kaide, wishing he was with her, wishing he was alive.

"You know what to do," she says when they are a block away, nodding to the orange neon sign just visible around the other signs and porticos. "I'll wait nearby."

Seth nods, eyes still darting around.

"You remember what to say?" she asks gently. He nods. She squeezes his hand and releases it. "You're not as well-known as I am; they won't recognise you."

He nods again, exhaling loudly.

"I'll see you in a bit," she says.

"See you in a bit."

His hesitancy doesn't show as he crosses the road, his posture finally straighter, his steps light. She waits until he is inside before she turns her attention to the streetscape. The afternoon energy is calm and the weight light. Long shadows criss-cross along the cracked pavement and the smell of cola-roasted pigeon drifts on a gentle southerly. It is enough to calm her nerves and allow her a rare moment to breathe.

And then Seth is walking towards her, his smile no longer forced, his light steps no longer an act. He throws an ugly grey jacket to her. "All unclaimed items are kept in the back."

Any washroom in a Peacekeeper district was just as likely to hold a kevlar uniform to steal. Some would have been easier to break into than others, but all would have raised an alarm that a Peacekeeper uniform had gone missing. Except this one.

She had almost forgotten about it—there was so much about the days before her realignment that was cast in technicolour, it should have been impossible to remember the little things. And yet, after months of living as an Earth Elemental, she has learned the most mundane activities have their own type of beauty. Like dragging a brush through knotted hair and straightening crumpled sheets on a bed. Like dropping her uniform into the washroom and never expecting to see it again.

"I'll come back before sunrise."

"And then?"

"And then we can strike our first target."

"We can't do this alone." Seth throws his arms up in frustration. The two of them sit on the floor of their dilapidated apartment, stitching pieces of Anaiya's old kevlar uniform into the insides of their shirts and pants. "We need access to technology—for maps and messages and just knowing what the Cooperative are putting out there. "

Anaiya scowls at him, but only because he speaks an uncomfortable truth. Logistics aside, they need people they can trust—to help them source nutrient boosters and medical supplies, to run distractions, and to help with target strikes.

"Whoever we bring in, we have to trust them implicitly. And we have to risk losing them, as well."

Seth sighs and sets down his handiwork. "That's the problem, isn't it? Choose the wrong comrade and we risk our Execution, choose the right comrade and we risk theirs."

"Is there anyone you trust who would be willing to help us? Anyone from the Resistance?"

Raking his hands through his hair, Seth looks past her, staring at the wall as if it will reveal the answers he needs. "There was a reason we limited the core resistance to only a few of us—most liked the idea of rebellion, but not the consequences or the responsibility. They just wanted to be associated with something new and exciting. To feel the thrill. There were others, like Lilith, and then Tomas and Issau, who became more invested after Rehhd's Execution, but I don't trust them—don't trust that they're not the reason I'm..." He throws his bandaged arm up, flicks at the kevlar-reinforced cottonex.

"So who does that leave?"

"Eamon, Rehhd, Kaide—they're all dead. Lilith, Tomas, Issau—they can't be trusted. It only leaves Cress."

Cress, the pixie-like Trainee that had gravitated to Anaiya as soon as she'd arrived in the Northern Area for her undercover mission. Except,Cress wouldn't be a Trainee anymore—would have graduated with the rest of her cohort into her assigned competency on Foundation Day a few months ago. It was strange to think of the lithe Dancer performing innocuous acts of entertainment after she had been so lethal at shutting down the city's power less than a year ago.

But even with Cress' infectious enthusiasm and proven battle skills, Anaiya remains unconvinced. She smiles grimly. "Not exactly the strength in numbers we need."

"No. But it is something. And it's not like *you* have anyone we can call on."

The thought of Lira blooms in her mind, but she doesn't say anything. Turning her attention back to her sewing, she finishes patching her shirt. "We don't need Cress for the first strike. No need to risk her so soon."

Seth sighs, but nods.

"We target the first string of Peacekeeper stations tomorrow," she says, with more confidence than she feels. "If all goes well, we reach out for reinforcements."

The shattering of glass rings out in the pre-dawn air. It crackles and sings with a satisfying clarity, carrying easily to the third-floor apartment where Anaiya sits perched on the windowsill. She lingers for the briefest moment, taking in the broken window of the Peacekeeper station in Precinct 5, the smallest destruction borne of an immense rage, and then she runs.

Her calves burn as she speeds up the stairwell to the rooftop, muscles resisting the exertion after sitting and waiting patiently for the three hours before the Peacekeeper skeleton-shift started.

The cold air pricks at her sweat-drenched skin as she bursts through the final door and into the open. She needs to move fast. Not that the Peacekeepers below will be looking for her up here— the paint bomb she lodged through their shattered window would have confused and disoriented them enough to focus their attention on what is immediately at their doorstep. Besides, as far as they know, the Heterodox Peacekeeper was Executed months ago; not only won't they be looking for her up here, they won't be looking for her at all.

Her haste comes not from fear of discovery, but urgency to hit the next target.

She dredges up every last reserve of her Peacekeeper skills and muscle memory, pushing her body to run faster, leap longer, land softer; never stopping until she reaches the tall building opposite the Peacekeeper station in the neighbouring precinct.

Dropping to a darkened balcony, she pulls another paint bomb from her hoodie. The smooth, plastic ball is heavy in her grip. Heavy, but fragile. She draws a blade from the sheath in her boot and attaches it to the ball, careful to secure it tightly enough to ensure it isn't dislodged, but not so tight that the thin plastic shatters before its time. She grimaces, remembering all the failed practice attempts she and Seth had suffered over the last few days.

That was the problem with no Kaide around to keep them grounded: they were both too hot-headed and impatient, pushing ahead when they should slow down and consider their options.

She was always going to be hot-headed; her Fire and Air conditioning guaranteed it. And Seth, who remained true to his Air nature. But Kaide's hypoxia had dulled his Air tendencies, gifted him some of a Water's sensibilities.

Stop it. It is too easy to fall down this well, to become distracted by thoughts of Kaide, to wallow in a strange kind of morbid desire. *Creator burn you, Niamh.* Her former patrol partner had taken everything from her—her dominance and confidence as a Peacekeeper, her alignment and identity, her life. And now Kaide.

She taps into the rage burning white hot in her core, tightens the blade a little tighter to the black sphere, and hurls it with a true aim to the station below. The blade hits the glass, the shattering of the window and the avalanche of fragments piercing the quiet night, sailing the paint bomb through the void and into the station.

Rage still filling her veins with fire, she secures the other paint bombs in her hoodie, checks the blades in her boot, and runs.

"There's no wallscreen coverage of it, but, being paint and all, there's no hiding it from the masses on the streets."

Cress sits perched on the arm of a lounge she had procured for Anaiya and Seth's neglected apartment. A week ago, Seth had found her living incognito as a street performer in the poorer districts of the Southern Area and brought her into the new plan.

Since then, they had hit another six Peacekeeper stations, bringing the total to nine.

"Is anyone talking about it?" Seth asks.

Cress shakes her head. "There might have been some initial chatter, but because the hits have been spread out across the Cardinal Areas, no-one's really pieced together the bigger picture. They think it's just a one-off strike."

"Don't worry about it, Seth," Anaiya says. "The strikes weren't about waking up the rest of Otpor; they were about taking control away from Niamh."

"And how's that working out?"

"Give it time. It's only been a week. The Peacekeepers are on alert, and the skeleton shifts are getting busier. They won't be able to cover everything."

"And?"

"And with a few more distractions, and a few more strikes, they'll be caught out." Peacekeeper numbers had always been kept low, the Nursery never conditioning more than what was needed. With the population so well controlled, so deeply lured into mindless compliance, the need for Peacekeepers had always been limited to patrolling for random Unorthodox acts. Even if the Nursery had conditioned more Peacekeepers after the Execution of Kane 148, they would still be locked away in the Nursery, too young to graduate and enter Otpor. "We just need to keep stretching them until they break."

"What are you thinking, Nisha?" Cress asks.

It still surprises Anaiya that Cress is not more shocked or overwhelmed at seeing her alive. She wonders if Kaide had told her something, or whether she had a hand in orchestrating her impossible resurrection.

"We need to use the same strategy as the power cuts."

Seth leans forward, no doubt remembering the rolling power

cuts the rebellion had orchestrated in the weeks before Anaiya's Execution. "You want us to attack the grid?"

She shakes her head. "No, they'll be too heavily protected after last time, or they would have installed a back-up. We don't need the grid. If there's enough Peacekeeper call outs for your average Unorthodoxy happening at the same time as the station attacks, they'll be spread too thin." She smiles. "Niamh won't be able to control all of it. And it will drive him crazy."

"What do you need us to do?" Cress asks.

"Snatch and grab stuff—stealing, property damage, noise complaints. Start a few fights, slash a few tires, break a few windows—anything that will get someone to call for Peacekeeper assistance and pull them away from their stations."

Cress grins. "I know a band of merry mischief-makers who would be perfect."

No doubt, Anaiya thinks. While they can't trust the members of the broader resistance movement with the bigger plan, there are scores of disaffected Air Elementals who are still devastated by the failure of their rebellion and no doubt looking for a way to get some payback.

"I don't know, Anaiya," Seth says. "It sounds pretty low-key. Are you sure it will be enough?"

"We get the Peacekeepers off-balance, we strip Niamh of his tightly held control, and then we turn up the heat. We strike the Enclave."

TWENTY-EIGHT

A week later, after every precinct's Peacekeeper station had been hit, and some more than once, the three of them return to the apartment.

"They're plugging the gaps," Seth says, sinking to the lounge.

Anaiya leans against the wall opposite, taking in the weary faces of her co-conspirators. The last seven days have been testing— physically demanding, dangerous, full of tension, and emotionally draining. While their efforts have been largely successful, leaving behind frazzled Peacekeepers and paint-drenched stations, the victory feels lacklustre.

"They're using Infrastructure Protectors to guard the stations," she replies. IPs are among the lowest ranking of Fire Elementals and the most abundant. It is a smart move.

"What do we do?" Cress sits next to Seth, heel tapping against the bottom of the lounge.

Anaiya walks over to the crate they have been using as a table. Picking up the red book, she throws it to Cress. "Battle is like a dance, a *minuet*."

Cress catches the book cleanly, her eyes shining as she thumbs the pages. "Minuet? The dance of tiny steps?"

"Being smaller and free of the confines of convention allows us to be agile," Anaiya says, recounting her understanding of the book's text. "If we change the dance, our opponent is slower to respond, burdened by the weight of structure, and rules, and bureaucracy. When they change the rules, we can move more quickly to react. To counter."

"Where are you going with this, Anaiya?" Seth's frustration sneaks into his voice. He is impatient to get on with things, to see bigger results.

"We live in a closed system," she says, trying hard to keep her own frustration out of her tone. "You give something to this hand," she throws her left hand up, "you have to take something from this hand," she throws her right hand up. "They're so busy protecting the stations, they're leaving other assets unprotected."

"How does that help us?" Seth demands, raking his hand through his hair in his go-to stress response. "How does an unprotected gallery, or demolition site, or warehouse…"

His voice trails off and his hand drops to his lap. He gets it.

Anaiya nods. "Some assets are worth more than others."

"Which assets are we targeting?" Cress asks, grinning no doubt at the promise of more chaos.

"Not the big ones," Anaiya cautions. "Not yet. They'll be guarded just like the Peacekeeper stations. Guerilla warfare is the way of the synthfly—stinging that annoys, that creates an unbearable itch, but isn't fatal."

Cress' grin falters and Seth opens his mouth to protest.

"The obvious targets aren't the best," Anaiya counters before they can voice their opposition. "And they're definitely not the best for us. We have to be smarter, more strategic. We don't have to hit a Commissioner's office, but we can hit her favourite brothel. Or a Peacekeeper izakaya. Or a Border Protector gym." Seth sighs and Cress fidgets uncomfortably, but Anaiya shakes her head, resolute in her plan. "We strike to frustrate, not disable. We don't have the resources or the capacity for one fatal strike. Our mission is death by a thousand cuts."

"Can we at least hit Niamh's favourite place first?" Seth asks.

Anaiya smiles. "I think that's a reasonable request."

A warped sense of nostalgia assaults Anaiya as the Wild Rover comes into view. The Peacekeeper izakaya had been the backdrop of so many between-shift drinking sessions. Most of them with Niamh. It was the place where her Fire culture had been celebrated and strengthened. Where she had felt the connection to her tribe was a perfect symbiosis, eternal and inviolable.

It is mid-morning, the brown Otpor sun beating down with intensity, pooling sweat between her shoulder blades and making her irritable. It is the salt in the wound, amplifying the unease she feels at being in a Fire-dominant precinct when there is little shadow to hide her.

She tugs at the Infrastructure Protector uniform and pushes a short, black ribbon of hair away from her cheek. The uniform had come from Cress, who'd orchestrated to steal it from a Trainee enjoying her first visit to a brothel. The hair style had been at Seth's hands. He had been surprisingly adept at cutting and shaping her black locks into something shorter and more inconspicuous for a Fire Elemental. *"I thought you were a Literary competent,"* she had said. *"I hear brain injuries have a way of messing with that,"* he had replied.

There is little chance a Peacekeeper will pay attention to an Infrastructure Protector, and the close-cropped hair should allow her to largely blend in, unless someone is looking more closely. Still, she avoids the busier streets, circumnavigating the blocks around the Wild Rover and approaching from the south.

Not for the first time, she wishes the quieter hours of the izakaya were not so… *illuminated.*

For over a week, she, Seth, and Cress had tried to come up with a disruption attack that wouldn't end with any of them dead, and yet be powerful enough to force Niamh to take notice of its message. Even now, just metres away from her target, she is not sure whether they have erred on the side of caution or recklessness.

"How do you piss off Peacekeepers without getting in their faces?"

It was the impossible question: Peacekeepers tended to ignore everything unless it was a known or visible threat.

"What do they love, but don't protect?" Cress had asked.

"They love nothing," Anaiya had replied.

"What do they desire, then?" Seth had asked. *"What do they chase,*

what do they enjoy?"

"Power, sex, competition, dodecahedrazine."

They had laughed, despite their frustration, and gone back to their planning. But, the questions, and her answers, had lingered in the background of her thoughts.

The service hatch is easy to access, left ajar by Earth Elementals too lazy to remember the eight-digit code to open it. The drop to the floor below is a simple one, even for an out-of-shape Peacekeeper.

Inside, she activates the diode on her fake wristplate and seeks out the vats of dodecahedrazine. They are easy to find, numerous among all the others and labelled clearly for the Cellar Dogs who change the vats and charge the distribution lines leading up to the bar. Easier still to unplug the lines and isolate them from the water supply. It is nothing she hasn't done a hundred times before on her black-market cleaning shifts.

She works quickly, removing the synth alcohol supply, splitting the vats of pituarmagn precursor that the Enclave had transported weeks ago, and charging the lines with water alone.

And, when it is all done, she smashes a single red paint sphere on the floor and uses the leaking vats to climb back out.

Over the next two weeks, they hit izakaya, brothels, gyms, and administration buildings; smashing windows, blocking access, detonating paint bombs, and cutting power; moving from precinct to precinct, striking the favourite places of Peacekeepers and high-ranking Elementals and then running away. Like a synthfly darting in to sting, and escaping before the hand can swat it away.

At least, that's what they'd thought. As the days ticked over, the three of them wondered aloud whether their sting was a mere annoyance, incapable of producing more than an itch; mildly irritating, but soon forgotten.

"They're not paying attention," Seth says, screwing up his face with obvious annoyance. "We need to hit harder or be bolder or, I don't know, do something bigger."

The cramped space of their apartment is oppressive. Situated on an abandoned floor of a dilapidated tower in an outer precinct, it is like all the ones that have come before; small, empty, broken, and dark. Even Cress has given up on bringing furnishings to lighten the mood, her normal exuberance growing dull as their efforts fail to generate any response from Niamh or his Peacekeepers.

So, it is unexpected when she bursts into the apartment flush with exhilaration. "Curfew is reinstated," she says breathlessly, barely able to form the words, her grin impossibly wide.

It takes Anaiya a moment to register what she is saying. "Curfew is back?"

"When?" Seth asks, his brow still furrowed.

"Tonight."

"Well, that's it then, isn't it?" he says, throwing his hands up in the air.

"Why aren't you happier?" Cress asks, walking over to poke at his shoulder. "It worked. They're responding."

"By shutting us down." He is softer with Cress, but his voice is still tight with frustration. "What are we going to do now? How are we going to hit them now? How do we kill them by a thousand cuts when we can't access them anymore, when they shut us down after only a few scratches?"

"But..." Cress throws a confused glance to Anaiya. "It's a good thing, right? The reaction, it's what we wanted?"

"It *is* what we wanted." Anaiya throws her hand up to block Seth's retort. "It is. We wanted to get Niamh's attention, to make him feel that his grasp on control is weakening."

"And how successful was that?" Seth interrupts. "Now that he's tightened his grasp, effectively around our throat?"

"That's the thing—he thinks the curfew is an easy fix, a simple way to demonstrate that he still holds the power. He knows that most Elementals will see this as confirmation that he's in control."

"Because he is," Seth says.

"Maybe. For now. But this is a desperate act, especially for Niamh. If he's resorting to curfew, if he can't shut this down using usual Peacekeeping vigilance and response, he's rattled."

"And how does that help us?"

"Because hits during curfew will cut deeper." Anaiya's voice pitches with her own frustration. Sometimes working with Seth feels a lot like working against him. "If we can hit unexpected targets with strategic or emotional importance, it will unravel him."

"And how are we going to do that with curfew in place?"

"Anaiya hit the Wild Rover mid-morning," Cress interjects. "Maybe we don't need the cover of night."

Anaiya smiles, but shakes her head. "The Wild Rover was always going to be a one-off. Niamh now knows we're bold enough to strike during daylight and he's still got his shadow assassins roaming around."

Seth groans and throws his hands in the air again. "So, if we can't strike during the day, and we can't move around during curfew—tell me again how this is what we wanted?"

"What can we do, Anaiya?" Cress asks.

"Well, there are ways to gain access to places without approaching at street level," she replies, thinking of the tunnels under the Western Area boulevardes that led to the Boileau Road Enclave. "And we're not the only ones who can do something."

Seth shakes his head. "Ordinary Air Elementals will not risk their otherwise debaucherous lives to attack targets in a locked-down Otpor."

"He's right, Anaiya," Cress says. "The Elementals I used were up for a bit of mischief; they're not revolutionaries."

"Maybe not, but everyone chafes against a heavy-handed authority. Everyone has an inner rebellion they want to unleash, even for just a bit."

TWENTY-NINE

Their hits in the ensuing weeks were more limited and less strategic. Even outside the curfew hours, Peacekeeper patrols were highly present and aggressive; minor Unorthodox acts—trading after hours, exceeding noise restrictions, jumping subworm turnstiles— were all restrained with violence and without hesitation.

With fear rampart in the streets, street traffic thinned out; Elementals stayed close to home—sticking to not only their precincts, but their specific quarters. And with the dwindling traffic, trading slowed; shops and galleries and drinking dens closed mid-afternoon, except for those in Fire dominated precincts frequented by Fire competencies.

It made movement around the city too conspicuous, and what little tunnels they could identify led nowhere important.

Maybe Seth was right. Anaiya can feel the choke-hold Niamh has on them. She expects to feel deflated, but all she feels is the frustrated anger of someone denied the chance to cross the finish line when they are only one step away.

And if she is frustrated, Seth is like a sand snake caught under a dog's paw—all of its potency constrained by something that is not more lethal, just bigger and heavier.

"It's everywhere," Cress says, sitting cross-legged on the apartment floor. "Frustration is rife. It feels just like it did…"

"Before we started with the murals," Seth finishes for her.

"Except, they weren't expecting us then, and hadn't mobilised to block us."

"Eventually they did," Anaiya says. "This isn't the first curfew we've lived through."

"But, we didn't survive it," Seth says, lowering his voice and dropping his head.

He doesn't need to add anything else. The mood in the room, already deflated, turns sombre. While the three of them have worked and lived closely with each other over the past couple of months, their recent connection is not enough to overshadow their damaged past. Sometimes the ghosts of their history—Rehhd, Eamon, Kaide—stay hidden in the corners. Tonight, they cast long shadows.

"Curfews weren't all bad," Cress says softly. Anaiya smiles gratefully at her attempt to ease the tension. "I mean, there were some great lockdown parties."

Anaiya looks to Seth, wondering if he is remembering the same lockdown party she is—the one that had started with music and drinking and kissing, and ended with Anaiya, Rehhd, and Eamon detained by Peacekeepers while a Trainee Peacekeeper sat shackled and blindfolded on the floor.

Seth looks over to her, his face unreadable, and then to Cress. "I don't know; seems to me they could shift on a wind change. That sometimes they caused more trouble than they should have."

Anaiya closes her eyes and leans back against the wall. It's all crumbling around her. She wishes, irrationally, that she could go back to that lockdown party at Veritas and change her path. In that first hour after curfew, even with the weight of betrayal and anticipation of detaining Rehhd, she had felt a release. Had left behind all the expectations and just enjoyed herself.

She opens her eyes. "Maybe it's not all lost. Niamh has had weeks of being reassured of his control and power. If we take that away from him now—"

"We've been here before, Anaiya," Seth yells, startling both her and Cress. "It hasn't worked. It *won't* work."

"It will if we target the Enclave," she says quietly.

"And how the fuck are we going to do that?" he says, the

muscles in his jaw tight. "The Enclave is protected by Border Watchers."

"We throw another party." The idea is starting to crystallise in her mind. Seth opens his mouth to scoff, or rail, or argue. She ignores him. "Outside the Second Enclave. In the square."

He doesn't reply, but his face doesn't soften either.

"I don't understand…" Cress says, her gaze flicking between Seth and Anaiya.

"It's like you said," Anaiya replies. "Everyone is reaching breaking point under this curfew and, unlike the last curfew, there's been no release. We can give them that release—throw a street party, like the one at the riverside, but this time outside the second Enclave. It will threaten the Enclave's anonymity, which will piss them off, and it will destroy the perception that Niamh has control of the situation, which will piss him off."

Seth shakes his head, no longer angry, but still not on board. "Who would risk detention, especially the kind of detention Peacekeepers are enforcing now, replete with lacerations and broken bones and long-term incarceration, for a street party?"

"Peacekeepers have been detaining Elementals for weeks; there aren't enough detention cells to maintain the kind of offensive they've been running. Plus, Niamh will be cautious about sending in too many Peacekeepers on the doorstep of the Enclave—he doesn't want to get them off-side."

Seth drums his fingers against his knees and Cress tugs at the strands of hair around her temples.

"Do you really think it can work?" Cress finally asks.

"It doesn't matter whether it can work," Seth says. "It's our only option, isn't it? That, or spend the rest of our lives wasting away in this shithouse apartment."

Anaiya stands up and walks over to the window. The view outside is mostly blocked by larger apartment buildings, but there is a narrow gap that opens up to the avenue. Three precincts away sits the Enclave. She can picture the imposing building and the large square at its doorstop.

"Let's start planning a party," she says.

"At least it's something we know we're good at," Seth

murmurs.

The next day, Anaiya leaves behind the confines of the apartment and heads north to Lira's apartment. She takes an indirect route and stops as often as she dares to stare into window reflections or step into doorways, checking for any sign of the shadow assassins.

Her heart skitters uneasily in her chest. Every detour, every stop along the way, keeps her longer on the streets and risks drawing attention from the roaming Peacekeeper patrols.

It takes every shred of self-control not to break into a sprint when she sees the familiar red-bricked building.

Once inside, she races up the stairwell three steps at a time and raps quickly on Lira's door.

Lira frowns when she lays eyes on Anaiya. "It's dangerous to be here," she says, but opens the door wider to let her in.

"It's dangerous to be anywhere," Anaiya replies, looking over her shoulder before stepping inside.

"You're more trouble than he ever was, you know that?"

"No, but I believe you." Anaiya sits down in one of Lira's uncomfortable chairs. "And, I think I'm about to cause more."

"Why do I think that this conversation is going to require genievre?"

"You know," Anaiya says when Lira brings back the drinks and sits in the chair opposite, "you're not entirely blameless."

"And how is that?"

"You gave me the red book."

"Ah, yes. Guerrilla Warfare. I hear you've been an adept student—word of paint-trashed Peacekeeper stations and exclusive brothels is gold-standard gossip. That kind of stuff races between drinking dens faster than the alcohol does."

Anaiya smiles. "It had some impact."

"And then curfew came along."

She nods and takes a drink of her genievre.

"So what's your plan now?" Lira asks, leaning back in her chair. "Obviously not giving up, since you're sitting here with that,"

Lira waves her hand around in the direction of Anaiya's face, "whatever that is you're calling a hairstyle."

Anaiya runs her hand through the short-cropped black hair and laughs. "No, not giving up. Going out swinging. But I need your help."

"You look happy," Anaiya says, catching Seth grinning to himself. They sit hidden behind the partially collapsed wall of a decommissioned construction platform. It is cramped; rusted bars jut out from the concrete rubble, pushing angrily into their arms and legs as if protesting their presence. And, yet, the mood between them is still light.

"The subworm stations are filling with Earth and Air Elementals," Seth says. "Subworm service is due to cease in twenty minutes, and curfew starts in an hour."

"Cress came through."

"And so did your Earth contact, it seems."

"Can always rely on the irrational, I mean *playful*, Elements to come to a party."

Seth smiles and then turns serious. "It was a genius move to use the subworm tunnels to move Elementals to the square undetected."

She nods her thanks at his unexpected compliment. It had taken her a while to reassess her earlier conclusion that Otpor's tunnels didn't lead anywhere important. *Was just thinking of the wrong tunnels.* With all the priority assets Peacekeepers and Infrastructure Protectors had eyes on, subworm tunnels didn't make the cut. With no subworms and no Peacekeepers, the tunnels were basically covert boulevardes. "I wish we could be there to see them all spill from the station and converge on the square."

Seth grins again. "It's going to be an epic party. But if all goes to plan, we'll be watching it on a wallscreen later tonight."

"That's a long time to play the waiting game."

"Good thing we have something to keep us occupied."

Anaiya follows his gaze across the road to the Peacekeeper

Station on the corner of Voegerard and Beuret. It's not the closest station to the Enclave, but it is close enough that if a Peacekeeper response is called to the curfew party, it will be the one to sacrifice some of its officers.

Opening up the opportunity for Anaiya and Seth to strike.

"How soon do you think they'll send out the call?" Seth asks, his eyes constantly scanning the immediate area.

"As soon as the revellers emerge from Montparnasse station."

Seth nods, his face now tight with anticipation. And then he sighs. "I wish Kaide was here."

She would have flinched if she hadn't been thinking the same thing. "He'd tell us we are being reckless, that we should wait a little longer."

Seth smiles sadly and shrugs. "Caution only gets you so far, and sometimes it gets you nowhere at all. *He who hesitates is lost.*"

"*He who hesitates is sometimes saved.*"

"*Doubt kills more dreams than failure ever will.*"

"*Doubt is the father of invention.*"

Seth cocks his head at her, his smile brief but genuine. "You've been reading."

"I've had some time on my hands."

"You were always different," he murmurs.

She stares across to the station, taking in the little details that are losing their sharpness in the waning light.

"Would he have been right?" she asks, not looking at Seth.

"Maybe… Maybe not. *Of all the words of mice and men, the saddest are, 'It might have been'*".

"I don't know that one."

"You've never died wondering."

There is nothing to announce curfew, no sirens or lights, no sudden increase in Peacekeeper presence, no sudden rush of Elementals from the streets. Nothing but the innocuous flash on their fake wristplates as the time changes from 19.59 to 20.00.

"I wish I could call Cress," Seth whispers.

Anaiya tears her gaze away from the Peacekeeper station across the road and throws him a sympathetic smile. It's been easy to forget that his experience would be so different from hers—he is more connected, has none of her Fire conditioning to temper his emotions, and is only weeks into a life without a lifeline.

"It will stop hurting after a while," she says. Hearing her own words takes her back to the night she had first met him, standing in the shadows at the Lavoir izakaya and watching him play pool as she and Kaide swapped stories about hypoxia. "It won't be better," she continues haltingly, recalling the words Kaide had murmured to her a lifetime ago. "It won't be worse. You will heal, but it will be different. *You* will be different."

He looks at her strangely. She looks away. Thinking about Kaide makes her act off-kilter, makes her vulnerable.

"I—" Seth doesn't get the chance to finish his sentence, silenced by the sudden thrum of footfalls on the road. Peacekeepers rush from the station, heading east towards Atlantic Square.

It is what she needs. A chance to shake off the awkwardness and let adrenalin burn away the vulnerability. "Looks like the party's started."

She glances over at him. He is still regarding her with a soft frown. "Being different isn't a bad thing," he murmurs. "When you're conditioned to be one thing, think one way, act one way, being different is the most powerful act of revolution."

The unexpected depth of emotion carrying in his words catches her off guard. She flushes, immediately grateful for the dark shadows.

"Smashing some windows and detonating paint bombs can be pretty effective too," she says, attempting to lighten the mood.

Seth laughs softly. "I still don't know why you need me here for that. You seem to have the smash-and-paint thing under control."

"I told you—I need you to keep track of how many Peacekeepers exit and which direction they run in."

"And if they are running in my direction?"

"They won't be. There's nothing about the attack that will lead them this way. This is the perfect vantage point, not the perfect attack point. Plus, the trajectory of the paint bomb will lead them down there." She cocks her head towards Voegerard Road.

"Hurry back, okay?"

She nods, tucking the paint bomb further into her pocket and standing to a half crouch. "I'll be back before you know it. Just keep count. We'll need to figure out the best way to retreat afterwards, especially if things get too hectic at the Square."

Her heart picks up pace as she steps out from behind the rubble. She keeps her eyes on the station as she ducks and weaves and creeps, sticking to the shadows and alternating between stealth and speed as she approaches her target.

Glancing up to the rooftops, she searches for any movement, knowing that Niamh's black-clad assassins are moving about the city looking for her. It is why she sticks to street level, even though it makes her skin crawl with the fear of it.

Finding nothing, she throws a quick glance over her shoulder to where Seth is hunkered down and hidden. The depth of trust inhabiting their fragile alliance should sit more uneasily. As it is, it seems the only thing calming her wilder emotions.

The Peacekeeper station is like any other—the same sharp lines, the same squat profile, the same narrow windows. The familiar exterior would be a blessing, if she wasn't so unsure of what lay behind it. Five Peacekeepers or twenty-five.

She takes a deep breath and appraises the landscape one last time. She'll need to move quickly once she tosses the paint bomb. The Peacekeepers will follow the trajectory of the impact, which should lead them east. If there are more Peacekeepers than less, some will fan out on a wider search, and she needs to anticipate that. But, thinking like a Peacekeeper is harder than it used to be—not because she can't, but because she can't differentiate her Fire analysis from her Air imagination, and everything in between.

Get it together, Anaiya. She can't stand out here all night second-guessing whether a pursuit down Voegerard makes sense from a tactical or an aesthetic perspective.

She pulls the cold, hard sphere from her pocket and ties it to a slender, fifteen-centimetre rod that used to hold up shelving in Cress' apartment.

"Fly straight," she whispers, and launches it at the nearest window.

She sprints from her position before waiting to see if it hits. The sound of shattering glass pierces the night seconds later, but she doesn't slow, racing between the shadows to circumnavigate the building.

The sound of yelling erupts soon after, but it is distant, muffled by the bricks and concrete between her and her pursuers.

Even with the adrenalin surging through her body and the blood thrumming in her ears, her core lightens. She presses north, already planning the next strike, but the whirring of a faulty generator nearby pulls at her attention.

She turns, expecting to see lights flickering in a nearby apartment building, but the buildings are dark, and what little lights are on, shine without interruption.

She pivots again, the sound growing louder, less like a generator, more like a swarm of synthflies next to her ear. Her earlier anxiety reignites, prickling the back of her throat.

The blade comes at her hard and fast, missing her throat and lodging in her kevlar-reinforced shirt. She feels the sting of the force and the tip of the blade, hears it clatter to the ground as its grip on the kevlar fails.

Another blade flies towards her, but she is ready for it, and her Peacekeeper skills aren't so dulled as to be felled by it. The arc of its flight path tells her the assassin is still some distance away. She needs to move fast and she needs to get to Seth.

Her lungs scream with the effort of outpacing her chasers. The whirring is louder now. She glances up and stumbles, her eyes taking in a sight her brain refuses to believe.

A metre-or-so above hovers a mechanical synthfly, at least two hand-spans wide and six long. White lights blink on and off, and Anaiya has no doubt that the tech abomination has her in its sights. And when the shrill siren bursts from its thorax, she finds a new depth to her fear and the last reserve of her energy.

She glances to her left, to the streets that will lead her directly to Seth, but her feet pivot right. Heading back to him will only doom them both. And, she has betrayed him too many times before.

THIRTY

The thought of the Edges comes quickly to her, but Anaiya ignores the instinct. The isolated borderland is a comfortable option, but not a smart one.

Instead she turns east, towards the Enclave, and the square full of Elementals who came to party, but who are likely now dancing with an aggressive contingent of Peacekeepers.

It seems mad to rush from one threat into the heart of another, but she has a better chance of evading a horde of Peacekeepers in a chaotic square than she does against a couple of elite assassins and their mechanical scout. With some luck, she will lose both in the melee she races towards.

The sound of the altercation emerges as a low rumble six blocks from the square, a dense bass note beneath the high-pitched whirring of the metal synthfly above her head. As she runs, she scans for a loose bit of concrete or a broken pipe, anything she can use as a projectile that will disable it, or at least damage its surveillance capacity. But she doesn't dare slow; she can't see or hear her true pursuers, but she knows they haven't slowed or abandoned their advance.

Hitting the perimetre of the square is like entering a fever dream. Earth and Air Elementals fill the space to capacity—more Elementals than she could have dreamed would have defied curfew. At least thirty Peacekeepers are dancing with them, taking down bodies with punches, leg sweeps, and syringes. It is easy to spot them—they move with a different stealth and precision than those around them.

Part of Anaiya wants to dance with them, engage in the fight, feed the fire. But it is a small part and one that is easily out-shouted by the part that urges her towards the subworm station.

A heavyset Earth Elemental stumbles into her, his frame slick with sweat and his eyes wide and glazed with some heady mix of dex and synth enhancers. She steps around him, wincing at the yelp that sounds as he crashes to the ground. The noise doesn't draw any attention from the Peacekeepers, who move with familiar precision and order through the crowd, even as the crowd streams towards the subworm tunnel to evade them.

Anaiya keeps her head down, resisting the urge to seek out the mechanical synthfly that she can no longer hear above the rising hum of activity around her. Resisting the urge to seek out the shadow assassins is a harder task—the itch between her shoulder blades grows with every step she can't turn to gauge whether they are upon her, or about to be.

Another cry sounds to her left and a slender Air Elemental stumbles to the ground. She is young and slender, a typical Dancer's body, except for the blade that sticks from her neck.

And this time, Anaiya can't help but look.

The crowd pushes her forward and Peacekeepers continue to detain Elementals and scan their wristplates. The synthfly hovers overhead, too high and dark to catch the attention of anyone else, its metal wings occasionally flashing in the muted glow of nearby lights.

Anaiya pulls the blade free. Ducking and weaving from the synthfly's scrutiny, she pushes sideways through the chaos instead of clearing a straight line to the tunnel ahead. It doesn't matter; when she looks up again, the synthfly is still there. The itch between her shoulder blades flares and she ducks her head again, hunching her shoulders and pressing deeper into the thicker parts of the crowd.

Step, push, side-step, duck, shove, weave, crouch, slink. She presses herself against other bodies, hides amongst the thicker-set

Earth Elementals, curls her body in as much as she can while moving in quick, smooth steps.

The synthfly continues to track her, hovering around five metres above; fixed in place when she stops, darting when she moves.

A shout from behind her draws her attention away. In her efforts to avoid the synthfly, she has stumbled into a cluster of Peacekeepers working their way through the western part of the square. The Peacekeeper closest to her is younger than the rest, not a Trainee, but only a year past graduation. She looks as overwhelmed as Anaiya feels, but is handling the pressure well; restraining the more aggressive revellers and scanning the wristplates of others around her.

The sight should be reassuring, but both options terrify Anaiya—either will lead to her detention, and detention can only lead to death.

No longer worrying about moving with stealth or staying hidden, Anaiya uses the adrenalin to race towards the only refuge where she can escape both the Peacekeepers and the synthfly, and maybe evade her shadow assassins.

Guilt lodges heavier in her core as Elementals fall at her jostling and desperate race to the station, but her need to escape obliterates it.

Something hard jams into her shoulder and the sharp fire that erupts in the muscle causes her to stumble. Her hand reaches frantically, against the pain, to pull the blade free. The kevlar reinforcement was only ever meant to protect the most vital body parts, not the most vulnerable.

She pivots clumsily to seek out her attacker, catching a brief glimpse of a dark-clad figure standing more stationary than it should amidst a rush of panicked Elementals. The assassin's arm is raised, the glint of a blade just visible. As Anaiya brings her arm up to protect her face, something else comes into view.

Like Anaiya, the assassin has unwittingly put themselves in the path of advancing Peacekeepers. The young Peacekeeper takes down the assassin, crash tackling them and jabbing at their jugular with a restraint syringe.

Anaiya turns away, caught up in the Elementals that continue to swell around her. Shaking off the residual panic from the attack, she sprints the last few metres to the subworm station. Even with the numbers of detained Elementals, the tunnel is densely packed. It is harder to move in and around the bodies, to find her way out.

She presses desperately against the wall of bodies, twisting her body and craning her neck to see where the next blade will come from. There is nothing but scared and trapped Elementals. No shadow assassins with lethal blades, no humming metal synthflies.

There is no relief in not finding them. If they are not pursuing her, they will not be sitting idle—they will look for the other missing piece.

She pushes harder, half barrelling, half crawling, to get to the nearest exit. To find her way back to Seth.

The apartment is quiet when Anaiya arrives close to an hour later. Roaming Peacekeeper patrols were not as abundant the further she tracked from the square, but the multiple detours and occasions where she just had to stay hidden until the Peacekeeper threat had passed have left her tired and on edge.

"Seth?" she calls out, moving from room to room, her anxiety spiking again. "Seth?" she calls louder.

Her chest tightens and the ache in her core swells despite her desperate attempts to beat it down. Thoughts of him detained and executed mix with the similar images of Kaide that have circled in her mind since he disappeared.

Distantly, she feels her legs shaking, as if her entire body has been hollowed out. Everything around her is too confined, too heavy. She knows this feeling, knows where it is heading; if she doesn't move now, she will collapse. Fighting against the resistance of her body, she runs from the apartment and back out into the night.

For the first few blocks, it is all she can manage to move through the street network with enough stealth to stay undetected. Eventually, the fear subsides, its hold loosening with the simple effort of staying in motion. She pushes aside the dire predictions and nightmares, and starts to work through what has happened and what she needs to do.

With every block that passes, three plausible options crystallise. Beyond the worst-case scenario, where Seth has been captured by Peacekeepers, there are only two other possibilities—he's stayed hidden in the same spot and avoided the Peacekeeper attention that had been drawn to the square, or he's moved away from whatever heat was generated from the paint bomb attack and found sanctuary elsewhere.

The street activity increases the closer she gets to the Precinct 14 station. A group of Infrastructure Protectors mill about, keeping a close eye on the Cleaners that weave between the Forensics carting out evidence from the paint-bomb blast. Peacekeepers are also out and about, canvassing the nearby buildings and interviewing potential witnesses.

Anaiya looks over to the hiding place where she had left Seth. It had seemed well-enough protected when she had first chosen it; now it seems small and exposed.

He wouldn't have stayed. If he'd stayed, he would have been found. And if he was found, he will be forever lost.

She turns from the scene and casts her gaze around, trying to think like he would have. If he didn't go back to the apartment, there is only one place he would have gone. Or tried to.

The Edges aren't exactly close, but close enough for him to attempt it.

Backtracking to the quieter streets, Anaiya heads south, struggling to find the right balance between taking a wide berth and getting there as quickly as possible. As she runs, she scans the landscape—the roads, the buildings, the sky—searching for signs of Peacekeepers, assassins, mechanical synthflies, Seth.

Three blocks from the Edges, she pulls up short. There is a glow on the horizon, where there should only be darkness.

Slowly, she sneaks forward, finding the darkest shadows to meld into, until the light is too strong.

Just like the square and the station, the streets that fringe the Edges are busy with Fire Elementals. Massive towers lined with strontium aluminate bars light the space up like a permanent lightning strike. Her last true refuge has been stolen from her.

She shuffles back, slinking in the shadows, keeping her gaze on the illuminated streets. And then she sees it. To the uninitiated eye, it would be invisible, just a random scattering of concrete debris. But, Anaiya's Air brain sees the structure to it, the abstract design, the connection.

Not just a random scattering. An arrow.

THIRTY-ONE

"Anaiya." The whisper is loud and sharp. She whips her head around, finding a collapsed wall, just like the one she had left him in twelve blocks away.

She races over, ducking behind, crashing into Seth.

"What happened?" he whispers harshly.

"The place is crawling with Fire Elementals."

"I know, that's why I'm here. What's going on with the Edges?"

"They're shutting us out. Lighting it up to stop us from hiding in the shadows."

"What do we do?"

"Well, we can't stay here." She pops her head up over the battered concrete, looking for the best retreat option. "About three blocks from here, things get a bit quieter. From there we can head back to the apartment. How are you holding up?"

"I can keep up, if that's what you're asking."

"Keep low, keep to the shadows, and just follow me, okay?"

"Got it, Peacekeeper."

She punches him in the shoulder and shuffles back to a crouch. "Ready?"

He rubs his shoulder and pushes himself up next to her. "Let's get out of here."

She keeps her back to the wall as she stands up, waiting for Seth to follow, and then steps out of the shadows. They move quickly, Anaiya keeping track of what's in front of them and behind.

Three blocks out, the glow from the light towers dissipates. Anaiya picks up the pace, checking that Seth is keeping up. He moves with an agility and grace she had forgotten about.

He flashes a smile, a kind of 'all good here' reassurance, and then frowns. She looks up, hearing the low-pitched whirring of the mechanical synthfly before she sees it.

"Seth, run!"

This time she doesn't wait to see if he keeps up, trusting her instincts that say he can.

"We need to hide," he calls to her.

"Won't help," she yells back, thinking of how the synthfly found her hidden among the Elementals in the square, face covered, body crouched behind a wall of Earths. "It will still find us."

"But our wristplates..."

And then the realisation hits. *That's how they find us.* Body thermal images without a wristplate signature. *The drones aren't looking for just any Unorthodox Elementals, they're looking for us.*

"Anaiya, we can't outrun it."

She finally slows and looks behind her. Seth stumbles along, distracted by the synthfly hovering above. But, Anaiya knows the synthfly is the least of their problems, her own gaze moving past Seth to the empty street behind, searching for shadowy movements of hidden assassins.

She falls into step with him, slowing to a jog. "We need to find a tunnel; the synthfly is vulnerable there."

"There's a subworm tunnel a few blocks away."

The subworm station is empty and the tunnel quiet when Anaiya and Seth barrel down the stairs and onto the tracks. The buzzing of the synthfly echoes against the walls as it follows them.

"Look for a loose piece of concrete," Anaiya yells, scanning the floor for a suitable projectile.

"Here," Seth calls, tossing up a jagged piece of stone the size of his fist.

She catches it cleanly, pins the synthfly in her sights, and launches it. The synthfly dips away, the concrete smashing against the wall opposite and splitting into smaller fragments.

Cursing, she scrambles around for another one, her hands grazing against rubble until she finds a decent-sized rock. She pelts it at the synthfly, but it darts again, the rock clipping the wing and bouncing away. It falters for the briefest of seconds, easily righting itself.

The rock that slams into its thorax doesn't come from her hand. The synthfly crashes to the floor and she sets upon it with the next rock she can find, smashing it until its lights blink off and the irregular whirring of wings stops.

"I think it's dead," Seth deadpans.

She stands up and kicks the broken metal away. "Nice aim."

He grins, obviously as surprised by the successful throw as she is.

"No time to celebrate, hot shot," she says, glancing towards the subworm entrance, grateful the assassins haven't yet arrived. "There may be more synthflies, and there are definitely assassins still after us."

Seth sobers. "What are we going to do?"

"We don't have a lot of time and we need to find a place where we can hide. Can be genuinely hidden." A place where heat signatures and fake wristplates weren't unexpected. "We need to get to Boileau Road."

THIRTY-TWO

"This is crazy," Seth whispers as Anaiya ushers him into the apartment building near Boileau Road that she had broken into weeks ago. With Peacekeepers occupied elsewhere, the building's entrance had been guarded by bored and lazy Infrastructure Protectors, who were easily distracted by noises half a block away.

"It's about to get crazier," she says, shutting the door behind him and leading him to the basement.

The door is not locked as she expects, the realisation not as comforting as it should be. At the bottom of the stairs, the basement is the same as when she first saw it. Except for the concrete floor.

"No, no, no, no…"

"What is it?" Seth glances nervously around.

Anaiya slumps down to the ground. "A dead end."

He follows her gaze to the floor. "That's our access point?"

"That *was* our access point." She beats her fist against the concrete, flinching at the pain that flares in her wrist.

"Well, don't just sit there. We need to find another one."

"There isn't another one."

Seth reaches down, offering her his arm. "Come on, Anaiya. There is always another way."

She looks up at him, his green eyes turned black in the darkened basement. Once upon a time she would have drowned in those eyes. Or clawed them out.

His grip is strong and he pulls her up easily. They stand there in the moment, a lifetime of shared experiences between them. And, even with everything between them, something has shifted. She trusts him and he believes in her.

She nods. "The tunnel is beneath us. If we're going to find another way, we have to go down."

He looks around. "Should we try accessing a ground-floor apartment?"

"Too risky," she says, looking around the basement. The space is relatively streamlined, largely empty except for the occasional stack of boxes and a few rows of industrial-looking shelves. Maybe Seth was right; maybe they should risk breaking into a ground-floor apartment.

She glances towards the staircase, still expecting to see Infrastructure Protectors or, worse, an assassin burst through. And then her gaze drops to the place where the stairs meet the wall.

"Help me dismantle the shelf," she says, walking over to the nearest stack.

"You need the whole thing?"

"I just need something to get through that wall."

Seth follows her gaze. "Breaking through that is going to attract some attention."

"I don't know," she replies slowly, pulling free her wristplate and jamming its metal edge into the screws of the nearest stack. "It's how I got in last time. No one came looking for me."

He stares at her in disbelief. "You mean, besides the Peacekeepers who chased you all the way to the Edges and then into the river?"

The first screw clatters to the concrete floor. "That was after I ran out of the building like an idiot. No-one came for me before that."

Seth slips off his own wristplate and attacks the screws on the other side of the shelf. "How bad was it at the square?" he eventually asks.

She looks up at him, sees the weariness and worry guarding his eyes. He doesn't know. There's been no time to tell him.

"She'll be alright," Anaiya murmurs, ducking her head against the flush of shame that comes from lying to him. "Cress is smart. She's stayed out of trouble this long."

The final screw falls to the floor, the weight of the shelf falling heavy now that it is untethered. She takes the brunt of it from Seth and walks it over to the staircase. Leaning the shelf against the wall, she looks back at Seth. "We'll go back for her."

He nods, but doesn't say anything, his face unchanged. Sighing, Anaiya leaves behind the shelf and walks over to him.

"I promise," she says softly. "Once we're safe and things are quieter. I'll go back for her."

"*We'll* go back for her." He still looks physically and emotionally spent, but his voice holds a quiet conviction.

"We will. And she'll be fine."

He steps past her, striding over to the staircase and lifting the shelf. The plaster wall is properly breached after only a few heavy collisions, and the two of them pull the rest of the sheeting away to reveal the cavity below the staircase. And its timber floor.

Seth picks the shelf up again to beat his way through, but Anaiya stops him. There is a heavy, musty stench to the space, and it is familiar. Images of broken pipes and a flooded room bubble up from her subconscious.

She shines her wristplate diode down to the timber boards, taking in the discoloration and testing it with her foot. Just like the plaster that had failed in one of the water-corrupted apartments she had squatted in a few months back, the timber floor breaks easily under the lightest of pressure.

She pushes her foot down again, relishing the sensation of the timber straining underfoot, feeling it bend and bow, and then crack.

The rest of the rotten boards give way easily, revealing a drop to the familiar subterranean space.

"What do we do with this big hole in the wall?" Seth asks.

The question catches Anaiya off guard. The last time she had broken into the tunnel below, there had always been the plan to return and escape before anyone noticed. She hadn't thought about needing to clean up her mess to avoid being pursued into the tunnel.

She stares at the two battered plaster panels lying discarded on the floor. "We can salvage this one." She pokes at the somewhat dented sheet with her foot.

"Mm," Seth says. "And what about this one?"

The other panel bears the full brunt of their attack; a hole, the diametre of her forearm, is punched through the centre.

She looks around the space, searching for a solution. "Help me move the shelves."

They drag the emptiest shelf across the floor, both of them wincing at the sound of metal grating on concrete.

"Won't they notice it?" Seth asks.

Anaiya shakes her head. "Even if they do, it won't raise any issues. Earth Elementals are the only ones likely to come down here, and they're not ones for details."

They settle the shelf unit in front of the wall, leaving enough space for them to squeeze behind it.

"Grab one of the boxes," she says, helping Seth manoeuvre it into place on one of the lower shelves. Looking up, she appraises the scene. It's not perfect, and anyone more alert than your typical low-level Cleaner would sense something was wrong, maybe report it, but it should be enough.

I would notice it, she thinks. *And Lira would notice it.* But, neither of them are typical low-level Cleaners.

And that is the problem, the reason for her lack of faith in her hastily structured plan. There is no way to know who or what is typical anymore, to know how strictly or loosely an Elemental will conform to their alignment and conditioning.

"Will it work?" Seth asks.

She nods, ignoring her own doubts, and picks up the two plaster panels. "You drop down first; I'll move the panels into place and follow you."

She waits for the heavy thud of Seth hitting the ground below, smiling at the string of curses that float up to her. Moving the intact panel into place, she shuffles along the gap with the other more firmly in her grip and secures it against the shelving structure.

The compromised timber groans, threatening to break under the constant shift in weight. There isn't enough time to stabilise herself, to work herself into the right position.

"Move!" she cries out to Seth as the floor gives way and she falls awkwardly to the real basement. Her feet slip out from under her and her hip slams heavily into the floor. She bites down on her lip to stop from cursing, the tang of blood rushing along her taste buds.

"You okay?" Seth asks from nearby.

She opens her eyes, finding him sitting against the floor less than a metre away.

"That was close," she murmurs, rubbing her hip and gingerly standing up.

"Did it work?" Seth shines his wristplate diode up the wall, the light bouncing around the well and landing on the plaster sheets covering the void they had created just minutes ago.

Anaiya looks away and flashes her own light down the tunnel that stretches away into darkness.

"Come on," she says. "I need a shower. And a bed."

She sets off down the tunnel, so consumed in her own thoughts and emotions that she doesn't immediately realise there are no following footsteps. Turning back, her wristplate diode shines a wide arc of light, landing on Seth who stands where she had left him, still staring up at the false basement above.

"Seth?" she asks quietly, sensing a different energy from him, an unfamiliar vulnerability.

"I don't know if I have the energy for this," he says, his voice soft and hoarse.

"For running away?"

"For running away, for always fighting, for sacrificing everything and everyone for this idea of a better Orthodoxy, or no Orthodoxy, or just a better fucking life."

He looks over at her, blinking against the bright light until she lowers her wristplate. "What good is a better life," he says despondently, "if I'm too corrupted to appreciate it?"

She shuts her diode off and walks towards him in the darkness, stopping until he is close enough to hear her whisper.

"Remember that night after we met at the Lavoir? After Rehhd and Eamon had danced with the Peacekeepers and you took me back to your apartment?"

"The night you pretended to be one of us? Pretended to be dropped by restraint serum?" His voice is bitter, but it lacks any heat. The wound is an old one.

"I was vulnerable that night. Genuinely. I was introduced to things that challenged my way of seeing the world and it was eating me from the inside out."

Seth turns his light off, plunging them both into darkness.

"I think you saw that," Anaiya continues, her own voice growing hoarse, with exhaustion or unspent emotion or the effort of reliving the moment. "And you caught me before I spiralled. You said to me—and I've never forgotten it—you said, 'there's still beauty in this world, you just need to know where to find it.'"

"I lied," he says. "Or even if it was true then, it's true no longer. True beauty has been ripped from this world. Everything has the same ugly taint to it, everything is corrupted by betrayal and failed connections and a broken Orthodoxy."

She knows this kind of despair; she's been on the brink of it and swallowed up by it before. Hesitantly, she steps forward, her eyes straining against the darkness to find his shadowy form.

"There is still beauty," she murmurs. "You were right—you just need to know where to find it."

Slowly, her eyes adjust to the darkness, making out details that were hidden to her before. He looks so broken.

"C'mon," she says softly. "Let me show you."

The two of them walk in silence through the isolated streets of the Enclave, past the terraced redstone apartment buildings that sit dark and empty.

"Anaiya…"

"Just trust me."

The intersection ahead is illuminated by a full moon, the cobblestone street stretching from darkness into light. With each step, Anaiya becomes more confident the Enclave is truly empty.

Even with all of Otpor's half-empty apartment buildings and quieter streets in run-down precincts, it is a surreal experience to be in such pure isolation. It heightens the anticipation, the thrill along her skin, as the intersection looms closer.

A metre-or-so from the crossroads, she shifts her gaze left, catching the first glimpse of the trees that line the street leading to the Danish Prince.

Memories of the exclusive izakaya are a jumble of different images—muted lighting, shimmering mirrors, run-ins with Seth, Lilith, and Eamon. And Kaide.

And, for the briefest of moments, she is transported to the street outside the Enclave, to the night she and Kaide had decided to go there together.

He had emerged from Jouvenay Street like a shadow, his messy hair and casual clothing replaced by curls that framed his face in dark waves, his body all curves and angles in dark threads that accentuated all the good parts, his eyes never leaving hers as they walked towards each other, his body moving with focused intensity. The low, seductive whistle; her pushing past his outstretched hand and into his chest...

"It's beautiful", Seth breathes. He stands still beside her in the real world, real time.

She sharpens her focus, leaving behind the ghosts of her memories, and fixes her gaze on a sight that still fills her with awe and wonder every time she sees it.

Seth presses forward, picking up his pace as he rushes to the trees. Anaiya hangs back, happy to watch his moment of uninhibited joy. Especially since moments of any joy are harder to come by.

"This is incredible," he calls out, his previous caution and despondency a fading shadow.

She smiles; only something as surreal as an actual, living tree could rob Seth of his Literature competency. She follows him, stopping beside him as he runs his hands over the smooth bark and presses his nose to the trunk to breathe in its scent.

"It's indescribable," he murmurs, face still pressed closed against the wood. "Like a dream, or a memory from a past you never had."

Anaiya reaches up and plucks a leaf from one of the low-lying branches. She lets it rest lightly in her palm, watching it twitch and shiver as she brings it up closer to her face. She clenches it in her fist, watching it crumple; she expects it to rip and tear like the pages of her books, and is surprised when it unfurls and bounces back—a little creased, but otherwise intact.

"Young leaves are more resilient," a familiar voice murmurs from behind her. She turns quickly, the leaf falling from her hand. Farasei emerges from the shadows. "It takes time to become corrupted and lose vitality."

Anaiya steps back with her right foot, settling into a basic fighting stance.

"Hello Anaiya," Farasei says, his voice clear and calm. "Seth."

In her peripheral vision, Seth step away from the tree. Anaiya brings her hands up, ready to strike.

"Stand down, soldier," Farasei says, holding his own hands up in submission. "I'm not your enemy."

"Should we run?" Seth's voice is tight, betraying his fear.

Anaiya shakes her head. Running will do them no good. They need to choose the lesser of two evils, engage in the fight they have a chance of winning.

"What are you doing here, Farasei? Shouldn't you be with your co-conspirators at Atlantic Square?"

"Atlantic Square is a little too hectic tonight for my tastes."

"You were there?"

Farasei shakes his head, with distaste or derision. "No, but I have contacts who keep me informed. It was a smart move, using guerilla tactics to piss off the Fire Elementals." The basic terminology sounds crude and uncharacteristic on his tongue. "But it seems your *anonymity* has come to an end. And what have you achieved for your efforts? Besides the annoyance of a synthfly sting?"

Anaiya presses up on the balls of her feet, ready to engage. Unless he has already alerted his contacts about their presence, disabling him is the only way to keep her and Seth safe.

"I'm not here to fight you, Anaiya." He puts his hands up again.

"Why *are* you here, Farasei?" She relaxes her stance a little, but stays alert.

"I figured you would return eventually. In a world enclosed by a wall, there are few places to evade a predator."

"You *are* the predator," she spits. "You and your Enclave take down any attempt to break down the lies and eliminate anyone who threatens your status quo."

Farasei silently regards her. "What do you *want*, wabi-sabi?"

She is unprepared for the rush of emotion that erupts at his calm question. "I want to burn it all down."

He doesn't laugh or scoff or recoil from her answer. Simply shakes his head and asks another. "Why do you want to burn it down? What will it achieve?"

She ignores the first answers that flash in her mind: *Because it burned me down, because I want to finally be the winner.* "I don't want to live in a world based on lies, lies that are fed to us to keep us starved while the likes of you feed like gluttons out of sight."

Farasei sighs and smiles sadly. "I never thought about the consequences, you know. Not really. Not until I saw them about to execute you on that makeshift stage out near the Edges. In truth, I'd never really given much thought to Elementals in general. I was happy in Le Hameau, happy and oblivious. Your kind were nothing more than a distraction; light entertainment for most of us, attractive playthings for those like Danai." He shakes out of his morosity, like shedding his skin. "In any case, what you're doing isn't going to give you what you really want."

"And what is it that you think I really want?"

"The same thing I want," he replies. "Revolution."

THIRTY-THREE

"There is no revolution," Anaiya says, leaning back in the plush chair and clenching her eyes shut with frustration.

Farasei had brought her and Seth back to one of his apartments in the Enclave. *Your first street party did wonders for my real estate portfolio,* he had said as he welcomed them across the threshold. There had been a moment of hesitation before they had followed Farasei back—he was the enemy they were railing against, the target they are trying to bring down. And yet, as he had reasoned with them, why approach them at the trees or rescue Seth from the Second Enclave, if only to hand them over to Peacekeepers? If not all Elementals were the same, maybe it was naive to think that all members of the Enclave were. Maybe Farasei was genuine when he'd said he wanted revolution.

In the end, their scepticism was overruled by the simple logic and the promise of rest after so many weeks of fighting and running. The promise of comfort and safety.

Farasei's apartment holds the same surreal opulence as the other Enclave apartments Anaiya had encountered; the freakish items, the abundance of organic and analogue objects. It is almost familiar to her, now. Almost Orthodox...

"There can *be* no revolution," she says, her anger turning weary. "Not when Niamh's Peacekeepers don't play by the rules and the Enclave exists outside them." She opens her eyes, but stares down at her feet. "There's no pituarmagn store large enough to manipulate the population, no way of accessing and distributing it even if there was. No way of hacking into the broadcast systems. We have access to *nothing*. And they hunt us with shadow assassins and mechanical synthflies. Will kill us without trial or witnesses as soon as they find our blank wristplate signature."

"The surveillance is… problematic," Farasei says after a while. "But, you're smart. Both of you. And you've obviously proven that you can evade it when you need to. The pituarmagn, well, it is an effective amplifier, undoubtedly. But, like all chemical manipulations, it merely triggers, escalates, or silences the natural processes of our bodies."

"You're saying there are other chemical amplifiers we could use instead of pituarmagn?" Seth asks, leaning forward. He sits on a white chaise, its legs carved from dark timber, its plush body upholstered in a material that lacks the normal sheen of synthetic Otpor fabrics.

"No, I'm saying you don't need an amplifier. Your original plan was an explosive one, but difficult to sustain; manipulating an entirely new emotion, against a completely unfamiliar enemy…" Farasei pauses and squints at them. "Ah, but you knew this?"

Anaiya nods. "We'd hoped it would transmit like Kane's Heterodoxy had."

"It might have," Farasei says, leaning back in his own chair, "if it had been a similar type of Heterodoxy. What do you remember about him? His ideology?"

"I… I…" She stops. It is too hard to disentangle what she remembers of Kane's Heterodoxy from her memories of him, her relationship with him, and the knot of emotions that still pull and tug at her mind every time she hears his name.

"He wanted us to break free of our chains," Seth says, filling the silence.

"What chains?"

"The chains of our oppressors."

"The chains of the Orthodoxy," Anaiya murmurs.

Farasei turns to her and smiles softly.

"That's why we wanted to bring you down," she says, staring

unflinchingly at Farasei. "You and your Principals created this Orthodoxy."

"True. But we do not maintain it."

"Bullshit," Seth spits.

Farasei chuckles. "Incongruous, I know. But, we don't need to maintain it. An object in motion tends to stay in motion, unless acted on by another force." He smiles and laces his fingers together. "Once the Orthodoxy was established, and the original generations of alignment and conditioning established, the wheels were set in motion, so to speak. You Elementals did all the work for us, blindly obeying your conditioning; all we had to do was maintain our anonymity and not interfere."

"Why are you interfering now?" Anaiya asks, still uncertain about his true motivation.

He threw his hands around as if to indicate the empty Enclave beyond. "You didn't leave me much choice. This isn't the status quo I signed up for—no *la belle vie*, no *joie de vivre*—just an empty shell in a world of ugly curfews and brutality. Danai thinks he is saving our way of life by setting the Peacekeepers after you like dogs, but look at what he has sacrificed—Otpor's belle epoch and our beautiful hameau, for a tall building and insipid parties." He shakes his head. "I want to push the reset button as much as you, my dear."

"You want to help us remove the Enclave's anonymity?" Seth asks. "We tried that before, it didn't work out so well."

"The Enclave is only one side of the Orthodoxy equation; alignment and conditioning are the other. I fear you've been focusing your efforts on the wrong side."

Now it's Anaiya's turn to laugh. "You think we should have focused on breaking alignment?"

"It seemed to work with you, my dear."

Anaiya opens her mouth to respond, to point out that it had taken weeks of isolation and realignment procedures, but Farasei isn't finished. "And him."

She looks away from Farasei and back towards Seth. Once, she couldn't have imagined him as anything but the quintessential Air Elemental—passionate, inspired, charismatic. But, Farasei's words scratch at a subconscious observation that has been quietly itching in her mind since his wristplate procedure. He is not the same Seth she once knew—he is quieter, more pragmatic, more pessimistic. His anger runs deep rather than burning hot. His emotions richer, but not as loud.

"It's more common than you are conditioned to notice," Farasei says.

Except she has noticed. Kaide and Lira were also anomalies within the strict profile parameters of their Elements: Kaide more analytical than he should have been, Lira more hedonistic.

"You aren't born with a single Element determining your personality, and your alignment and conditioning doesn't erase the other facets. It just mutes them. They're still there—the full spectrum of Elements within your mind. The Cooperative has just chosen one to amplify."

"You think we should amplify the others?" she asks.

Farasei shakes his head. "You're still thinking about it back to front. Stop trying to build additional constructs. Stop adding to the manipulation."

He stands up and walks over to the grand column of timber shelves embedded in the wall behind him. Moments later, he returns with a rectangular box made of enamel and plucks a small white tube from its depths. Twisting off the red cap, he squeezes the tube. Paint, deep and red and thick, spills over the top of the low-lying table that sits between him and them.

"That is your conditioning, your alignment," he says. "If you were going to 'fix' it, would you do this?" He reaches into the box and pulls more tubes, spilling more colours over the table—different hues of green, blue, purple, orange—and mixing them together with his fingers. "Or would you do this?" He reaches again into the box and retrieves a large cloth square. Wiping the paint off his finger, he scrunches the cloth into a ball and drags it across the table, leaving long swathes of the original-coloured lacquer in its wake. "Don't build on the corruption. Just uncover the truth."

"And how would we do that?"

Farasei smiles. "Have you had a splinter, well no, not a splinter in your case, a metal shard maybe. Have you ever had a metal shard lodged in your skin? Or sand embedded in a cut?"

Anaiya nods and, in her peripheral vision, sees Seth do the same.

"Did you notice how your body actively rejected it? How it fought to expel what didn't belong, what was harmful? Infection, fever, blisters, pustules. Natural, *instinctual*, responses your body uses to expel unwanted invaders."

Anaiya fights the urge to scratch at her skin.

"It's doing that now." Farasei continues. "Not with me, and likely not with you either, Anaiya, but with you Seth, and all the other Elementals out there. There is a primal part of your brain—underneath all the alignment and conditioning—that is fighting, futilely but doggedly, to reassert its true nature."

Anaiya sits silent and rigid. She knows the truth of what he is saying because she has lived it. The fracturing of her brain, the resistance to every attempt to compress her identity into a small box. Even when it had been herself that had tried to keep it within its confines.

"That impulse, that natural instinctual response, has been overwhelmed by conditioning—original and ongoing."

"Ongoing?" Seth asks, his knees bouncing with anxious energy.

"The tailored music, wallscreen entertainment, even those nutrient boosters that you only purchase if they appeal to your Element. It's all reinforcement."

"So we just disrupt the reinforcement?" Seth asks.

"That would assuredly help. But, it will only be as effective as picking away a scab. You need to dig deeper and attack the original conditioning."

A thrill races along Anaiya's spine. The same kind of thrill that had attacked her when Seth had showed her the view from the air recycler in the Edges, when Kaide had pressed the pages of Kane 148's notebook into her hand, and when she had first set her gaze on the trees of the Enclave. The thrill of something true but dangerous.

The sun has lost some of its heat as Anaiya walks the final blocks to the drinking den in Precinct 17. It is unnerving; like most hard truths, it seems to defy logic that this is the better path.

As she steps into the muted lighting of the den, she thinks of Seth stepping into the Lavoir izakaya in the next precinct. He had seemed more nervous than she'd expected when they left Boileau Road. In a way, she concluded, it was harder for him—she would be more nervous too if she was going back to a Peacekeeper izakaya instead of a den full of Earth Elementals.

"Nanshe? Where have you been?" Sharna steps into view. The Cleaner's eyes glow with a warmth that can only come from alcohol and ignorance.

"I picked up a contract in the Southern Area," Anaiya replies above the din, relaying the story she had crafted the night before as she and Seth had worked out their plan. "Curfew has made it hard to get back."

"Curfew means nothing. No one knows the difference between night and day in here; where there are no windows, there's no such thing as time."

Anaiya smiles. She has missed the deprecating ways of Earth Elementals. And forgotten how poetic they can be, contrary to what society expected of them.

On a whim, she breaks from her rehearsed plan, and asks Sharna a question. "Do you remember your time in the Nursery? Before you were assigned your competency?"

Sharna cocks her head, a slight frown, from confusion or the effort of remembering a memory buried under old time and recent alcohol. "You know, I do remember this one thing. I was really young, like early in my second lustrum. A rat had found its way into the play yard and I scooped it up and hid it in my jumper." Her glassy eyes turn soft. "I kept it in a spare shoe under my bunk, wrapped it up in a pillow case, fed it all these soylent leftovers I was saving. Remember the soylent bricks we used to get at the Nursery? Those weird, wet bricks we used to drink out of those pyramid-shaped containers?"

Anaiya smiles. "They were always cold and the label colour would rub off on your hands, staining them red."

"Exactly! Except they were yellow labels, remember?"

Anaiya nods slowly, caught by surprise that the Nursery's conditioning had extended to their basic nutrition supplement.

"I called him Ratolio and he would sleep on my pillow at night. But that's the thing with rats, they don't do well with being hidden away from sunlight, and feeding on soggy soylent, or kept from scurrying around the place.

"I knew he wasn't doing so good. And I was going to put him back in the yard. But, there was something about keeping him with me… I couldn't let him go." She squeezes her eyes shut briefly. "But, the longer I kept him, the worse he got. He would cry—this awful squealing. It was soft at first, I could only hear it when he was on the pillow next to my ear. But then it got louder, and I started to worry someone would find him and that I'd get in trouble, so I used to shove him back in my shoe.

"And one night, I shoved him back so far that he squished against my hand. I remember that feeling so clearly." She pauses, her whole body, once languid with alcohol, now rigid and still. "I'd forgotten it, you know?" she murmurs, barely loud enough to be heard over the noise of the den. "Forgotten that feeling of my fingers pushing through skin to squelch that sick, damaged body to pulpy flesh and broken bones. Forgotten how my heart clenched and my stomach turned a quick somersault like a Peacekeeper on a roof." She presses her hand to her stomach, caught in the full throes of the memory.

"And after it had passed, I picked up the shoe, without looking inside, and swapped it for another Premie's shoe under another bunk, and spent the next day curled up in the corner of the yard where I first found him."

Sharna exhales, a tiny movement that seems to carry an impossible weight of memory and emotion.

"Fuck," she exclaims. "Ten minutes ago, I didn't even remember that fucking rat, and now it feels like it's burrowed a hole into my stomach. I need another fucking drink."

Sharna turns a wobbly pivot and heads back to the bar without a backward glance at Anaiya. Childhood memories were messy—full of uncontrolled emotion and overwrought anxiety. Even without the pituarmagn that had been harmlessly imbibed by

Elementals in the weeks since its distribution and finally ran dry, pre-conditioning memories held an unnatural power. Like her own memories of being at the Nursery and competing with Niamh— memories and emotions that created deep undercurrents and continued, mostly hidden, into her adult life.

Anaiya shakes her mind clear of its own unsettled vortex and walks to the bar, away from Sharna and towards the less crowded end. This is what she had come here for, to trigger a better future, not get dragged down a messy past.

"What can I get you?" the Earth Server asks, never really looking at her.

Anaiya plants her feet firmly, stealing confidence from the stability it affords her. "A dodecahedrazine."

It has been an age since she has ordered one. A lifetime. *Literally.* The Peacekeeper favourite would be unheard of in Earth drinking dens, except amongst the Serving competency who waited on all Elements, not just their own.

The Server doesn't react, not initially. Only when he drops the edrazine enhancer in the tumbler of blue liquid does he look up, squinting back at her.

"Interesting choice," he says, sliding the glass across the bar top.

"Ever tried it?" she asks, working hard to keep her voice light against all the synthflies in her stomach.

"Poured a thousand, but never tasted one."

She slides the drink back to him. "All yours. And pour two more."

He takes the glass hesitantly, but takes a decent swig. His eyes open a little wider and he smiles. "That's actually pretty good."

She smiles back. "Then get the other two."

He grins, eyes shining already with the edrazine, and turns back to the rows of synthetic alcohol on the shelves behind.

Emboldened, Anaiya unwraps the lifeline of her unfamiliar wristplate. Farasei had gifted it to her the night before. *"All of the functionality of your Elemental wristplates, none of the traceability."* She plugs it into the music upload station, tapping and swiping at the terminal screen to add her song to the den's playlist, exhaling deeply when the transaction is done and the lifeline disconnects with the slightest resistance.

The Server returns with two more glasses brimming with dodeca.

"Viva la belle epoch," he says, raising his glass.

"Viva la chaos," she murmurs into her own.

THIRTY-FOUR

A week goes by. And then another. Seth finds Cress, her cheery resilience an echo of their growing optimism.

"We're so close," Anaiya says, sitting cross-legged on the generous window sill, foregoing the comfortable lounges and plush chaises. "We just need a way to amplify it."

Their plan had been successful, in a way: the weeks had brought an awakening and confusion in the Elements, the beginnings of a collective crisis of identity. Earth Elementals downloaded music designed for the Fire Element, Air Elementals took nutrient boosters branded for Water Elementals. Cracks were widening in the spaces between the Elements, and between the Elementals within them. But it wasn't enough.

"We can't amplify it," Seth countered, raking his hand through his hair. "No pituarmagn."

"That's not necessarily the case," Farasei interjects.

Seth whips his head around. "What do you mean, *not necessarily the case*? You sat here three weeks ago and told us exactly that."

"No," Farasei says slowly, leaning back in the armchair. "I said that pituarmagn was a manipulation, and that you needed to move beyond temporary and unsustainable shifts in behaviour if you wanted to birth a revolution."

"What is he talking about?" Cress mumbles to Seth. Seth

shakes his head and shrugs with exaggeration.

Anaiya turns her gaze to Farasei, trying to recall their earlier conversation. As the weeks had passed, bringing with them with no Peacekeepers to detain them, and gifting them with more progress towards their goal of revolution, it had become easier to trust him. "So, using chemicals to manipulate an unnatural reaction is off limits… but using chemicals to remove an unnatural conditioning is fair play?"

Farasei grins. "You were always too smart to be a Peacekeeper. I can see why they chose you for realignment."

"So, we need a chemical that does the opposite of pituarmagn?" she asks, ignoring the hollow flattery.

"Not exactly the opposite. But there are two chemicals that should be capable of turning off the selective amplification you find in conditioning."

"Should?" Seth asks, obviously still frustrated by the vagueness and ambiguity.

"Well," Farasei replies with exaggerated patience, "it's not like anyone has ever tried it, is it?"

"What are the two chemicals?" Anaiya asks, ignoring the rising tension. "And where can we find them?"

"One, is the very complex-named gamma-Aminobutyric acid, found in the very simple root system of a honeysuckle plant that lives in the Wasteland. And the other is the simpler-named serotonin, which is found in unfiltered sunlight."

"What is he *talking about?*" Cress says again, louder.

"I still don't know," Seth grumbles. "But, every time he says the word 'simple', I hear the word 'trouble'".

"Unfiltered sunlight is an easier proposition," Anaiya muses. "We could shut down power to the factories and divert it to the air recyclers; boost their production and reduce the level of contamination in the air. But, getting to the Wasteland—it's impossible."

"Not for everyone."

"You have an Enclave tunnel to the Wasteland?"

Farasei laughs. "It doesn't always have to be cloak and dagger, wabi-sabi. The best solutions are always the ones right in front of you."

Cress sighs loudly and stands up. "I'm out. Come find me by the trees when all of this makes sense."

Seth waits until she has left the apartment before he turns back to Anaiya and Farasei. "We don't need to go to the Wasteland."

"They're growing this plant in an Enclave?" Anaiya asks.

Seth's eyes widen and he looks back to Farasei. "Are you?"

The man grins and shakes his head.

"Doesn't matter," Seth says, switching his focus to Anaiya. "*We* don't need to go to the Wasteland to get it."

"What?" Anaiya scoffs. "We'll just get the Border Watchers to get it for us?"

"Yes."

"Yes?"

"Yes. Because they already do. Well, not exactly; they don't get *honeysuckle*."

Anaiya frowns, trying to disentangle his coded meaning. And then she realises there is no coded meaning. "The tequila."

He nods, grinning. "The tequila." For decades, Border Watchers had been collecting the Wasteland's agave to make some black-market on the side, selling it to izakaya owners who turned it into rare and lucrative tequila. If the Border Watchers were procuring agave, it would be easy to turn their attention to finding the honeysuckle.

"We'll need to—"

"Get Yve on board," he says, jumping in over the top, bouncing off her energy.

"Will she do it? Can we get to her without compromising her?"

"Cress can go; there's no risk there."

"How much do we need?"

They both turn to Farasei, who sits comfortably in the armchair, regarding them thoughtfully.

"How much do we need?" Anaiya repeats, directing the question to him.

"I'm not entirely sure. Like I said, it's never been tried before. I'm not even sure it can work—I'm merely speculating after doing some limited research from the pre-Singularity texts."

"How much do you *think* we'll need?"

"How much of an unsynthesised chemical from a raw, organic source does one need to undo years of conditioning?"

"Fine," she says, exasperated, and turns back to Seth. "We'll ask Yve to get as much as she can without it being suspicious. We'll test it. And we'll take it from there."

"Still leaves the seratarny."

"Serotonin," Farasei interjects softly.

They both ignore him.

"You think your crew can still pull off strategic power outages?" she asks Seth.

He nods. "But, how do we divert the power to the air recyclers?"

"We won't need to. The grid will do it for us; it will need to redirect the excess power somewhere, and it will default to the infrastructure drawing down the most at the same time."

"But, what if the air recyclers aren't the biggest drawers? What if it's an administration building or a sewage treatment facility?"

"We game the system."

"And how do we do that?"

"If there's one place we both know how to navigate, it's the Edges."

"This is crazy," Seth whispers harshly. "You know that right?"

Anaiya glares at him. "Of course I know that. We're in kevlar-reinforced clothes, ten metres up a random air recycler in the middle of the Edges, trying to manoeuvre a fucking *demon* of a... a... what the fuck is this, anyway?"

The thick sheet of coarse material is unwieldy in her grasp, seeming to take on a life of its own as it struggles to escape from her hold and then Seth's, impatient to get to the vent embedded in the recycler's collar. They have spent too long trying to manipulate it into place, their patience worn down to its finest thread.

Seth grunts and pulls the material tighter. Anaiya curses and clenches her fists, her fingers biting with the effort to just hold on.

Fuck it. In an unlikely moment of abandon, she gives up—gives up the need to fix something, or control it, or wrangle it into a shape it just does not want to be wrangled into. And, she lets go.

The sheet pulls from Seth's grasp, too chaotic to be held in place now that Anaiya has let go.

It rushes like a zephyr into the grate, bunching and bundling up, sticking in places and leaving massive gaps in others.

Seth stares at her. "What the fuck, Anaiya?"

She shrugs and throws her hand towards it. "Look, it's still working." The air around them has shifted, turned sluggish whereas moments ago it raced. Somewhere inside the metal casing, the recycler's internal monitoring system will be registering the insufficient air drag, and somewhere in a Water monitoring facility, the inefficiency will trigger an algorithm to monitor for other anomalies. Once enough of them are registered, that same algorithm will push excess network power to meet the recyclers' extra demands, even after the obstructions are gone. "It doesn't have to be perfect; it's doing what it needs to."

Seth rolls his eyes but picks up the large backpack at his feet and hoists it onto his shoulder. Anaiya does the same, and they both scale down the recycler's shell in silence.

There is enough light in the pre-dawn hour to see the tension in Seth's face as they reach the gravel below. She doesn't say anything, mindful of the tension in her own body that pulls at her shoulders and makes her chest tight. There are a lot of memories for them both in the Edges and a lot of expectation riding on their latest effort to bring down the Orthodoxy.

The silence stretches long into the hours it takes them to drag the other nine sheets to recyclers dotted around the Edges in the Northern Area. Only when they have made their way through the back streets and into the tunnel system does Seth voice his concerns.

"Do you think it will work?" His voice, only a murmur, echoes against the tight brickwork.

Anaiya doesn't respond straight away. They had decided to target about a third of the city's recyclers; enough to make a dint in the oppressive pollution, but not enough to cause a bored Water Analyst to investigate further. It was a reasonable plan, but it was still just speculation.

"I mean, it won't last forever," Seth says. "Even if it does work, won't everything just go back to the way it was once the power anomaly is fixed?"

Anaiya reaches out to drag her hand against the rough texture of the curved walls less than a metre away. "Maybe. But, if there's anything I've learned from all of this messed up, insane, *heterodox* experience, it's that once you turn off the conditioning, it's hard to switch it back on."

"But, how is a couple of Earth Elementals preferring blue nutrient boosters, or listening to dense Peacekeeper beats, going to bring down Orthodoxy?"

"Because if their conditioning is disrupted, it won't be able to manipulate them anymore. They'll be able to think for themselves. They'll be able to determine their own identities, their own futures."

Seth doesn't respond, the silence between them broken only by the echo of their footfalls.

"Was it the change in your alignment that pushed you to set your own path?" Seth says eventually. "Or was it being confronted with the truth?"

She knows he isn't trying to rile her; his voice is calm and soft, his posture a little rigid but not confrontational. And yet, she feels her body tense with a sudden frustration.

"What are you trying to say, Seth?" she snaps, unable to keep the tightness out of her voice.

Seth doesn't react as strongly, but she still sees his posture stiffen. "I'm just saying that shuffling around Elemental traits won't change the impact of the Orthodoxy. What good is being able to think for yourself, if the only thing you contemplate is what you watch on your wallscreen or whether you drink a lys or a dodeca?"

Anaiya slows her pace, belatedly realising she has been striding for most of their conversation. She stops and stares at him, trying to work through the implications of what he has just uttered.

He was right. Fuel alone didn't create a fire; it needed a spark.

"There's no way we can do it," she says. "There's no way Farasei would go for it; even with all his talk of revolution and pushing the reset button, he's as addicted to his anonymity and privilege as much as Danai and the rest of the Enclave are. We can't access the broadcast system without him." She shakes her head. "We tried to broadcast the truth last time, and they shut us down. It put us on Niamh's radar. It killed Kaide."

Seth sighs and leans back against the wall. Anaiya follows his lead and leans against the wall opposite him. They stare at each other across the narrow gap, illuminated by the soft glow of their fake wristplates.

"Maybe we don't need to broadcast it," Seth says.

Anaiya shakes her head. "A simple message painted on some walls won't work. The resistance murals were a call to fight for people who *wanted* to fight. This truth—the Enclave, the Principals, the corrupted Orthodoxy—it is a more complex truth. One that will not fit on a wall."

She expects him to take offence or become defensive, but he merely falls silent and turns away. The two of them go still, unable to continue on their path back to the Enclave with the unsolved problem hanging between them.

After a while, Seth kicks his foot against the wall and pushes himself forward to stand. "Perhaps the eroded conditioning will help them see the truth, eventually."

She smiles at his poor attempt at optimism and pushes away from her own wall. "I doubt it. But, we don't need to have all the answers right now. You were right to point out that breaking the conditioning is only part of the solution. But it's still a part we need."

"One step at a time," he says, throwing her a rueful smile as they recommence their underground journey towards Boileau Road.

The silence they lapse into is an easier one this time, but Anaiya's mind keeps returning to Seth's words and the heavy truth behind them. Not needing all the answers at once is not the same as not needing them at all. At some stage, they will have to find their spark. And it seems, with everything teetering on a precipice, that they will need it sooner than they are prepared for.

The sky is dark when Anaiya and Seth climb up through the well and into the empty streets of the Enclave. As she always does, Anaiya immediately turns her head to seek out the trees, pausing when she sees activity at the base of the largest.

"Is that Cress?"

Seth follows her gaze to where the younger girl is kneeling beside the tree. "What is she doing with Farasei?"

It is strange to see the younger girl so still and Farasei so animated. As Anaiya and Seth get closer, Cress turns around, the smile on her face a sharp rebuke to the negative thoughts drowning Anaiya's brain.

"Seth!" she cries out, the wariness of her early days in the empty Enclave evaporated like so much water in the Wasteland.

Seth picks up his pace and rushes towards Cress, the heaviness gone from his footsteps. Anaiya is warier; she keeps her pace steady and her eyes on Farasei.

"Why the excitement?" she says when she reaches the line of trees.

Farasei turns and smiles at her. "It's beautiful, no?"

He steps aside to allow Anaiya a closer look. The road is littered with discarded and broken cobblestones. A rich, dark soil lies scattered around the row of broad-trunked trees, interrupted by five clusters of straggly green sticks bearing a low crown of star-shaped leaves and topped with a misshapen globe of impossibly small white flowers.

The sight alone is arresting, but it is the scent hanging heavy in the cool morning air that forces her to bend closer.

"Is it the honeysuckle?" she murmurs, breathing in the rich, sweet scent of the flowers.

"The ancients called it *Valerian*," Farasei says, reaching down to pluck a small floret from the nearest stand and twirl it in his fingers. "They used it to cure sleeplessness."

Anaiya crouches to inspect the fragile flowers. "I can't believe it survives in the Wasteland. How did you know it was out there?"

Farasei plucks at one of the tiny flowers, and then another, pinching them between his fingertips and letting them fall. "In the early days of the Border Wall, the Principals would send out scouting parties, worried about groups of marauders also looking for a new life, a place to find prosperity. They documented everything—the terrain, the water sources, what little vegetation survived the Singularity."

"How did you know it was *still* out there?"

Farasei drops the denuded stem and brushes his hands. "I didn't. But, I knew that it was the right time for it to flower. It only flowers for two days before the heat of the Wasteland destroys the blossoms, but it can flower any time between the last week of Aresa and first week of Taurino. And it will always flower close to the river in the shadows of the eastern wall."

"So, what do we do now?" Seth asks. "How do we get more?"

"More?"

Seth frowns, looking from Farasei to the flowers and back again. "There's no way there are enough flowers to dose all of Otpor."

"There aren't enough flowers to dose a precinct," Anaiya murmurs, feeling the return of her earlier misgivings. "Not enough to remove the inhibitions of conditioning."

Farasei laughs. "Don't be deceived. Valerian's potency comes from the part you can't see. Beneath all those pretty white flowers, covered by the soil, is a mess of taproots thicker than your wrist. And a piece half the size of your fingernail would put a fully grown Demolitioner to sleep in less than a minute."

"Still," Anaiya says, unconvinced. "They would need taproots the size of your thigh, and we would need five times as many of them for this to work."

"If it was agave and we were trying to make tequila, then yes. Or, if we were trying to do this with the plants that grew pre-Singularity. But, we are doing neither. Trust me—there is enough concentrated valarenic acid in those thirty plants to inhibit the effectiveness of conditioning for every fourth, fifth, sixth, and seventh lustrum."

"But, that's only half of Otpor," Cress says as she fixes a cluster of flowers behind her ear.

Anaiya smiles and feels some of the negativity lift from her core. "It's the half that maintains the Orthodoxy."

Farasei nods. "It's the half that matters."

While the sun completes its arc in the sky, Anaiya sleeps around bad dreams in an empty apartment building. Farasei had handed over the 'keys' to the apartments in his own building—small, heavy metal rods carved in strange geometric shapes—and the apartments themselves were luxuriously appointed with their soft furnishings and even softer beds, but Anaiya found it claustrophobic being so close to Farasei.

Tonight she escapes to the upper balconies of a group of red-brick buildings located as far away from Farasei, the Danish Prince, the trees, and everything else that reminds her she is living on borrowed time in an open-air prison.

She jumps and cat vaults from balcony to balcony, losing herself in the pull of her muscles and the rush of air against her skin. Finding a smaller balcony oriented west, she settles down on to the polished tiles and slides off her wristplate. The cuff is made of a lighter polymer than the metal cuff she had worn after her Execution, and it folds out along invisible hinges to become a small glass screen. Farasei had casually unfolded his own wristplate a few days earlier, oblivious to her amazement. Just when she thought she had peeled off the final layer of the world beyond the Orthodoxy, there was always something else to throw her off-balance.

The music composition function she taps open is a much simpler program than the one on her glass screen at her old apartment. She had been tempted to go back there and retrieve it, but thoughts of dark-clad assassins and metal synthflies had stayed her feet.

She shifts to find a comfortable position, eyes scanning the rooftops that signal the end of the Enclave. Even from her vantage point on the top floor of the apartment building, there is no indication of the city beyond.

Sighing, she plugs the screen's slender audio cords into her ears and turns her attention back to the glass screen. For hours now, her earlier conversation with Seth has been circling in her mind, putting an edge to all the optimism about yellow suns and valerian boosters. He had been right—it wouldn't matter if they finally brought free thought to Otpor, if there were no changes in the facts and narratives that would continue to saturate communication channels.

Without access to the broadcasting system, the only avenue she can see is the same one she had been using all those weeks ago when the pituarmagn plan was still in play. And, yet, relying on organic movement of music downloads and random playlists in izakayas and drinking dens seems desperate. And delusional.

But, it is all she has to work with, so she shuts out the spiralling negativity and starts tapping and swiping at the screen, experimenting with sounds, trying to hit upon something that will create a sense of questioning or disbelief or critical judgement in the listener. Even though she knows it is impossible, she keeps messing around with the composition, emphasising a bass track, stretching out and contracting notes, warping chords. None of it is working.

Frustrated, she pulls the cords from her ears and disengages them from the glass screen. It would be so much easier if she could just plaster Otpor's walls with Kane 148's notes. His ideology has always been the alternative narrative that Otpor needs.

"What are you working on?"

Seth and Cress materialise on a balcony two apartments over.

"How did you find me?"

Seth holds up his arm and taps on the wristplate Farasei had gifted him, the screen flashing bright in the evening's dusky shadows. "Tracking capability."

"Do you mind if we join you?" Cress calls.

Anaiya shakes her head, surprised to find that, despite her self-imposed isolation, she is grateful for the offer of company.

They arrive on the balcony a minute later, and the three of them shuffle around until they all sit like interconnected pieces of an unlikely puzzle.

"What brings you two here?" Anaiya asks, ignoring the easy familiarity between Seth and Cress and the uneasy reminder that she is truly alone in this new world.

Cress shrugs. "This world doesn't suit us."

Anaiya looks to Seth to see if he agrees. He holds her gaze, sombrely. It is an emotion she hasn't seen on him before. "I guess we came to the conclusion," he says, "that we finally knew what you had felt when you became an Air Elemental."

She smiles sadly at him, and then turns to Cress. "But, life as an Air Elemental held beauty and laughter. This life, as luxurious as it is, holds no comfort."

"Is that what you're doing?" Cress asks. "Finding comfort in music?"

Anaiya laughs. "No. I was trying to find a way to create a new narrative in music, one that would give Otpor an alternative to the Orthodoxy once their mental manipulation was stripped away. But, it won't work—it is too vague, it only operates on an emotional level. "

She recalls her earlier thought about Kane's notebooks. "I need something concrete, something to offer an intellectual alternative. I need words…"

Cress quirks her head, the same gesture Anaiya had seen and smiled at a lifetime ago in just another izakaya. Anaiya draws a sharp breath, the memories of that night exploding in unexpected clarity in her mind. Cress laughing, Eamon with his charismatic charm and subtle overtures, Kaide with his easy confidence and prescient scepticism—even then, he had been an anomaly—and Seth, distantly observing, struggling and failing to contain the emotions within. Anaiya had gone to the Rabid Dog that night to escape the burden of her realignment mission and left more entangled in it than ever.

"Remember that night at the Rabid Dog?" she asks. "At the spoken word?"

Cress looks to Seth, no doubt remembering the tension that had plagued that night. Before it can get awkward, Anaiya swipes on the glass screen, turning up the volume, and plays a thread of the symphony she had been playing around with minutes earlier. "I am," she says, her voice light and sonorous, the words recalled from that night in the izakaya, "a person, not an Elemental."

"A citizen without a government," Cress chimes in, her voice pitched higher against Anaiya's, finding harmony in the difference, "a scorched and barren land."

The effect of their voices melded together and with the music, speaking forbidden words that call for a familiar resistance—it stuns the three of them into silence.

"I always said Music and Literature are the greatest companions," Cress says after a while.

"That was *powerful*," Seth says.

Anaiya nods. "Imagine if we used Kane's words instead."

THIRTY-FIVE

Two weeks later, Anaiya sits on the same balcony, her wristplate forgotten. The sky is changing from day to dusk and she can't tear her eyes away from it; the bright yellow orb exploding in a medley of pinks, reds, and oranges.

Cress and her crew had been hitting the power lines for the last week—their targets always close to other critical infrastructure so as to obscure their true targets. In just three days, the sky had turned from its deep brown to a faded beige and the sun from a ball of dirt to a ball of fire.

The change had quickly shifted the mood in Otpor—a portent of hope and doom within the more superstitious Air and Earth Elements, a sign of progress among Water Elementals, and a call to battle for the Fire Element.

From Cress' reports, Peacekeepers had been out in force and Infrastructure Protectors were more aggressive. Even the normally elusive Border Watchers had become more visible, leaving their posts atop the Border Wall and Enclave roofs to walk the streets as a secondary Peacekeeping force.

Every day she had come to the Enclave with news of the outside—elation and adrenalin radiating from her in the aftermath of the initial strikes, then excitement and high-energy hubris from evading the growing patrols. But lately, there had been another shift; the younger Elemental's energy turning darker and heavier.

"Hey." Seth steps out on to the balcony. For the last two weeks it has been their ritual—finding a space of their own in this borrowed place to talk about what is happening in the world beyond their grasp.

"Hey."

He settles on the tiles next to her, both of them facing west to catch the new colours of the sunset.

"Farasei's confirmed the enhanced nutrient boosters have shipped."

Anaiya nods; she had seen the cluster of valerian plants around the base of the Enclave's trees reduced to just one on her way to the balcony.

"You don't seem too elated about that."

"How's Cress?"

Seth shifts uncomfortably next to her, stretching out his legs and raking his hand through his hair. "Still not back."

"She's changing." Over the last few days, Anaiya has noticed a shift in Cress' demeanour; more reserved and withdrawn, quick to anger, often intoxicated, and suddenly cautious about the new world that is starting to unfold.

Seth sighs and lays his hands in his lap. "I guess that was the point of all of this, wasn't it?"

They both fall silent. Only when the sun lets out its last spectacular breath of colour and the sky turns its familiar shade of black does Anaiya speak again. "Don't you want to see what's going on out there? Don't you want to be part of it?"

"I am part of it. I don't need to be painting murals on crumbling concrete walls to be part of the resistance."

He rolls his shoulder against hers in a good-natured jostle. She smiles reluctantly and jostles him back. And, for the briefest of moments, they are the old Anaiya and Seth. The jostling over, the two of them fall still again, comfortably leaning against each other.

"I want to see it for myself," she says eventually. "I want to know what's happening, I want to see it working."

She waits until the next morning, until the sun is a hot ball of gold in the sky, before slipping down into the tunnel and heading out of the

Enclave. She has learned by now that the night is no longer as safe as it had been; worse, it is now where they expect to find her. Her heart is thundering by the time she reaches the empty basement at the end of the tunnel, not from the effort, but from the new fear that assaults her.

Stepping out onto the empty, riverside service road, she resists the urge to slouch and glance furtively around. With her heart still pummelling her ribcage, she walks quickly to Boulevarde Exelmans, ready to blend in the normal crowd until she can get to the subworm station a few blocks away.

Reaching the intersection, the anxiety in her chest explodes into the all-too-familiar white heat of fear; there are no crowds, no clusters of Elementals, no meandering and haphazard groups she can use as her shield. The boulevarde is empty of all but a few random Elementals.

Her first thought is to rush back to the safety of the tunnel and the Enclave, but returning will not yield answers to the questions that continue to plague her.

It is easy to ascribe the empty boulevarde to simpler changes, to Elementals simply avoiding the new and more oppressive heat. But, Anaiya recalls the changes she has seen in Cress and wonders if something more is at play. And the thrill that comes with that possibility, that their plan has worked, tempers her fear and she keeps her course towards the subworm station.

There is a growing drop in temperature as she descends the steps to the station, but the platforms are similarly empty. She doesn't wait for the subworm, instead jumping down to the tracks and making her way north.

Six stations in, the subworm tunnel turns dark, explaining the lack of subworms rattling along the tracks. Cress had spoken about hitting a target near the old necropolis ruins, but that was at least three days ago, just before her change in mood. *Surely, they would have fixed it by now.*

Slowing down, she taps on her wristplate to activate the diode and continues in the half-darkness the rest of the way. Five stations on and she arrives at Ternes station. Like all the stations that came before, it is empty.

She switches off her diode and peers down the tunnel, looking for a sign of light and finding none. Taking a deep breath, she taps the diode back on, squares her shoulders and leaps up to the platform. She pauses before she steps out, shielding her eyes against the sunlight and looking around for Earth Elementals that can grant her access to Precinct 17's drinking den, while constantly scanning for the threat of Peacekeepers.

To her chagrin and relief, there are none of either. She stares at the den's door, surprised to hear the sounds of the Earth Elementals inside more clearly than she should. And then she realises it is because the door is open.

It makes sense; when the original power outages had struck in the early days of Seth's rebellion, she had opened every window of her apartment and still sweltered in the oppressive heat.

No power, no air conditioning, no access panels to deny her entry.

She scans the street one last time and then strides across to the den. Even with the heat and lack of air conditioning, there are enough Elementals inside to fill the space with sound. The volume is as loud as she expects, but the tone is not the usual boisterous mess of laughter and bawdy jokes. Angry voices and arguments fill the space, but come only from a few Elementals. The rest of the patrons sit around staring morosely into their glasses, lines of empty glasses littering the tables in front of them.

This is not what she expected. Where is the enlightenment? The revelling in a truth that had been unfairly hidden from them?

"Long time no see, Nanshe." Jiran stands up from a nearby table, swaying a little before grabbing its edge.

"What's with the mood, Jiran? Heat's not that bad, is it?"

"The heat's fucking unbearable. And the power outages aren't helping. But it's that fucking yellow sun—it's causing all sorts of demons to squirm their way up." He presses his hands to his belly and screws his face up, dragging his hands to his throat. He stops and drops his hands, his face blank. "Most times, alcohol is the only thing that quietens it."

"You want to quieten it?"

"I want to rip it from my gut and feed it to the river."

Anaiya steps back and looks around the den, seeing the despair and the self-medication, the wretchedness that comes from finding something inside yourself you do not like and can not stomach.

She should have known better. She had lived the same wretchedness in the weeks after she had lost her Fire alignment, and her Air.

Failure is a thick oil slick that coats her skin and curdles her stomach.

"You feel it," Jiran says, pointing at her face. "*Everyone* feels it."

A flash of light and sound announces the return of power and a half-hearted cheer erupts from one of the emptier tables.

It's enough to shock Anaiya back to her senses. *I did feel it.* "It doesn't last forever."

Jiran barks a mirthless laugh. "Anything feels like forever when you can't see its end."

Or an alternative. Without thinking, she reaches out and grabs his wrist. He starts to pull away.

"Trust me, Jiran. This will help you find an end to it."

She presses her own wristplate to his, swiping and tapping it to download the demo piece she, Seth, and Cress had created in the Enclave. It is still rough—Seth had pulled together the words from Kane 148's notebooks, arranging them to fit Anaiya's symphony, and Cress had given them life with her voice. It still needs refinement; there are other words they could use and the music needs to be tighter, denser. But, it is all she has, and it will do.

Her wristplate flashes green to signal the download has completed. She drops her arm and smiles softly at Jiran. "Hang in there. It will get better." She steps past him. "And slow down on the alcohol—synth toxin is a bitch."

She unravels her wristplate's lifeline equivalent as she walks to the bar, her focus moving easily past the drunken Elementals loitering nearby and fixing-+ solely on the music terminal. She is mere steps from the bar when loud shouts barrel into the space.

"Peacekeepers. Cease and desist all activity."

Anaiya turns slowly, taking in the two Peacekeepers striding into the den. They are unfamiliar, which is of some relief, until the older one squares his gaze on her. He recognises her; not as the resurrected Resistor, but as a priority target of interest that needs to be detained.

The younger one, a Trainee, glances at her partner; not as sure, not as confident.

Anaiya seizes the opportunity, running to her left and leaping onto the nearest table. Both Peacekeepers leap to stop her, the younger wanting the glory, the older not trusting his protege to get the job done. The result is a less than smooth advance, which Anaiya uses to her advantage.

Vaulting over their grasping hands, she jumps to the closest table, kicking past empty glasses and leaping to the next table. And then it topples.

She crashes awkwardly to the floor, shoulder slamming into the hard tiles. A rough hand picks her up by her hoodie and she lashes out, her fists blocked by a coarse hand.

"Get out of here," Jiran yells, throwing her towards the exit.

Anaiya stumbles forward, throwing a backwards glance over her shoulder in time to see Jiran land a punch square on the jaw of the Trainee Peacekeeper. Sounds of a melee break out, but Anaiya doesn't stick around to watch it unfold. She pushes through the door and out into the sunshine, legs stretching into a sprint.

The blade that whirrs past her ear pulls her up short. The next one thunks into her chest, burying itself into her kevlar-reinforced shirt. She pulls it free and throws it back towards the black-clad figure advancing on her.

The figure bends and twists out of the blade's trajectory, the metal clattering harmlessly to the road beyond. And then they are running at her again.

Anaiya crouches to absorb the impact, pushing up against her aggressor and rolling to avoid the retribution.

The punch she throws connects with a rib.

"Fucking bitch."

Anaiya rolls away and stands up. "Lumen?"

The assassin rips off their black keffiyeh and stands up. "Hello, Anaiya."

She and Lumen stand off against each other. They had been

partners on occasion; had shouted rounds of drinks at Fire izakayas, shared cola-roasted pigeon at the Samedi markets, shut down public disturbances together.

"You're missing your metal synthfly." Anaiya's voice is rough, her body screaming for oxygen.

"Don't need it when you're wearing a tracking beacon," Lumen replies, glancing down at Anaiya's wristplate.

"Did you know I was the target when they recruited you? Can't imagine it's a secret Niamh wants too many people to know about." She's stalling, trying to find an exit.

"I've never had a mission like this, Anaiya. I thought finding the dead would have been easier."

The street is still empty and Anaiya knows that her best chance of escaping Lumen is the subworm tunnel. But to reach it, she will have to turn her back on her assailant, and the thought of a blade buried between her shoulders keeps her where she is.

"Is that the order? To find me? Because your blades are telling me something different."

"Retrieve or terminate, it doesn't ma—"

Lumen falls heavily to the ground, the chunk of rock that had struck her clattering to the ground behind her. Anaiya looks past the fallen body. "Lira?"

The older woman steps from out of the shadows. "What are you waiting for, you stupid girl? Run!"

Shaking out of her stupor, Anaiya spins on her heel and races towards the subworm station, bringing up her wristplate and punching in Seth's number.

"Anaiya?" His voice crackles and echoes against the walls of the staircase.

"Seth, are you alone?"

"Yes, wh—"

"Ditch your wristplate now."

"What?"

"Farasei's betrayed us. And he's tracking us. Ditch your wristplate. I'll meet you at the place where we recorded the music."

She doesn't wait for him to answer, ending the call and ripping the cuff from her wrist. She throws it to the ground and tramples it underfoot. It would have been enough to discard the wristplate to disable the covert surveillance, but smashing it helps to sharpen her rage to a fine point. *I'm coming for you, Farasei.*

THIRTY-SIX

"What's going on, Anaiya?" Seth whispers harshly as she enters the apartment at the edge of the Enclave.

She glances down at his wrist, relieved to see that he has heeded her advice and ditched the wristplate.

"Where did you leave it?"

"I tossed it in the izakaya. Now, what's going on?"

"He used the wristplate to send the assassins after me."

"Why? Why would he do that?"

"Same reason the Enclave do anything—because it suits them and their designs for power."

"I don't know, Anaiya. If Farasei wanted to kill you, he could have done it at any time. I mean, he's had us here cornered for weeks, now."

Anaiya sighs and leans against the wall. It didn't make sense. Why would Farasei help them only to betray them? *What had changed?*

"He knew I was going to play the music." Of course he knew— she had recorded it on the wristplate and had used the wristplate to transfer it to Jiran's.

"Why would that matter? He was helping us to change the status quo, anyway—the sunlight, the valerian."

Anaiya slumps down to the floor and Seth follows.

"Are you sure it was Farasei?" Seth murmurs.

Anaiya nods. "Lumen—the assassin—called the wristplate a 'tracking beacon'. Farasei was the only one who knew I had it. Only he could have told Niamh."

"I don't get it," Seth says. "He was the one with the plan. All of it was his idea: the sunlight, the nutrient boosters."

It was all his idea. It was all his idea. "He's been playing us, making us think that he was helping us. But we were helping him. He *needed* us. To shut down the power. To get the valerian."

"To what end?"

"I don't know. Maybe it's time we asked him."

The sun is past its zenith and long shadows cover the cobblestone streets when Anaiya and Seth leave the apartment to seek out Farasei.

"I don't know whether we should be more stealth or more casual," Seth murmurs as they walk side-by-side through the empty Enclave.

Anaiya stays silent, her vision tunnelling until she sees only the stretch of road before her.

"Do you think we're walking into a trap?" His voice floats to her, running along the edges of her intense focus.

It had been one of the first things she had considered when she'd started to make her way back to the Enclave. If Farasei had hacked the wristplate, he knew about the encounter with Lumen and the emergency call patched through to Seth.

But, she also knew he safeguarded his Enclave and protected his anonymity. There is the possibility he has called for Peacekeeper backup, but there are not many Peacekeepers with the knowledge or the clearance to answer that call.

She is confident she can evade two Peacekeepers, three at a stretch, but less confident about her ability to do that *and* protect Seth.

"Hang back when we get there," she says, her voice distant and cold. "Run when I say run, and always protect your face. Everything else that is important is protected by the kevlar. If we get separated, I'll meet you back at—"

"Veritas," he says.

"No. They'll check there; they'll be checking any place that has a direct connection to either of us. I'll meet you where you showed me the mural."

"Got betrayal on your mind, huh?" he murmurs.

The words break her out of her singular focus. He isn't talking about his betrayal, he is talking about hers.

She steals a sidelong glance at him. There has always been something that has connected her to Seth—a shared vision, a shared emotion, but always from the opposite side of the mirror, always in reverse.

Anaiya's gut twists in a faint echo of the visceral revulsion she had felt when Seth had shown her the ten-metre-high Resistance mural. Kaide and Cress had also been there, watching her, waiting for her reaction. It had taken every shred of self-control to push down her emotions, to keep her from showing Seth her true response. She had been so devastated he could have been so intimately connected to the Resistance that she had fallen into delusion. A delusion that had led her to Rehhd's Execution, and eventually her own.

In her memory, it had always been Seth that had betrayed her in that moment. And while she knew she had betrayed him later on, it surprises her to realise that, from his perspective, she had betrayed him then.

"Betrayal is a complex thing," she murmurs. "Full of threads and knots and tangles."

Seth's hand darts out to grip her forearm. He opens his mouth to speak and then snaps it shut, opens it again, and sighs. He loosens his grip but doesn't let go. "I used to think that following your heart was the only way to truth. And then, after Rehhd, I thought the only way to victory was through ignoring your heart and following your mind. But, I've come to realise that the truth can only be found in the place where they both meet." He sighs again. "We've both been on the same trajectory—swinging from one extreme to the other. And it's caused us nothing but hurt and heartache. But, the last few months—since your Execution, since you found connection with Kaide, since I removed my wristplate and joined you in this insane mission—it feels like we've found the balance." His green eyes are piercing, his voice raw with emotion. "There's a litany of betrayals in our past, but that's the best thing about the past—we don't need to live in it. I'm not asking for your forgiveness or offering mine. We buried the past a long time ago. I'll never betray you again."

Anaiya pulls from his grip. His face falls with hurt and confusion. She smiles and throws her arms around him, pressing him in a fierce embrace.

"I couldn't have done this without you," she says, pushing her voice past the rock in her throat.

"I've been lucky to know you," he murmurs against her shoulder. "And Kaide was lucky to have loved you."

Before the emotion can undo her, she pushes him away and locks her gaze onto his. "You're right," she says through a tight throat, her voice husky. "Truth and power come from a balance between heart and mind. And right now we need both of them to be sharp to take down Farasei and his Enclave."

THIRTY-SEVEN

There are no Peacekeepers waiting for them when Anaiya and Seth enter Farasei's apartment. The space is as it always is—impeccably appointed, everything in its place, light and shadows playing on thick carpet and timber furniture. Everything beautiful and unfamiliar and cold.

Farasei emerges from an adjoining room and his flinch when sighting Anaiya confirms her suspicions.

"Not expecting us?" she says.

He looks down at her wrist. "You've lost your wristplate."

"It was starting to chafe."

Farasei glances down at his own, quickly tapping and swiping at the panel.

"Niamh didn't give you the head's up?" she murmurs, watching as his pretence of a calm demeanour slips entirely.

"You shouldn't have come here." He reaches for his wristplate again, but Anaiya is quicker. She brings her foot around in a sweeping roundhouse kick, connecting with his forearm. He howls and drops his arm to his side. His gaze snaps to a table where five syringes lie perfectly arranged in a neat row. He steps forward, but she strikes again, the impact doubling him over.

Anaiya rushes to him and wraps him up in a restraint hold, fingers pressing into the soft spot of his neck. He falls limp in her arms and she lowers him more gently than intended to a nearby chair. His wristplate comes away easily in her hands and she tosses it to the floor.

"Seth. Seth?" She turns to find him scouring the room, turning over objects and rummaging through drawers. "What are you doing?"

He strides over to the windows and pulls the rope-like sashes from their anchor points.

"Here," he calls, throwing one to her.

She catches it easily and joins him in tying Farasei to the chair.

"How long before he wakes?"

Anaiya pulls the knot tighter and peers into Farasei's face. "Not sure. The last time I restrained someone like that, I didn't stick around to see them regain consciousness."

Seth raises his eyebrows at that, but lets it slide. "So, what do we do in the meantime?"

"Well," she says, wiping her hands on her jeans and standing up, "it's unlikely Farasei is just going to tell us everything we want to know. Unless he thinks we already know most of it anyway."

"But, we don't know *any* of it."

Anaiya looks around. "Not yet. But I've learned that Unorthodox people tend to keep their secrets close."

Seth ties the last knot and looks up at her. "You think he would be that reckless?"

"The Enclave is empty," she says, throwing her hands towards the window. "It's not reckless if there's no-one around to find anything."

"What are we looking for?"

She scans the space, taking in the myriad of places that Farasei could have hidden his secrets.

"Anything that can tell us what Farasei's real plan has been all along."

With Farasei tied up, the two of them begin their search, rifling amongst bric-a-brac and thumbing through dull-coloured books, their efforts becoming less careful and more frantic as time wears on.

"There's nothing here," Anaiya says at the same time Seth calls, "I think I've found something."

He holds up one of the dull-coloured books, its cloth cover faded and patchy.

"I've already checked it," she says, shoulders slumping as the hope of finding answers evaporates. "It's just another ancient text. No handwritten notes; just scientific studies and diagrams of plants that no longer exist."

"Except this one," he says, walking over and showing her the pages opened in his hands. One side is covered in lines and lines of finely printed text, but the other is illustrated with a vibrantly rendered picture of valerian, its delicate form captured in perfect and painstaking detail.

"You did hear me say 'real plan', not 'the plan we've all been following this whole time'?"

Seth laughs. "You've turned all Earth on me, Anaiya."

"Ha. Alright, *Water Elemental*, tell me how this helps us."

He pulls the book back and tracks his finger down the lines of text. "Farasei told us the truth when he said that valerian would break down conditioning, but he didn't tell us the whole truth—like that it only works as a sedative, that it would take thousands of plants to dose Otpor, and that a dose strong enough to break years of conditioning would also put half the population in a coma."

"There were only twenty-odd plants…"

"Enough to dose maybe two or three Elementals, at best."

"I was out there," Anaiya protests. "People were acting differently. They were despondent and angry and all kinds of frustrated…"

What had Jiran said? *It's that fucking yellow sun—it's causing all sorts of demons to squirm their way up.*

"What is it?" Seth asks.

"I don't know," she replies, frustration bubbling up to her tongue. "I don't know whether they've changed because of the sunlight alone, or whether they've changed at all. Maybe what I saw was just resistance to a new environment they weren't expecting and didn't want."

A sharp, hacking laugh draws her attention away from Seth and the book.

"It's a conundrum, isn't it?" Farasei rasps. "Hard to tell the cure from the placebo. I didn't really think the sunlight would work. But, your Elementals have certainly reacted." He tugs at the restraints against his wrists, grimacing as they chafe against his skin. "Not the repayment I expected for my generous hospitality."

"Turns out your hospitality wasn't so generous," Anaiya says. "What game have you been playing, Farasei? What was the real purpose of all of this?"

"Enough with the trite questions, wabi-sabi," he says, the real emotion twisting his pretty face into a snarl and tightening his voice. "Let's just cut to the chase, shall we?"

"Alright, Farasei," Anaiya says, steel in her voice. "No more pretense. What is the fucking valerian for? Because we all know it wasn't to start a revolution."

Farasei's glance cuts to the book in her hands. "So, you figured that one out, did you?"

"Not enough to dose a population, and it's more likely to sedate you than uncondition you…" She stares at him. "Is that what it was about? You were trying to eliminate someone?"

Farasei falls still, no longer tugging at the restraints or throwing his head around.

"Not us," Anaiya continues, sorting her thoughts into order. "Not by valerian in any case—you've got your Peacekeeper connections to do that for you. So who were you trying to eliminate?"

"Let's just say that I don't like what Danai and his sycophantic entourage have done with the place. Or what he's trying to establish in his second rate Enclave in Precinct 14. Even we have our rules, and *normal* means of disposal only leads to discovery. I needed something more subtle. Something no-one could find, or would even know to look for."

"And you needed us to do your dirty work."

"You Elementals always do," he crows. "Although I didn't expect you to be so compliant or effective. But, then again, you were so single-minded, so self-righteous, so *desperate* for a solution that would make all this better. That would make it something it has never been. But, you never stopped to think, did you? Never conceived that no-one wants this change you are so adamant to bring about."

She thinks of Cress and Jiran and all the Elementals in the

drinking den with their despondency and desperation overflowing.

"Everyone else is happy. You think changing this will make *you* happy. But it won't. People will always disappoint you, wabi-sabi. At least with conditioning, you know the exact ways they will."

Anaiya picks up one of the syringes from the table. "I should destroy you and your lies by your own designs."

Farasei laughs. "You can't hurt me. You'll never find your precious Kaide without me."

She stares at him, unwilling to fall victim to another one of his lies.

"Why are you so surprised?" he continues. "I plan for all contingencies. And I wanted to have another bargaining chip in case this didn't go exactly to plan. Which it obviously hasn't…"

Anaiya's mind races with scenarios of where Kaide could be kept. "There's only so many places you have access to. And we both know he is not here."

"Ah, but the second Enclave is bigger than la hameau; you'll never get access, and even if you did, it would take you years to search every—"

Anaiya steps forward and pierces his jugular with the syringe, Farasei's eyes widening briefly before drifting shut.

"What did you do?" Seth says, panic bright in his voice.

Anaiya grabs the remaining four syringes and threads them in the waistband of her jeans in a poor, but effective, approximation of the belt she had worn as a Peacekeeper. "Call Lilith; she's the only access point we have to the second Enclave. And go find Kaide."

"You're not coming with me?"

"Lilith doesn't trust me. And I need to dismantle this fucking Orthodoxy once and for all."

THIRTY-EIGHT

Anaiya isn't sure where the idea to target the Nursery first originated. As she runs towards Precinct 1, it seems that it has been building fragment by fragment since her first realignment. The memory of sitting in one of the Nursery's training rooms, surrounded by hypoxic Elementals learning a new competency and starting a new life, flashes clear and bright.

With all the lies Farasei has fed her, there is one truth she believes—a real revolution can not be built on manipulation; it needs for the manipulations to be stripped back and destroyed. She has learned how difficult it is to take away conditioning from those who have become connected to it, who *depend* on it; has seen first-hand how they resist the truth and bury themselves in alcohol and mindless entertainment just to escape it. She has known that same despair and desperation to return to 'normal', even if that normal is a crippling lie.

A revolution, in order to be successful, to be *sustainable*, needs to be entered into willingly. Needs to be championed and supported by those who have the capacity to see what the world of Otpor is truly like and to want to rebel against it with every fibre of their mind and body. And to be able to imagine a different future and work towards achieving it.

The Nursery is not only the best option, it is the easiest—no need for impossible chemical distributions or complex musical manipulations, no benchmark of 'normal' to chafe against or raise the alarm, no discernible changes in behaviour until it is too late to correct them.

Yes, it is the ideal pathway to igniting a revolution, but it is not the reason she is running to it now instead of towards the second Enclave with Seth. Farasei's claim that Kaide was still alive had filled her with an irrational hope. One she was not willing to chase blindly. If it turned out to be another of Farasei's lies, she would never recover from it.

An itch between her shoulder blades pulls her from her thoughts. She is only two blocks from the Nursery, but she pulls her gaze from it and glances over her shoulder.

The street is empty of all but the black-clad figure. Anaiya opens her mouth to call out Lumen's name, but stops. The figure that slowly advances on her is more broad-shouldered than her old friend-turned-assailant, and almost a head taller. And then the figure stops, the casual arrogance of their stance more pronounced than usual for even a Peacekeeper.

"Niamh."

"No mutt to give you an advantage this time around, Anaiya. It's time we make your death more permanent."

He twirls his blade casually in his hand and steps forward, no doubt expecting her to run. Instead, she reaches for one of the syringes at her waistband and sprints towards him. His brief hesitation confirms she has taken him by surprise. It is all the advantage she needs.

She doesn't waste time with feints or fancy footwork—it will only slow her down and give Niamh time to recover and attack. Instead, she barrels towards him.

She has no consideration for the blade he wields and barely acknowledges the sting of its edge as it rips into the flesh along her forearm. She raises her arm and tries to manoeuvre the syringe into a position where it can disable him.

The blow that comes as Niamh brings his elbow up sends her head ricocheting back. Another blow to her stomach bends her over, the blade slicing thickly against her hip before she crashes to the ground, the syringe skittering away from her grasp.

She lies on the street, winded and bleeding, unable to move; her body prioritising the need to breathe over the need to avoid Niamh's next blow.

Seeing her disabled, he takes his time advancing, confident enough to remove the mask that had been hiding his face. "You have never known when to just sit down and accept your position in this world. You've always overreached. Always thought you were better than what you were, or could be." He kneels down beside her and presses the blade to her neck. She feels the cool metal and the wet, sticky itch it leaves behind as blood springs from its cut. "You've always been in the shadows, Anaiya—my shadow, Kane's, and now the one of your own making." He leans in close until his face is just centimetres from hers. "But there is no greater shadow than death, and it's time we returned you to it."

The blade begins to press more firmly against her neck, but unbeknownst to Niamh, her breath has returned to her and, with it, her ability to finally fight Niamh off. She grasps one of the remaining syringes and, with as much force as she can muster, slams it against his neck and depresses the plunger.

The knife at her own neck sinks deeper, from shock or desperation. There is a moment when the pressure fades, but the respite is brief and the pressure quickly returns as Niamh's full weight bears down and threatens to suffocate her.

With the last reserve of her energy and desperation, she rolls him off and plunges another syringe into his jugular.

Leaping to her feet, her body sways and a dark, fuzzy static blooms in her vision. She presses a hand to her neck, recoiling as it comes away slick with blood. On unsteady feet, she stumbles to where Niamh's discarded keffiyeh lies and ties it tightly around her neck.

Fear and panic still crawling along her skin, she injects Niamh with the last of her syringes to ensure he doesn't wake any time soon, picks up his blade from the road, and slowly makes her way to the shadows.

He had been right to call her out for living in the shadows. And, once, she would have rejected them just to prove him wrong. But, the shadows have kept her safe, and she needs them to keep her safe a little longer if she is to survive the next few hours to see her plan executed.

Accessing the Nursery is easier than it should be. The Cooperative has never really seen it as an asset to be protected; it was designed to keep the real assets in, rather than non-existent threats out. And, as far as the Cooperative is concerned, the assets the Nursery keeps secure don't reach their value until the end of their conditioning, at which point they leave its walls.

Anaiya finds the service lane and stumbles to the large metal doors that lead to the subterranean storage room. Despite the functioning access panel on the wall, the doors open without resistance thanks to the wedge of metal jammed between them. She makes her way slowly down the ladder, gripping the metal treads tightly to maintain purchase. The wound at her neck is throbbing, but the fact she has made it this far reassures her that there has been no fatal damage.

Once her feet touch the concrete floor, she scrambles as quickly as she can; the open doors above will attract attention with no delivery truck present. The storage room is vast, extending into crowded maintenance areas that control electrical supply and plumbing.

Large vats are arrayed in orderly rows, connected by thick, black tubes to the pipes overhead. She pauses, trying to push her mind past the fog of adrenalin and cortisol to figure out what she needs to do. Knowing that the conditioning chemicals mix freely in the water distribution lines is only part of the puzzle. Her initial plan, ill-conceived and rapidly constructed, had been to disconnect the vats and let the water flow uncontaminated above. But, that would have been a short-term solution—one easily identified and rectified. She needs a better plan, one that can be sustained.

How to interrupt the flow of chemicals for ten years without detection...

Every week a truck would arrive here to collect empty vats and deposit new ones. Any unexpected volumes in the vats or disconnected pipework would draw suspicion. The manipulation needs to be hidden. Something taken for granted, an unchallenged assumption.

REVOLUTION

Her eyes track to the pipes above. One for pure water, one for chemical distribution, one for sewage. It is something she has done a hundred times before in her Cleaner role—connecting one line, disconnecting another—and more recently with her Wild Rover efforts at cutting the alcohol distribution. It's not exactly the same—this time she needs to switch the lines, push the chemical line to the sewage, and connect the pure water to the chemical distribution line—but it is similar enough to give her confidence.

The isolation valves for all three pipes are easy to find. She pushes them to the 'off' position and turns her attention to the stash of plumbing supplies stacked nearby. Using Niamh's blade, she hacks away at a piece of pipe until it is cut to two lengths and fits both with the connectors she needs.

It is messy work disconnecting and restructuring the lines, but she does it quickly and silently. When it is finally done, she steps back to admire her work, suddenly overcome with exhaustion and resignation.

After all the fighting and violence and betrayal and death, it is strange to think that the solution with the highest chance of success is as simple and unobtrusive as rearranged plumbing.

Stranger still that the answer had been in front of her the whole time. Kane 148 had been right—the success of the revolution lied with the Premies. When she had first read that in his journal, she had assumed he was referring to her. While Anaiya doesn't doubt Lira had been genuine when she'd said that Kane had seen her as the lifeline out of Otpor's lies, it is easier to realise now that Kane had seen her as a symbol of the uninitiated generations, the Elementals who could escape their conditioning before it ensnared them forever.

With a sigh, she returns the valves to their 'on' position and makes her way up the access ladder and back to street level. As she closes the large metal doors and secures the rock wedge in place, she pulls her hood up, her hand grazing the blood-soaked cloth at her neck. For the first time in as long as she can remember, she doesn't feel the weight of Kane 148's legacy, the shadow his Heterodoxy has cast for so many years. Stepping out into the sunlight, she heads west along the river, away from Niamh and back to the Enclave.

THIRTY-NINE

Anaiya enters Farasei's apartment with trepidation. She had toyed with the idea of not returning at all, but trying to find Seth at the Second Enclave would be like handing her enemies a second knife because they missed her with the first one. And, besides, there are questions she needs him to answer.

The door is still unlocked when she arrives. She enters slowly, even knowing it is unlikely Niamh has yet woken from his valerian dose and ordered a Peacekeeper assault. There is no sound or movement to alert her to anything untoward, but she still startles at the sight of Farasei bound where she had left him.

She treads softly towards him, her hand shaking as she reaches out to touch him. The nudge is gentle, becoming more vigorous as every prod and shake is met with no response.

Grabbing at his wristplate, she taps on it relentlessly, trying to bring up his vitals. With each tap, the wristplate flashes with a black cross, denying her access.

She unclasps it from his wrist, to no avail—the black cross still flashes with every attempt. "Damn it, Farasei."

In a moment of desperation, she grabs his hand and presses it against the wristplate. It flashes again, not with a black cross, but a white circle. She swipes his finger against it, but the circle flashes again.

Not a denial of access, but not an open invitation.

She slips the wristplate back on his wrist, gaze firmly on his face for any movement, expecting him at any second to open his eyes, and jumpy with the anticipation of it. With the cuff returned, she swipes at the plate again with Farasei's hand, the screen flashing to life with a burst of life and an array of icons.

Tapping on the body icon brings up Farasei's vitals. She taps again, thinking the connection is broken again. And then, when it doesn't change, she presses her own fingers to his wrist.

It is hard to perceive the pulse with her own heart beating so heavily. She holds her breath, trying to hold at bay her nerves.

Nothing.

She lessens the pressure of her grip, worried she is cutting off the blood flow.

Nothing.

She stares down at the statistics on his wristplate. He is not dead, but from the numbers he has less than an hour to live.

And then her mind turns to Niamh. She had injected him with three syringes. If one had left Farasei close to death…

She pushes the thought from her mind; there are precious few minutes left to utilise her access to his wristplate. Scrolling through the call history, she sees Niamh's name, pushes past the pang of guilt, and keeps scrolling. There are no familiar names, no evident patterns.

Switching to the messages is more rewarding. The most recent, sent just fifteen minutes ago from an unlisted contact, is brief but damning.

Seth has made contact. Wants to know about our holding. What's our move?

Anaiya's hands shakes as she hastily taps a reply.

Release the holding. Tell Seth to return him to Boileu without delay.

Three seconds after she sends it, a shrill beeping erupts from the wristplate. She tears it from his arm and flings it from her, the noise stopping immediately.

She looks to Farasei. There is no observable change, but she knows, without needing to check, that he is dead.

It is not the first time Anaiya has been in the same room as a dead body, but the body has never been one that she has killed.

She steps away, stumbling on shaky legs to the bathroom where she throws up a meagre stream of bile into the sink. Drawing water from the tap, she splashes it into her face and holds her palms against her eyes.

When she pulls them away, she is confronted by a face she doesn't recognise; black hair in disarray, eyes glassy, face pale and bruised after her altercation with Niamh. She pulls at the mirror to reveal the cabinet behind, pushing past small jars of creams and pills to find a vial of skin-mending serum.

With her hands still shaking, she pulls the keffiyeh from her neck, grimacing as the cloth pulls at the wound and causes fresh blood to ooze again. She stares at it, unable to reconcile how such a small cut can produce so much blood.

She sprays the serum in three sharp bursts, watching her reflection in the mirror as her eyes widen at the rush of cold and the skin at her neck knits itself together. Ignoring the dirty cloth in the sink, she grabs the soft and luxurious towel to her left. Running it under the water still streaming from the faucet, she drags it carefully over the wound, wiping away the residual blood in long, deliberate strokes.

Only when the wound is reduced to a faint white line does she sink down to the cold, blue tiles.

Farasei is dead. Niamh is almost certainly dead. Kaide has been alive all along, and right now he could be on his way to her with Seth. Or they both could be detained or dead at the second Enclave.

And there is nothing for her to do but wait.

Without her wristplate or Farasei's, there is nothing to mark the passing of time, and so it seems that the wait is interminable. Thoughts of death and hope, betrayal and second-chances, swirl in her mind with nothing else to distract her.

She stands up, still unsteady on her feet. She has never been good at waiting.

The room spins and she grips the basin to stop from swaying. Not from the pain, which has become distant and muted, but from something more primal. She can't remember the last time she had a nutrient boost; at least twenty-four hours, maybe longer.

She grits her teeth and makes her way to the oversized kitchen located down the hallway. There is no chance of finding a nutrient shot, or even a stale soylent brick like the ones she used to prop open her old apartment door, but she knows she'll find something to make do.

In the early days of finding refuge in the Enclave, she had tried the food that Farasei had offered; rich, dense, textured. He had called it *le pain*, Seth had called it *bread*. After a week of eating it, she had been sick, her body not equipped to deal with the non-synthetic nourishment. But that first night, it had been exquisite.

"We are accounted poor citizens," Seth had said after finishing the first loaf they had shared, quoting from one of his ancient and obscure texts, *"the patricians good. What authority surfeits on would relieve us: if they would yield us but the superfluity..."*

Farasei had laughed. "You two are some of the most intriguing Elementals I have ever met." And then he had walked over to his wall of shelves, plucked a grey-bound book almost randomly, and tossed it to Seth. *"The Tragedy of Coriolanus.* Not one of Shakespeare's most notable works in the early centuries after his death, but one more suited to our circumstances, wouldn't you agree?"

Later on, she had taken it from Seth's possession and poured over its pages, intrigued by the music of the sentences but unable to decipher any real meaning in the strings of unfamiliar words. Instead, she returned over and over to the first page, the words searing into her mind as she tried to unlock their secrets.

The leanness that afflicts us, the object of our misery, is as an inventory to particularise their abundance; our sufferance is a gain to them. Let us revenge this with our pikes, ere we become rakes: for the gods know I speak this in hunger for bread, not in thirst for revenge.

There is a half loaf of bread tucked away in a cloth bag on the countertop. She tears off a large chunk and bites into it, fighting the urge to gag as she forces it down her throat.

Seth should have returned by now.

She swallows roughly, turning to the sink and running the water to help wash down the hard lump.

There are only two possible reasons for him not returning — the message didn't transmit from Farasei's wristplate in time, or whoever received it did not believe it, and Seth is now detained with Kaide; or Seth had extracted Kaide from the Second Enclave but feared that returning to Boileau Road would be walking into a trap.

Holding her breath and averting her eyes, she rushes past Farasei's dead body and out of his apartment. She doesn't want to believe the first possibility, so she concentrates on the second, and heads to the only place she knows Seth would feel safe.

FORTY

The stone steps down to Lei Zhardan pull Anaiya into the shadows and lead her to a deeper darkness. The concrete garden is silent and cold; she navigates her way to the ablutions basin by memory alone.

Tears, hot and stubborn, spring unannounced, their presence made sharper by the chill of the place seeping into her skin.

Her knee smashes into the low wall, the pain an added defeat that snaps the final thread holding her composure. Her tears flow freely now and she sinks down onto the edge of the basin, burying her head into her hands and sobbing. The sound comes out strangled, catching in her chest before erupting under all the pressure of trying to suppress it.

She doesn't have the strength anymore. The Orthodoxy has defeated her. She may have dealt it a death blow, but it has fatally wounded her as well.

Once, the thought would have rallied her, would have called to her pride and defiance, and she would have pushed forward with a new plan. But, she has no more energy for it. And there is no more fight.

"Anaiya?"

The word whispers to her in the midst of her despair. In this place of ghosts, she doesn't trust herself to know dreams from waking.

Hands gently pull her own away from her face. And there it is again, the whisper of her name.

She keeps her eyes closed. Her heart is in a vice, caught in the impossible limbo of two equally devastating options: keeping her eyes closed and denying the potential of a beautiful truth, or opening them and having the last remnant of hope unequivocally shattered.

"Anaiya. It's me."

She can't deny it any longer; every fibre of her body knows that voice, responds to it. And when she opens her eyes, she sees Kaide kneeling before her.

"Hey," he murmurs.

In a rush, she falls into his arms. He holds her tight against his chest and buries his face into her shoulder.

"I missed you, Anaiyasha," he says, his voice soft and muffled. "Did you manage to save the world while I was gone?"

She pulls away from him and runs her hand against his cheek, testing reality. "Early days yet; ask me again tomorrow."

"I hate to interrupt the reunion," Seth murmurs, breaking into the moment, "but we can't stay here—there are still assassins and metal synthflies hunting us."

Kaide frowns and looks from Seth to Anaiya.

"Long story," she murmurs.

"So where do we go?" Kaide asks.

"Can't go back to the Enclave," Seth says. "Too much of a risk."

"Farasei's dead." Anaiya's voice sounds flat and cold to her own ears.

Kaide's frown deepens, but she looks to Seth. "And maybe Niamh as well."

"Do we go back to the Enclave?" Seth asks.

She shakes her head. "I never liked that place. And the other Enclave members will turn up eventually, looking for Farasei."

"Where then?" Kaide asks. "Where do we go?"

And suddenly, she is overwhelmed by the enormity of that question. Not just *where do we go, now?* But *where do we go?*

Where will they be safe? Where will they be able to carve out a life in a world that demands obedience and compliance? Where can they go to not just survive, but to live? Where can they shelter not just for the next few crazy, surreal, tenuous days, but the rest of their lives?

"There's somewhere we can go," she says slowly, still not sure it is a real option.

"How far away is it?" Seth asks.

"Nine or ten subworm stations, and then two blocks."

"Are there records of you being there?"

"No—I only ever went there with my fake wristplate."

"The synthflies won't be expecting us?"

"Nothing to track them there. Nothing interesting to draw their attention."

"Alright. Let's do it. Lead the way."

She turns back to Kaide. Her eyes have adjusted to the shadows and she can see the look of confusion and concern painted across his face in broad strokes. He has returned to a world he doesn't understand and threats he has yet to witness.

"I'll explain everything, I promise."

He stands up and pulls her up with him. "I know. I trust you."

Anaiya's hand is still in Kaide's when the three of them arrive at Brochant station.

"Wait here," she says, glancing around the empty platform. "If I'm not back in thirty minutes, go to Boileau Road. If there's any suggestion of Peacekeeper presence, go to Boileau Road." The words are for Seth, even though she looks at Kaide. She can't rely on Kaide to follow through on her instructions, she needs Seth to be the pragmatic one if things turn bad. "The first chance you get, remove your wristplate."

"Anaiya…" The first hints of anguish clouding his face.

She puts on a brave smile and shakes her head. "It's okay. I'll be okay. I'm just going to scout a place for us; in thirty minutes I'll be back here. And if I'm not…" Her voice cracks at the last moment, betraying the rush of emotion pooling in the pit of her belly. How many times will she have to lose her life, lose what she loves…

He pulls her in quickly and embraces her tightly. Part of her would stay in that embrace forever, but she pulls away.

"I'll come back for you. Just give me thirty minutes."

He smiles sadly at her. "I won't leave without you."

"Unless I'm late. Or there are Peacekeepers."

He shakes his head, but doesn't say anything, and she doesn't have the conviction to press the issue. With every bit of self-restraint she has, she pulls away.

"Don't let him stay," she murmurs to Seth, moving past both of them and heading up the stairs to the street level.

It takes her less than five minutes to reach Lira's apartment. Like all good Earth Elemental buildings, the access panel is easily bypassed to gain entry. She hurries up the stairs, rapping twice on the door and whispering a quick plea to the Creator that Lira is behind it.

The door cracks open, the older woman peering out from behind it. Her sigh is audible as she widens the opening and ushers Anaiya in.

"What's going on, Anaiya?"

"A lot. But I can't explain right now. I have two friends hiding in the subworm station. We need a place to stay."

"Were you followed?"

"No."

"What about the Elemental that attacked you? She'll be looking for you."

Anaiya holds up her naked wrist. "No way for them to trace me."

"What about your friends?"

"One is untraceable like me, the other won't be tracked for a while."

"How can you be sure?"

"He has a kind of amnesty; he's like a black-market commodity." It is the only way she can describe how Kaide would be unmissed by the Second Enclave, who could only assume he was in Farasei's charge, and off-limits to the Cooperative. "And the only person who would alert the Peacekeepers is dead, and the only Peacekeeper who would be alerted is also dead."

"Anaiya…"

"I know it's a lot to ask. And I know you don't owe me anything. But there's nowhere else to go, and there are still assassins looking to eradicate me."

Lira sighs again. "Not here. There's an empty apartment building three floors above. It will be vacant for the next few weeks—the occupant is in the Southern Area on a blue-rounds job. I'll drop off nutrients. The electricity and plumbing are still connected. It's the best I can offer."

"It's all we need. Thank you."

Lira grabs her arm. "Revolution does not come easy."

Anaiya laughs, the sound discordant and lacking any joy. "I don't know whether it will come at all."

FORTY-ONE

"You okay?" Anaiya and Kaide sit atop an air recycler in the Edges, the same place where their paths had first converged after Rehhd's Execution. Even now, a week after they had reunited again, she still can't believe he has been returned to her unbroken.

All this time, she had thought Peacekeepers had taken him from his studio, but it had been Unorthodox Water Elementals working for Farasei who had sedated him and dropped him into a delivery van bound for the Second Enclave. No solo detention cell, no torture, no clandestine Execution. He had spent his weeks locked in an apartment, but otherwise untouched; physically, at least. But even without the bruises and broken bones, something has changed in him. He is quieter, less optimistic, more distant. She looks to his hands resting in his lap, the scars on his left covered by his fake wristplate. Like her and Seth, he has been cut off from everything that makes him an Elemental.

"I'm okay," he murmurs, but doesn't look at her, keeping his gaze on the cityscape that stretches ahead. A rare nor-westerly has blown a scattering of clouds across the sky, and the yellow sun has turned a brilliant red as it drops to the horizon, setting the sky on fire.

"How long do you think it will last?" Kaide asks softly.

It is impossible to know whether he is talking about the brilliance of the red skies, the yellow sun, or the general discontent and chaos lingering in Otpor's streets. It doesn't matter; the answer is the same for all of them.

"Not long," she says, turning away from Kaide and following his gaze to the city. "Without the power cuts, the excess power will be redistributed and the recycler power levels will drop to normal. Without the yellow sun, people won't be so agitated, which means less call outs for Peacekeepers. It will die out eventually, just like it did after Kane's Execution."

"Until the next attempt," he says. "Until it starts all over again."

She looks over to him. *Is that what's behind the melancholy?*

"We don't have to start it again," she says.

"Who would lift all the misaligned Elementals from their identity prisons, then?" he asks bitterly.

"Let Seth rescue them—he needs a new project."

Anaiya hadn't seen Seth so energised as he had been over the past few days. With Farasei gone and Niamh's demise confirmed (his death broadcast in nightly bulletins as a dex restraint gone wrong), Seth had scored his victory in surviving his oppressors and was keen to take advantage of the void they had left behind. He had a thousand plans for finding others on the fringes of alignment, and a thousand more for bringing them into the fold. But that was his project—Anaiya was happy to let him have it. She had finished her own.

Kaide laughs, low and hollow. "You will never give up your revolution."

The words sting and she looks away. His faith in her has been shattered; she wonders if she will ever regain it. "The revolution was never mine. It was never ours. People resist change—not because their conditioning requires it, but because of that primal survival instinct we've carried with us for millennia. People resist uncomfortable truths and cling to the easy lies that make them feel safe."

"Not all," Kaide counters.

"No, not all. And not all of the time. But most people, and most of the time. Even me—who had opened my eyes and seen the Orthodoxy for what it was, seen the lies of my Peacekeeping corps, seen beyond the lies of 'Kane 148, the Ultimate Betrayer'—still resisted the truth and vulnerability of growing close to you."

He looks over to her at that, his frown of dejection replaced with a softer kind of hope.

"Peeling away lies is like peeling away a scab," she continues, looking out as the sun dips below the horizon and the brilliant colours start to fade, "it's ugly and it hurts. You have to want to do it, and if you don't, it will only hurt more."

How long had she resisted her re-alignment? How long until it had stopped chafing and she could see the truth that had been in front of her the whole time?

"The truth we broadcast didn't make Elementals free, it made them miserable. Forcing truth on people who don't want to see it only ever yields resistance, and stealing that fight from them only hurts us and any chance at revolution. Farasei was right—a revolution built on manipulation isn't a revolution as much as the Orthodoxy painted in a different colour."

"So, you are giving up the revolution?"

She turns her gaze eastward, finding the silhouette of Stricken Core and then the slender obelisk on the Avenue of the Elysian Fields. Somewhere nearby is the Nursery; she imagines it as she last saw it, imagines the vats of conditioning chemicals flowing into the sewage system while uncontaminated water flows up to the many levels above. Two, maybe three, generations of Premies, untainted by the chemical manipulation. Primed for free-thinking and resistance. Open to the Heterodox words and music she will need to prepare for them when they graduate. Capable of bringing down the Orthodoxy and the Enclave. *I am peppered, I warrant, for this world. A plague o' both your houses.*

She smiles and turns back to Kaide. "No, not giving it up; just handing it over. Entrusting it to generations that won't fight it, won't be manipulated to want it, but who will choose it freely."

"Can't fool the children of the revolution," Kaide murmurs. "What if they don't choose it?"

Anaiya turns back to the growing darkness, the clear skies pricked with the first tiny stars. "The fact that they choose at all is the real revolution."

ABOUT THE AUTHOR

MIKHAEYLA KOPIEVSKY is an independent speculative fiction author who loves writing about complex and flawed characters in stories that explore philosophy, sociology and politics. She holds degrees in International Relations, Journalism and Environmental Science. A former counter-terrorism advisor, she has travelled to and worked in Asia, the Middle East and Africa.

Mikhaeyla lives in the Hunter Valley, Australia, with her husband and son. *Divided Elements* is her debut offering.

For exclusive content and VIP access to new releases, reader events and advance copies, sign up at
www.kyrija.com

Loved *Divided Elements | Rebellion* ? Spread the word by leaving a review on Goodreads and Amazon.

www.ingramcontent.com/pod-product-compliance
Lightning Source LLC
Chambersburg PA
CBHW021643110726
47902CB00007B/1803